Praise for ~~Patricia Davids~~ and her novels

"Quaint characters and tender moments combine in this...sweet tale."
—*RT Book Reviews* on *A Hope Springs Christmas*

"Davids' deep understanding of Amish culture is evident in the compassionate characters and beautiful descriptions."
—*RT Book Reviews* on *A Home for Hannah*

"Davids' latest beautifully portrays the Amish belief that everything happens for a reason, which helps one focus on the most important things in life."
—*RT Book Reviews* on *The Christmas Quilt*

Praise for Kit Wilkinson and her novels

"[A]n engaging, well-paced tale."
—*RT Book Reviews* on *Lancaster County Target*

"This excellent story builds an intriguing mystery."
—*RT Book Reviews* on *Sabotage*

"Plenty of action, a heartwarming love story and a good mystery make this a compelling read."
—*RT Book Reviews* on *Protector's Honor*

After thirty-five years as a nurse, **Patricia Davids** hung up her stethoscope to become a full-time writer. She enjoys spending her free time visiting her grandchildren, doing some long-overdue yard work and traveling to research her story locations. She resides in Wichita, Kansas. Pat always enjoys hearing from her readers. You can visit her online at patriciadavids.com.

Kit Wilkinson is a former PhD student who once wrote discussions on the medieval feminine voice. She now prefers weaving stories of romance and redemption. Her first inspirational manuscript won a prestigious Golden Heart® Award. You can visit Kit at kitwilkinson.com or write to her at write@kitwilkinson.com.

USA TODAY Bestselling Author

PATRICIA DAVIDS

Katie's Redemption

&

KIT WILKINSON

Plain Secrets

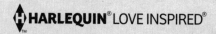

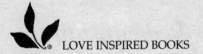 LOVE INSPIRED BOOKS

Recycling programs
for this product may
not exist in your area.

ISBN-13: 978-0-373-83816-5

Katie's Redemption and Plain Secrets

Copyright © 2016 by Harlequin Books S.A.

The publisher acknowledges the copyright holder
of the individual works as follows:

Katie's Redemption
Copyright © 2010 by Patricia MacDonald

Plain Secrets
Copyright © 2012 by Kit Wilkinson

www.Harlequin.com

Printed in U.S.A.

CONTENTS

KATIE'S REDEMPTION

Patricia Davids

This book is dedicated to my family.
You have supported me every step of the way
and I couldn't do it without you.

Even the sparrow has found a home, and the swallow a nest for herself, where she may have her young—a place near Your altar, O Lord Almighty, my King and my God.
—*Psalms* 84:3

Chapter One

"Lady, you sure this is where you wanna get out?" The middle-aged bus driver tipped his hat back and regarded his passenger with worry-filled eyes.

"This is the place." Katie Lantz glanced from his concerned face to the desolate winter landscape beyond the windshield. A chill that owed nothing to the weather crawled over her skin.

It was her destination, but rural Ohio was the last place in the world she wanted to be. She had agonized over her decision for weeks. Now that she was here, the same worries that had robbed her of sleep for endless nights cartwheeled through her mind.

Would her brother take her in? What if Malachi turned her away? What would she do then? If he did allow her to return to his home would she ever find the strength to leave again?

"It don't feel right leaving a gal in your condition out here alone. You sure I can't take ya into town?"

"I'm sure." She pressed a protective hand to her midsection. Her condition was the only reason she was here. She didn't want to get off the bus, but what choice did she have?

None.

All her plans, her dreams and her hopes had turned to ashes. She took a deep breath and straightened her shoulders. "I'd just have to walk back if I went into Hope Springs. Thank you for letting me off. I know you aren't supposed to make unscheduled stops."

The driver pulled the lever to open the doors with obvious reluctance. "I don't make a habit of it, but I figured it was best not to argue with a gal that's as pregnant as you are."

A gust of wintry wind swirled in, raking Katie's face with icy fingers. A tremor raced through her body. She turned up the collar of her red plaid coat, prolonging the moment she would have to actually step out of the bus and back into the life she dreaded.

The driver seemed to sense her unwillingness to leave. "Is someone meeting you?"

She hadn't bothered to write that she was coming. Her previous letters had all been returned unopened. Proof, if she needed any, that her family hadn't forgiven her for turning her back on her Amish heritage.

She lifted her chin.

I don't have to do this. I can stay on the bus and go to the next town.

And then what?

As quickly as her bravado appeared it evaporated. She closed her eyes. Her shoulders slumped in defeat.

All she had in her pocket was twelve dollars. All she owned was in the suitcase she clutched. It wasn't enough, not with her baby due in three weeks. For her child's sake, returning home was her only option.

For now.

Clinging to that faint echo of resolve, she drew a steadying breath, opened her eyes and faced her bleak future. "My brother's farm is just over the hill. It's not far. I'll be fine."

Oh, how she hoped her words would prove true.

She didn't belong in this Amish world. She had escaped it once before. She would do so again. It would be harder with a baby, but she would find a way.

With no money, without even a driver's license and nothing but an eighth-grade education, the English world was a hard place for an ex-Amish woman on her own.

Matt had taken her away and promised to take care of her and show her the wonders of the modern world, but his promises had been empty. He'd disappeared from her life three months ago, leaving her to struggle and fail alone.

The bus driver shrugged. "All right. You be careful."

"*Danki*. I mean...thank you." When she was upset the language of her childhood often slipped out. It was hard to remember to speak English when the words of her native Pennsylvania Dutch came to mind first.

Gripping her small case tightly, Katie descended the steps and walked toward the edge of the roadway. The doors slammed shut behind her. The engine roared as the driver pulled away, followed by a billowing cloud of diesel fumes.

There was no turning back—nowhere left to run.

Shivering as the frigid air found its way inside the coat she couldn't button over her bulging stomach, she pulled at the material to close the gap. Now she was truly alone. Except for the child she carried.

Standing here wasn't helping. She needed to get moving. Switching her suitcase to her other hand, she arched her back to stretch out a persistent cramp. When it eased, she turned and glanced up the long lane leading over the hill. For her baby she would do anything. Endure anything.

With the late-March sky hanging low and gray overhead, Katie wished for the first time that she had kept some of her Amish clothing. If she at least looked the part of a repentant Plain woman, her family reunion might go better.

She had left before her baptism—before taking her vows to faithfully follow the Plain faith. She would be reprimanded for her errant behavior, but she might not be shunned if she came asking forgiveness.

Please, God, don't let them send me away.

To give her child a home she would endure the angry tirade she expected from her brother. His wife, Beatrice, wouldn't intercede for Katie. Beatrice would sit silent and sullen, never saying a word. Through it all Malachi wouldn't be able to hide the gloating in his voice. He had predicted Katie would come to a bad end out among the English.

How she hated that he had been right.

Still, she would soon have the one thing her brother and her sister-in-law had been denied in their lives— a baby. Was it possible the arrival of her child might heal old wounds? Or would it only make things worse?

An unexpected tightening across her stomach made her draw in a quick breath. She had been up since dawn, riding for hours on the jolting bus. It was no wonder her back ached almost constantly now. She started toward the lane that led north from the highway. There could be no rest until she reached her brother's house.

The dirt road running between twin fences made for rough and treacherous walking. Buggy wheels and horse's hooves had cut deep ruts in the mud that was now frozen. Tiny, hard flakes driven by the wind stung

her cheeks and made it difficult to see. She shivered and
hunched deeper into her too-small coat.

As much as she wanted to hurry toward the warm
stove she knew was glowing in her brother's kitchen,
she couldn't. She had to be careful of each step over
the rough ground. The last thing she wanted to do was
fall and hurt the child that meant everything to her.
When her son or daughter arrived, Katie would have
the one true thing she had always longed for—a family of her own.

Her stomach tightened again. She had to stop to catch
her breath. Her pain deepened. Something wasn't right.
This was more than fatigue. Had her long day of travel
hurt the baby? She'd never forgive herself if something
happened to her child.

After a few quick, panting breaths the discomfort
passed. Katie straightened with relief. She switched her
suitcase to her other hand, pushed her frozen fingers
deep into her pocket and started walking again. She
hadn't gone more than a hundred yards when the next
pain made her double over and drop her case.

Fear clogged her throat as she clutched her belly.
Breathing hard, she peered through the blowing snow.
She could just make out the light from a window up
ahead. It wasn't much farther. Closing her eyes, she
gathered her strength.

*One foot in front of the other. The only way to finish
a journey is to start it.*

With grim determination, she pressed on. Another
dozen yards brought her to the steps of the small front
porch. She sagged with relief when her hand closed over
the railing. She was home.

Home. The word echoed inside her mind, bringing
with it grim memories from the past. Defeat weighed

down her already-low spirits. She raised her fist and knocked at the front door. Then she bowed her head and closed her eyes, grasping the collar of her coat to keep the chill at bay.

When the door finally opened she looked up slowly past the dark trousers and suspenders, past the expanse of pale blue shirt to meet her brother's gaze.

Katie sucked in a breath and took a half step back. A tall, broad-shouldered Amish man stood in front of her with a kerosene lamp in his hand and a faint puzzled expression on his handsome face.

It wasn't Malachi.

Elam Sutter stared in surprise at the English woman on his doorstep clutching a suitcase in one hand and the collar of her coat with the other. Her pale face was framed by coal-black hair that ended just below her jawline. The way the ends of it swung forward to caress her cheeks reminded Elam of the wings of a small bird.

In his lamplight, snowflakes sparkled in her hair and on the tips of her thick eyelashes. Her eyes, dark as the night, brimmed with misery. She looked nearly frozen from her head…to her very pregnant belly.

He drew back in shock and raised the lamp higher, scanning the yard behind her for a car, but saw none. Perhaps it had broken down on the highway. That would explain her sudden appearance.

The English! They hadn't enough sense to stay by a warm fire on such a fierce night. Still, she was obviously in trouble. He asked politely, "Can I help you?"

"Would you…" Her voice faltered. She swallowed hard then began again. "I must speak with Malachi."

"Would you be meaning Malachi Lantz?"

She pressed her lips together and nodded.

"The Lantz family doesn't live here anymore."

Her eyes widened in disbelief. "What? But this is his home."

"*Jah,* it was. He and his wife moved to Kansas last spring after he sold the farm to me. I have his address inside if you need it."

"That can't be," she whispered as she pressed a hand to her forehead.

"Who is it, Elam?" his mother, Nettie, called from behind him.

He spoke over his shoulder, "Someone looking for Malachi Lantz."

A second later his mother was beside him. She looked as shocked as he at the sight of a very pregnant outsider on their stoop, but it took only an instant for her kindheartedness to assert itself.

"Goodness, child, come in out of this terrible weather. You look chilled to the bone. Elam, pull a chair close to the fireplace." She nudged him aside and he hurried to do as she instructed.

Grasping the woman's elbow, Nettie guided her guest into the living room and helped her into a straight-backed seat, one of a pair that flanked the stone fireplace.

"*Ach,* your hands are like ice." Nettie began rubbing them between her own.

The young woman's gaze roved around the room and finally came to rest on Elam's mother's face. "Malachi doesn't live here anymore?"

Nettie's gaze softened. "No, dear. I'm sorry. He moved away."

Pulling her hands away from the older woman's, she raked them through her dark hair. "Why would he move? Was it because of me?"

Elam exchanged puzzled glances with his mother. What did the woman mean by that comment? Nettie shrugged, then took the girl's hands once more. "What's your name, child?"

The dazed look on his visitor's face was replaced by a blankness that troubled him. "My name is Katie."

"Katie, I'm Nettie Sutter, and this is my son, Elam."

Katie bent forward with a deep moan. "I don't know what to do."

"Don't cry." His mother patted the girl's shoulder as she shot Elam a worried glance.

After several deep breaths, Katie straightened and wiped her cheeks. "I have to go."

"You haven't thawed out yet. At least stay for a cup of tea. The kettle is still on. Elam, bring me a cup, too." Nettie caught his eye and made shooing motions toward the kitchen with one hand.

He retreated, but he could still hear them talking as he fixed the requested drinks. His mother's tone was calm and reassuring as she said, "Why not stay and rest a bit longer? It's not good for your baby to have his mother turning into an icicle."

"I need to go. I have to find Malachi." Katie's voice wavered with uncertainty.

"Is he the father?" Nettie asked gently.

Elam didn't want to think ill of any man, but why else would a pregnant woman show up demanding to see Malachi months after he had moved away?

"No. He's my brother."

Elam stopped pouring the hot water and glanced toward the living room. He had heard the story of Malachi's willful sister from the man's own lips. So this was the woman that had left the Amish after bringing shame to her family. At least she had done so before her baptism.

Elam placed the tea bags in the mugs. Malachi had his sympathy. Elam knew what it was like to face such heartbreak—the talk, the pitying looks, the whispers behind a man's back.

He pushed aside those memories as he carried the cups into the other room. "I didn't see your car outside."

She looked up at him and once again the sadness in her luminous eyes caught him like a physical blow. Her lower lip quivered. "I came on the bus."

Elam felt his mother's eyes on him but he kept his gaze averted, focusing instead on handing over the hot drinks without spilling any.

Nettie took a cup from Elam and pressed it into Katie's hands. "Have a sip. This will warm you right up. You can't walk all the way to Hope Springs tonight. Elam will take you in the buggy when you're ready."

Katie shook her head. "I can't ask you to do that."

"It's no trouble." He tried hard to mean it. He'd already finished a long day of work and he was ready for his bed. He would have to be up again before dawn to milk the cows and feed the livestock.

Returning to the kitchen, he began donning his coat and his black felt hat. It was a mean night for a ride into town, but what else could he do? He certainly couldn't let her walk, in her condition.

Suddenly, he heard Katie cry out. Rushing back into the room, he saw her doubled over, the mug lying broken on the floor in a puddle at her feet.

Chapter Two

Through a haze of pain, Katie heard Elam ask, "What is it? What's wrong?"

She felt strong arms supporting her. She leaned into his strength but she couldn't answer because she was gritting her teeth to keep from screaming.

"I believe her baby's coming," Nettie replied calmly.

Panic swallowed Katie whole.

This can't be happening. Not here. Not with strangers. This isn't right. Nothing is right. Please, God, I know I've disappointed You, but help me now.

A horrible sensation settled in the pit of her stomach. Was this her punishment for leaving the faith? She knew there would be a price to pay someday, but she didn't want her baby to suffer because of her actions.

She looked from Elam's wide, startled eyes above her to his mother's serene face. "My baby can't come now. I'm not due for three weeks."

Nettie's smile was reassuring. "Babies have a way of choosing their own time."

Katie bit her lower lip to stop its trembling. She'd never been so scared in all her life.

"Don't worry. I know just what to do. I've had eight

of my own." Nettie's unruffled demeanor eased some of Katie's panic. Seeing no other choice, Katie allowed Nettie to take charge of the situation.

Why wasn't Matt here when she needed him? It should have been Matt beside her, not these people.

Because he'd grown tired of her, that's why. He had been ashamed of her backward ways. Her pregnancy had been the last straw. He accused her of getting pregnant to force him into marriage, which wasn't true. After their last fight three months ago, he walked out and never came back, leaving her with rent and bills she couldn't pay.

Nettie turned to her son. "Elam, move one of the extra beds into the kitchen so Katie has a warm place to rest while you fetch the midwife."

"Jah." A blush of embarrassment stained his cheeks dark red. His lack of a beard proclaimed his single status. Childbirth was the territory of women, clearly a territory he didn't want to explore. He hurried away.

Nettie coaxed Katie to sit and showed her how to breathe through her next contraction. When Elam had wrestled a narrow bed into the kitchen and piled several quilts on one end, Nettie helped Katie onto it. Lying down with a sigh of relief, Katie closed her eyes. She was so tired. "I can't do this."

"Yes, you can. The Lord will give you the strength you need," Nettie said gently.

No, He won't. God doesn't care what happens to a sinner like me.

"Is the midwife okay, or will you be wanting to go to a hospital?" Elam's voice interrupted her fatalistic thoughts.

She turned her face toward the wall. "I can't afford a hospital."

"The midwife will do fine, Elam. I've heard good things about Nurse Bradley from the women hereabouts. Go over to the Zimmerman farm and ask to use their phone. They'll know her number. What are you waiting for? Get a move on."

"I was wondering if there was anyone else I should call. Perhaps the baby's father? He should know his child is being born."

"Matt doesn't care about this baby. He left us," Katie managed to say through gritted teeth. The growing contraction required all her concentration. The slamming of the outside door signaled that Elam had gone.

When her pain eased, Katie turned back to watch Nettie bustling about, making preparations for her baby's arrival. The kitchen looked so different than it had during the years Katie had lived here. She could see all of the changes Elam and his mother had made. She concentrated on each detail as she tried to relax and gather strength for her next contraction.

Overhead, a new gas lamp above the kitchen table cast a warm glow throughout the room. As it had in her day, a rectangular table occupied the center of the room. The chairs around it were straight-backed and sturdy. The dark, small cabinets that once flanked the wide window above the sink had been replaced with new larger ones that spread across the length of the wall. Their natural golden oak color was much more appealing.

Setting Katie's suitcase on a chair, Nettie opened it and drew out a pink cotton nightgown. "Let's get you into something more comfortable."

Embarrassment sent the blood rushing to Katie's face, but Nettie didn't seem to notice. The look of kindness on her face and her soothing prattle in thick German quickly put Katie at ease. Elam's mother seemed perfectly willing to accept a stranger into her home and care for her.

Dressed in a dark blue dress covered by a black apron, Nettie had a sparkle in her eyes behind the wire-rimmed glasses perched on her nose. Her plump cheeks were creased with smile lines. No one in Katie's family had ever been cheerful.

Nettie's gray hair was parted in the middle and coiled into a bun beneath her white *kapp* the way all Amish women wore their hair. Katie fingered her own short locks.

Cutting her hair had been her first act of rebellion after she left home. Amish women never cut their hair. It had been one way Katie could prove to herself that she was no longer Amish. At times, she regretted the loss of her waist-length hair. She once thought she despised all things Amish, yet this Amish woman was showing her more kindness than anyone had ever done. Only one person Katie knew in the neighborhood where she'd lived with Matt would have taken her in like this, but that friend was dead. The English world wasn't always a friendly place.

After she had changed into her nightclothes, Katie settled back into bed. Nettie added more wood to the stove. The familiar crackle, hiss and popping sounds of the fire helped calm Katie's nerves. Until the next contraction hit.

Elam wasted no time getting Judy hitched to the buggy. In spite of her master's attempts to hurry, the black mare balked at the wide doorway, making it clear she objected to leaving her warm barn. Elam couldn't blame her. The windblown sleet felt like stinging nettles where it hit his face. He pulled the warm scarf his mother had knitted for him over his nose and mouth, then climbed inside the carriage.

The town of Hope Springs lay three miles to the east of his farm. He had Amish neighbors on all sides. None of them used telephones. The nearest phone was at the Zimmerman farm just over a mile away. He prayed the Mennonite family would be at home when he got there or he would have to go all the way into town to find one.

Once he reached the highway, he urged Judy to pick up her pace. He slapped the reins against her rump and frequently checked the rectangular mirror mounted on the side of his buggy. This stretch of curving road could be a nerve-racking drive in daylight. Traveling it in this kind of weather was doubly dangerous. The English cars and trucks came speeding by with little regard for the fact that a slow-moving buggy might be just over the rise.

Tonight, as always, Elam trusted the Lord to see him safely to his destination, but he kept a sharp lookout for headlights coming up behind him.

It was a relief to finally swing off the blacktop onto the gravel drive of his neighbor's farm. By the time he reached their yard, his scarf was coated with ice from his frozen breath. He saw at once that the lights were on. The Zimmermans were home. He gave a quick prayer of thanks.

Hitching Judy to the picket fence near the front gate, he bounded up the porch steps. Pulling down his muffler, he rapped on the door.

Grace Zimmerman answered his knock. "Elam, what on earth are you doing out on a night like this?"

He nodded to her. "*Goot* evening, Mrs. Zimmerman. I've come to ask if I might use your telephone, please."

"Of course. Is something wrong? Is your mother ill?"

"*Mamm* is fine. We've a visitor, a young woman who's gone into labor."

"Shall I call 911 and get an ambulance?"

"*Mamm* says the midwife will do."

"Okay. Come in and I'll get that number for you."

"My thanks."

The midwife answered on the second ring. "Nurse Bradley speaking."

"Miss Bradley, I am Elam Sutter, and I have need of your services."

"Babies never check the weather report before they decide to make an appearance, do they? Has your wife been into the clinic before?"

"It is not my wife. It is a woman who is visiting in the area, so she hasn't been to see you."

"Oh. Okay, give me the patient's name."

He knew Katie's maiden name, but he didn't know her married name. Was the man she spoke of her husband? Deciding it didn't matter, he said, "Her name is Katie Lantz."

"Is Mrs. Lantz full term?"

"I'm not sure."

"How far apart are her contractions? Is it her first baby?"

"That I don't know. My mother is with her and she said to call you," he stated firmly. He was embarrassed at not being able to answer her questions.

"Are there complications?"

"Not that I know of, but you would be the best judge of that."

"All right. How do I find your place?"

He gave her directions. She repeated them, then

cheerfully assured him that she would get there as fast as she could.

As he hung up the phone, Mrs. Zimmerman withdrew a steaming cup from her microwave. "Have a cup of hot cocoa before you head back into the storm, Elam. Did I hear you say that Katie Lantz is having a baby?"

"*Jah*. She came looking for her brother. She didn't know he had moved." He took the cup and sipped it gratefully, letting the steam warm his face. Mrs. Zimmerman was a kindhearted woman but she did love to gossip.

"Poor Katie. Is Matt with her?" She seemed genuinely distressed.

"She's alone. Is Matt her husband? Do you know how to contact him?"

Mrs. Zimmerman shook her head. "I have no idea if they married. Matt Carson was a friend of my grandson's from college. The boys spent a few weeks here two summers ago. That's how Katie met Matt. I'll call William and see if he has kept in touch with Matt or his family."

"Thank you."

"I never thought Katie would come back. Malachi was furious at the attention Matt paid her. If he hadn't overreacted I think the romance would have died a natural death when Matt went back to school. I don't normally speak ill of people, but Malachi was very hard on that girl, even when she was little."

"'Train up a child in the way he should go: and when he is old, he will not depart from it.' *Proverbs* 22:6," Elam quoted.

"I agree the tree grows the way the sapling is bent, but not if it's snapped in half. I even spoke to Bishop Zook about Malachi's treatment of Katie when she was about ten but I don't think it did any good. I wasn't all that surprised when she ran off with Matt."

Elam didn't feel right gossiping about Katie or her family. He took another sip of the chocolate, then set the cup on the counter. "*Danki,* Mrs. Zimmerman. I'd best be getting back."

"I'll keep Katie in my prayers. Please tell her I said hello."

"I will, and thank you again." He wrapped his scarf around his face and headed out the door.

By the time Elam returned home, the midwife had already arrived. Her blue station wagon sat in front of the house collecting a coating of snow on the hood and windshield.

He lit a lantern and hung it inside the barn so his mother would know he was back if she looked out. He took his time making sure Judy was rubbed down and dry before returning her to her stall with an extra ration of oats for her hard work. When he was done, he stood facing the house from the wide barn door. The snow was letting up and the wind was dying down at last.

Lamplight glowed from the kitchen window and he wondered how Katie was faring. He couldn't imagine finding himself cast upon the mercy of strangers at such a time. He had seven brothers and sisters plus cousins galore that he could turn to at a moment's notice for help. It seemed that poor Katie had no one.

Knowing his presence wouldn't be needed or wanted in the house, he decided he might as well get some work done if he wasn't going to get any sleep. Taking the lantern down, he carried it to the workshop he'd set up inside the barn. Once there, he lit the gas lamps hanging overhead. They filled the space with light. He turned out the portable lamp and set it on the counter.

The tools of his carpentry and wooden basket-making business were hung neatly on the walls. Everything was in order—exactly the way he liked it. A long, narrow table sat near the windows with five chairs along its length. Several dozen baskets in assorted sizes and shapes were stacked in bins against the far wall. Cedar, poplar and pine boards on sawhorses filled the air with their fresh, woody scents.

Only a year ago the room had been a small feed storage area, but as the demand for his baskets and woodworking expanded, he'd needed more space. Remodeling the workshop had been his winter project and it was almost done. The clean white walls were meant to reflect the light coming in from the extra windows he'd added. When summer took hold of the land, the windows would open to let in the cool breezes. It was a good shop, and he was pleased with what he'd accomplished.

Stoking the coals glowing in a small stove, he soon had a bright fire burning. It wasn't long before the chill was gone from the air. He took off his coat and hung it on a peg near the frost-covered windows. Using his sleeve, he rubbed one windowpane clear so he could see the house.

Light flooded from the kitchen window. They must have moved more lamps into the room. Knowing he couldn't help, he pick up his measuring tape and began marking sections of cedar board for a hope chest a client had ordered last week.

He didn't need to concentrate on the task. His hands knew the wood, knew the tools he held as if they were extensions of his own fingers. His gaze was drawn repeatedly to the window and the drama he knew was being played out inside his home. As he worked, he prayed for Katie Lantz and her unborn child.

Hours later, he glanced out the window and stopped his work abruptly. He saw his mother hurrying toward him. Had something gone wrong?

Chapter Three

❧

"You are so beautiful," Katie whispered. Tears blurred her vision and she rapidly blinked them away.

Propped up with pillows against the headboard of her borrowed bed, she drew her fingers gently across the face of her daughter where she lay nestled in the crook of her arm. Her little head was covered in dark hair. Her eyelashes lay like tiny curved spikes against her cheeks. She was the most beautiful thing Katie had ever seen.

Amber Bradley, the midwife, moved about the other side of the room, quietly putting her things away. Katie had been a little surprised that the midwife wasn't Amish. That the women of the district trusted an outsider spoke volumes for Amber. She was both kind and competent, as Katie had discovered.

When Amber came over to the bed at last, she sat gently on the edge and asked, "Shall I take her now? You really do need some rest."

"Can I hold her just a little longer?" Katie didn't want to give her baby over to anyone. Not yet. The joy of holding her own child was too new, too wonderful to allow it to end.

Amber smiled and nodded. "All right, but I do need

to check her over more completely before I go. We didn't have a lot of time to discuss your plans. Maybe we can do that now."

Reality poked its ugly head back into Katie's mind. Her plans hadn't changed. They had simply been delayed. "I intend to go to my brother's house."

"Does he live close by?"

"No. Mr. Sutter said Malachi has moved to Kansas."

"I see. That's a long way to travel with a newborn."

Especially for someone who had no money. And now she owed the midwife, as well. All Katie could do was be honest with Amber. She glanced up at the nurse. "I'm grateful you came tonight, but I'm sorry I can't pay you right now. I will, I promise. As soon as I get a job."

"I'm not worried about that. The Amish always pay their bills. In fact, they're much more prompt than any insurance company I've dealt with."

Katie looked down at her daughter. "I'm not Amish. Not anymore."

"Don't be worrying about my fee. Just enjoy that beautiful baby. I'll send a bill in a few days and you can pay me when you're able."

The outside door opened and Nettie rushed in carrying a large, oval wooden basket. She was followed by Elam. He paused long enough to hang his coat and hat by the door, then he approached the bed. "I heard it's a fine, healthy girl. Congratulations, Katie Lantz."

"Thank you." She proudly pulled back the corner of the receiving blanket, a gift from Amber, to show Elam her little girl.

He moved closer and leaned down, but kept his hands tucked in the front pockets of his pants. "*Ach,* she's *wundascheen!*"

"Thank you. I think she's beautiful, too." Katie planted a kiss on her daughter's head.

Nettie set the basket on the table, folded her arms over her ample chest and grinned. "*Jah,* she looks like her Mama with all that black hair."

Reaching out hesitantly, Elam touched the baby's tiny fist. "Have you given her a name?"

"Rachel Ann. It was my mother's name."

Nodding his satisfaction, he straightened and shoved his hand back in his pocket. "It's a *goot* name. A plain name."

Katie blinked back sudden tears as she gazed at her daughter. Even though they would have to live with Malachi for a while, Rachel would not be raised Amish as Katie's mother had been. Why did that make her feel sad?

Amber rose from her place at the foot of the bed. "I see you've got a solution for where this little one is going to sleep, Nettie."

"My daughter, Mary, is expecting in a few months. She has my old cradle, but a folded quilt will make this a comfortable bed for Rachel. What do you think, Katie?"

"I think it will do fine." All of the sudden, Katie was so tired she could barely keep her eyes open.

"I will make a bassinet for her," Elam offered quickly. "It won't take any time at all."

Overwhelmed, Katie said, "You've been so kind already, Mr. Sutter. How can I ever thank you?"

"Someday, you will do a kindness for someone in need. That will be my thanks," he replied, soft and low so that only she could hear him.

Katie studied his face in the lamplight. It was the first time she had really looked at him. He was probably twenty-five years old. Most Amish men his age were married with one or two children already. She wondered why he was still single. He was certainly handsome enough to please any young woman. His hair, sable-brown and thick, held a touch of unruly curl where it brushed the back of his collar.

His face, unlike his hair, was all chiseled angles and planes, from his broad forehead to his high cheekbones. That, coupled with a straight, no-nonsense nose, gave him a look of harshness. Until she noticed his eyes. Soft sky-blue eyes that crinkled at the corners when he smiled as he was smiling now at the sight of Rachel's pink bow mouth opened in a wide yawn.

"Looks like someone is ready to try out her new bed." He stepped back as Amber came to take Rachel from Katie.

"I know her mother could use some rest," Amber stated with a stern glance in Katie's direction.

Katie nodded in agreement, but she didn't want to sleep. "If I close my eyes for a few minutes, that's all I need."

"You're going to need much more than that," Nettie declared, placing the quilt-lined basket on a kitchen chair beside Katie's bed.

Amber laid the baby on the table and unwrapped her enough to listen to her heart and lungs with a stethoscope. Katie couldn't close her eyes until she knew all was well. After finishing her examination, Amber rewrapped the baby tightly and laid her in the basket. "Everything looks good, but I'll be back to check on her tomorrow, and you, too, Mommy. I'll also draw a little blood from her heel tomorrow. The state requires certain tests on all newborns. You'll get the results in a few weeks. I can tell you're tired, Katie. We'll talk about it tomorrow."

Katie scooted down under the covers and rolled to her side so that she could see her daughter. "Will she be warm enough?"

"She'll be fine. We'll keep the stove going all night," Nettie promised.

"She's so sweet. I can't believe how much I love her already." Sleep pulled Katie's eyelids lower. She fought it, afraid if she slept she would wake and find it all had been a dream.

The murmur of voices reached her. She heard her name mentioned and struggled to understand what was being said.

"I'm worried about Katie." It was Amber talking.

"Why?" came Elam's deep voice.

Opening her eyes, Katie saw that everyone had gone into the living room. She strained to hear them.

Amber said, "It's clear she hasn't been eating well for some time. Plus, her blood loss was heavier than I like to see. Physically, she's very run-down."

"Do you think she should go to the hospital?" Elam asked. Katie heard the worry behind his words.

He was concerned about her. She smiled at the thought. It had been a long time since anyone had worried about her. As hard as she tried, she couldn't keep her eyes open any longer.

Concerned for his unexpected guest's health, Elam glanced from the kitchen door to the nurse standing beside his mother.

Amber shook her head. "I don't think she needs to go to the hospital, but I do think she should take it easy for a few days. She needs good hearty food, lots of rest and plenty of fluids. I understand she was on her way to her brother's home?"

"Jah," Nettie said. "When she realized he wasn't here, she said she was going to the bus station."

Amber scowled and crossed her arms. "She shouldn't travel for a while. Not for at least a week, maybe two. If having her here is an inconvenience, I can try to make other arrangements in town until her family can send someone for her."

Elam could see his mother struggling to hold back her opinion. He was the man of the house. It would have to be his decision.

At least that was the way it was supposed to work, but he had learned a valuable lesson about women from his father. His *dat* used to say, "Women get their way by one means or another, son. Make a woman mad only if you're willing to eat burnt bread until she decides otherwise. The man who tells you he's in charge in his own house will lie about other things, too."

His father had been wise about so many things and yet so foolish in the end.

Elam's mother might want Katie to remain with them, but Elam was hesitant about the idea. The last thing he needed was to stir up trouble in his new church district. Katie wasn't a member of his family. She had turned her back on her Amish upbringing. Her presence might even prompt unwanted gossip. His family had endured enough of that.

"I certainly wouldn't mind having another woman in the house." It seemed his mother couldn't be silent for long.

This wasn't a discussion he wanted to have in front of an outsider. He said, "Nothing can be done tonight. We'll talk it over with Katie in the morning."

The faint smile that played across Nettie's lips told him she'd already made up her mind. "The woman needs help. It's our Christian duty to care for her and that precious baby."

Mustering a stern tone, he said, "You don't fool me, *Mamm.* I saw how excited you were to tell me it was a little girl. The way you came running out to the barn, I thought the house must be on fire. You're just happy to have a new baby in the house. I've heard you telling your friends that you're hoping Mary's next one is a girl."

His mother raised one finger toward the ceiling. "*Gott* has given me five fine grandsons. I'm not complaining. I pray only that my daughters have more healthy children. If one or two should be girls—that is *Gotte wille,* too, and fine with me. Just as it was *Gotte wille* that Katie and her baby came to us."

Her logic was something Elam couldn't argue with. He turned to the nurse. "She can stay here until her family comes to fetch her if that is what she wants. She can write to Malachi in the morning and tell him that she's here."

Amber looked relieved. "Wonderful. That's settled, then."

For Malachi's sake and for Katie's, Elam prayed that she was prepared to mend her ways and come back to the Amish. If she was sincere about returning, the church members would welcome her back with open arms.

Amber gathered up her bag. "I'll come by late tomorrow afternoon to check on both of my patients. I'm going to leave some powdered infant formula with you in case the nursing doesn't go well, but I'm sure you won't need it. Please don't hesitate to send for me if you think something is wrong. Mrs. Sutter, I'm sure you know what to look for."

"Thank you for coming, Miss Bradley."

"Thank you for calling me."

Elam hesitated, then said, "About your bill."

She waved his concern aside. "Katie and I have already discussed it."

After she left, a calm settled over the house. Nettie tried to hide a yawn, but Elam saw it. The clock on the wall said it was nearly two in the morning. At least it was the off Sunday and they would not have to travel to services in the morning. "Go to bed, *Mamm.*"

"No, I'm going to sleep here in my chair in case Katie or the baby needs me."

He knew better than to argue with her. "I'll get a quilt and a pillow from your room."

"Thank you, Elam. You are a good son."

A few minutes later he returned with the bedding and handed it to her. As she settled herself in her favorite brown wingback chair, he moved a footstool in front of it and helped her prop up her feet, then tucked the blanket under them. She sighed heavily and set her glasses on the small, oval reading table beside her.

When he was sure she was comfortable, he quietly walked back into the kitchen. Before heading upstairs to his room, he checked the fire in the stove. It had died down to glowing red coals. The wood box beside it was almost empty. The women must have used most of it keeping the room warm for Katie's delivery. Glancing toward the bed in the corner, he watched Katie sleeping huddled beneath a blue-and-green patterned quilt.

She looked so small and alone.

Only she wasn't alone. Her baby slept on a chair beside the bed in one of his baskets. And what of the child's father? Katie had said he didn't care about them, but what man would not care that he had such a beautiful daughter? There was a lot Elam didn't know about his surprise guest, but answers would have to wait until morning.

Quietly slipping into his coat, he eased the door open and went out to fetch more wood. He paused on the front steps to admire the view. A three-quarter moon sent its bright light across the farmyard, making the trees and buildings cast sharp black shadows over the snow. High in the night sky, the stars twinkled as if in competition with the sparkling landscape.

Elam shook his head. He was being fanciful again. It was a habit he tried hard to break. Still, it had to be good for a man to stop and admire the handiwork of God. Why else did he have eyes to see and ears to hear?

Elam's breath rose in the air in frosty puffs as he loaded his arms with wood and returned to the house. He managed to open the door with one hand, but it banged shut behind him. He froze, hoping he hadn't disturbed his guests or his mother. When no one moved, he blew out the breath he'd been holding and began unloading his burden as quietly as he could.

After adding a few of his logs to the stove, he stoked up the blaze and closed the firebox door. He had taken a half-dozen steps toward the stairs and the bed that was calling to him when the baby started to fuss. He spun around.

Katie stirred but didn't open her eyes. He could hear his mother's not-so-soft snoring in the other room. The baby quieted.

He took a step back and grimaced as the floorboard creaked. Immediately, the baby started her soft fussing again. Elam waited, but neither of the women woke. The baby's cries weren't loud. Maybe she was just lonely in a strange new place.

He crossed the room. Squatting beside the basket, he rocked it gently. The moonlight spilling in through the kitchen window showed him a tiny face with bright eyes wide open.

"Shh," he whispered as he rocked her. Rachel showed no inclination to go back to sleep. Her attempts to catch her tight fists in her mouth amused him. What a cute little pumpkin she was. Another of God's wonders.

Glancing once more at Katie's pale face, he picked the baby up. She immediately quieted. He crossed the room and sat down at the table. "Let's let your mama sleep a bit longer."

He disapproved of the choices this little one's mother had made, but none of that disapproval spilled over onto this new life. Settling her into the crook of his arm, he marveled at how tiny she was and yet how complete. The cares and worries of his day slipped away. A softness nestled itself around his heart. What would it be like to hold a child of his own? Would he ever know? Rachel yawned and he smiled at her.

"Ah, I was right. You just wanted someone to cuddle you. I know a thing or two about wee ones. You're not the first babe I've held."

Babies certainly weren't new to him. He'd rocked nephews aplenty. He raised her slightly to make her more comfortable.

"My sisters think nothing of plopping a babe in my arms so they're free to help *Mamm* with canning or gardening, but I know what they're up to," he whispered to the cute baby he held.

"They think if I'm reminded how wonderful children are I'll start going to the Sunday night singings again and court a wife of my own. They don't see that I'm not ready for that."

He wasn't sure he would ever be ready to trust his heart to someone again. If that time did come, it would only be with a woman he was certain shared his love of God and his Plain faith.

"Once burned, twice shy, as the English say," he confided to his tiny listener.

He waited for the anger to surface but it didn't. For the first time in over a year he was able to think about his broken engagement without bitterness. Maybe the sweet-smelling babe in his arms had brought with her a measure of God's peace for him. To her, life was new and good and shouldn't be tainted with the sins of the past.

He began to sing a soft lullaby in his native tongue. Rachel stared back at him intently for a few minutes, but she eventually grew discontent with his voice and the fingers she couldn't quite get in her mouth. Her little fussing noises became a full-fledged cry.

"I guess I can't fix what ails you after all. I reckon I'll have to wake your mother."

"I'm awake." Katie's low voice came from the bed.

He looked over to find her watching him with dark eyes as beautiful and intense as her daughter's. How long had she been listening to him?

Chapter Four

Katie met Elam's gaze across the room. Moonlight streaming through the windows cut long rectangles of light across the plank floor. It gave her enough light to see the way Elam held her daughter. With confidence, caring and gentleness. Would Matt have done the same? Somehow, she didn't think so.

Her boyfriend's charm had evaporated quickly, once the novelty of having an Amish girlfriend wore off. When he found himself stuck with a "stupid Amish bumpkin" who couldn't use a microwave and didn't know how to work a cell phone, he reverted to his true nature. The harder Katie tried to make him happy, the more resentful he became. The harder she tried to prove her love, the louder he complained that she was smothering him. Looking back, it seemed that their relationship had been doomed from the start.

Her elderly landlady back in Columbus once said, "Honey, that man's a case of bad judgment. Dump him before he dumps you."

Katie hadn't wanted to believe Mrs. Pearlman, but it turned out she knew what she was talking about.

Elam spoke as he rose to his feet, yanking Katie's attention back to the present. "I was trying to get Rachel to go back to sleep without waking you."

"The song you were singing, what's it called?"

"You don't know *In der Stillen Einsamkeit?*" He sounded genuinely surprised.

"No."

"I thought every Amish child had heard it. My mother sang it to all of us and still sings it to her grandchildren."

"There wasn't a lot of singing in my house. I don't remember my mother ever singing. I have very few clear memories of my family. My father died before I was born in some kind of farm accident. I do remember my brother Hans playing with me. He was always laughing. He gave me a doll that I loved, and he gave me piggyback rides. I remember someone scolding him to be careful. I think it was my mother."

"What happened to your family?"

"Everyone except Malachi and I died in a fire when I was four."

"I'm sorry."

Katie shrugged off his sympathy. "It was a long time ago."

Rachel gave another lusty cry. Elam said, "I think she's telling me I make a poor substitute for her mother."

Katie shifted into a sitting position in the bed and held out her arms. When Elam laid her daughter in her embrace, she said, "I'm afraid she's going to think I'm a poor substitute for a mother when she gets to know me."

"My sisters all worried that they wouldn't make good mothers, but they learned. You will, too."

"I hope you're right." He sounded so matter-of-fact. Like it was a done deal. She wanted to believe him, but she had made such a mess of her life up to this point.

"My mother will help as long as you're here. If you let her."

"I'm not sure I could stop her. She's something of a force of nature."

Chuckling softly, he nodded. "*Jah,* that is a good description of *Mamm.*"

As their eyes met, Katie experienced a strange thrill, a sizzling connection with Elam that both surprised and delighted her. Rachel quieted. Elam's expression changed. The amusement left his gaze, replaced by an odd intensity that sent heat rushing to Katie's cheeks.

Since the baby had quieted, Katie simply held and admired her. Stroking one of her daughter's sweetly curved brows, Katie said, "This wasn't the way I planned for you to come into the world."

Elam folded his arms. "Our best laid plans often come to naught."

"My landlady used to say, 'Man plans, God laughs.'" Katie tried to imitate her friend's broad Yiddish accent.

"She sounds like a wise woman."

Katie nodded sadly. "She was a very wise woman."

If Mrs. Pearlman had lived, Katie wouldn't be in this mess. Her kind landlady would have taken her in until she found a job. God had once again taken away the person who truly cared about her, leaving Katie where she had always been. Alone, unwanted, belonging nowhere.

She glanced up at Elam as he towered over her bed. "Your mother reminds me of my friend. She had the same kind eyes."

When he didn't say anything, Katie sighed. "I know what you're thinking."

Frowning slightly, he asked, "And what would that be?"

"You're thinking I didn't plan very well at all."

He crossed his arms and looked at the floor. "I didn't say that."

"No, you didn't, but it's the truth. I kept thinking that Matt would come back for me. For us."

"How long ago did he leave you?"

"Three months. After that I got a part-time job working for our landlady, but she died and the place was sold. I waited for him to come back until my rent ran out. I only had enough money left to buy a bus ticket here."

"Your husband should not have left you."

It was her turn to look away. The shame she'd tried so hard to ignore left a bitter taste in her mouth. "Matt Carson wasn't my husband."

"Ah." It was all Elam said, but to her ears that one syllable carried a wealth of condemnation and pity.

After a long moment, he said, "You should know that Grace Zimmerman mentioned Matt was a friend of her grandson when I went there to use the phone. She said she would have her grandson try and contact Matt. Perhaps he will come for you when he finds out you are here."

Rachel began to fuss again. Katie bounced her gently. "Matt had plenty of time to come for us when we were in the city. I don't expect he will come now. We won't be a burden to you or your family any longer than necessary."

"We will not turn you out. That is not our way. The Bible commands us to help those in need."

"I'm grateful for all you've done, but I'll go on to my brother as soon as possible."

Nettie appeared in the living room doorway rubbing her neck. "There's no need to speak of traveling yet. The nurse says you're to rest. You can write to Malachi and tell him your situation, but you will stay here for a few days. Or more if you need it."

Katie bit her lip. Writing her brother would not be enough. She had to go to Malachi in person. He'd made that abundantly clear the day she left with Matt. His angry words still echoed inside her head.

"You ungrateful harlot, you've brought shame on me since the day you were born. You'll not last six months out in the English world. When you come to your senses you'll be back. But know this. You are dead to me until I see you kneeling in front of me and begging my forgiveness."

At the time, she felt only relief at getting away from her brother's strict control. In the months that followed, when it became clear that running away with Matt had been a bad decision, Katie came to realize that she did still care about her brother and she was sorry for the way she'd left.

Matt laughed at her and called her spineless when she decided to try and mend things with her only sibling. She had written several long letters of apology, but each one came back unopened. After two months, she gave up trying. When Matt left she didn't bother writing to her brother. She knew he meant what he'd said.

Rachel started crying again. Nettie waved a hand to send Elam on his way. "We'll talk about this tomorrow. Right now this little one is hungry and she doesn't want to wait any longer."

Elam bid her good-night, then turned away and headed for the stairs leading to the upper story.

Katie was sorry their quiet talk had ended. She would have enjoyed spending more time with him.

As soon as the thought occurred, she chided herself for such feelings. The last thing she needed was to complicate her life with another man. She appreciated Elam's kindness, but she wouldn't mistake those feelings for anything more.

After that, all Katie's attention was taken up trying to satisfy her daughter's hungry demands. Later, as Katie fell asleep again, she dreamed about Elam rocking her baby in his arms and singing a soft lullaby. In her dream, the sound of his voice soothed her spirit and brought with it a quiet peacefulness.

For most of the next two days all Katie did was doze and feed the baby. Nettie took over the job of nursemaid, in addition to running her household, without missing a beat and with undisguised gentle joy. At her insistence, Katie was allowed to rest, drink plenty of hearty chicken soup, nurse her baby and nothing else.

Elam had moved a folding screen into the kitchen and placed it in front of her bed to give her and the baby some privacy, then he vanished for most of the day to do his chores and work in his woodshop.

Katie saw so little of him that she began to wonder if he was deliberately trying to avoid spending time with her. When he was in the house, she felt none of the closeness they'd shared the night Rachel was born. She began to think she'd simply imagined the connection they had shared.

The midwife returned as promised to check on Katie and the baby. Amber came bearing a gift of disposable diapers, several blankets and baby gowns which she insisted were donations made by the community for just such an occasion. While Rachel scored glowing marks and was pronounced as healthy as a horse, Amber wasn't quite as pleased with Katie's progress.

"At least another day of bed rest is in order. If your

color and your blood pressure aren't better by tomorrow, I may send you to the hospital after all."

"I promise I will take it easy," Katie assured Amber. It was an easy promise to keep. Deep fatigue pulled at her limbs and made even the simplest task, like changing diapers, into an exhausting exercise.

"Mrs. Sutter will tell me if you aren't." Amber glanced at Nettie, who stood at the foot of the bed with her arms folded and a look of kindly determination on her face.

Amber was on her way out the door when another car pulled into the drive. She said, "Looks like you have more company. Don't overdo it."

"I'm sure they aren't here to see me."

Looking out the door, Nettie said, "I believe that is Mrs. Zimmerman talking to Elam."

Katie sat up as hope surged in her heart. Had Mrs. Zimmerman been able to contact Matt? Was he on his way here? "Is she coming in?"

"No. It looks like she's leaving, but Elam is coming to the house."

Unwilling to let hope die, Katie threaded her fingers together and held on tight. As soon as Elam walked in and she saw his face, her last tiny reservoir of hope faded into nothingness. "He's not going to come, is he?"

Elam shook his head. "Mrs. Zimmerman's grandson says the family has gone abroad. He sent a computer message to Matt, but he hasn't answered."

Katie nodded. "I think I'd like to rest now."

She slipped down under the covers and turned her back on the people standing beside her bed.

From her place inside her small alcove in the corner of the kitchen, Katie could hear Nettie and her son speaking in hushed tones, and the sounds of housework taking place, but she was simply too tired to care what they were saying.

Her beautiful daughter was her whole world now. Rachel was all that mattered.

It was the smell of cinnamon bread baking that woke Katie on the morning of the third day. She opened her eyes to the sight of bright morning light pouring in through the kitchen windows. Someone, Nettie perhaps, had moved the screen aside. Warm and comfortable beneath the quilts, Katie rested, feeling secure and safe for the first time in weeks. She knew it was an illusion, but one she desperately wanted to hold on to.

Nettie was busy pulling a pan of steaming hot bread from the oven with the corner of her apron. The mouthwatering smell was enough to make Katie's empty stomach sit up and take notice with a loud rumble. Nettie glanced her way and began to chuckle. "I reckon that means you feel *goot* enough to have a bite to eat."

"If it tastes as good as it smells, I may wolf down the whole loaf."

"You'll have to fight Elam for it. This is his favorite."

Katie sat up and swung her bare feet to the cool plank floor. As she did, the room dipped and swirled, causing her to shut her eyes and clutch the side of the mattress.

"Are you all right?"

Katie opened her eyes to find Nettie watching her with deep concern. "Just a touch of dizziness. It's gone now."

"You sit right there until I get a cup of hot coffee into you. I don't want you fainting when you stand up."

Katie took several deep breaths and waited for the room to stop spinning. When everything settled into place, she looked down at her daughter sleeping quietly in her basket. The sight brought a thrill of delight to Katie's heart. This was her child, her gift. Matt had been wrong when he said a baby would only be a burden.

If he saw Rachel now, would it change how he felt? The thought pushed a lump of regret into her throat. She had made so many bad decisions.

Nettie, having poured the coffee from a dark blue, enameled pot on the back of the stove, laced it liberally with milk from a small pitcher on the table and added a spoonful of sugar before carrying the white earthenware mug to Katie.

Katie didn't take her coffee sweetened, but she didn't mention the fact. Nettie had done far too much for her. Grasping the cup, Katie sipped the hot drink slowly, feeling the warmth seep into her bones.

Nettie stood over her with her hands fisted on her hips. Looking up, Katie said, "I'm fine. Really."

"I will tell you when you are fine. When the color comes back to those cheeks you can get up. Not before. Now drink."

"Yes, ma'am." Katie blew on the cup to cool the beverage and took another sip.

Nettie nodded, then left the room. She returned a few minutes later with a large black shawl, which she wrapped around Katie's shoulders. That done, Nettie turned back to the stove.

Upending the bread pan, she dumped the loaf onto a cutting board and pulled a knife from a drawer. Cutting off thick slices, she transferred them to a plate. Setting the dish aside, she began breaking eggs in a bowl. "Are you drinking?" she asked without looking.

"Yes." Katie took another quick sip and pulled the shawl tighter, grateful for its soft warmth.

She thought she detected a smile tugging at the corner of the older woman's mouth, but she didn't have a clear view of Nettie's face.

After a few minutes of silence, Nettie asked, "How's the coffee?"

"It's good. Better than my sister-in-law ever made on that stove. I used to think her bitter coffee gave Beatrice her sour face."

"You don't like your sister-in-law?"

"She's okay." It was more that Beatrice didn't like her. Katie had felt Beatrice's resentment from the moment she came to live with them, although she never understood why.

"I've got a sister-in-law I don't care for. It's not right to speak ill of her, but she thought my brother married up when he married into her family. That, and she claims her peach preserves are better than mine. They aren't. I use my mama's recipe."

"And riper peaches?"

Nettie's eyes brimmed with humor as she shot a look in Katie's direction. "Can you keep a secret?"

Taken aback slightly, Katie replied, "I guess. Sure."

"I use canned, store-bought peaches."

Katie laughed, feeling oddly pleased to be let in on a Sutter family joke.

Chuckling, Nettie continued. "I hate to think of the hours that woman has slaved over a hot stove stewing her fresh fruit and trying to outdo me. It's prideful, I know. I reckon I'd better confess my sin before next communion."

Katie's mirth evaporated. She bowed her head. She had so much more than a little false pride to confess. What must Nettie think of her?

If Mrs. Sutter hoped her admission would prompt Katie to seek acceptance back among the Amish, she was sadly mistaken. Katie had no intention of talking to a bishop or anyone else about the choices she'd made in her life. She had made them. She would live with them.

After a few minutes of silence, Nettie said, "It must feel strange to see another family living in your child-hood home."

Relieved by the change of subject, Katie looked up to find her hostess watching her closely. "It was a bit of a shock."

"It's a good house, but I'd like a bigger porch. Elam has promised to build it this summer. I love to sit out-side in the evenings and do my mending. That way I can enjoy a cup of coffee and the flowers in my garden while I watch the sun go down. Speaking of coffee, are you finished with yours?"

"Almost. Do you miss the home you left behind?"

"*Jah,* at times I do, but my oldest son and his wife still live on our farm in Pennsylvania, so I can go back for a visit as often as I like."

"What made you leave?"

A fleeting look of sadness crossed Nettie face. "Elam wanted to come west. There's more farm ground out here and it's cheaper than back home. That, and there was some church trouble."

Nettie busied herself at the stove and began scram-bling eggs in a large cast-iron skillet. Katie waited for her to elaborate, but she didn't. Although Katie found herself curious to hear more of the story, it was clear Nettie wasn't willing to share.

Suddenly, Nettie began speaking again. "My daughter-in-law's parents were talking about mov-ing into the *dawdy haus* with one of their children. I would have welcomed the company, but then Elam told me he'd found this property."

The Amish welcomed their elderly relatives and nearly all Amish farms had a second, smaller, "grandfather house" connected to the main home. Grandparents could live in comfort and remain a part of the family, helping to care for the children or with the farm work if they were able.

"Elam is my youngest, you know, and he's without a wife yet. All my others are married. It just made sense for me to come with him and to keep house for him until he finds a wife of his own."

"Not all men want to get married." Katie was thinking more of Matt than Elam, but she did wonder why Nettie's son was still single. Besides being a handsome man, he was kind, gentle and seemed to love children.

Nettie stopped stirring and stared out the window. "Elam was betrothed once."

Katie recalled Elam's comment about "once burned, twice shy" the first night when he was holding Rachel. Now she knew what he meant. "What happened?"

Nettie began stirring her eggs again. "Salome wasn't the right one for him. It was better that they found it out before they were married, because she left the church."

"After her baptism?"

"Jah."

Katie knew what that meant. "She was shunned."

"It was very hard on Elam. Especially after…" Nettie paused and stared out the kitchen window as though seeing unhappy things in the past.

"You don't need to explain anything to me," Katie said, gently. She considered Nettie a friend, and she was willing to respect her privacy.

Nettie glanced her way. The sorrow-filled look in her eyes touched Katie's heart deeply. "It is no secret. You may hear it anyway. I'd rather you heard it from me. My husband also left the church a few months before he died."

While the Amish religion might not be something Katie wanted for herself, she understood how deeply spiritual true believers were and how painful such an event would be to Nettie's entire family. "I'm so sorry."

"*Danki.* How are you feeling?"

"Better."

It was true. Katie finished her drink, rose and carried her cup to the table, happy to find her dizziness didn't return. As she sat down she thought she understood better why Elam disliked that she had left the faith. "That can't have been easy for Elam or for any of you."

Nettie looked over her shoulder with a sad little smile. "Life is not meant to be easy, child. That is why we pray for God's strength to help us bear it."

Katie didn't want to depend on God for her strength. She had made her own mistakes. She was the one who would fix them.

The front door opened and Elam came in accompanied by a draft of chilly air. In his arms he held a small bassinet. He paused when he caught sight of Katie at the table. She could have sworn that a blush crept up his neck, but she decided she was mistaken. He nodded in her direction, then closed the door.

Nettie transferred her eggs from the stove top to a shallow bowl. "I was just getting ready to call you, Elam. Breakfast is ready."

"*Goot,* I could use some coffee. The wind has a raw bite to it this morning. March is not going out like a lamb. At least the sun is shining. The ground will be glad of the moisture when this snow melts. It will help our spring planting."

He hung his coat and black felt hat on the row of pegs

beside the door, then he approached Katie. "I made your Rachel a better bed. It'll be safer than setting her basket on a chair and it will keep her up off the drafty floor."

The bassinet was about a third the size of the ones Katie had seen in the stores in the city when she had gone window-shopping and dreamed about things she could never afford for her baby. The picnic basket-size bed was finely crafted of wooden strips sanded smooth and glowing with a linseed oil finish. It had a small canopy at one end. "It's lovely. You didn't have to do this."

"It was easy enough to make out of a few things I had on hand. It has double swing handles and the legs fold up so you can take it with you when you leave. Have you had time to write a letter to your brother? I'll carry it to the mailbox for you."

He wasn't exactly pushing her out the door, but he was making it plain she couldn't expect to stay longer than necessary.

She didn't blame him. Katie knew she had been dependent on the Sutters' charity for too long already. She'd never intended to take advantage of them and yet she was.

How could she explain that her brother—her only family—wouldn't come to her aid? She might find shelter for herself and her baby at his home, but it would be on his terms and his terms alone.

Elam was waiting for her answer. She wouldn't lie to him. Nor could she write and pretend she was waiting for an answer when she knew full well the letter would come back unopened.

She glanced at Elam. Two important people in his life had betrayed the faith and he had shunned them.

If he knew her brother had disowned her would he allow her to stay?

Chapter Five

"Let the girl get a little food in her before you start pestering her, Elam."

Elam didn't miss the grateful look Katie flashed at his mother. He kept silent, but only out of respect for Nettie. His unexpected visitor had aroused his curiosity and a niggling sense of unease. Katie didn't seem at all eager to contact her brother. That bothered him.

That and Grace Zimmerman's comments about Malachi's harsh treatment of his young sister.

Elam was well aware that some men held to the idea that being the head of the house gave them the right to be stern, even cruel. He also knew such behavior was against God's teaching.

If Katie had been subjected to that type of treatment in the past, it might explain a lot. But even if her life had been difficult, it was no excuse for turning her back on her religion.

Nor was it his place to pass judgment on her or on her brother, he reminded himself sternly. He stepped up to the sink and began to wash. When he was finished, he pulled a white towel off the hook on the end of the counter and dried his hands.

Whatever troubles Katie had, she would take them with her when she left. Then the peace he tried so hard to cultivate would once again return to his life.

Nettie set a bowl in the center of the table. "Take a seat, both of you. Don't let my eggs get cold."

Elam took his place at the head of the table, and Nettie sat in her usual spot at his right. Katie was already seated in the chair to his left. In the morning light her color was still pale, made more so by the black woolen shawl she had wrapped about her shoulders. The dark circles under her eyes added to the impression of sadness he saw in her face.

Her dark eyes looked too big for her thin face. What she needed was some of his mother's good cooking to put a little meat on her bones. He wasn't a man who liked scrawny women.

She quietly clasped her hands together and bowed her head. The movement sent the ends of her short hair swinging against her cheeks. The sight brought a sudden tightening to his chest. She might be a thin waif, but she was also a woman. There was no mistaking that or the odd pull of attraction he felt when she was near.

He tore his gaze away. He'd made a fool of himself over a woman once before and once was enough. Closing his eyes, he bowed his head as a signal to the others, then he began a silent blessing over the meal.

When he was finished, he cleared his throat to signal the prayer was done, then reached for the cinnamon bread. Katie stretched out her arm at the same moment and their hands touched. He felt the shock of the contact all the way up his arm.

She jerked her hand back as quickly as he did. A flush stained her cheeks, giving her back some much-needed color.

"I'm sorry," he mumbled. "Help yourself."

"You first. You've been out working already."

"And you're eating for two."

Following their exchange neither of them moved. Finally Nettie pushed the plate closer to Katie. "I thought you were starving?"

Katie smiled shyly at her. "I am."

"Then eat," Elam added sternly. When Katie still didn't move he took her plate and loaded it with scrambled eggs, two sausage patties and two thick slices of cinnamon bread. When the plate was filled to his satisfaction, he set it in front of her and folded his arms over his chest.

Her blush deepened, but she picked up her fork and began eating. She kept her head down and her gaze focused on her meal so she didn't see the look of triumph on his mother's face, but Elam did.

He had seen just that look when his mother had convinced his oldest sister that her two boys needed and deserved to keep the muddy stray puppy they'd found in the orchard on their last visit. His mother had a big heart and she often thought she knew what was best for everyone.

In the case of the puppy she had been right, but her desire to mother Katie and her little girl wasn't the same thing at all. Having Katie in their home could easily bring the censure of the community to bear on them. Katie's rejection of her faith placed all of them in an awkward position. He and his mother had few friends among their new acquaintances who would speak up for them.

His mother had endured enough heartache back in Pennsylvania. He wanted it to be different here.

From the far corner of the room, Rachel began crying. Katie quickly started to rise, but Nettie stopped her by saying, "I'll get her this time. You finish your meal."

Katie sank back into her seat. "Thank you."

Elam noticed she didn't take her eyes off Rachel as his mother picked the child up. Nettie said, "I see what's wrong, *moppel*. You need your diaper changed."

She carried the child to her bedroom as she crooned, "We had better send Elam to the store for more."

Elam turned his attention back to Katie. "If you make a list of things you need I'll be happy to make a trip into town."

She stared at her plate and pushed a piece of sausage around with her fork. "I don't have the money to repay you."

"I asked for a list, not for money. Your brother will settle with me when he comes for you. I'm not worried about it."

When she made no comment, he resumed eating, but she didn't. The silence in the room lengthened uncomfortably. Every time he brought up the subject of her brother she clammed up. He wasn't sure what to make of her withdrawal. He wasn't sure what to make of Katie Lantz at all.

He could understand her reluctance to admit to her family how far she had fallen, but the time for such false pride was past. She had a child to care for now and no way that he could see to support herself, let alone her baby. If she couldn't bring herself to write her brother then Elam would do it for her.

That might be best. He could mail a letter today.

He would not include the details of her plight. That would be for Katie to do. He'd only say that she had come looking for her family and that she needed her brother's assistance to get home.

When Katie found the courage she could say what she needed to say to her family, but the sooner they came for her the better it would be for everyone.

Elam studied her as she picked at her food. He'd heard not one word of complaint from her. She didn't bemoan her fate, that was commendable. She was certainly attentive to her baby. The love she had for her child shone in her eyes whenever she looked upon her babe's face. There was much he liked about Katie. It was a pity she had turned her back on the Plain life.

As if aware of his scrutiny, she self-consciously tucked her hair behind her ear, then gave up any pretense of eating. She laid her fork down and folded her hands in her lap. "I'll make a list of things the baby needs. It won't be much."

"*Goot.* Now eat or my mother will scold us both." He gestured toward her plate with his fork.

A hint of a smile tugged at her lips, but it vanished quickly. She picked up her slice of cinnamon bread and took a dainty bite.

A few minutes later, Nettie returned with a quiet baby nestled in her arms. Katie started to rise. "I'll take her."

Nettie waved her away. "I can manage. You've barely touched your food."

"And you haven't eaten a thing," Katie countered.

Elam pushed his empty plate aside. "I'll take her, then you can both eat."

"Very well." Nettie handed Rachel over reluctantly.

Elam took her and settled her upright against his shoulder. He liked holding her. Leaning back in his chair, he glanced down at her plump cheeks and tiny mouth. Each day it was easier to see the resemblance between her and her mother, except Katie's cheeks were hollow, not plump and healthy-looking. They shared the same full bottom lip, but Rachel's curved naturally into a sweet smile.

His gaze was drawn to Katie's face. She was watching him, an odd expression in her eyes. What would it take to make her smile as freely as her baby did?

Katie returned to her bed for the rest of the day. Physically she was stronger, but when night finally came the hopelessness of her situation pulled her spirits to a new low. She was homeless and penniless with a new baby to care for and a growing debt to the people that had befriended her.

The memory of Nettie and Elam's tender care of Rachel brought tears to her eyes. For one horrible instant she wondered if her baby wouldn't be better off without her.

Turning over, she muffled her sobs in the pillow as she gave in to despair.

The following morning she stayed behind the screen until Elam had gone outside. She didn't want to answer his questions about why she hadn't written to Malachi. It was cowardly and she knew she couldn't avoid the subject much longer, but she didn't know how to explain.

She had been a trial to Malachi and his wife all her life. Even though the Sutters were aware she had made bad choices, she didn't want them to know Malachi had disowned her. She was too ashamed to admit it. If she had to grovel before Malachi, for her child's sake she would, but what little pride she had left kept her from admitting as much to the Sutter family.

The day passed slowly, but when Elam came in for supper he didn't mention her brother or ask her for a letter. Relieved, but puzzled, she was able to eat a little of Nettie's excellent beef stew and listen as Elam talked about plans for planting pumpkins to sell in addition to their normal produce.

"Pumpkins?" Nettie cocked her head to the side. "Would you sell them through the organic farming co-op?"

"*Jah.* The demand is growing."

Katie's curiosity was aroused. She knew most of the area's Amish farmers sold their produce from roadside stands and at the local produce auctions. Every year her brother had complained bitterly about how hard it was to earn a living competing against the large, mechanized English farms. She asked, "What's an organic co-op?"

Nettie passed a bowl of her canned pears to Katie. "Last year Elam persuaded several dozen farmers to switch from conventional agriculture to organic, using no chemicals, no antibiotics, none of those things."

Katie could see the spark of interest in his eyes. "There's a good market for organic vegetables, fruits and cheeses. I had heard about such a co-op near Akron. Aaron Zook and I contacted them. They helped us find a chain of grocery stores in Cleveland that were interested in selling our crops. They even helped us obtain our organic certification from the U.S.D.A."

"The government men came and inspected the barns and the fields of everyone involved," Nettie added.

Frowning slightly, Katie asked, "Isn't it more expensive to farm that way?"

He gave a slight shake of his head. "Not if it's done right."

"Elam attended seminars on soil management to learn what organic products would give our soil the best nutrients. He learned how to make the plants strong, so they wouldn't fall prey to insects and disease without chemicals to protect them. It has already saved two of our families from losing their farms." Nettie beamed, clearly pleased with her son's accomplishments.

It seemed there was more to Elam than the stoic farmer Katie had assumed he was. The Amish were known as shrewd businessmen, but it was plain Elam was also forward thinking.

Nettie picked up her empty plate and carried it to the sink. "If our people can make a living from the farms and not have to work in factories, then our families will stay intact. It's a win-win situation."

After the meal was over Nettie retired to her sewing room, and in what seemed like no time she emerged with a stack of baby gowns for Rachel and two new cotton nightgowns for Katie.

"You shouldn't have." Katie managed to speak past the lump of gratitude in her throat.

Nettie smiled. "You might as well accept them. They're much too small for me and I'm not going to rip out all those stitches."

It seemed that every minute Katie stayed here she became more indebted to Elam and his mother. She needed to be on her way. It was doubtful that Malachi would pay back any of the money the Sutters had spent on her or Rachel. In time, when she found a job, she would make sure she repaid them herself as soon as possible.

The following days passed in much the same fashion. Katie took care of Rachel and tried to regain her strength. Nettie fussed over the both of them.

Whatever Elam thought of Nettie's pampering, he kept it to himself, but Katie could tell he was ready for her to be on her way. Elam had done his Christian duty by taking her in, but he wanted her out of his home. He avoided looking at her when he was in the same room. A faint scowl creased his brows whenever his gaze did fall on her.

Nearly a week after her arrival, Katie was helping clear the lunch dishes when Nettie announced that she and Elam were driving her out to her daughter Mary's farm some five miles away. That explained why Nettie had been baking all morning.

"Mary is pregnant and expecting in a few months. She's been feeling low. I've several baskets of baked goods and preserves I want to take her and her family. Nothing makes a person feel more chipper than a good shoofly pie they didn't have to bake themselves."

Grateful as Katie was for Nettie's care and mothering, she was excited to hear she would finally have some time alone. "When will you be back?"

"I think about four o'clock. Will you be okay without us? I could have Elam stay with you."

"No, I'll be fine."

"I'm sure you will. You should rest. You still look washed-out."

"Oh, thank you very much." Katie rolled her eyes, and Nettie chuckled.

Thirty minutes later, with Rachel asleep and the quietness of the house pressing in, Katie put down the book she couldn't get into and began looking for something to do. Memories of her life in this same house crept out without Nettie's happy chatter to keep them at bay.

It wasn't so much that her brother had been cruel. It was that he had been cold and devoid of the love she saw so freely given by Nettie to her son. The Sutters were the kind of family Katie longed to be a part of. Malachi and his wife hadn't given her that. Neither had Matt.

With sudden clarity, Katie realized she would have to

see that Rachel grew up knowing she was loved, knowing happiness and hearing laughter. A new determination pushed aside the pity she had been wallowing in. She would raise her child on her own. She would get a job and make a life for the two of them. They would have to live with Malachi for a while, but it wouldn't be any longer than absolutely necessary.

Katie walked into the kitchen with a new sense of purpose. In her rush to leave, Nettie had left a few pots and pans soaking in the sink. Smiling, Katie pushed up the sleeves of her sweater and carried a kettle to the sink. She filled it with water and put it on the stove to heat. It was time to stop feeling sorry for herself and do something for someone else.

It wasn't long until she was putting the last clean pot in the cupboard and closing the door. Looking around the spotless kitchen, she bit the corner of her lower lip. Would Nettie think it was clean enough? Would Elam?

That was a silly thought. Why should she want to impress Elam with how well she could manage a home? He wouldn't care. He wasn't at all like Malachi.

Many was the time she'd scrubbed this same kitchen until her hands were raw only to have her brother come in, look around and begin shouting that she couldn't do anything right, that if she wanted to live in filth she could live in the barn.

How many nights had she spent locked inside the feed room listening to the sounds of scurrying mice in the darkness? Too many to count.

She pressed a hand to her lips to hide the tiny smile that crept out of hiding. Malachi would have been furious to know she hadn't really minded sleeping there. The old sheet she had been given was much softer stuffed with hay than the thin mattress in her room upstairs. The mice had been quieter than her brother's heavy snoring in the room next to hers. She often wondered how her sister-in-law ever got a wink of sleep.

Folding the dish towel carefully, Katie hung it on the towel bar at the end of the counter. Nettie and Elam were not like Malachi. She didn't have to be afraid while she was here.

Two hours later Katie's solitude was interrupted when Amber arrived to check on her patients. To Katie's chagrin, the nurse caught her sweeping the porch and steps free of the mud that clung to everything now that the weather had warmed up enough to melt the snow.

Amber advanced on Katie and took the broom out of her hands. "What do you think you're doing? I gave you strict orders to rest."

Katie sighed. "I'm not used to lying around. Besides, I wanted to repay Nettie's kindness in some small fashion. She and Elam have gone to visit his sister and I thought I'd clean up a little while she was gone."

"I understand, but you won't repay her if you overdo it and get sick. That will just make more work for her. Come inside and have a seat. I want to check your blood pressure. At least your color is better today."

"I feel fine." Maybe if she kept repeating the phrase it would remain true.

Inside the house, Katie hung up her coat and took a seat at the kitchen table. Amber did the same and opened the large canvas bag she carried slung over one shoulder. "How's your appetite?"

"It's good."

Amber narrowed her eyes as she wrapped the black cuff around Katie's arm. "If I ask Nettie, what will she say?"

"She'll say I pick at my food like a bird."

"I thought so." Placing her stethoscope in her ears, Amber inflated the cuff and took her reading.

"Well?" Katie asked when she was done.

"It's good, and your pulse is normal, too. You Amish women amaze me the way you bounce back after childbirth."

"I'm not Amish."

"I'm sorry. That was thoughtless of me." Amber leaned back to regard Katie intently. "I know you grew up here and I've lived in Hope Springs for almost six years, yet I don't remember seeing you."

"How can you tell us apart in our white caps and dark dresses?" Katie didn't mean to sound bitter, but she couldn't help it.

"I think I would have remembered you. There aren't too many women in this area with black hair and eyes as dark as yours. I don't think I remember your brother and his wife."

"They didn't have any children."

"Then they'll be excited to have a baby in the house."

"I'm not so sure."

Amber leaned forward and placed a hand on Katie's arm. "I will tell you something I've learned in my years as a nurse midwife. No matter how upset a family may be at the circumstances surrounding the arrival of a baby, once that child is born…the love just comes pouring out. It's the way God made us."

Would that be the case for her and Rachel? Would her daughter bring love and happiness to her brother's home? Would Rachel help her mother find the sense of belonging she craved?

They were big hopes to pin on such a small baby.

One step at a time, Katie cautioned herself. First, she

had to get home, and soon. She had been a burden on the Sutters long enough.

"Amber, do you know what day the bus leaves that I'd need to take to go to Kansas?"

"As a matter of fact I keep copies of the bus schedule in my car. You have no idea how often I'm asked about that when people want to make plans for family members to come see a new baby. I should just memorize it. It isn't like Hope Springs is a major hub. I think we only get four buses a week through here."

After she checked on Rachel, Amber went out to her car and returned with a laminated sheet of paper. "It looks like the bus going west leaves on Monday and Friday evening at six-ten. The buses going east leave on Wednesday and Saturday afternoon at five forty-five. There's no Sunday service."

Today was Friday. Katie glanced at the clock. It was half past two now. If she hurried, she could make today's bus. Otherwise, she wouldn't be able to leave until Monday. As much as she had grown to like Nettie and even Elam, she didn't want to burden them with her presence for three more days.

The only problem was that she was broke. She didn't have enough money to pay for a ticket to the next town, let alone to go across four states.

Amber tucked the sheet in her bag. "Actually, the bus isn't the best way for you to travel. The best thing would be if your brother could arrange to send a car."

The Amish often hired drivers for long trips. It was a common occurrence in a society devoted to the horse and buggy. One was permitted to ride in an automobile for such things as doctor visits or to travel to see relatives that lived far away. One could even take an airplane if they obtained the bishop's permission.

Katie had heard that a few Amish churches permitted owning and driving a car, but that certainly wasn't accepted by her brother's church. "Hiring a driver to come all this way would be expensive."

Amber fisted her hands on her hips. "True, but you can tell your brother that's what the nurse recommends."

Katie forced a smile, but she knew her brother wouldn't send anyone for her. She would have to make her own way home.

Only…what if she didn't go. What if she stayed in Hope Springs?

The kindness and caring she'd been shown over the last few days had given her a different vision of what her life could be like. A new sense of energy swept through her. "Amber, do you know of any jobs in the area?"

"For you?"

"Yes. Perhaps someone who needs live-in help. I'm not afraid of hard work. I can clean and cook. I know my way around a farm. I'll take anything."

"I don't know of any work right offhand, but I'll keep my ears open. Are you thinking of returning to Hope Springs?"

"I just need a job as soon as possible."

Stepping close, Amber laid a hand on Katie's arm. Her eyes softened. "If you're worried about paying me, don't be. I can wait."

She pulled a card from her coat pocket. "This is my address. Just send what you can…when you can."

Katie took the card, but her heart sank. It seemed that God wanted her to return to her brother's house after all. She considered asking Amber for the loan of enough money to reach her brother's but quickly discarded the idea. She already owed the woman for her midwife services. She couldn't ask for anything else. Except perhaps a ride into town.

"Amber, are you heading back to Hope Springs now?"

Taking her coat from the hook by the door, Amber slipped it on and lifted her long blond hair from beneath it, letting it spill down her back. "No, I've got a few more visits to make. I'm on my way to check on Mrs. Yoder and her new baby. I'm worried that the child is jaundiced. I may end up sending them to the hospital. Why? Was there something you needed in town?"

Katie shook her head. "It's nothing that can't wait until the Sutters get home."

"Are you sure?"

"I'm sure."

After Amber left, Katie pulled out the newspaper that Nettie had finished reading that morning. Quickly, she looked over the help wanted ads in case there was something listed that Amber didn't know about. As she read the few listings her heart sank. There were few jobs available, and none for a woman without education or skills.

Folding the paper, Katie returned it to Nettie's reading table. Rachel began crying in the other room. Katie picked her up and sat on the edge of her bed. "I feel like crying, too."

So much for her renewed sense of optimism.

Looking around the room, Katie couldn't believe how much she had dreaded coming to this place. Now she dreaded leaving. In a strange way her arrival here had turned out to be a blessing. What else could I call this family's kindness?

Cradling her baby, she looked down at her child's wonderful bright eyes and beautiful face. "I just have to believe that God has more blessings in store for us when we reach Malachi's new home."

Reaching that home would require money they didn't have. Besides her clothes and shoes, she didn't own anything of value. As much as she dreaded it, she would simply have to tell Elam why she hadn't yet written to Malachi.

Perhaps Elam and Nettie knew of some work she could do to earn her bus fare. No doubt Nettie would offer to pay Katie's way home, but she couldn't take advantage of the woman's kind heart any more than she already had.

After feeding her daughter, Katie laid the baby in her bassinet. "At least you own a fine place to sleep. Never take it for granted."

Lifting the handles, Katie started to carry the baby's bed into the living room, but stopped in the doorway and looked down. She did own something of value. The bed Elam had made for Rachel was beautifully crafted, but was it worth more than a bus ticket out of town?

Could she bring herself to sell it?

No, Elam had made it clear that it was a gift to Rachel. He'd even made it to travel, so Katie could take it with her.

She bit her lip. Selling it would solve her immediate problem. Should she?

The memory of Elam gently holding her baby in the moonlight came rushing to mind.

His kindness to her daughter had touched something deep inside Katie. Thoughts of him stirred vague longings, but she refused to examine those feelings. She had no right to be thinking about her own happiness. Rachel was her first priority.

Malachi would give them a home where Rachel

would be safe. She'd have a roof over her head and food to eat. What did it matter that her mother had cold-hearted relatives? Rachel would be taken care of and one day soon they would both leave again. For good.

Katie sat in the chair before the fireplace and considered her options. The weather was decently warm today. She would make sure Rachel was snugly dressed and wrapped in one of Nettie's old but warm quilts. As soon as she could, Katie would send the quilt back with a letter of thanks for its use.

It was only a three-mile walk into town. She could easily get there before the bus left that evening. Unless things had changed drastically in Hope Springs, there were several stores in town that catered to the tourist trade by selling Amish furniture, gifts and quilts. The thought of parting with Elam's beautiful gift gave Katie pause, but she didn't see any other choice.

No. This was the only way.

Chapter Six

It was nearly four o'clock in the afternoon when Elam and his mother returned home. Leaving Judy tied up near the gate, he helped his mother unload her empty baskets and carried them up the steps for her. Inside the front door, he stopped. The house had an odd, empty feel to it.

He glanced around the kitchen. The folding screen had been pushed back against the wall. Katie's bed was stripped and empty. The quilts and sheets sat neatly folded at one end. Rachel's cradle was gone along with Katie's suitcase. It was clear they had left.

His heart sank. He'd tried not to become attached to them, but it seemed that he had failed.

Nettie came in behind him. "Just set those baskets on the table, son. I'll get them washed in a few minutes. Are you still planning to go to the lumberyard?"

He didn't move, couldn't take his eyes off the empty corner. "Yes. I need to pick up some more cedar to finish the chest I'm working on."

Where had she gone? Had she found someone to take her to her family or was she going back to the city and Rachel's father?

"What's wrong?" Nettie asked as she stepped around him.

"I think our little birds have flown." He couldn't believe how disappointed he was. In only a few days he'd become deeply attached to little Rachel...and to her mother, although he hated to admit that, even to himself.

Walking to the table, he set the baskets on it and slipped one hand into his pants pocket. He withdrew the pink-and-white wooden baby rattle he'd made and simply stared at it.

"She can't be gone." His mother's distress was clear as she carried her burdens in and set them next to his. A letter sat in the middle of the table. Nettie picked it up and read it.

She pulled her bonnet from her head and laid it and the note on the table, then turned to Elam. "That girl doesn't have a lick of sense. She isn't strong enough to be gadding about. She's gone to the bus station. You have to go after her."

That was exactly what he wanted to do. He wanted to bring her back where she and her baby would be safe, but perhaps this was for the best. Perhaps it was better that Katie went away before he grew any fonder of her and her child. He knew what heartbreak lay in that direction.

"She's a grown woman, *Mamm.* She has made up her mind."

"She's not thinking straight. She's putting herself and her baby in danger."

"What do you mean?"

"The baby blues have muddled her thinking. Tell me you didn't notice how depressed she has been. What if she collapses on the way, or worse?"

"The town is only three miles away. Amish children

walk that far to school every day." He slipped the rattle back in his pocket.

"Please, take the buggy and fetch her back. It will get cold as soon as the sun goes down."

"By then she'll be on a bus headed for Kansas. She will be happier with her own family."

Nettie paced the length of the kitchen and back with her hands pressed to her cheeks. "I'm not sure that's true."

He frowned. "Do you know something you aren't telling me?"

"It's not what I know. It's what I feel. She didn't want to write to her brother. Why? Something isn't right."

"You can't know that."

"Even if I'm wrong, we at least need to make sure she made it to the bus depot. I couldn't rest without knowing that she and that precious baby are all right. Katie isn't strong enough to be traveling. What will become of Rachel if anything happens to her mother?"

Everything Nettie said was an echo of his own concerns, but still he hesitated. "Katie has the right to live her own life as she sees fit. She has made her choice. She chose to leave us."

He turned to the bed in the corner and began dragging off the mattress.

"Elam, what are you doing?"

"I'm putting the bed back in the spare bedroom. We have no need of it in here anymore."

The little bassinet, which seemed like such a wonderful way to carry Rachel, had become horribly heavy long before Katie had finished the first mile. By the time she reached the outskirts of town she'd already stopped to rest a dozen times. Now, outside the Amish Trading Post, she simply had to stop again.

After setting Rachel down gently on the sidewalk, Katie used her suitcase as a seat. Rubbing her aching arms, she willed her nagging dizziness away. She was stronger than this. She had to be.

The hollowness in the pit of her stomach made her wish she'd had the forethought to bring something to eat. The sun was low in the western sky and the chill had returned to the air. She had no idea what time it was, but it was getting late. She couldn't rest for long. She had to make it to the bus station on time.

Glancing down, the sight of her sleeping daughter brought a little smile to Katie's lips. At least the baby had slept the whole trip. Lifting Rachel from the bassinet, Katie swaddled her tightly in her blanket. Rising, she pushed her suitcase beneath the branches of a nearby cedar tree, picked up Elam's gift and crossed the street to the store.

At the door, she hesitated. Rachel's bed was the only thing she owned that had been given to her out of kindness. Keeping it meant hanging on to a small part of Elam.

No, I've already been over this. It has to be done. Open the door and go in.

Selling the bassinet proved to be easier than she had hoped. In fact, the woman behind the counter asked if Katie could supply her with several more. Pocketing the cash, Katie thanked the saleswoman and gave her Elam's name. If she helped him earn some extra income, it might make up in some small way for the fact that she'd had to part with his gift like this.

Once outside the building, Katie retrieved her suitcase and hurried toward the bus station. Main Street in

Hope Springs ran north and south past shops, a café and small, neat homes with drab winter yards. Traffic was light. Only an occasional car passed her. Each time she heard the fast clip-clop of a buggy coming up behind her she couldn't help but think of Elam and Nettie and how kind they had been to her.

In a secret place in her heart, Katie foolishly wished that Elam would come after her. She knew better, but the wish remained.

She prayed he and his mother were not offended by her abrupt departure. She'd tried to explain herself in the note she'd left, but words were inadequate to thank them for all they had done.

The bus depot lay at the far side of town just off the highway. Relief flooded through her when she saw the large blue and gray vehicle still idling beneath the corrugated iron awning outside the terminal. A man in a gray uniform was stowing a green duffel bag in the luggage compartment. She stopped beside him. "Is this the bus going west?"

"It is."

"Can I still get a ticket?"

He slammed the storage lid shut. "If you hurry. I'm pulling out in five minutes."

"I'll hurry."

Inside, she rushed to the ticket window, but had to wait for a couple, obviously tourists, to finish first. She glanced repeatedly at the large clock on the wall.

When it was finally her turn, she said, "I need a ticket to Yoder, Kansas."

The short, bald man with glasses didn't look up, but typed away at his keyboard. "We don't have service to Yoder. The nearest town is Hutchinson, Kansas. You'll have to make connections in St. Louis and Kansas City."

"That will be fine. How much is it?" She pulled the bills from her pocket.

"One hundred and sixty-nine dollars."

Her heart dropped to her feet. That was thirty dollars more than she had. This couldn't be happening. She'd come so far. She'd even sold Elam's gift to her child. Rachel began squirming and fussing. Tightening her grip on her daughter, Katie said, "Are you sure it's that much?"

He looked over his glasses. "I'm sure. Do you want a ticket or not?"

"I don't have enough, but I have to get on this bus." What was she going to do?

"We take credit cards."

"I don't have one," she admitted in a small voice.

"Then I can't sell you a ticket. I'm sorry."

"Please, I have to get on this bus today."

"Do you want to buy a ticket to St. Louis instead of Hutchinson?" he suggested.

"No." What good would it do to arrive in a strange city with no money and no one to help her? It would be jumping from the frying pan into the fire. She turned to look over the waiting room. Besides the tourist, there were two Amish men, both in black suits with wide-brimmed, black felt hats and long gray beards. The only other person waiting to board was a young soldier in brown-and-green fatigues.

Rachel began crying in earnest. Any pride that Katie had slid away in the face of her growing desperation. She left the ticket counter and approached the Amish men first praying they would treat her with the same kindness the Sutter family had shown her.

"Sirs, I must get on this bus, but I don't have enough

money to reach my destination. Could I beg you for the loan of thirty dollars? I will pay you back, I promise."

The men stared at her a long moment, then one spoke to the other in German, but Katie understood them. "She looks like a runaway. We shouldn't help her. We should send her back to her family."

"*Jah.*"

The bus driver pushed open the outside door and said, "All aboard."

Katie clutched the black gabardine sleeve of the Amish elder. "I'm not a runaway. I mean... I was, but I'm trying to reach my brother's home. Malachi Lantz. Perhaps you knew him before he moved away from here."

"We are not from Hope Springs. We came on business and now we must go home." They picked up their satchels and moved toward the doorway.

Katie spun around to face the English tourists. "Please. I only need thirty more dollars to get home. Won't you help me?"

The man hesitated, then started to pull his wallet out of his pocket, but his wife stopped him. "She probably wants it for drug money. I've heard plenty stories about these Amish teenagers. Let's go."

Tears filled Katie's eyes as she watched them leave. The young soldier stopped at her side. "I've only got ten bucks on me, but you're welcome to it. I won't need it. I'm headed back to my post."

She shook her head. "It's not enough, but bless you."

He shrugged and said, "Good luck."

As the people filed up the steps of the bus outside, Katie sank onto one of the chairs. Exhaustion rushed in to sap what little strength she had left.

The man behind the ticket counter came out and

began turning off the lights. "We're closing, ma'am. You'll have to leave."

Rising, she picked up her small suitcase and walked out with lagging steps.

The bus pulled away in a cloud of diesel fumes. The sight reminded her so much of her arrival only days ago that she started to laugh. Only her chuckle turned into a broken sob. She couldn't do anything right. Everything she touched turned to ashes. She couldn't run away. She couldn't even run home. How was she going to take care of her daughter?

Dropping her suitcase, she sat on it and leaned back against the wall of the depot. She pressed a hand to her lips to stifle the next sob.

Rachel began crying but Katie was too tired to do more than hold her. Closing her eyes, she rocked back and forth. "What will become of us now?"

Chapter Seven

Elam finished loading the lumber he needed into the back of his farm cart. His gray Belgian draft horse, Joey, stood quietly, his head hung low, waiting to carry the load home. As Elam closed the tailgate of the wagon, he heard someone call his name. Turning, he saw Bishop Joseph Zook approaching.

"Good evening to you, Elam." The bishop touched the brim of his black felt hat.

"And to you, Bishop," Elam replied, feeling uneasy at the man's intense scrutiny.

"Mrs. Zimmerman mentioned that Katie Lantz has been staying with you. I didn't know she was a friend of the family."

"She returned expecting to find her brother still farming here. The shock of finding him gone brought on her labor and she delivered a little girl, but they left today."

"She's gone, then?" The bishop seemed relieved.

"*Jah,* she's gone." Saying the words made it seem so final. Katie had dropped into his life without warning. She had stirred up feelings he'd tried to keep buried. Now she was gone and he felt her loss keenly.

He hesitated, then asked, "Did you know her well, Bishop?"

"I did not. Once she was of age, she rarely attended services or gatherings. Her brother used to lament how stubborn and how selfish she was, how she thought herself better than the others in our Plain community. He expressed much worry that she meant to leave us and to entice other youth away, as well."

Her brother's description didn't match the quiet, meek woman that had come to Elam's door. Still, her family would know her best.

Bishop Zook hooked his thumbs in his suspenders. "I wish that I might have spoken to her to see if she has come back to the faith. My cousin lives near Malachi in Kansas and he has written that they are happy in their new home. It would be good news for them to hear Katie has found redemption."

Elam shook his head. "She was in trouble and seeking her family's help, but I fear she does not mean to stay among the Plain people."

"It was commendable that you rendered her assistance, but it is better that she has left your home if she has not repented. Perhaps she will see the error of her ways. Until then all we can do is pray for her."

"*Jah,* we can do that. I'd best be getting on my way or it will be dark before I get home." Elam nodded toward the bishop and climbed up to his seat.

"Please tell your mother I send my regards."

"I will. She's looking forward to holding church services at our home come Sunday."

"I know God will bless the gathering. It will not be long until spring communion is upon us. We must select a new deacon before then."

"I was sorry to hear of Deacon Yoder's passing. I did not know him well, but I'm told he was a good man."

"He is with God now, and we must all rejoice in that."

Besides the bishop, Elam's church district had two preaching ministers and one deacon. The deacon's responsibilities included helping the bishop and preachers at church services and assisting needy members of the community, such as widows, by collecting alms. It was also the duty of a deacon to secure information about errant members of the community and convey those to the bishop.

It had been the deacon in Elam's old church that had brought the pronouncement of Elam's father's excommunication and later the news of his fiancée's shunning.

"You are new to our congregation, Elam. If you feel you don't know our men well enough to nominate someone for the office, I can offer you some guidance. My cousin in Kansas writes that they too have lost their deacon and that Malachi Lantz has been chosen to take his place."

Being single, Elam knew he was ineligible to be nominated, and for that he was glad. Only married men could serve. A deacon would be chosen by lots from among the nominated men. It was a lifelong appointment.

Nodding to the bishop, Elam said, "I will visit with you after services this Sunday."

Slapping the lines against Joey's broad rump, Elam left the lumberyard and headed down Lake Street toward Main. Pulling to a halt at the traffic light, he glanced up Main toward the bus depot at the other end of town. Had Katie already left? Was she on her way to her brother's or was she going back to the city and Rachel's father?

Either way it was none of his business, so why did he care so much? The light turned green, but he didn't notice until a car honked behind him. The English, always in such a hurry.

He clucked his tongue to get Joey moving, but as they entered the intersection Elam suddenly turned the horse left instead of right.

What would it hurt to make sure Katie had gotten on the bus? If he could tell his mother he knew for certain Katie had left town Nettie might feel better and give up worrying over Katie and Rachel. He didn't closely examine his own motives for going out of his way. He simply assumed he wanted the chance to say goodbye.

As he neared the station, he saw the lights were off and the closed sign had been hung on the door. Sadness filled him. The bus had already gone, taking puzzling, pretty Katie Lantz with it.

Pulling on the reins, he started to turn around when he caught the sound of a baby crying. Drawing closer to the building, he saw Katie sitting huddled against the side of the depot. She had her head down, her face buried in one hand as she cradled her baby with the other. Her shoulders shook with heavy sobs.

He stopped the wagon and jumped down. Reaching her in three long strides, he dropped to his haunches beside her.

Her head jerked up and he found himself looking at her red-rimmed eyes and tearstained face, partially obscured by the curtain of her dark hair. Even in her pitiful state he couldn't help but think how beautiful she was. Reaching out with one hand, he gently tucked her hair behind her ear. "Ah, Katie, why couldn't you have been on that bus."

"I tried…but I didn't have…enough money."

Her broken sobs twisted his heart like a wet dishrag. He had no business caring so much about this woman. He said, "Mother wants me to bring you home."

"I can't…go with you. I've been…too much trouble…already. We'll be…fine."

"You are a prideful woman, Katie. Would you stop me from doing what the Bible commands of me?"

At her look of confusion, he said, "It is my duty to care for anyone who is destitute and in need, even if it be my bitter enemy—which you are not. Now, let me have Rachel." He eased the baby from her arms.

"Besides, if Mother found out that I left you and Rachel here alone she would tan my hide. Or make me do my own cooking, which would be worse." His attempt at humor brought a fresh onslaught of crying.

"Don't cry, Katie." Slipping his free hand under her elbow, he helped her to her feet. She swayed, and for a second he feared she would crumple to the sidewalk. He pulled her close to steady her, wondering how he could manage to carry both of them to the wagon.

"Be strong just a little longer," he whispered.

She nodded and moved away from him, but he didn't let go of her arm. Helping her up onto the wagon seat, he glanced toward the street as a horse and buggy trotted past. What kind of rumors would soon be flying about him and the weeping English woman he'd picked up at the bus station? Hope Springs was a small town with a well-oiled rumor mill. By tomorrow, speculation would be flying over the fences.

More gossip was the last thing he wanted for his family in their new community, but leaving Katie and her baby on the side of the road was out of the question. He briefly considered taking them to the medical clinic and leaving them in the care of the midwife and the town doctor, but he dismissed the idea.

He hadn't been kidding when he said his mother would be upset if he didn't bring Katie back. It was easier to blame her than to admit he wanted Katie and Rachel back under his roof as much as his mother did.

When Katie was settled on the seat, he handed her the baby, then picked up her suitcase and swung it into the wagon bed. After glancing around, he asked, "Where is Rachel's *babybett?*"

"I sold it," Katie answered, her voice low and filled with anguish.

"You did what?"

"I sold it to the woman who runs the Amish Trading Post to pay for my ticket but it wasn't enough. I'm so sorry. I had to do it."

And you left Rachel without a place to lay her head.

He bit back the comment he wanted to make and climbed onto the seat beside Katie. Picking up the reins with one hand, he clucked to Joey.

The big Belgian swung the wagon around and began plodding toward the edge of town. Before long, a line of cars started stacking up behind them, but he didn't care.

At the Trading Post, Elam drove into the parking lot and stopped near the front of the store. Katie withdrew a wad of bills from her pocket and silently held them out. He ignored her.

He jumped down from the wagon without saying a word and entered the building. The bassinet was on display near the counter. He picked it up, haggled the outrageous price down to one he could afford and left the store with the bed slung over his arm and his anger simmering low and hot. Outside, he climbed onto the wooden bench and set the basket between them.

As soon as Joey had them back out on the highway, Katie said. "I'm sorry. It was all I had. Please take the money."

He glanced at her from the corner of his eye. Her lips trembled pitifully. Her face was pale, her eyes red-rimmed and swollen from crying. His anger evaporated. How could he stay angry with her in the face of her obvious distress?

"Keep your money."

"But you bought back the bed."

"I bought it for Rachel, not for you. It is hers. Put your money away."

Katie extended the bills toward him. "I can't let you do that."

"Repay me by explaining why you ran off today."

Her eyes widened. She looked like a rabbit caught in the open, with nowhere to hide and a hawk swooping in for the kill.

"I wanted to reach my brother. The next bus wasn't until Monday. I didn't want to impose on you for that long."

"Since you have not given me or my mother a letter to mail to your brother, I'm going to ask why not."

She looked down at the child she held in her arms. "I have to go to Malachi in person."

"What are you not telling me, Katie Lantz?" Elam's firm tone demanded a truthful answer.

She looked away and stared at the barren fields awaiting their spring planting. "I am dead to my brother until I kneel in front of him and beg his forgiveness."

Elam could only wonder at the behavior that had forced her brother to make such a pronouncement. Church members who had committed serious offences were required to kneel in front of the congregation or the bishop and confess their sins before they could be forgiven. Her brother was not a bishop.

"Surely a letter would suffice under these circumstances," Elam said. "Had you written to him when you first came to us, you might have a reply by now."

"I wrote my brother several times in the first months after I left home. I was sorry for the things I said and the way we parted. He sent my letters back unopened. After that, I stopped trying."

"So that's why you didn't know he had sold the farm and moved away."

"Yes."

"He will open a letter from me," Elam stated firmly.

Katie said nothing. Her eyes were closed and she swayed on the seat. She looked utterly exhausted. He said, "Why don't you put the baby in her bassinet before you drop her."

Katie's eyes shot open. "I won't drop her."

"You're both bone tired. I think she'll rest better in her bed."

"She does seem to like it. The woman at the Trading Post wanted you to make more of them."

"Is that so?" Some additional orders for his work would be welcome. He hadn't considered making baby beds. Perhaps Katie's actions would bring some good after all.

Elam let the lines go slack, but the horse continued on his way without faltering. He needed no urging to head home where there would be hay, grain and a rubdown at the end of the trip. Elam held the baby bed steady while Katie laid her daughter in it. Rachel made little grunting noises as she squirmed herself into a comfortable position and drifted off to sleep.

Once he was sure she wasn't going to start fussing

again, he carefully set her bed on the floorboard under the seat, where she would be out of the wind.

"She's beautiful, isn't she?" Katie asked, her voice barely audible. "I don't know what I did to deserve her."

"*Jah,* she's a right pretty baby." A baby with a young and foolish mother and a father who didn't want her. As Elam picked up the reins again, he prayed that Rachel and her mother would come to know God's love in their lives.

They rode on in silence as the last rays of sunlight cast long shadows toward the east. Elam began to make an inventory of the supplies he'd need to make more beds like the one Rachel slept in.

Suddenly, Katie slumped against Elam. He grabbed her to keep her from tumbling forward off the wagon seat and jerked Joey to a halt.

"Katie! Are you all right?"

He cupped her chin and lifted her face so he could see her. She was deathly pale. Dark circles under her eyes stood out like vivid bruises. Her eyelids fluttered open and she tried to focus on his face.

"I'm…so tired…." Her words trailed off and her eyes closed again.

Poor thing. She was all done in. It was no wonder. She'd had a rough time of it today. He shifted his weight and settled her head against his shoulder, keeping one arm around her to hold her steady.

Elam spoke softly. "Hup now, Joey. Get along."

The horse moved forward once more. Elam tried to concentrate on the road ahead, but the feel of Katie's slender body nestled against him drove all coherent thoughts out of his head. How could something that felt so right be so wrong? She wanted no part of his faith or his way of life. He knew that, but he couldn't deny the attraction he felt for her.

He'd only held one other woman this way. Salome, the night he'd asked her to marry him. The memory of that day came rushing back.

He had nervously proposed marriage as he was driving her home in his buggy after the barn raising at Levi Knopp's farm. She'd said yes as she sat bolt upright beside him, looking straight ahead. He'd draped his arm around her shoulder wanting to hold her close.

Instantly he'd sensed her withdrawal. At the time, he put it down to her modesty and promptly withdrew his arm. It wasn't until much later that he understood she didn't return his regard. If only she'd been able to confide in him that night, a great deal of heartbreak could have been avoided.

He glanced down at Katie. She and Salome were nothing alike. Where Katie was small, slender and dark-haired, Salome had been tall, blonde and sturdy. A hard-working farm girl, she and Elam had known each other their entire lives, attending the same church and sitting on opposite sides of the one-room schoolhouse until they'd finished the eighth grade.

As with all Amish children the eighth grade was the end of their formal education. Salome had cried inconsolably the final day of school. A year later, he took her home after Sunday singing. He had only been sixteen, but he knew then that he was going to ask her to marry him someday.

Joey turned off the highway into Elam's lane and picked up the pace without urging. Katie moaned softly when the wagon wheels hit a deep rut in the dirt road.

Pushing the painful memories of Salome to the back of his mind, he again pondered Katie's situation. Why had Malachi cut her out of his life? Had it been because he felt the censure of the community over Katie's rejection of her Amish heritage? Elam found that hard to believe.

The community of Hope Springs had been welcoming and supportive. A few Amish families in the area had children who didn't follow the faith. His uncle Isaac had two children out of ten that had never been baptized. They maintained cordial relations with their parents and visited back and forth often. Uncle Isaac referred to them as his English sons. He loved and enjoyed seeing his English grandchildren.

Not all Amish felt that way. Many families simply couldn't come to terms with children who jumped the fence and never reconciled with them. Yet, for Malachi to move to another state without leaving a way for his sister to contact him spoke of a very serious breach. There had to be more to the story than Katie had told them. Perhaps his letter to Malachi would bring some answers in the return mail.

Would Katie be angry that Elam had written to her brother without her consent? He suspected she might, and that made him smile down at her. If he had learned anything about Katie Lantz, it was that she had a large measure of pride. Perhaps today's troubles had shown her the error of such thinking. Perhaps—but he doubted it.

As the wagon rolled into the farmyard, his mother rushed out of the house. "You found them. Thanks be to God. Are they all right? Where is the baby?"

"She's sleeping in her bed under the seat. Can you get her? I'm afraid to let go of Katie."

Looking up at him, Nettie seemed to notice for the

first time that he had his arm around Katie. A quick frown put a crease between her brows. "Is she ill?"

"I think she's just exhausted."

Nettie stepped up to the side of the wagon and extracted the baby and her bed. "Come here, precious one. I've missed you."

Elam shook his passenger. "Katie, wake up. We're home."

"We are?" she muttered against his shoulder. Sitting up straighter, she wavered back and forth, but didn't open her eyes.

"We are. If I let go of you, will you fall off the wagon?"

It took her a long moment to reply. She pushed her hair out of her eyes and blinked hard. "I'm fine. Where's Rachel?"

"I have her," Nettie said.

Elam stepped down and held up his arms to Katie. At first he thought she intended to refuse his help, but she changed her mind. Leaning toward him, she braced her hands on his shoulders as he lifted her out of the cart.

Her knees buckled when her feet hit the ground. He scooped her up into his arms to keep her from falling.

"Put me down. I'm fine." Her slurred words and drooping eyelids said otherwise.

He shifted her higher. The feel of her slight body in his arms made him catch his breath. She was a woman who made him all too aware that he was a flesh-and-blood man. The last thing he wanted was to become involved with a woman outside his faith.

She put her arms around his neck and laid her head on his shoulder. "I said I'm fine, Elam."

She wasn't, but neither was he. Without replying, he turned and carried her into his home.

Chapter Eight

Katie woke in a familiar room. Her own room. The room she'd slept in all through her childhood. The same white-painted, unadorned walls surrounded her. The ceiling over the bed sloped low because of the roof's pitch. The series of cracks that had developed in the plaster over her head hadn't changed. When she was little, they had reminded her of stair steps leading to heaven, the place where her parents had gone.

It had been a comfort to a lonely little girl to believe that she might be able to follow them up those steps someday. Now Katie knew they were only cracks in the plaster.

She turned her head. Sunlight was streaming through the tall, narrow window because the green shade was up. It must be late.

She sat up. The room was chilly but not unbearable. The heat from the stove in the kitchen below had always kept this room warmer than any of the other upstairs bedrooms.

She winced as she threw off the covers. Rubbing her aching arms, she quickly realized almost every part of her body throbbed with dull pain. She felt as if she'd been run over by a bus.

The bus! She'd missed the bus.

And Elam had found her weeping in the terminal parking lot.

Embarrassment flooded every fiber of her being as she recalled being carried up the narrow stairs in his arms, followed by Nettie's gentle scolding as she had readied Katie for bed.

Where was Rachel? Where was her baby?

Katie quickly checked the room, but her daughter was nowhere in sight. She noticed her suitcase beside a dark bureau along the opposite wall. Rising, she dressed quickly in a red cable-knit sweater and dark skirt, then ran her fingers through her tousled hair.

At the top of the stairs she heard women's voices. As she descended the steps, she heard laughter and banter exchanged in German. Stepping into the kitchen, she saw Nettie and three other Amish women all hard at work cleaning the room.

Nettie was the first to catch sight of Katie. "You're up. How are you feeling?" she asked in English.

Instantly, Katie found herself the focus of the other women's attention. "I'm feeling much better. Where is Rachel?"

"Elam is keeping the little ones entertained in the living room while we get our work done. Katie, these are my daughters, Ruby and Mary, and this is Ruby's sister-in-law, Sally. All of them work with Elam in his basket business."

Although farming was considered the best work, Katie knew many Amish families needed more than one income and small, home-based businesses were the norm.

Katie glanced around the room. The two women in their late twenties to early thirties were carbon copies of their mother, with blond hair, apple-red cheeks and bright blue eyes. Katie thought the youngest woman must be fifteen or sixteen. She had ginger red hair parted in the middle beneath her white *kapp* and a generous sprinkling of freckles over her upturned nose.

One of the older women stepped forward. Katie saw she was pregnant. "I'm Mary. My mother has told us about your daughter's unexpected and exciting arrival."

Mary glanced over her shoulder toward her mother then leaned closer. "I shouldn't say this, but I'm grateful you've given her something to do besides hover over me and fuss."

"I don't hover or fuss," Nettie declared.

The two sisters looked at each other and burst into giggles.

"When one of us is pregnant that's exactly what you do," Mary countered.

"*Ach,* pay them no mind, Katie. Would you like something to eat? You must be starving. You've nearly slept the clock around." Without waiting for a reply, Nettie began gathering a plate and silverware to place on the table.

Katie frowned. "I'm okay, but Rachel must be starving."

"No need to worry," Nettie answered. "I gave her some infant formula the nurse left with us. Rachel took it fine."

"I could use a bite to eat. I'm as hungry as a horse," Mary interjected.

"And as big as one," Ruby added, then ducked away from her sister's outrage.

"You just wait. Your turn will come round again, sister."

"Everyone sit down," Nettie commanded. "I have cinnamon rolls, and I can fix coffee in a jiffy."

Mary eased into a kitchen chair at the table. She looked at Katie and patted the seat beside her. "*Mamm* tells us you used to live here."

"I did. My mother died in a fire when I was just a toddler. My brother Malachi and his wife took me in. This was his house."

Before Katie sat down to eat she had to check on Rachel. She moved to the living room doorway. Looking in, she saw Elam with the baby in his arms and three little boys playing with blocks around his feet. Elam hadn't noticed her as he was trying to keep the oldest boys from squabbling over the ownership of a carved wooden horse.

Her daughter looked so tiny balanced against his broad chest. For Katie, it was odd to see a man who wasn't intimidated by a newborn baby. Elam firmly but kindly settled the brewing quarrel and sat back in his chair to keep a watchful eye on the bunch. Rachel looked quite content where she was, so Katie returned to the table and sat down.

She was hungry so she made short work of the delicious cinnamon bun and the glass of milk Nettie placed in front of her.

While Mary and Ruby seemed at ease with their mother's houseguest, Sally remained quiet. She had a hard time meeting Katie's eyes. The young Amish girl obviously hadn't had much exposure to the English or an ex-Amish who was trying to be English.

Finally, Sally worked up the nerve to speak. "Did

you really live in Cincinnati? What was it like in such a big city?"

How do I answer that question? My experience was colored by so many different things, Katie thought.

She smiled at Sally. "When I first moved there it was very exciting. Especially at night. You can't imagine the lights. They glow from every tall building and many stay on all night long."

"It sounds so exciting." Sally's tone was wistful.

Katie knew just how it felt to wonder about forbidden things so far away. "Although it can be pretty, it was also terrifying. It was far, far different than I imagined."

Sally leaned forward eagerly. "Are you going back there?"

"I'm not sure what I'm going to do."

"I would like to see the city. My *dat* sometimes travels there for his furniture business, but he's never taken me. Are the buildings really so tall that they block out the sun?"

"It's a place filled with wickedness ready to ensnare the unwary." Elam spoke from the doorway to the living room. He still held Rachel in his arms.

Katie felt the heat rising in her cheeks. He was talking about her. She raised her chin, refusing to give in to the need to keep her head down. Amazed at her own daring, she replied, "Wickedness can ensnare the unwary no matter where they are. Even on the family farm."

He met her gaze, then nodded slightly. "That is true."

An awkward silence ensued until Sally asked, "Elam, my *dat* wants to know when you need me to start weaving again."

"I'll be ready to start the middle of next week, if that's okay with everyone."

All the women nodded. One of the boys, the littlest one, who looked to be about a year old, crawled over to Elam's leg and pulled himself upright and babbled away. Elam reached down to steady the child. "Monroe thinks he is hungry, Ruby."

Nettie came and took the boy from him. His older brother wriggled between Elam's leg and the doorjamb. "I'm starving, *Mamm*."

"You don't fool me, Thomas. You heard the words *cinnamon roll*."

A wide grin split his cheeks, and he bobbed his blond head.

Elam rubbed his stomach. "I'm hungry, too. It's hard work watching the children. I've worked up an appetite."

Ruby threw up her hands. "That's what I tell my Jesse, but he doesn't believe me."

A shout from outside drew everyone's attention. Elam looked out the window. "The bench wagon is here."

Nettie, dishing out rolls to each of the women at the table and their assorted children, said, "Oh, my, and I'm not done with the cleaning."

Katie realized the arrival of the bench wagon meant that the family was making preparations for the *Gemeesunndaag*, the church Sunday, to be held in their home.

The Amish had no formal house of worship. Instead, a preaching service was held every other Sunday in the home of one church family. Up to a hundred and twenty people had attended services in the house when Katie was growing up. In fact, the wall between the kitchen and the living room was constructed so that it could be moved aside to make more space for the benches that were lined up for the men on one side and the women on the other.

In their district, the church owned the benches required to seat so many people and transported them from home to home for each service as they were needed. In the summertime, church was occasionally held in the cool interiors of large barns in the area.

"I'll have the men stack the benches on the porch." Elam approached Katie and handed over the baby. She took care not to touch him, as her heart skipped a beat and then raced ahead of her good sense at his nearness. When he was close, the memory of his strong arms around her brought the heat of a blush rushing to her face. She glanced around covertly, hoping no one noticed her reaction.

There was something about Elam that stirred feelings she didn't want to acknowledge. What a fickle woman she must be. Once she'd imagined herself in love with Matt. Now she was wrestling with those same emotions when Elam was near.

No. These were not the same emotions.

Elam was kindness and charity. He was strength and faith. He was as different from Matt as day was from night.

How had she been fooled into thinking that what she felt for Matt was love? It had been a shallow substitute. She understood that now. Why hadn't she been smart enough to see it before she'd made such a mess of her life?

With her daughter in her arms, Katie rose, wanting to escape the turmoil of her own thoughts. "I'll feed

Rachel and then I'll be back to help you get ready for church."

Nettie shook her head. "We can do this. You need to rest."

"I've already slept the clock around. How much more rest do I need?" Katie countered.

"A lot. You go take it easy," Ruby said, gathering up the plates.

What Katie really wanted to do was race up to her room and hide under the warm quilt on her bed. It would have been easy to withdraw and hide, but she couldn't do it. She wanted to earn the respect this family was showing her. And she wanted to show Elam that she was more than a helpless, sobbing woman in need of rescue.

Elam escaped outside and drew a deep breath—one filled with the smell of a muddy farmyard, not with the sweet, womanly scent that was so uniquely Katie's.

What was wrong with him? Why did his thoughts continually turn to her? The memory of carrying her in his arms had haunted him long into the night and came rushing back the moment he'd seen her today.

Was he so weak in his faith that he was only attracted to the forbidden fruit? Katie had chosen to be an outsider. He should have nothing to do with her.

Be ye not unequally yoked together with unbelievers: for what fellowship hath righteousness with unrighteousness? And what communion hath light with darkness?

The Plain people were to live apart from the world. He must harden his heart against Katie's dark eyes so full of pain and loneliness. He had to resist the need to make her smile. To touch her soft skin, to kiss her full lips. She was not for him.

Eli Imhoff stepped down from the bench wagon. "*Goot* day, Elam. Jacob and I have brought the benches for your house."

"*Danki,* Mr. Imhoff, and my thanks to you, as well, Jacob." Elam nodded to the teenage boy sitting on the back of the wagon.

The boy nodded and held out a bundle of letters and the newspaper. "The mailman was dropping this off as we came by. I thought I'd save you a trip down the lane."

"*Danki,* Jacob." Elam took the mail and laid it on his mother's rocker near the front door.

Walking to the back of the wagon, Mr. Imhoff lowered the tailgate. "Shall we get started?"

Elam hurried to join them. "*Jah,* and then you must stay for a cup of coffee. My mother has just made some."

Mr. Imhoff, a widower, glanced toward the house. "How is your mother getting along? Is she liking Hope Springs?"

Perhaps it was his awareness of Katie's effect on him that made Elam notice the odd quality in Mr. Imhoff's simple questions.

"Mother is well. She misses her friends back home, but I think she likes the area well enough."

"*Goot.* Very *goot.*" Mr. Imhoff grinned and began pulling off the first seat. After unloading the sturdy wooden benches and stacking them together on the porch, Elam invited Mr. Imhoff and his son into the house.

Elam picked up the mail as he followed them inside. He laid the letters on the counter, more interested in the looks and shy smiles that passed between his neighbor and his mother. How long had this been going on? His mother had been a widow for three years now, but he'd never considered that she might be interested in another man.

After accepting a cup of coffee, Mr. Imhoff said, "I was just asking your son if you're adjusting to our community."

"I find it much to my liking, especially since two of my daughters and my son are here."

"It's a blessing to have your family close by." Mr. Imhoff blew on his coffee to cool it.

Jacob was drawn into the other room by Elam's nephews. The next time Elam glanced that way, the strapping boy was down on the floor with them. Mr. Imhoff followed Elam's gaze. "He's used to having little ones underfoot."

The sound of someone descending the stairs made Elam tense. He hadn't thought of how he would introduce Katie to the members of his church.

She came through the door holding Rachel on her shoulder. Her English clothing and uncovered head made her stand out in the room filled with Plain women. She nodded politely at the visitors.

Elam's mother stepped in to fill the awkward silence. "This is our visitor. Mr. Imhoff, perhaps you remember Katie Lantz."

He nodded in her direction. "Quiet little Katie with the dark eyes? I do, but you are much changed. How is your brother? Is he happy in Kansas? My cousin moved there a few years ago. He says a man can own land and not farm it, but make a living by renting his grass out for other men's cows to graze on."

"I have not seen my brother in quite a while," Katie admitted.

"I'm sorry to hear that. Family is so very important."

Katie looked lovingly at the child she held. "I'm beginning to understand that."

Mr. Imhoff sighed. "I wish God had seen fit to leave mine with me longer."

Nettie laid a hand on his arm. "We take comfort in knowing they are with God."

He patted her hand, allowing his fingers to linger on hers longer than Elam thought necessary.

Elam knew that Mr. Imhoff's wife and three of his seven children had been killed when a car struck their buggy several years ago. His oldest daughter, Karen, had taken over the reins of the family and was raising her younger siblings.

Nettie caught her son looking her way and withdrew her hand. Mr. Imhoff said quickly, "My daughter wants you to know she'll be happy to help with the meal and the cleanup after church if you wish it."

Nettie cast a sly look at Elam before she replied. "Tell Karen her help will be most welcome."

Even his sisters exchanged speaking looks and little smiles. Mary said, "*Jah,* we always welcome Karen's help."

A possible reason for their covert glances suddenly dawned on him. Karen was single and close to his own age. Had the women of his family decided on some matchmaking?

Shaking his head, he turned away and picked up the mail. Sorting through it, he froze when his glance fell on a long white envelope. The return address was Yoder, Kansas. It was an answer from Malachi Lantz.

Elam's heart dropped to his boots. He glanced to where Katie was happily showing her daughter to Mr. Imhoff.

Her brother had written. That meant she would be leaving soon.

Elam leaned back against the counter. That was what he wanted, wasn't it? So why wasn't he glad?

Chapter Nine

When Mr. Imhoff and his son left, Katie excused herself from the group in the kitchen and carried Rachel into the living room where the bassinet was set up. When Katie attempted to put her down, her daughter displayed an unusual streak of bad temper and threw a fit. The young boys were immediately intrigued by the baby and crowded around, their toys forgotten.

"Why is she crying?" the older boy asked in Pennsylvania Dutch. He, like all Amish children, would not learn more than a few words of English until he started school.

She answered him in kind. "I think she is tired, but she's afraid she'll miss something interesting if she goes to sleep."

"Can I hold her?"

"If you sit quietly on the sofa, you may."

The boys scrambled onto the couch and sat up straight. Katie laid Rachel in Thomas's arms. The baby immediately fell silent as she focused on the unfamiliar face. The difference between her dark-haired baby and the boys with their white-blond hair was striking.

Thomas grinned at Katie. "She likes me."

Katie smiled back at him. "I think she does."

She was sitting beside Thomas showing him how to support Rachel's head, when Elam came into the room. Katie looked up and froze when she saw the expression on his face. He drew a chair close and sat in front of her.

He glanced at the boys. "Thomas, I need someone to gather the eggs today. Can you boys do that?"

Thomas puffed up. "Sure."

Katie took Rachel from the boy. Clearly Elam wanted to talk to her without the children in the room. A sense of unease settled in the pit of her stomach.

"*Gut.* Get a basket for the eggs from your grandmother." Elam ruffled Thomas's hair. The boy hurried to do the chore with his younger cousin following close behind.

Katie held Rachel and rocked her gently, waiting for Elam to speak.

"I wrote to your brother shortly after you came to us."

Her heart sank. "You did what?"

"It was clear you couldn't find the words. I did not tell him anything about Rachel. I only said that you were staying with us, but had not the means to get to Kansas."

"I wish you hadn't done that, Elam."

"I know. I'm sorry I didn't tell you sooner." After a moment, he held out a white envelope. "This came this morning."

Katie tried to hide her trepidation, but she could feel Elam's gaze on her as she stared at the envelope without moving. She asked, "What does he say?"

"I haven't opened it. I thought perhaps you would like to do that."

"It's addressed to you. You should read it." She lifted her chin, expecting the worst but praying for the best.

"All right."

She struggled to maintain a brave front. He tore open the envelope and read the short note inside.

His expression hardened. He pressed his lips together.

"Well?" Katie asked.

He read aloud. "'Dear Mr. Sutter, I am sorry to hear Katie has burdened your family with her presence. Please understand it is with a heavy heart that I tell you she is not welcome in our home.'"

Elam stopped reading to look at her. "Perhaps it would be better if you read the rest in private."

She shook her head and clutched Rachel more tightly. "No, go on."

Swallowing hard, Elam resumed reading. "'I will not make arrangements for Katie to travel here. Beware of her serpent's tongue. She has fooled us too often with her words of repentance uttered in falsehood. I pray God will take pity on her soul. She is no longer kin of mine. Your friend in Christ, Malachi Lantz.'"

Katie cringed as Elam lowered the letter. Though she had tried to prepare herself for Malachi's response, it still hurt. She turned her face away as tears stung her eyes.

She was disgraced with nowhere to go. All her struggles to reach her family had been in vain.

Looking into Elam's sympathetic eyes, she said, "I had hoped Malachi would take us in, but if he has publicly disowned me…he won't. I did not believe he would do this."

"Perhaps when he learns you have a child."

She shook her head. "I don't see how that will make him think better of me."

"What about Matt's family?"

"I never met any of them. I think Matt was too ashamed of me."

"Ashamed or not, he has a duty to provide for his child."

"I don't know how to reach him or his family. Mrs. Zimmerman said they were out of the country."

Katie looked up at Elam through her tears. "I truly had nowhere to go."

Elam longed to gather her into his arms and comfort her, but he couldn't. It wouldn't be right. How could a brother be so coldhearted? And Matt! To cast aside a woman and ignore his own child. What kind of man could do that? Elam wanted to shake them both.

Now was the time for her family to show Katie compassion, to welcome her back as the prodigal child and show her the true meaning of Christian forgiveness.

While he had no way of knowing what had transpired between the siblings before Katie left home, this didn't seem right. Many young people made mistakes and fell away from the true path during their *rumspringa,* the "running around" time of adolescents, but it was unusual for a person to be disowned by their family because of such activity.

Elam stared at Katie, trying to see her as her brother saw her. Tears stained her cheeks. She couldn't disguise the hurt in her eyes. She was simply a young woman struggling to find her way in life.

"Is what your brother said true?"

"About my serpent's tongue? Maybe it is. I was ready to pretend to be Amish again so that Rachel and I would have somewhere to live."

"So you were going to lie to your brother when you faced him."

"I don't know what I would have done. I was so desperate."

Would she have lied? Elam wanted to believe she would have found the strength to tell the truth. "What will you do now?"

"I'll find work. I'll take care of Rachel."

"What if you can't find work?"

She managed a crooked half smile. "I have a little money put back that I won't have to use on a bus ticket. If I can't find work here, then I'll go to the next town and the next one until I do find something."

"You can't wander the country with a baby."

She shot to her feet. "I'll do whatever I have to do to take care of my child."

Elam stared at her dumbfounded as she stormed out of the room and up the stairs.

A few minutes later, his mother came in the room and began picking up toys. "Your sisters are leaving. Ruby has some baby clothes for little Rachel. I thought Katie was in here? Where did she go?"

Elam held up Malachi's letter. "I heard from her brother today."

Nettie's happy smile faded. "Oh. I knew she wouldn't be with us long, but I had hoped she could stay a few more days. I've grown so fond of her and of that baby. How soon is Malachi coming?"

"He's not."

"What?"

"He says that she is no longer kin of his."

"That's ridiculous."

Elam held out the paper. "Read for yourself."

Taking the note, Nettie settled herself in the chair beside him and adjusted her glasses. After reading the short missive she handed it back. "Well, I never. His own sister is destitute and begging for his help and he is refusing to acknowledge her. No wonder *Gott* sent that child to us."

"Her brother may have his reasons. We can't know his heart, only God can."

"You think this is right?"

"No, but what we think isn't important."

Nettie stood. "She is going to need friends now that she has no family."

His mind told him he could be a friend to Katie, but he realized in his heart he wanted to be much more. Unless she gave up her English ways, that would never happen.

Sunday morning dawned overcast and gray. The warm spell had come to an end. Winter reclaimed the land for a little while longer, sending a cold, drizzling rain that fit Katie's mood. She would have to make some kind of decision soon. Without her brother, she had no one to turn to now. She needed a new plan.

As much as she wanted to be angry with Malachi, she couldn't. She'd never felt like she belonged in his home.

Gazing at her baby sleeping sweetly in her arms, Katie tried to block out the despair that threatened to overwhelm her. She was bone tired. Between Rachel's frequent night feedings and the lingering effects of her hike into town, she could barely keep her eyes open. Any sleep she did get was filled with nightmares of what would happen to them now. No matter what, she had to protect her child.

Outside, buggy after buggy began to arrive. Katie watched the gathering from her upstairs window. Families came together, the men and boys in their black suits and hats, the girls and women in dark dresses with their best black bonnets on their heads.

While most came in buggies, a number of people arrived on foot. Before long the yard was filled with black buggies and the line stretched partway down the lane. The tired horses, some who'd brought a family from as far away as fifteen miles, were unhitched and taken to the corrals.

Nettie had invited Katie to attend services, but she had declined. She didn't belong among them. She didn't belong anywhere.

What was she going to do? How would she take care of Rachel? How would they live?

Why had God sent her this trial?

She turned her limited options over and over in her mind. Perhaps Amber had learned of a job Katie could take? It didn't matter what it was. She'd do anything. Anything.

She turned away from the window. Knowing that the services would last for several hours, she was prepared to stay in her room the entire time. What she wasn't prepared for was the tug of emotion she felt when the first familiar hymn began.

Downstairs, the slow and mournful chanting rose in volume, as voices blended together in one of the ancient songs that had been passed down through the generations. No music accompanied the singing. The Amish needed only the voices of the faithful.

Listening to the words of sorrow, hope and God's promise of salvation, Katie felt a stirring deep within her soul. She knew sorrow, she needed hope, but she was afraid to trust God's mercy.

Moving to the door, Katie opened it a crack. The song continued for another few minutes, then silence fell over the house. She opened the door farther and caught the sound of a man's voice. The preaching had begun, but she couldn't quite make out the words.

Moving outside her room, she stopped at the top of the stairwell where she could hear better. Standing soon grew tiring and she sank down to sit on the top riser.

Cuddling Rachel close to her heart, Katie closed her eyes and listened to the words of the preacher. The scripture readings and preaching were in German, but she had no trouble understanding them.

When the second hymn began, Katie found herself softly singing along as she pondered the meaning of the words for her own life.

When the three-hour service concluded, she heard the rustling of people rising and the flow of social talk getting underway. Shortly, the gathering meal would start.

Suddenly, an Amish woman started up the stairs. When she looked up, Katie recognized Sally.

The young woman stopped a few steps below Katie. "Nettie says you have to eat and it's time to come down. She won't take no for an answer."

Nodding, Katie rose. It was time to face the community she had turned her back on.

She had no illusions that everyone would be as welcoming as Elam and his mother had been. Drawing a deep breath, she descended the stairs with Rachel in her arms.

When she came out of the stairway, she saw Elam off to one side of the room with several other men who were rearranging the benches and forming tables by stacking them together. Not knowing what to do, Katie simply stood out of the way.

It wasn't long before Nettie caught sight of her. "Katie, come help me set the tables."

Sally returned to Katie's side and reached for Rachel. "I'll take her."

Handing over her daughter, Katie smiled at Sally. "Thanks."

Now that she had two free hands, Katie joined Nettie and her daughters in the kitchen. Other women came in carrying hampers laden with fresh breads, meat pies, homemade butter and jams as well as cheeses. Many covert glances came Katie's way, but no one made comments.

Katie and Ruby began setting a knife, cup and saucer at each place around the tables. Since there wasn't enough room to feed everyone at once, the ordained and eldest church members would eat first. The youngest among them would have to wait until last.

Katie was amazed at how natural it felt to be doing such an ordinary task with Nettie and her family. No one chided her or scolded her for sloppy work. She laughed in response to some story Ruby relayed about her boys. Looking across the room, she met Elam's gaze. He gave her a small smile and a nod. She felt the color rush to her cheeks, but she smiled back.

Looking down, she laid another knife by a cup and saucer. She could almost pretend this was her family and this was where she belonged.

When she looked up again, Elam stood across the table from her. He said, "It is good you're not hiding anymore."

She glanced toward the women gathering in the kitchen. "I'm not sure the worst is over."

"I pray that it is, Katie." It seemed as if he wanted to say more, but he didn't.

She watched as he went out to the barn to wait his turn to eat with the other young men. She couldn't help but wonder how he would explain her presence to his friends.

Elam stood just inside the wide-open barn doors amid a group of ten other young men near his age. He was the only clean-shaven one in the group. They were all farmers and his neighbors, and all were married with growing families. A number of those children raced by playing a game of hide-and-seek in the barn. The dreary weather hadn't put a damper on the jovial mood of those around Elam.

"Heard you planned on planting pumpkins this year," Aaron Zook remarked. The bishop's son farmed sixty acres across the road from Elam's place.

Aaron had been the one to help Elam develop the area's newly formed organic food cooperative. Limited to small acreages by their reliance on horses, the local Amish farmers had been struggling to compete with the commercial produce farms in the area. But thanks to Aaron and Elam's efforts, they were finding a niche in a new, fast-growing market as certified organic farmers.

"Prices aren't what they were last year," Samuel Stutzman cautioned.

Elam fought back a smile. Samuel always thought last year's prices were better. "I'm going to try a small field of pumpkins. They're a good fall cash crop, but mostly I'll be sticking to cabbage, potatoes and onions."

Aaron pushed aside his black coat to hook his thumbs in his suspenders. "I'm going to plant more watermelon and cantaloupe. They did the best for me."

Elam kept one ear in the conversation, but planting and cash crops weren't what was foremost on his mind. He looked past the array of black coats, beards and black hats to the house. He had no trouble picking Katie out among the throngs of women on the porch waiting their turn to eat. Her simple gray skirt and red sweater made her stand out like a sore thumb. The women of his family surrounded her.

They were making it plain that Katie was a friend and accepted by them. Part of him was proud of their actions, but another part feared their public display of support would bring disapproval down on them. Katie's history would keep many of the women from acknowledging her.

His mother was talking to Karen Imhoff. Karen's father, rather than gathering with the men, was helping move the tables where Elam's mother directed him.

"Elam, might I have a word with you?"

He turned to find Bishop Zook at his elbow. "Of course, Bishop."

"Come. Walk with me."

Chapter Ten

Elam walked silently alongside the bishop until they were out of earshot from the men in the barn.

The bishop spoke at last. "I see that Katie Lantz is still with you."

"*Jah*. She missed the bus."

"I had hoped to hear she was turning from her English ways?"

"Not yet, but my mother is a good influence on her."

"Let us pray so." He took a deep breath and then continued. "There has been talk, Elam. I tell you this because I value you as a member of the church. You have done much to preserve our way of life."

"I can assure you that nothing unacceptable has happened in my home."

The bishop stopped walking and turned to face him. "I believe you. You are an upright man, but such talk can take on a life of its own. Some are saying that your family cares more about outsiders than our own people."

Anger rose up in Elam, but he worked to suppress it. "Because of my father?"

"Word has reached us of your troubles back in Pennsylvania. Perhaps that is why members of the district have scrutinized you so closely. Taking in this woman wasn't a good idea. We must limit our contact with those who do not believe as we do."

"What would you have me do? Turn her and her child out to beg on the roadside?"

"Of course not, but surely you could arrange for her to travel to her brother's home."

"He has disowned her. The baby's father has abandoned her. She has nowhere to go."

The bishop frowned as he rubbed his neck. "Malachi has disowned his own sister? I had not heard this."

"The letter came yesterday. My mother is only doing her Christian duty in caring for Katie and her baby. Perhaps you can stem this gossip."

"I will do what I can, but I can only do so much."

Elam nodded, but his frustration boiled beneath the surface. It was so unfair. He hadn't lived a blameless life, but he had always loved his faith and tried to do God's will. His mother was a good and kind woman. That should not be held against her.

The bishop began walking back toward the house. "If Katie's brother would change his mind it might solve this problem."

"She does not believe he will. From the tone of his letter, I fear she is right."

"I will write to Malachi and the bishop of his district and explain the situation. Perhaps Malachi can be persuaded to listen to wiser counsel. So you are thinking of planting pumpkins. I've been considering that myself."

Elam followed the bishop's lead and changed the subject back to spring planting.

As they walked back to the gathering, Elam related what he knew about the new variety of pumpkins available, but inside he was deeply worried.

He would not turn Katie and Rachel out of his home, but neither could he stand by and watch his family be shunned again.

Katie was acutely aware that she was the focus of much speculation among the district members. A few of the younger women, friends of Mary and Ruby, came up to be introduced. Some of them Katie remembered from her school days. For the most part, the older women of the group ignored her. Katie recognized many of them as friends of her sister-in-law, Beatrice.

From the covert glances cast her way, she knew most, if not all, were aware that she was an unwed mother.

Another poor Amish girl come to no good in the English world. They would point her out to their teenage daughters as an example of why English men weren't to be trusted.

She glanced toward Elam. Did he see her as spoiled goods?

As she watched, Bishop Zook left Elam's side and came toward her. The bishop looked pensive, but Elam had a deep scowl on his face. Apprehension crawled across her skin.

She folded her hands and lowered her gaze. "Hello, Bishop Zook."

"Hello, Katie. It's been a long time."

"Yes, it has."

"Might I have a word with you in private?"

"Of course." She folded her arms to keep her hands from trembling.

They left the porch and walked to where a large oak tree provided some shelter from the light mist.

"I'm sorry to hear of your troubles. What are your plans now that you are back in Hope Springs?"

"I will be looking for work."

"I see. It won't be easy with a new baby to take care of."

Katie glanced toward the house. "Life is not meant to be easy. That is why we pray for God's strength to help us bear it."

"That is true."

She studied Bishop Zook's lined face and saw only kind concern. His long gray beard was considered a sign of wisdom. She hoped that was true. "Is my presence causing trouble for the Sutters?"

"You wish to protect them?"

"I would not hurt them for the world."

"Let me ask you this. Do you plan to join the church?"

If she gave the bishop that impression, would it prevent the censure of Elam and his family? She didn't want to lie. She chose a middle ground and hoped it would be enough.

"I have been gone a long time. I need to reaccustom myself to the community before making a decision. Joining the church is not a step to be taken lightly."

He rocked back on his heels. "That is wise. Since you were not a member when you left, you will not be expected to make a confession to the church should you decide to begin instructions for baptism. Don't hesitate to come to me if you feel you are in need of guidance."

Relief swept over her. She had bought herself more time without an outright lie. "I will keep that in mind."

As the bishop walked away, Katie headed back to the house. She reached the steps just as Mrs. Zook and several women came out after having finished their meal. The stark expressions on their faces sent a bolt of apprehension through Katie.

Lifting her chin a notch, Katie nodded toward the bishop's wife. "Good day, Mrs. Zook."

She didn't reply. She and the other women turned

their faces aside. The brims of their black bonnets effectively blocking their faces from Katie's view as they walked past her without a word.

Katie's smile slipped as humiliation drained the blood from her face. She could feel the eyes of everyone watching her. Glancing across the yard, she saw Elam staring at her. He stood without moving for a long moment, then he turned away. Her whole body started shaking.

A second later, Nettie was at her side. "Sally says that Rachel is getting fussy. Why don't you take her upstairs and I'll bring you something to eat."

Grateful for Nettie's quick intervention, Katie tried to smile, but her throat ached with unshed tears. She quickly fled into the house where Sally was watching Rachel in Nettie's room.

"I tell you, Elam, I was shocked. The bishop's wife snubbed Katie in front of everyone."

Sitting in his living room that evening, Elam pondered what to tell his mother about his conversation with the bishop. He glanced at the ceiling. Katie had gone to her room and hadn't come down.

Sighing deeply, he said, "The bishop told me talk is already circulating in the community. Some people are saying we are going against the *Ordnung* by allowing Katie to stay here."

"Are you worried about a few gossips who have nothing better to do? And the bishop's wife is the worst offender."

"Which means her words will carry much weight with him. You must take care."

"Are you trying to protect me or yourself? Search your heart, Elam. Katie is a lost sheep, but she wants to find her way back to God."

"I have not heard her say this."

"That's because you aren't listening. We must be a light for her, Elam. We can show her God's goodness and His kindness. If we send her away, we only prove that she doesn't belong here. That child wants so much to belong somewhere. She has been made to feel apart her whole life. Her heart is crying out for someone to care about her, but she is afraid."

"Afraid of what?"

"She's afraid of the same thing that frightens you. She's afraid that she doesn't deserve to be happy."

"I'm not afraid."

She took his hands between her own. "I know your heart has been broken. I know your trust was betrayed. None of it was your fault, Elam. You must forgive."

"I have."

"You say that, but I think there is still bitterness in your heart."

There was, and he hated himself for it. "Have you forgotten how much we all suffered when we had to shun *Dat?* How we begged and pleaded with him to come back to God? Do you remember how your friends stopped seeing you? Of standing on the porch and hearing Deacon Hertzler tell both of you that you were excommunicated because you could not bear to shun your own husband. I heard your weeping, *Mamm,* night after night."

"I have not forgotten, Elam," she answered quietly. "But I made my confession, and I was welcomed back into the church after your father died."

He struggled to bring his agitation under control. "But it was never the same. It must be different here or we have uprooted our lives for nothing."

"And Katie? What part did she play in those sorrows?"

The breath whooshed out of his lungs. He hung his head. "None."

"She has been abandoned by everyone she loved. You and I, we know the pain of that. Of trusting and loving someone only to find that love isn't enough."

"What would you have me do?"

"I would have you show her the compassion I know lives in your heart."

Chapter Eleven

"What will you do now?" Nettie hung a pair of Elam's pants on the clothesline and secured them with wooden clothespins. Monday was wash day.

Beside her, Katie hung up one of Rachel's gowns and reached into the basket for another. "I can't continue living on your charity."

"Don't worry about that," Nettie mumbled around the clothespin she held in her mouth. She secured another pair of pants and said, "You've been a help to me. My wash is going twice as easy with your help."

Katie rolled her eyes. "You could do Monday wash with one hand tied behind your back."

Chuckling, Nettie said, "I've done it with one toddler on my hip and two at my ankles, but I appreciate your help anyway. I'm not as young as I used to be."

Picking up a pair of her own slacks, Katie said, "All I've done is add to your work."

"Your few pants and blouses add very little to my workload. You need more clothes."

Katie was thankful she had packed a few of her pre-pregnancy outfits in her suitcase. "If I keep eating your good cooking, I'm going to have to start wearing my maternity pants again."

"You don't eat enough to make a mouse fat. I would loan you some of my dresses, but they'd be much too big. You are welcome to borrow some things from my daughters. Mary will be happy to loan you a few dresses. The two of you are about the same size."

She'd sworn she would never wear Plain clothes again. After shaking the wrinkles out of one of Nettie's navy dresses, Katie pinned it to the line. The simple designs and solid colors didn't seem as restrictive as she'd once thought them. Wearing sweatshirts and jeans hadn't made her happy or made her feel she belonged in the English world.

She picked up a white sheet. Tossing it over the cord, she adjusted it until it hung evenly. The wind that set it to flapping was cold. The sun played peekaboo behind low gray clouds.

Securing the sheet, Katie said, "Thanks for the offer, but what I need is to get a job. Then I can buy my own clothes and pay rent on my own place."

"Who will take care of Rachel while you work?"

"I'll find someone. There must be a day-care center in Hope Springs."

"It's not right to let others raise your child."

Katie sighed. "What choice do I have?"

"Perhaps your brother will reconsider." Elam's deep voice startled Katie and she nearly dropped the pillowcase she was holding.

Why did he have such an effect on her? She took a deep breath to quiet her rapid pulse. "He might if I go to him in person."

"And if he won't take you in, then you've gone all the way to Kansas for no reason and you'll be worse off than you are now because you'll not have a single friend there." Nettie scowled at her son.

Nettie pulled a shirt from the laundry basket at her feet and shook it vigorously. "What your brother needs is a serious attitude adjustment!"

Katie's mouth fell open. She looked at Elam and they both started laughing. He said, "*Mamm,* where did you hear such talk?"

Her gaze darted between their startled faces. "I heard Jacob Imhoff say it about his little brother. Why? Doesn't it mean he must change his mind?"

Smiling at her, Katie said, "It means you'd like someone to beat him up and change his mind for him."

Taken aback, Nettie raised her eyebrows. "Is that what Jacob meant? Well, I hope and pray your brother finds it in his heart to offer you aid, but I certainly don't wish him harm."

Neither did Katie. With her limited options, she knew she needed to find work as soon as possible. "Would it be all right if I borrowed the buggy this afternoon?"

Elam nodded. "I won't be using it."

"I'd like to see if I can find work in town."

"I will drive you." Elam started to leave.

Katie stopped him by saying, "I can drive myself. I've not been among the English so long that I've forgotten how to handle a buggy."

He scowled at her. "Very well. Have it your way. What time will you be wanting to leave?"

She gestured toward the baskets of laundry waiting to be hung on the clotheslines. "As soon as we are done here."

"Then I'll get Judy hitched up now."

As he strode away, Katie said, "I'm sorry if I made him angry."

"He doesn't know how to handle a woman who wants to make her own way in life."

"I've spent my whole life waiting for a man to take care of me. I thought that was the way it should be, but if I hadn't been so dependent on Matt, and on my brother before that, I wouldn't be in this situation. I'm not going to blithely put my life in the hands of another man. I'm going to take care of myself and I'm going to take care of Rachel."

"I believe you will," Nettie said.

Katie's irritation faded. "It's just bold talk. I haven't a clue how to take care of myself or a baby. Nettie, what am I going to do?"

"Pray to God for guidance and take things one day at a time."

One day at a time. Nettie's advice repeated itself over and over in Katie's mind as she drove toward Hope Springs an hour later. There was little else she could do.

On Main Street, people turned to stare as she drove past. A woman dressed in a red plaid coat and blue jeans driving an Amish buggy was an odd sight to say the least.

At the Trading Post, the same woman that had bought Elam's bassinet was rearranging items on a clearance rack. She looked up at the sound of the bell over the door. "Welcome to the Trading Post. Is there something I can help you with? Oh, you're the young woman who came in with that adorable little bassinet. I sold it the very same day. I don't suppose you've brought more, have you?"

Katie decided not to tell her she'd sold it to the man who made it. "Actually, I've come looking for a job."

"I'm sorry. We aren't hiring now, but we usually take

on summer help starting about mid-May. If you want, I can give you an application."

Hiding her disappointment, Katie said, "That would be great."

"I'm sure I can sell more of those baby carriers."

"I'll tell the man who made mine." Katie filled out the application and left it with the woman, but the idea of waiting another month and a half for a job was discouraging.

The responses at the other merchants and eateries in town were pretty much the same. No one needed help, but most said they would be hiring when the tourist season got underway.

Dejected, Katie left a half-dozen applications with various merchants and turned Judy toward home.

Katie was unhitching the horse when Elam appeared at her side. He said, "Let me give you a hand with that."

"I can manage."

"I know you can, but I'm going to help anyway." He took the heavy harness out of her hands. "How did your job hunting go?"

"Not well. You may be stuck with me until the tourists arrive."

"I thought as much."

Katie pulled off Judy's headstall and paused to draw her hand down the horse's silky black neck. Unlike her brother and some Amish, Katie knew Elam took good care of his horses. He was kind to animals and stray women. She shouldn't read anything into the way he'd cared for her and her baby. "I'm sorry, Elam. If I didn't have Rachel, I'd just go, but I have to think of her welfare."

"You are being foolish to worry about this. God will provide."

"He hasn't done such a good job so far."

"Do not mock Him. He brought you to my mother, didn't He? What better care could He have provided than that?"

"I'm sorry. I'm just frustrated and angry."

"Angry about what?"

"Everything. I'm angry with Matt for leaving me. I'm angry with my brother for disowning me. I'm angry at the people in town who don't need help until summer."

"Are you angry with me?"

She turned to face him. "Of course not. You and your mother have been kindness itself."

"But you still wish to leave and go back among the English."

Did she? There were times when her previous life seemed like an unreal dream. She hadn't truly been happy on this farm, but she hadn't been happy in the city, either. What was wrong with her? What was missing inside her that made her feel she was always on the outside looking in?

Katie led Judy into her stall, turned the mare loose and closed the gate. Facing Elam, Katie knew only the truth would satisfy him.

"I don't belong here, Elam. I never fit in, not with my family, not with the other Amish kids. I was always different. Sometimes I used to wonder if I'd ever find a place where I did belong."

"Would staying here really be so bad?" he asked softly.

Did she imagine the soft pleading in his voice? She must have. It was only wishful thinking on her part. He had no interest in her as a woman. She wasn't of his faith. It was foolish to consider there could be anything between them.

Katie moved to hang up the harness, needing to put some distance between herself and the man who disturbed her peace of mind. She needed to get a handle on her wayward emotions. "I don't want to be a burden on anyone. I need to make a life of my own. To do that, I must find work."

He was silent for so long that she thought he'd gone. When she turned around, he was standing with his hands in his pockets and his head bowed.

Finally, he said, "I've been thinking of hiring more help for my woodshop. I've been getting a fair number of orders for my baskets. More than I'll be able to fill once spring planting starts. Ruby, Mary and Sally all work with me in the business."

"Why haven't I seen them working?"

"I've been remodeling my workroom, but it's done now. They'll all be back to work the day after tomorrow. Of course, once Mary has her baby she'll be at home, but by then you should be able to pick up her slack. Would you be interested in work like that?"

Katie couldn't believe her ears. "Are you offering me a job?"

"You will get paid a commission for each piece you make. It won't be much to start with. Not like the jobs you could get in Cincinnati."

"A woman with nothing but an eighth grade education doesn't earn much, even if she can *find* a job in the city."

"So, do you want to work for me?"

Katie hesitated. "Aren't you afraid of what people will say?"

He sighed deeply. "Katie, I'm sorry about yesterday."

"I was expecting it from people like Mrs. Zook and her friends." She just hadn't expected it from him. It hurt, but she couldn't sustain the anger she wanted to feel. She knew he was simply protecting his family.

"I should have shown you the same support my mother did. Let me make up for my lapse of courage. Come work for me."

She needed work, but she hadn't planned on having to work beside Elam. She was already much fonder of him than was good for her. Whenever he was near, her heart charged into a gallop that left her feeling elated and breathless. Hopefully he didn't suspect. She would die of mortification if he realized how often her thoughts turned to him.

She glanced at his face as he waited for her reply. "I'll have to think on it. I've never done any weaving. I might not be any good at it."

"I can teach you what you need to know. You'll get the hang of it in no time. Come. I'll show you how it's done." He turned on his heels and strode toward the front of the barn. Surprised by his confidence in her ability to learn a new skill, Katie followed him.

He opened a door and stood aside for her to enter. Katie paused at the doorway. She rubbed her hands on her jeans. "This used to be the feed room."

"*Jah,* I turned it into my workroom because it had a good big window."

"Wasn't the window nailed shut?"

"I took the old one out and added more. Come in and see what else I have done. Here is where I keep the wood I use for the baskets. I like working with poplar. There's a big stand of them around the pond, so I don't have to buy the wood." His voice brimmed with eagerness to show her his work.

"I remember the poplars." She recalled their shiny

green leaves reflected in the calm waters of the pond in the summertime.

"I also use brown ash. These are some of my finished baskets." He gestured toward a bin beside the window.

Katie stepped inside the room. The aromatic scent of cedar and wood shavings enveloped her. Elam had painted the walls a bright white. Tools hung from pegs neatly arranged on one wall. A nearly completed cedar chest sat on a worktable. Its lid and a long hinge lay beside it waiting for him to assemble them. In the far corner of the room a tall cabinet stood open.

On the top shelf, Katie spied an Amish doll in a faded purple gown and black apron. It looked out of place among the tools and baskets.

She crossed the room and picked up the doll. Once she'd had one just like it. It had been a gift from her brother Hans. One of her few memories of him.

As she stared at the toy she noticed a small burn hole in the hem of the dress. Her doll's dress had had just such a hole. A burst of excitement sent her pulse racing. It couldn't be. Not after all these years. With shaky fingers she turned back the edge of the bonnet.

Thrilled, she spun around clutching the doll to her chest. "You found Lucita."

The delight in her voice and the happiness shining in her eyes took Elam's breath away. He'd once wondered what it would take to make her smile at him. It seemed that he'd found the answer.

"Clearly, she must be one of your long-lost toys."

"It's my Lucita. Where did you find her?"

"She had been stuffed inside the wall through a gap in the boards. I found her when I was remodeling the place."

She was still hugging the toy. "My brother Hans gave her to me. It's the only thing I have from before the fire."

Elam stepped closer, happy that he had found the toy and kept it all these months. It was a simple Amish doll. The absence of facial features and hair was in keeping with the Amish obedience to the biblical commandment that forbade the creation of an image. It was dressed in typical Amish clothing, a deep purple gown that had faded over the years and a black apron and bonnet.

He said, "Lucita is an odd name for an Amish doll."

"Hans named her."

"Hans was the brother who died in the fire?"

She smiled sadly. "Yes. Hans saved my life that night. He carried me out wrapped in a blanket. I had Lucita in my arms. I suffered a few burns on my legs, but Hans was badly injured. Malachi told me he died a short time later."

"I'm sorry."

She shrugged. "It was a long time ago."

"How can you be sure it's your doll?"

She gave a guilty grin and pulled back the doll's bonnet to reveal a secret. "Hans used a marker to give her black hair like mine. I wanted someone who looked like me. All my family had blond hair. I always felt like I stuck out."

"Now you can give the toy to your daughter."

"I will, and I'll tell her it's a gift from her uncle Hans." Katie's smile was bright as the summer sun, and Elam basked in its warmth.

"You must tell her to take better care of Lucita than you did and not lose her."

Katie's smile faded. "Malachi took her away from me when I was seven. He said I was too old to play with dolls. He told me he threw her in the rubbish fire. Why would he hide her inside the wall?"

"I don't know. Perhaps he meant to give her back to you one day."

"I'd really like to believe that, but I don't think I can. He used to make me sleep out here when I did something that upset him. I think he enjoyed knowing he'd hidden the one thing that could give me comfort just out of sight."

"Why would your brother do something so cruel?"

"Because I caused the deaths of our whole family."

He stared at her in shock. "How could you? You were only a child."

"Malachi said I was the one who knocked over a kerosene lamp and set the house on fire. I don't remember doing it, but I remember seeing flames everywhere and screaming for help. Besides my mother, I lost Hans and two sisters, Emma and Jane. I can barely remember their faces. Malachi had recently married and had moved into this place. If he hadn't, he might have died, too."

Elam was deeply affected to hear how much she had suffered. He wanted to comfort her, but wasn't sure how. "Such things happen. It was a terrible tragedy, but it was God's will. It was not your fault. Your brother was wrong to blame you."

She straightened the bonnet on her doll's head. "I know. I tried so hard to earn his forgiveness when I was little. As I grew older, I resented his coldness and pretended I didn't care what he thought. The sad thing is… I really did care. I still do."

"Forgiveness is our way, Katie. Even if your brother cannot forgive you, you must forgive him."

"Easier said than done."

How could he ask it of her if he had not been able

to do it himself? He sighed and smiled gently. "I know that well. But it does not change what is right."

Katie Lantz had brought turmoil into his orderly world, but she'd brought something else, too. She had a way of making him take a closer look at his own life, his own shortcomings. He strongly suspected that by the time she left, he would be a better man for having known her.

She drew a deep breath and looked up. "You were going to show me how to weave a basket."

He allowed her to change the subject, but he would always remember the sadness in her voice. It touched a place deep inside him. A place that he'd kept closed off after the death of his father and Salome's excommunication. He wasn't the only one who had suffered a loss.

Katie moved about the room looking at the tools. She stopped at the stove. "What are these trays for?"

"For soaking the wooden strips so they can be bent easily."

"Tell me everything I need to know." She gestured toward the stacked poplar logs.

He focused on his work and pushed his need to comfort her to the back of his mind. "My baskets are unique. They're handmade from strips of wood. I buy the plywood for the base, but I do all the cutting here. After a log is trimmed and the bark stripped off, I pound the log with a mallet to loosen the growth rings."

"Will I be hammering logs?"

"No."

"I'm stronger than I look."

"I've seen baby barn swallows hanging out of their nests who look stronger than you."

She opened her mouth to reply, but seemed to think

better of it. Instead, she turned back to the wood on the sawhorse. "What do you do next?"

"Then I peel off splints, or strips. The splints are then shaved to get rid of the fuzzy layer between the growth rings. They are rolled up in coils and stacked here. I cut them to size when I'm ready to start a basket."

Picking up a splint, she laid it on the workbench. "Now what?"

"This is one of the forms we use." He began setting the strips in place to form the ribs of the basket. Katie moved to stand close beside him. The top of her head barely reached his shoulder. She tucked her hair behind her ear and leaned over his work to inspect it.

Among his people women never cut their hair. Out of modesty and reverence, they wore it in a bun under a *kapp*. Katie's head was uncovered. She had cut her hair.

She was not Amish. He had to remember that. He had to harden his heart against the influence of this woman who chose to be an outsider.

Only the more he was near her, the more impossible that became. How was he going to work with her day after day?

Chapter Twelve

Two days later, Katie found herself seated at the long table in Elam's workshop. The air, already filled with the smell of fresh-cut wood and simmering dyes, was being flooded with giggles. Mary, Ruby and Sally sat at the same table watching Katie's fledgling attempts to weave.

"I thought you were making a candy basket." Ruby picked up Katie's project to examine it.

"I am."

"Aren't you afraid the candy will fall though the gaps?" Ruby chuckled as she pushed her fingers through the loose slats and wiggled them at Katie.

Snatching her work away from Elam's oldest sister, Katie said, "Very funny. It's better than my last one."

Sally rose to Katie's defense. "I'm sure she'll improve in time."

"Before I run out of trees?" Elam came in carrying an armload of freshly cut wooden splints.

Katie rolled her eyes. "Another comedian in the family."

After slipping the poplar pieces into a large vat of warm water, he came to stand at Katie's elbow. "You aren't doing so badly. You should have seen Ruby's first piece. In fact, I think *Mamm* still has it in the attic. Shall I go get it?"

Ruby wove another band between the upright stakes of her heart-shaped basket. "Go. You can spend all day looking through that dusty place. I don't care."

"Because she burned it." Mary's honesty was rewarded with an elbow to the ribs. She promptly swatted her sister with a long wand of reed. Ruby grabbed it. The ensuing tug-of-war ended when the reed broke in two.

"Oops." Ruby held out her broken half to Elam.

He sighed and grinned at Katie. "See what I've had to put up with all my life? It's no wonder this venture isn't making much money."

"But it keeps you close as a family," Sally said.

"*Jah.* It does that." Mary snatched the reed from her sister and tossed both pieces in the trash.

Elam moved to the stove. "The poplar should be ready."

The women all rose to select the plywood bases and molds for the unit they would be working on. Katie didn't bother to get up. Working with the woods instead of the more pliable reeds required some skill. Looking at her poor example, she knew she wasn't ready to tackle a complicated piece, but she was determined to learn.

She watched closely as Elam and Mary began to construct large hampers. Ruby and Sally both worked on picnic baskets. Their labors didn't stem the flow of chatter. More than once Katie found herself chuckling at the women's stories of family life.

"Just the other day, Thomas smeared mud all over Monroe so he could stick straw on him and make him look like a porcupine crawling across the floor." Ruby added a double band of scarlet color to the middle of her piece.

Mary smothered a laugh. "Now where did he get such an idea?"

Ruby shot a look at her brother. "It seems *Onkel* Elam told the boys a story about finding a porcupine in the woodpile."

"I didn't tell Thomas to make Monroe into one."

Pointing at him, Ruby said, "No, but you told me to drop an egg on *Dat's* hat from the haymow. Do you remember that?"

"I remember scrubbing milk cans for a month because you hit Bishop Stulzman."

Ruby held up her hands. "How was I to know the bishop had come to talk to Papa? Besides, from the hayloft door I could only see the hat, not the man. I shouldn't have let you take the blame for that one."

"It *was* my idea. You just had better aim."

Mary began cutting the top of her basket ribs in preparation for setting the rim in place. "No wonder your boys are so ornery."

Sally began looping strands of rattan over her rim. "*Jah,* Jesse says they get their high jinks from their mother."

Ruby's eyebrows shot up. "Oh, he does, does he?"

Startled by her tone, Sally looked up to find her sister-in-law scowling at her. She opened her mouth, but closed it again.

A smile tugged at the corner of Elam's lips. "I didn't realize your husband was so smart, Ruby."

Ruby's jaw dropped. Mary snickered.

Katie, quietly turning and tucking the ribs of her basket, said, "He must be smart. He married Ruby."

Ruby's eyes lit up. "That's right." She poked her brother's arm.

Elam's face reflected his surprise. "I did not know you could be so sassy, Katie."

Sitting back with satisfaction, Ruby grinned. "I like you, Katie Lantz. You're a quick wit."

"But not a quick basket weaver. I'm stumped. How do I attach the rim?" Katie was amazed at how easily she fit in with this family, and how accepting of her they were.

Sally moved her chair closer to Katie. "Use the thicker strips of flat, oval reed. One on the inside and one on the outside."

"I don't have enough hands to hold it all in place."

From her pocket, Ruby pulled a half-dozen wooden clothespins and slid them across the table. "Use these to clip the reed in place. They'll be your extra hands."

Sally demonstrated and Katie leaned in to watch as the younger woman used dyed sea grass to lash the rim pieces to the top row of the basket. When Sally was done, she handed it to Katie. "It's yours to sell now."

Katie looked at Elam. "Speaking of selling, how does that work?"

"Once a month, I take our products to a shop in Millersburg. The owner sells them for us. He takes orders at his shop and from mail catalogs and also from their internet site, then he gives them to me to be filled."

"How many kinds of baskets do you make?" She looked at the variety in the bins.

"We have twenty different types, from laundry hampers to little trinket boxes." Mary stood and placed her hand in the small of her back as she stretched.

"Our best sellers are these picnic baskets. What do you think?" Ruby held up her finished container. It was the fanciest piece on the table, with double bands of scarlet color in the middle and a strip of scarlet rattan lashed around the top.

Katie tipped her head to the side. "It's very nice, but not plain."

Ruby smiled. "It's for the tourists."

Elam took it from his sister. "They come to see us Plain folk, but they like bright colors in their quilts and souvenirs. I'll put a lid and handles on this."

As Elam went to work with his small hand drill at the adjacent workbench, Katie couldn't help but admire the view of his broad shoulders, slim waist and trim hips. His homemade dark trousers and shirt accentuated his physique. She especially liked the way his hair curled in an unruly fashion, defying the typical "bowl style" haircut Amish men wore.

"He is a fine-looking man," Sally said quietly.

Katie, feeling the heat of a blush in her cheeks, glanced at Sally. Both Mary and Ruby were busy teasing each other and hadn't heard the remark. "He's well enough, I guess."

That produced a smothered giggle. "Far better than some I've met here. He will make a fine husband."

Katie tried to sound nonchalant. "Is there someone special?"

"Elam doesn't attend the singings on Sunday nights. Ruby and Mary fear he plans to remain single. They are hoping he'll be interested in Karen Imhoff, but I don't think he will be," Sally said.

"Why not?"

"She's *en alt maedel,* an old maid. She's twenty-five and never been married."

At twenty-two, Katie didn't consider twenty-five to be that old. Katie decided it was best to steer the subject away from Elam's single status. "Do you attend the singings?"

"*Jah.* I'll be seventeen next month. My mother says it's time I started looking for a husband."

"Don't be in a big hurry to give up your freedom."

Sally scooted her chair closer. "I'm not. I want to see and do things before I settle down. You've lived among the English. What was it like? Tell me about the music and dancing and movie stars."

Katie glanced at Elam's back. "I don't think I should."

"You're the only one I know who has lived away from this place."

It was hard to ignore the pleading in Sally's eyes. Katie, too, had dreamed about a world beyond the farm and the endless work. "I understand how you feel. Believe me, I do."

The door opened and Nettie came in, a bright smile on her face. "Rachel is awake and she wants her mama."

"I'm coming." Happy for any excuse to leave, Katie rose and left Sally's questions unanswered.

While she wouldn't mind satisfying Sally's curiosity, she knew Elam would object. The last thing she wanted was to upset the man who was giving shelter to her and her child.

"How goes life on the Sutter farm?"

Katie smiled at Amber as she began undressing Rachel for her one month examination.

"It's okay, I guess."

Elam had insisted on bringing her and the baby into Hope Springs for Rachel's visit with the doctor. Katie had enjoyed the ride seated beside him, but they had both remained silent. It seemed whenever they were together a kind of tension filled the air between them.

Amber glanced at Katie closely. "You don't sound like it's okay."

"You mustn't think I'm ungrateful. I can't begin to repay the Sutters for all they have done for me."

"So what's the problem?" Amber placed Rachel, naked and kicking, on the infant scale. The baby promptly voiced her disapproval with a piercing cry.

Katie leaned forward. "How much does she weigh?"

"Eight pounds nine ounces."

"That's good, right?"

"Very good. She's passed her birth weight. The doctor will be in in a few minutes." After measuring the baby, Amber swaddled her in a blanket and handed her back to her mother.

Katie shouldered the baby and patted her until she stopped fussing. "Amber, did you learn of any work in the area?"

Picking up a spray bottle of antiseptic, Amber misted the scale and then wiped it down with a paper towel. "I thought you were working for Elam Sutter and his mother?"

"I am, but I thought maybe I could find something else."

Amber regarded Katie closely. "Is Mr. Sutter working you too hard? Because if he is…"

Katie quickly shook her head and looked down. She couldn't stop the soft smile that curved her lips. "No, it's nothing like that. Elam has been very kind."

"Is Nettie chafing to have you out of the house?"

"Not that I can tell. She spoils the baby every chance she gets."

The puzzled expression on Amber's face changed to a look of understanding. "Oh. I see how it is. You poor thing."

Katie frowned at her. "What's that supposed to mean?"

"Elam's very kind, but you don't want to work for him. His mother adores your baby and spoils her, but you don't want to live with her. I'm getting the picture."

"I don't know what you're talking about."

"You know, it shows when you say his name."

Katie dropped her gaze. "You're talking nonsense."

"I don't think I am. Your eyes light up when you say Elam."

"They do not. You're being ridiculous."

"No, I'm not. Say his name."

"Stop it."

Amber propped her hands on her hips. "You can't do it without blushing."

"Because you're embarrassing me."

Pulling over a chair, Amber sat beside Katie. "I'm sorry to tease you. Are you thinking of joining the Amish church?"

"I've considered it, but I'm not sure. Sometimes I think it would make things easier."

"Don't do it if you're not certain that's where your heart lies."

"It's hard to know what to do. I wanted to get away from here so badly, yet now that I'm back things are different. No matter what I want, I have to think of what's best for Rachel. It isn't that I want material things for her. I want her to know she is loved and accepted. I want her to feel safe and secure."

"She can have those things in the Amish world or in the English one."

"I'm not sure that's true. I couldn't have given her any of that without Matt to help me in the city. Here, you've seen how Nettie dotes on Rachel. It's the same with everyone in the Sutter family. Rachel will be taken care of in this community. She will belong."

"Joining a church for your daughter's sake isn't the same as doing it because you feel God has called you to that life. Do you feel called?"

It was a question Katie couldn't answer. Was she being called or was she just searching for something she'd never had?

The outer door opened. Katie looked up in relief as a white-haired man in a pale blue lab coat walked in. His smile was kindly and vaguely familiar. "Good afternoon. I'm Dr. Harold White. You must be Katie Lantz."

Katie shook the hand he held out. "It's nice to meet you, Dr. White."

He sat down on a metal stool and rolled it close. "I remember you now. You were only three or four at the time, so I shouldn't be surprised if you don't remember me. I treated your burns after your family's house fire. Terrible, sad business that was."

Katie still bore the scars on her legs. "I think I remember you. Did you know my family well?"

"Not really. Your mother hadn't been in the area very long. I do remember hearing that she had immigrated to the United States from Belize."

This was the first that Katie had heard of such a thing. "My family came from Central America?"

"I believe so. I know several colonies of Old Order Amish exist in Belize."

Amber handed Dr. White Rachel's chart, then grinned at Katie. "That's the fun thing about working with Dr. White. You learn something new every day."

He chuckled. "A day I don't learn something new is a wasted day."

Katie smiled, but her mind was reeling. Why hadn't

Malachi told her this? Was it possible she still had family in another country? She'd often wondered why she didn't have grandparents and cousins when everyone else at school had such big extended families. All Malachi ever said was that all her family was gone. If they had come from Central America, her doll's Spanish name made much more sense.

Dr. White placed his stethoscope in his ears and directed his attention to Rachel. "Let's have a listen to this little one."

After he had checked her over and pronounced her in excellent health, Katie asked, "Dr. White, is it possible to find out exactly where my family came from?"

He rubbed his chin. "I reckon the State Department would have to have some kind of records. Would you like me to check into it for you? I know a fella that used to work for them."

"I don't want to make extra trouble for you." Katie wasn't going to get her hopes up. Surely, if they had family anywhere Malachi would have mentioned it.

Dr. White chuckled. "I enjoy a challenge. It keeps me young. Besides, everything can be done on computers these days. Amber, have you drawn blood from Rachel?"

"Not yet, Doctor."

Katie frowned. "Why does she need blood drawn?"

Turning aside to make a note on the chart, Dr. White said, "It's just routine newborn screening."

"Shall I do the extended panel?" Amber asked.

He looked at Katie. "Is the baby's father of Amish or Mennonite descent?"

Katie shook her head. "No. What difference does that make?"

Gathering her supplies and pulling on a pair of latex

gloves, Amber said, "Because the Amish and Mennonites are almost all descended from a relatively small group of ancestors, there are some inherited diseases that show up more frequently in their children."

Dr. White closed the chart and rose. "It's unlikely that you'll have to worry about any of those. Just do the regular lab, Amber. I'd like to see Rachel again in three months and at six months."

"I may not be here then."

"Where will you be?" he asked.

"I'm not sure."

"Well, wherever you settle, she needs her well-baby checkups at least that often."

Katie had been focused on earning enough money to pay back the people who had helped them. She hadn't considered where she would go if she left Hope Springs. Where did she want to settle?

Out in the waiting room, Elam put down the gardening magazine he'd been leafing through and glanced at the clock. What was taking so long? Rachel was a happy, healthy baby. Surely there wasn't anything wrong with her.

He had work to do. If he'd been thinking clearly, he would have let his mother bring Katie and the baby to town. The truth was, he hadn't been able to pass up this chance to spend time alone with Katie.

He had no idea how long she'd be staying with them. He had begun to cherish the minutes and hours he spent in her company, knowing it would end soon. It was foolish—he knew that—but his heart could not be persuaded otherwise.

He heard a door open and glanced toward the hallway leading back to the exam rooms. Katie came out with Rachel in her arms. Amber walked beside her. The two women exchanged hugs and Katie turned to him. She was grinning from ear to ear.

He smiled back as his heart flipped over in his chest. No amount of rationalization or denial could change the fact that he was falling for this woman. And those feelings were growing every day.

Rising to his feet, he waited until she reached him. "You look happy about something."

"I've been learning so much about my family. My mother brought us here from Central America."

With her at his side, they left the doctor's office. He helped her into the buggy, using the excuse to hold her hand as she stepped up. "Your brother never mentioned this?"

"No, and I can't imagine why not. Dr. White is going to find out exactly where we came from and if any of my family still live there. I could have aunts, uncles and cousins I never knew about." Her eyes sparkled with exhilaration.

"I suppose it's possible." If she found she had family in Central America, would she travel there? Sending her to Kansas would be hard enough, but he at least had some hope of seeing her again if she stayed with her brother.

She gripped her hands together. "It's so exciting."

He hated to burst her bubble, but he didn't want her getting her hopes up. "It's possible, but don't you think it's unlikely?"

As he feared, the excitement drained from her face. "I guess it is. I'm being silly, aren't I?"

"No. I don't think you're silly at all." He maneuvered Judy out into traffic.

She looked at him and said, "I am being silly. It's just—"

"Just what?" he prompted.

She blushed and looked down. He longed to lift her chin and see what was in her eyes, but Judy shied at a passing car and he turned his attention back to his driving.

Sitting up straighter, she asked, "When will you start planting your pumpkins?"

"In the next week or two."

The rest of the way home, they talked about everything from pumpkins to his mother's interest in Mr. Imhoff. It was a pleasant journey, but he got the feeling Katie was deliberately steering him away from her conversation with Dr. White.

Chapter Thirteen

Over the next weeks, Elam found himself constantly making excuses to spend time with Katie and Rachel. Holding the baby and playing with her became his normal evening pastime. He was pleasantly surprised by Katie's aptitude and fast-growing skill at weaving. She had a good eye for color combinations and weaving patterns, and she had nimble hands. Some of her pieces were as good as Ruby's, and his sister had been weaving for over a year.

Late one evening, he was leaving the barn after tending to a sick colt when he passed the workroom and saw a light shining from under the door. He opened it to find Katie seated at the table with pen and paper in front of her, making a sketch. He almost left without disturbing her, but something drew him in.

"What has you up so late, Katie?"

Her gaze shot toward him. She laid both hands over her drawing. "I couldn't sleep. I had an idea and I wanted to see if I could make it work."

"Let me see this idea." He entered the room, but she snatched the paper and held it behind her back before he could get a peek.

"It's nothing. You'll think it's silly."

"I've been making baskets for many years. If the idea has merit, I will know."

He approached the table and took a seat across from her. It was just the two of them. The lamp made a cozy circle of light. For an instant, it was almost possible to believe they were alone in the world. She was so beautiful it hurt his heart to look at her, but neither could he look away.

Nervous under his scrutiny, she licked her lips.

Ah, Katie. You have no idea how much I want to kiss you.

He forced his eyes away from her full red lips and held out his hand. "Let me see it. I may save you hours of frustration later."

Unfortunately, there would be no one to save him from the frustration of having her near and not being able to touch her. He'd been foolish to give her this job, to let her stay in his home. The price he would have to pay for such foolishness was becoming more apparent day by day. His heart was breaking by inches.

She smiled shyly and pushed the paper across the table. On it he saw a sketch of a bowl basket with a spiral weave curving around the sides like the stripes on a peppermint candy. "I saw one like this a long time ago and never forgot it. Is it possible to make one like this?"

As he studied it, he could see how a new mold would need to be made to shape the bowl just so. It might take some trial and error to find the right angle to form up the ribs. "What type of wood are you planning to use?"

"I don't know. What do you think?"

"Maybe a mix of light and dark maple. I could make a solid wood lid with a wooden knob on it for a top. It would be very fancy."

"Too fancy?" She reached to take the paper from him, but he held on to it.

"Not too fancy to sell."

It was definitely different from anything he'd seen in the gift shops. It was an eye-catching piece. "If they do well, I'll have to give you a larger commission."

"You really think it's *goot?*" The delight in her eyes shone as bright as the lamp.

He couldn't believe how happy it made him to see her smile. "*Jah,* Katie. It is very *goot.*"

She dipped her head. "*Danki,* Elam. More money is what I need."

His smile faded. Allowing Katie to earn more money meant that she would leave that much sooner.

It was the thing he wanted…and the thing he now dreaded.

Katie watched the play of emotions across Elam's face. What was he thinking? She knew the local gossips were linking his name with hers. His mother and his sisters tried to downplay the impact of the talk, but she wasn't fooled. They were beginning to worry. The family had suffered so much when their father was shunned. She didn't want to cause more pain.

He rose to his feet and picked up the lamp. "It is late. You should get some rest."

She stood and walked to the door with him. "Rachel will be awake soon. Once I've fed her I'll go back to bed and try to sleep."

"What troubles your sleep? Or is it that our beds are not as soft as the English like."

"The bed is fine. I just have a lot on my mind."

"Give your cares over to God."

Pulling her coat from a peg by the door, she slipped into it. "Good advice, but hard to follow."

As she walked out the door he nodded. It was true for him, as well.

At the house, they found Nettie reading her Bible in the living room. She held Rachel in the crook of one arm. Peering over the top of her glasses at them, she asked, "What have you two been up to?"

"Katie has been drawing up plans for a new basket design."

Blushing, Katie said, "I was just playing with an idea. Elam saw how to make it work."

"I'd like to see this plan. Elam, would you take this child. She's put my arm to sleep."

He lifted Rachel from his mother and carried her to the sofa where he sat down. "You are getting heavy. What are we going to do about that? Oh, I see. It's your eyelids that are getting heavy. Well, don't mind me. Go back to sleep."

Katie smiled at the pair. Elam was so good with Rachel. He was never impatient, always gentle. It was easy to see he cared a great deal for her daughter. He would make a good father someday.

He glanced up at her. As their eyes met, an arch of awareness passed between them. She knew by the look in his eyes that he felt it, too. How had this happened? When had she fallen in love with Elam?

On the last Saturday in April, Elam packed his baskets into the back of the buggy and prepared for the three-hour round trip into Millersburg. He wasn't surprised when Nettie announced that she and Katie would be joining him.

Attired in her newest dress and her Sunday bonnet and cape, Nettie climbed into the buggy. "What a nice spring day we have for our trip. I can't believe it's already the middle of April."

Elam found it hard to believe that Katie and Rachel had been with them for over a month. Katie had proven herself to be a hard worker and he knew she was making his mother's life easier by helping her with household chores. "I'll be able to get started with planting soon if the weather holds."

"And I need to get my garden in, but first we'll have a fine shopping trip. I want to go to the superstore and then I may need to stop at the fabric store. What are you needing, Elam?"

"Some new drill bits and blades for my wood plane. I also want to pick up some new dyes and coils of maple splints."

"Maple?" His mother looked at him in surprise. "I thought you only used poplar and ash in your baskets."

"We are trying something new with Katie's design. What about you, Katie? What are you needing in town?" Taking the baby from her, he helped her in and then handed up Rachel when Katie was settled.

"A few things for Rachel and a new pair of jeans. It shouldn't take me long to find what I need."

"*Goot,* then we will not have to spend much time in the city."

The buggy rocked in his direction when he stepped in, tipping Katie toward him. With Rachel in her arms, she couldn't catch herself. He threw up a hand to steady her. It landed at her waist. Her cheeks flamed crimson. When she regained her balance he withdrew his hand, but the feel of her slender torso remained imprinted in his mind.

Katie moved as far over as she was able, but it was still a tight fit with her sandwiched between him and his mother. It was going to be a long ride. He didn't know how he'd keep his attention on the road with her soft body pressed against his.

Each jolt in the road threw them against one another and sent waves of awareness tingling along his nerve endings. The sweet fragrance of her hair was like a tempting flower beside him. Judy tossed her head anxiously each time a car passed them, and he knew he was communicating his nervousness to the animal. Fortunately, they soon turned into the lane leading to Ruby's home.

Ruby had volunteered to keep Rachel so Katie would be free to enjoy her shopping trip. She came out of the house to meet them. "Sally is wanting to go with you, Elam. Do you mind one more?"

Sally came flying out of the house. "Please say I can go!"

Elam cast his gaze skyward. "What do you need in the city?"

"Some new shoes."

He frowned at her. "You can't find them in Hope Springs?"

"They'll be cheaper in Millersburg. I won't be any trouble. I promise."

"You'll have to squeeze in back with my cargo."

"That's fine. Thank you." She quickly climbed in the backseat, pushing aside several of the baskets.

Ruby moved to stand beside Elam. "Thanks for taking her. Can I have that fine baby girl now?"

Katie handed Rachel to him, a look of apprehension on her face. "I've never left her for so long."

Elam knew exactly how she felt as he handed the baby to his sister. "Don't let the boys turn her into a porcupine."

Gathering Rachel close, Ruby smiled at her. "Don't worry. I'll keep a good eye on her."

Katie handed out a bag with diapers and formula in it. "I know you will. Thanks again for watching her."

"My pleasure." Ruby waved as Elam turned Judy and drove out of the yard.

Back on the highway, the mare managed a brisk trot, but she was no match for the cars that went zinging past. It wasn't the local drivers he minded. They shared the road with only occasional complaints. It was the out-of-towners and teenagers he worried about. The ones who didn't know enough to slow down when they crested a hill, in case a buggy was just over the rise and out of sight. At fifty-five miles an hour, a car could run up on an Amish vehicle before the driver knew it. In such crashes, the car always won.

They had been on the road for an hour when a white van came flying past and honked loudly. The noise spooked the horse, but Elam was able to keep her under control. His temper was harder to hold in check. "Foolish English. They're looking to get someone killed."

"Calm yourself, Elam," his mother said.

She was right. What good did it do to show his temper to his family?

The next car that passed them slowed when it drew alongside. As soon as he saw the camera aimed his way, he pulled off his hat to shield his face. The Plain People felt photographs were graven images and forbidden by the Bible. His mother turned away, as well. To his surprise, so did Katie. As the car sped on, he looked at Katie with a new respect. It was good to see she still practiced some of the Amish ways.

After another half hour of travel, Sally, sitting behind him, leaned forward. "Does anyone know some new jokes?"

For the next mile they exchanged funny stories and jokes that had all the women laughing. Elam put up with it.

Finally, Katie prodded Elam with her elbow. "Knock, knock."

"This is silliness," he stated firmly.

"'A merry heart doeth good like a medicine: but a broken spirit drieth the bones,'" his mother quoted from *Proverbs*.

Katie repeated, "Knock, knock."

He rolled his eyes heavenward. "Who's there?"

"Amish."

He glared at her from the corner of his eye. "Amish who?"

She playfully draped her arm around his shoulders. "Ah, I miss you, too."

Katie regretted her impulsive hug the moment she felt Elam stiffen. Self-consciously, she withdrew her arms and folded her hands in her lap. Nettie and Sally were laughing, but he wasn't. Had she made him angry with her forward behavior?

"That's a good one," Nettie declared.

"A bunch of silliness," Elam stated again, but as Katie glanced his way she saw the corner of his mouth twitching.

She said, "The English don't think the Amish have a sense of humor."

"Oh, but we do," Nettie declared, still chuckling.

"Have you heard the one about the Amish farmer with twin mules?" Elam asked.

"No." Katie relaxed and listened to his joke with a light heart. It felt good to be included and accepted by

Elam and his family. The trip into town became a happy jaunt as they all tried to outdo each other with funny stories. Katie was sorry when the outskirts of Millersburg came into view.

The first stop was a busy gift shop where Elam carried in his baskets. Katie followed, eager to see how her weaving design would be greeted. Of course, it had been Elam who perfected the pieces, but she had had a hand in their creation. The owner showed enough interest to order a dozen more bowls and to add a photo of one to his online catalog.

With the cargo disposed of, Katie joined Sally in the backseat. Sally, eager to see as much of the small city as possible, rolled up the rear flap and was almost hanging out. "Did you see the dresses in that store window?"

"I saw them." Katie was sure the prices were well above what she could afford.

Sally checked to make sure Nettie and Elam weren't listening. In a low voice she said, "My friend Faith has clothes like that. She sneaks out of the house and goes out on dates with English boys. They go to movies and smoke cigarettes. Faith says she's going to make the most of her *rumspringa*."

It was a common enough occurrence in Amish communities. Teenagers often rebelled against their strict upbringing. Most families in Katie's more liberal district tolerated such behavior and waited for it to end. When the teenagers reached marrying age, most settled down, made their baptisms and led quiet lives. Most, but not all.

"Is that what you want to do?" Katie asked.

Sally averted her gaze. "I don't know. It sounds like fun, but my folks would be so disappointed and ashamed if I was caught doing something like that."

"Only if you were caught?"

Sally's eyes snapped to meet Katie's. She didn't reply, but her mood became pensive. After a while, she said, "I noticed you weren't at the last church service. Will you be going tomorrow?"

"I'm not sure." Katie had been considering it but she didn't know if she was ready to face Bishop Zook again. He was sure to ask if she was ready to start instructions for baptism.

At the superstore, Elam secured Judy to one of the dozen hitching rails in a special section of the parking lot, and the group headed through the large sliding glass doors. By unspoken consent, the women became reserved and quiet. When they were out in the English world, they did nothing to attract attention to themselves.

Inside, Elam turned to his mother. "I will not be long. I know where the tools are. Where shall we meet?"

Sally turned around slowly, awe written on her face.

Nettie pulled a red shopping cart from the line. "I may be a while. I need several bolts of fabric and some thread. Hopefully they will have the sewing machine needles I need here and we won't have to go to another store."

Spinning to face her, Sally said, "I don't mind if we have to visit more stores."

"I'm sure it won't take me long to find things for Rachel. Why don't we meet in the food court," Katie suggested, gesturing to a collection of booths and fast-food counters off to the side of the doorway.

Elam smiled and rubbed his stomach. "*Jah,* a cheeseburger and French fries sounds yummy."

Katie grinned. Eating out was a rare treat. One enjoyed by every member of the family.

Nettie took Sally's hand. "Let's see if we can find you some shoes that fit. Then you can help me pick the fabric for my new dresses."

Elam strode toward the hardware department as Nettie and Sally went in the other direction. Left alone, Katie strolled through the store. Row after row of bright summer clothes in every color of the rainbow beckoned her. After trying on several pairs of jeans and finding one that fit, Katie draped them over her arm and left the dressing room.

A pair of teenage girls were holding up tank tops and shorts in front of a mirror. Katie stopped beside them to hang up a pair of pants she didn't want. As she did, one of the girls began snickering and pointing. Katie followed their gaze to see what was so funny. She saw Sally admiring the shimmering material of a dress on one of the mannequins.

What a contrast. Sally wore a simple dark blue dress beneath her black cape. Black stockings and sturdy black shoes with little heels adorned her feet. Her head was covered with a wide-rimmed bonnet. They were the same style of clothes every Amish woman wore. Yet so much more than clothes separated Sally from these other young women.

Katie's thoughts turned to Rachel. Which world did she want for her daughter? Until Katie had met Elam and his family, her choice seemed simple. Now she was seeing the Amish in a new light. Her brother's views weren't the views of all Plain people. Malachi was an unhappy man who took his sour mood out on those around him. She understood that now.

One of the shopping teens pulled out her cell phone and snapped a picture of Sally. "Why do they dress so stupid?"

Katie answered the girl, although she knew the question hadn't been directed at her. "They dress that way because they wish to be separate from the world. Their clothing and even the shape of their head coverings identify them as part of a special group."

"What does being separate from the world mean?" the other girl asked.

"That they have chosen to live a life they believe is pleasing to God. To do that, they must reject worldly things such as electricity and cars, bright colors and jewelry, even phones."

"No electricity, no TV, no iPods—that's just dumb." The taller girl shook her head and the two of them laughed as they resumed their shopping.

Katie threaded her way between racks of clothes on her way to the infant department. How funny was it that she should be the one explaining about Amish practices? Matt would be laughing his head off if he were still around.

With a start, she realized she hadn't thought about Matt in days. The man occupying her thoughts lately had been Elam. She thought about his ready smile, the way he was always willing to help his mother or his sisters with their work in addition to his own. The way he enjoyed talking to and rocking Rachel in the evenings. He was so different from her brother. So different from Matt.

Katie had to admit she was falling hard for Elam. Her head told her there was no future there, but the heart rarely paid attention to what was smart.

As Katie rounded the corner into the infant section, she stopped short at the sight of a beautiful baby dress on display. Pink satin with short, puff sleeves trimmed with lace, it had a row of pearl buttons and bows down the front. Katie reached out to finger the silky cloth.

"Is that how you want Rachel to grow up?"

She turned to see Elam leaning on a shopping cart behind her.

He nodded toward the dress. "Do you want her to value fancy clothes, to think our ways are stupid?"

"Of course I don't."

But once she had felt that way. Until a few weeks ago Katie had been determined to return to the outside world. She had a choice now.

Elam straightened and stepped closer. "I heard what you said to those young women. You said we have chosen to live a life that is pleasing to God."

"That's what I was taught."

"But is it what you believe?"

Was it? It was hard to put into words what she believed. No one had ever asked her that question. Elam stood quietly waiting for her answer. She said, "I believe people of all faiths can choose to live a life that is pleasing to God."

His eyes bored into hers. "Is that what you are doing, Katie? Are you living a life that pleases God?"

Chapter Fourteen

Katie had no answer for Elam's questions. Instead, she said, "It won't take me long to get what I need for Rachel, then I'll be ready to leave."

"All right. I'll wait for you in the food court." As he turned away, she glimpsed a deep sadness in his eyes and couldn't help wondering why he cared so much.

When she had what she needed, she crossed the store to the sewing center. She found Nettie talking to another Amish woman next to a table of solid broadcloth bolts in an array of colors. Lavenders, purples, darker greens, mauves and even pinks were all acceptable colors for dresses in their church district.

Nettie caught sight of Katie and nodded in her direction. The other woman glanced her way, said something else to Nettie and then walked off without acknowledging Katie.

Nettie held up a length of green fabric. "What do you think of this one?"

"I like the mauve better."

"For me, yes, but for you this dark green would be a good color."

"You don't need to make me a dress."

"No, but I want to. I'm tired of seeing you in those jeans all the time. Now don't argue with me."

Katie debated a moment, then said, "All right."

Nettie's brows shot up in surprise. "You aren't going to argue?"

"If you want to make me a dress, I won't stop you."

A slow smile spread across Nettie's features. "And you will wear it to church services tomorrow?"

So that was the hitch. Katie's conversation with the young shoppers and with Elam came to mind. Perhaps it was time she started living a better life and not just existing in her present one.

Anyway, just because I go to a church service doesn't mean I'm thinking of joining the Amish faith. Does it?

Was she really considering returning to the strict, devout life she once hated? To her surprise, she found that she was.

She met Nettie's hopeful gaze and nodded. "*Jah*. I will wear the dress to tomorrow's preaching."

"*Wundervoll*. I was worried you would refuse." Nettie's relief was so evident that Katie instantly became suspicious.

"Who was the woman you were talking to when I came up?"

Nettie busied herself with choosing thread to match her fabric. "Oh, that was the new deacon's wife."

"What did she want?"

"Eada was shopping for fabric, the same as me."

"But she said something that upset you. I saw your face."

"Eada likes to repeat gossip, that's all."

"And the gossip was about me." A horrible sensation settled in the pit of Katie's stomach.

"It's nothing. Nothing. Where did I put my purse?"

"Nettie, you don't lie well."

Sighing in resignation, Nettie said, "Some of the elders don't like that you are staying under the roof of an unmarried man. I said, 'What am I? A doorpost?' I chaperone you."

"Oh, Nettie, the last thing I want is to make trouble for you and Elam."

"Talk will die down when they see what a fine woman you have become."

Katie wasn't so sure. Her old insecurities raised their ugly heads. She'd never fit in before. What made her think she could fit in now?

The following morning Katie was the last one to leave the house. Nettie was already waiting in the buggy. Elam stood at the horse's head.

Katie slanted a glance in his direction. He gave her a gentle smile. "You look Plain, Katie Lantz."

From Elam, it was a wonderful compliment. She knew she had to be blushing.

The dark green dress and white apron she had on fit her well enough. Made without buttons or zippers, the dress required pins to fit it to the wearer. To Katie, it felt strangely comforting to be back in Plain clothes. It was the only thing comforting about the morning. Worrying about how she would be accepted at the service had her stomach in knots.

Katie handed Rachel up to Nettie. The baby, swaddled in a soft, white woolen blanket, wore a small white bonnet. Katie had borrowed a *kapp* from Nettie for herself, but wisps of her short hair kept escaping her hairpins. She might pass for an Amish woman to an outsider, but the church members would know differently.

The trip to services took nearly half an hour. With

each passing mile Katie became more nervous. When the farm came into view, she drew a deep, ragged breath and tried to brace her failing courage.

Suddenly, she felt Elam's hand on hers. He didn't say anything, but the comfort in his simple touch gave her the strength she need. After a long moment, he let go to guide the horse into the yard. When he pulled the horse to a stop, Katie was ready.

She took her place beside Nettie and her daughters on one side of the room. After the first hymn the preaching started. As she listened to the minister, she noticed two little girls in front of her squirming on hard benches. Some things never changed.

At one point, Katie left to nurse her baby. In one of the bedrooms at the back of the house, a second young mother on the same mission joined her.

Katie learned the woman was Bishop Zook's daughter-in-law, the wife of Aaron Zook and a neighbor of Elam's. As the two of them exchanged pleasantries, Katie learned their children were almost the same age. Discussing their infant's temperaments, their funny quirks and motherly concerns made Katie see she wasn't that different from any mother, Amish or otherwise.

When Rachel was satisfied, Katie returned to her place beside Nettie. The second sermon, conducted by Bishop Zook, was heartfelt and moving.

A great sense of peace came over Katie. She held tight to the presence of Christ in her heart for the first time in a long, long time. All that she had worried about drifted away. She was one of God's children and she had been called to this place by His will.

Throughout the long service, Elam was constantly aware of Katie across the room from him. What was she thinking? Was she only pretending piety to stem the gossip or to appease his mother? He didn't want to believe it, but how could he be sure?

In spite of his best intentions, he had grown fond of Katie and Rachel. In his mind, it was easy to see them all becoming a family. What would it be like to spend a lifetime with Katie at his side? To see her bear his children? How he wanted to watch Rachel grow into a young woman, to see her marry and have children of her own.

These were things he wanted, but he kept them closed off inside his heart. He didn't dare give voice to them for if Katie took Rachel and left their community, he would grieve their loss more deeply than any other in his life.

When church came to an end, he followed the other men outside. It was warm enough that the homeowners had decided to set out the meal picnic style in the yard.

A volleyball net was soon up in place between two trees on the lawn. Several dozen of the younger boys and girls quickly began a game. The cheering and laughter from participants and onlookers filled the spring afternoon with joyous sounds.

Elam spied Katie watching the game, a wistful look on her face. She stood on the edge of the lawn by herself, except for Rachel in her arms.

Elam loaded two plates with fried chicken, coleslaw, pickled red beets, fresh rolls and two slices of gooey shoofly pie. He carried them to where she stood. "I've brought you something to eat."

She smiled and rolled her eyes. "What is this *thing* you have about feeding me?"

"I don't like skinny women." He held out one plate.

Lowering herself to the ground, she leaned back

against the trunk of the tree and placed Rachel on her outstretched thighs.

"If you think I'm going to get fat just to make you happy, think again."

"One plate of food will not make you fat."

"Ha! Do you know how many calories are in that peanut butter and marshmallow spread?"

He sat beside her. "No, and I don't want to know."

She took the plate from his hand, set it on the grass and picked up the slice of homemade bread covered with the gooey spread. She bit into it and moaned. "Oh, this is good."

The words were no sooner out of her mouth than the volleyball came flying toward them. Elam threw out his hand to protect Rachel as the ball landed beside her. Katie caught it on the bounce. Holding her chicken between her teeth, she threw the ball back to the players.

Elam sat back, relieved they were both okay.

"Nice toss," Sally said as she dropped down at Katie's feet.

"It was a fluke. I don't have an athletic bone in my body."

"You didn't play ball when you were younger?" Elam asked.

"No." Shaking her head, Katie took another bite of her meal.

Sally scowled. "Why not?"

"Malachi didn't like it."

"Your brother sounds…*premlijch*."

Katie laughed. "Yes, *grumpy* is a good word for him."

Sally shot to her feet and grabbed Katie's arm. "Well, he's not here, so come and play."

"I can't. I have a baby to watch."

Laying his plate aside, Elam held out his arms. "I'll watch her."

"There! Now you have no excuse." Sally clapped her hands together.

After a moment of hesitation, Katie gathered Rachel close and turned toward Elam, a look of uncertainty in her eyes. "Are you sure you don't mind?"

In that moment, he knew Katie had wormed her way past all the defenses he'd set around his heart. He smiled and said, "Go."

Grinning, she handed him the baby and shot to her feet. Elam leaned back against the tree with Rachel propped against his shoulder as Katie joined the game in progress.

She missed the first ball that came her way. Hiding her face behind her hands, she doubled over laughing at her own foolishness. The second time the white ball came flying toward her, she hit a creditable return.

Hearing cheering for her, he twisted his head to see his mother and sisters sitting on a bench near the house. Nettie and Ruby, their hands cupped around their mouths, were yelling instructions.

It seemed that Katie had wormed her way into more hearts than just his.

He glanced down at Rachel's sleeping face. "What have I let myself in for, little one?"

There was no help for it now. He was well and truly on his way to falling in love with Katie Lantz.

Katie felt like a kid again. No, she felt like the kid she'd never been allowed to be.

Racing over the fresh new grass, she chased a ball that she'd hit out of bounds. It rolled to a stop at the feet of Bishop Zook.

He said, "You are out of practice, Katie."

Breathless, she scooped up the ball and nodded to him. "*Jah,* I am."

"When your game is over, come and speak with me for a little while."

She felt her smile slip away. "Should I come now?"

Shaking his head, he said, "No, it will wait. Go and enjoy this beautiful day that God has made."

Katie returned to the game, but some of her enjoyment was lost. At the end of the match, she checked to see that Elam was still okay holding Rachel, then she excused herself and went to seek the bishop. She found him loading a large picnic basket into the back of his buggy.

"Are you leaving?" Maybe she could put off this conversation.

"In a little while. My wife and I are taking some food to Emma Wadler. Her mother is recovering from a broken hip and Emma is having a tough time running the inn and taking care of her."

"I think I remember Mrs. Wadler." It was easier to make small talk than to find out why the bishop wanted to see her.

"It was good to see you back among us, Katie, dressed Plain and attending services. It makes my heart glad. For we know there is more rejoicing in Heaven over one sinner who repents than over ninety-nine righteous ones who do not need to repent."

She looked down, unable to meet his gaze. "Thank you, Bishop."

"Many of us have doubts about the path God wishes us to follow."

Looking up, she asked, "Even you?"

"You have no idea how I struggled with my decision to become baptized."

"Really?"

He smiled at her. "Really."

"But you're a bishop."

"It was a path I never wished to trod, but *Gott* chose me. Without His help, I could do none of this. Let *Gott* be your help, Katie. Be still. Be at peace and listen with your heart to His council."

"I'm trying to do that."

"If you find *Gott* wishes for you to stay among us, we shall welcome you with open arms." He began rolling down the rear flap on his buggy.

Katie glanced to where Elam sat talking to Aaron Zook and his wife. Both men held the babies while the women of the congregation were busy packing up their hampers of leftover food. Numerous children, reluctant to give up their games, were kicking the ball across the grass with shouts of glee.

Wasn't this what she wanted? Didn't she long to be a part of a family, a part of a community? It wouldn't be an easy life, but it would be a life of belonging.

Impulsively, she turned back to the bishop. "When does *die Gemee nooch geh* begin?"

He paused in the act of fastening the leather flaps. "The class of instruction to the faith will be starting after the next church day."

"Thank you, Bishop."

He looked over her head. "Ah, here is my wife. I believe there is something she wishes to say to you."

Chapter Fifteen

Elam unharnessed his draft horses on Monday evening and led them to the corral beside the barn. Turning them loose, he watched as they each picked a spot and began to turn around with their nose at ground level. Finally, they dropped to their knees, then rolled their massive bodies in the dirt. Wiggling like puppies, they thrashed about to scratch their backs and shake off the sweat of their long day in the fields.

Elam spared a moment to envy them. Planting was hard work, and he still had things in the woodshop waiting for him. After hanging and cleaning his harnesses, he strode to the front of the barn and opened the workroom door. Katie was seated at the table with a small heart-shaped basket in front of her.

He saw she had finished several already. "You are getting faster?"

"But am I getting better?" She held up one for inspection.

He examined it closely "*Jah,* you are getting better."

Handing it back, he moved to his workstation and selected the tools he needed. A nearly finished rocking chair was waiting for him to carve a design into the headrest. He glanced over his shoulder. The frown of concentration on Katie's face made him smile.

Was she happy here? He wanted to ask, but he was afraid of the answer. Although she rarely talked about leaving any more, he'd never heard her mention another plan.

Would she stay if he asked her to? He looked back to the wood in front of him. He was afraid to ask. Afraid she might say no, and equally afraid she might say yes for all the wrong reasons. Instead, he said, "I thought Bishop Zook did a good job of preaching yesterday."

"He did. It was long and the benches haven't gotten any softer since I left, but I did find it comforting."

"I saw Mrs. Zook talking to you. Was she rude again?"

"No. She apologized for her earlier behavior."

He picked up his chisel. "Did she?"

"I can tell you I was stunned."

He chuckled. "You and me both."

"She said she'd let hearsay form her opinions and that she was aware that people could change."

"I reckon they can. What did you think of the service?"

"I enjoyed it."

"Enough to attend again?"

"I'm thinking about it."

He spun around to look at her. "You are?"

"*Jah.* I can tell you're stunned."

Moving to stand beside her, he said, "Maybe a little stunned but mostly happy."

They stood staring at each other for a long time. He wanted so badly to kiss her. He sucked in a quick breath and moved back to his workbench.

"Elam, can I ask you a personal question?"

"*Jah.*"

"What was she like, the girl you were betrothed to?"

He leaned forward and pushed his gouge into the wood, wondering how to answer that. "She was quiet. A hard worker."

"Was she pretty?"

"Yes." He kept his eyes on his task.

"How did you meet?"

"We grew up together. How did you meet Matt?"

"Matt and I met at the drugstore in Hope Springs. He was visiting some friends in the area. They were sitting at a booth and making fun of a young Amish boy who had come in."

"Is that what you liked about him? That he poked fun at us?"

"No. I felt sorry for the boy and I told Matt and his friends to stop it. I know I shouldn't have. We are to turn the other cheek."

"Rude behavior doesn't have to be tolerated."

"Anyway, after I left, Matt followed me and apologized. I thought it was very fine of him."

Her voice took on a soft quality. "He could be like that. One moment a good man, the next moment a spoiled child. I don't know what it was about him that blinded me to his true self."

"It is our own feelings that blind us."

"Were you blind to Salome's feelings?"

"*Jah.* When I finished school, my parents sent me to my uncle Isaac in Ontario to learn the woodworking trade. During those years I wrote to Salome every week. I told her about my plans for our life together."

"And she wrote back?"

"She did, but her letters were filled with the day-to-day things. I should have known then that something was wrong, but I wasn't looking for the signs." It was the first time in a long time that he was willing to examine his feelings about those days.

"I know what you mean. Matt seemed so interested in me. The more I resisted his advances, the more interested he became. I was so flattered. I snuck out of the house to see him. Malachi caught us together one night. He was furious. He grabbed my arm and ordered Matt to leave. That's one thing about Matt—he hates to have anyone tell him what to do."

"And so it is with you, too."

"Perhaps that's true. To be honest, I jumped at the chance to defy Malachi."

"So you left with Matt."

"I did. I was honestly determined to make our relationship work, but he wasn't. He soon grew tired of being saddled with a stupid Amish girlfriend who couldn't drive a car or work the DVD recorder."

He turned around and came to sit beside her. Taking her hand, he said, "You aren't stupid."

She stared into his eyes for a long time. She had such beautiful dark eyes. He could almost see his future in them. Finally, she looked down. "It took me a while to start believing that. What happened between you and Salome?"

"It isn't important anymore." He started to rise, but she laid a hand on his arm and stopped him.

"It is important. Past wrongs have the power to hurt us if we don't let go of them."

The warmth of her small, soft hand on his skin sent a wave of awareness coursing through his body. He focused on her concerned face. "What makes you think I haven't let go?"

She tipped her head to the side. "Have you?"

"Perhaps not."

He longed to reach out and touch her face. How would she react? Would she pull away?

Such thoughts were folly. He should go. He had work to do. But he didn't rise. He sat there looking into her eyes and he saw himself as he had been when he was young and impressionable and sure of his place in the world. He wanted to share that part of his life with Katie.

"I returned home from my uncle's at the age of twenty-one, ready to settle down, start my own business…and marry. That spring I was baptized and took my vows to the church. Salome did the same. If only she had waited until she was certain of what she wanted."

"Don't judge her too harshly."

"I've begun to forgive her." As he said it, he realized it was true. She had hurt him, but how much more would they both have suffered if she had gone ahead with the wedding?

Glancing sideways at Katie seated beside him, he said, "When the date for our marriage approached she finally admitted the truth. She had used our engagement to keep her parents from pressuring her into marrying anyone else. She didn't love me."

"I'm so sorry."

"I thought maybe she saw some flaw in me."

"I don't see how. You're a good man, Elam."

She thought he was a good man. Well, he wasn't, Elam reflected bitterly. He struggled every day to live a life pleasing to God. Perhaps she understood that better than anyone, for she openly admitted her own struggles.

Katie said, "Why did she leave the church?"

"All the time I had been working for my uncle, Salome had been working for an English family as a nanny. I believe she tried to give up her life among the English, but she couldn't do it. Not when her employer offered to help her further her education. She told me she longed to go back to school, to learn things beyond what she needed to know to keep house and rear children."

Salome had turned her back on her family, on Elam and on his hopes and dreams. "My family, her family, we all tried to reason with her, but after several months it was clear that she wasn't going to return to the church. She was shunned, not because we didn't love her anymore, but in the hopes of making her reconsider her choices."

"Your mother told me your father also left the faith."

Elam bowed his head. "He did. I had to shun my own father. My mother couldn't bear it and asked to be excommunicated, too, so that they could live together as man and wife. It was a dark time."

Katie's heart went out to Elam. She squeezed his hand. "I'm so sorry. Was that why you moved to Ohio?"

"After *Dat* passed away, my mother came back to the church, but it was not the same for us. I saw an ad in the paper for farms for sale in Ohio. My brothers-in-law and I came to look the places over. Your brother was eager to sell to me. I got the land for a good price. We were blessed that Mary and Ruby found homes here, as well."

Katie hesitated before voicing the question she couldn't ignore. Finally, she asked gently, "Elam, was your mother wrong to leave the church to stay with your father?"

The sadness in his eyes was replaced by anger. "My father was wrong to leave the church."

"Your mother must have loved him very much."

"*Jah,* she loved him, but did he love her? I'm not so

sure. What kind of love is it to make another suffer for your own doubts?"

He shot to his feet and left. Katie didn't try to stop him. She was happy that he'd been able to share this much about himself. All she wanted was to be near him and to make him happy.

She loved him, but loving a person was not enough. They had both learned that the hard way. He wasn't indifferent to her. She was woman enough to read the signs in his eyes, but he never spoke of it. She knew why.

Even if she found the courage to tell him of her love, she knew he'd never consider marriage to someone outside his faith. If she became Amish would it change how he felt about her? Or was she breaking her own heart by staying here?

The following afternoon, Katie was working in the woodshop when Elam poked his head in the door. She laid the basket aside, loving the way her heart skipped a beat each time he was near.

He said, "Katie, you have a visitor. Dr. White is here."

She frowned. "Dr. White? Why has he come to see me?"

Elam stepped closer, a look of concern on his face. "I don't know. Is Rachel okay?"

Katie rose to her feet. "He did take a blood test from her."

Had the results been serious enough to bring him out to the farm? She was aware that some Amish children suffered from inherited birth defects, but she hadn't seen any signs that Rachel was sick.

Please, God, don't let there be anything wrong with my baby.

Katie darted past Elam and hurried toward the house. Inside, Nettie had the good doctor settled at the kitchen table with a cup of coffee and a slice of her homemade cherry pie in front of him. He already had a forkful in his mouth.

Katie halted inside the door, striving to keep calm. Elam came in and stood behind her. To her surprise, she felt his hands on her shoulders offering comfort and support.

She said, "Dr. White, what brings you out here?"

He finished chewing, then tapped his plate with his silverware. "If I had known that there was pie this good here, I've have come much sooner."

Nettie beamed. "I'm glad it's to your liking."

"If your family ever has need of medical care, you may pay the bill with pies, Mrs. Sutter."

Katie took a step forward. "Is there something wrong with Rachel's tests?"

The doctor shook his head. "No, everything is fine. After your visit, I got to thinking about your family and I did a little investigating with the help of my old college roommate. He's retired from the State Department, but he still has connections there. It turns out your family immigrated from a place called Blue Creek in Belize. Unfortunately, that's all my friend could find out. There isn't anyone left in the area with the name of Lantz or Eicher, which was your mother's maiden name. I'm sorry. I know you were hoping for a different answer."

Katie struggled to hide her disappointment and hold back tears. She knew the chances of finding more of her family had been remote, but she couldn't help getting her hopes up.

After the doctor thanked Nettie for her hospitality, he donned his hat and headed outside to his car. He opened the car door, then stopped. "I almost forgot. Nettie's pie drove it right out of my mind. Amber said to tell you she found a job you might like."

"She has? Where?"

"At the Wadler Inn. Now, it's only a temporary position, but it could turn into more. Emma Wadler is needing help because her mother has broken her hip, and Amber thought of you."

"I'll go and see her today."

As the doctor drove away, Katie heard the screen door slam. She looked toward the house to see Elam approaching. When he was close enough, he said, "I'm sorry, Katie. I know how much finding more of your family meant to you."

She turned and began walking toward the bench beneath the apple tree at the back of the yard. "It's just that I've wanted to be a part of a real family for as long as I can remember. I wanted to be a part of a family like yours. A place where people laugh and talk about their worries and their hopes. Where they get together on Sundays and travel to visit each other in their homes. I took that away from Malachi. I have to accept that he is my only family."

Elam grasped her arm and turned her to face him. "Katie, you can't keep blaming yourself."

"Oh, I know. I used to think I didn't deserve a family after what I'd done. I just needed to know there was someone out there who wanted me."

He opened his arms and she went to him. "Katie, you are already a part of a family. You are one of God's children. That makes you a part of His family. Wherever you go, no one can take that from you."

Wherever I go. He doesn't believe I will stay here.

She laid her cheek against his chest, drawing strength

from him and comfort from his embrace. "You are a good man, Elam."

"And you're a good woman, Katie."

Giving a tiny shake of her head, she said, "A lot of people will disagree with that."

From the porch, his mother called his name. He slowly drew away from Katie. She missed his warmth like a physical ache. He gazed at her intently. "I stand by what I said."

She watched him walk to the house. She had been searching for a place to belong somewhere in the world, but what she really wanted was to belong here.

Was it possible? Elam's embrace had just given her a bright ray of hope.

Chapter Sixteen

"What is that long face for?" Nettie demanded as she sprinkled a packet of flower seeds into the freshly turned earth bordering the walkway.

On her knees clearing away last year's old growth, Katie sighed. How was she going to break the news to her friend? Pulling out a few early weeds, Katie said, "What if I told you I was moping because… I'm moving out."

"What is this? Where are you going?" Nettie propped her fists on her hips.

"I have a job at the Wadler Inn starting the day after tomorrow. Emma Wadler also owns a small apartment that I can rent starting in two weeks."

Turning away, Nettie wiped at her eye with her forearm. "I'm happy for you, but I will miss you."

"I'll come to visit often and you will see me at church. I've already talked to Bishop Zook about taking instructions."

Nettie turned back, a wide smile on her face. "That's wonderful news."

"I thought you'd be happy to hear that."

"Have you told Elam?"

"Not yet." Katie looked down. She wasn't sure how Elam would take the news. Would he think she was only doing it because of her feelings for him?

There had been no repeat of the closeness they'd shared the day the doctor came to see her. She was half-afraid her growing love was making her see things that weren't there. Did Elam care for her the way a man cared for a woman, or was she reading what she wanted to see into his simple kindness?

Nettie brought up a hand to shade her eyes. "It looks like Elam is home from town."

Sitting back on her heels, Katie dusted off her hands and tried to calm her rapidly beating heart. She was surprised when he stopped the buggy in front of the house instead of driving it to the barn.

Stepping down, Elam came toward her, a pensive expression on his face. She stood, a sense of unease tickling the back of her neck. He held out a thick white envelope. "This came for you in the mail today."

"For me?" She took a step closer.

"It's from your brother."

Stunned, she took the letter from him and stared at the return address. Why had Malachi written? What did he want?

"Aren't you going to open it?" Elam prompted.

"Yes." She turned away and walked across the new green grass to the bench beneath the blooming apple tree. The pink flowers of the tree scented the air with their heady perfume. The drone of bees inspecting each open bud mingled with the soft sighing of the breeze in the branches.

Sitting down, she opened the envelope with trembling hands and began to read.

Dear Katie,
I hope this letter finds you well. We are settled in
Kansas. Beatrice finds it too hot and dusty here
in the summer.

I have been asked by my bishop and by Bishop
Zook to seek a mending between us. Bishop Zook
has written to tell me you have a daughter named
Rachel, for our mother. When I heard this I knew
God had chosen this time for me to reveal the
truth to you, Katie. Rachel was not your mother's name.

Katie stared at the words in shock. What did he mean?
Fearfully, she continued reading.

Our family farm was in the hill country of Belize. A young native woman, an orphan named
Lucita, worked for us. She was much loved by my
mother. One day she came to my mother to confess she was pregnant. She did not want the child.
She asked my mother to take you and raise you.
We never learned who your father was. Lucita
died when you were born and my mother took you
in as Lucita had wished and raised you as her own.

Because my father was dead, speculation
began to circulate in the church that the child was
Mother's. Such gossip caused her great distress.
She denied it, but some women who did not like
her kept the gossip alive. The bishop asked Mother
to repent, she refused and was shunned. It finally
drove us to leave.

Katie laid the letter down without reading more. Her
mind reeled. She wanted to pinch herself and wake from

this bad dream. No wonder she'd never felt as if she fit in. She wasn't a Lantz. She wasn't Amish. Her black hair and eyes were a gift from a mother she'd never known. She stared at the grass littered with apple blossoms in front of her without seeing it. After a few minutes, she began reading again.

I did not wish to leave Belize. There was someone I planned to marry there, but as father was dead, I was the head of the house. It was my responsibility to take care of my mother and the rest of the family. When everyone died in that fire, I could not look upon your face without seeing all I had lost because of you.

Perhaps I was too hard on you when you were growing up. If I was, it was because I saw your mother's wildness in you and wished to stem it.

Beatrice and I have come, at last, to accept that God does not mean to bless us with children of our own. It will not be easy for you, an unwed mother, to raise a child by yourself. Please consider letting us raise her for you. We have a good home. She will not want for anything. You may see her often if you wish. I know of work nearby if you choose to move here.

As I told you the day you left, if you had come to me in person, Katie, and shown repentance, I would have taken you in. I shall now tell my bishop all is mended between us.

Malachi Lantz

Katie wadded the letter up and threw it into the grass. How dare Malachi offer to take her baby after making her miserable her entire life! Rising to her feet, she paced back and forth. Pausing to calm herself, she saw Elam watching her.

Elam asked, "What does he say?"

She wanted to run to Elam's embrace and cry out her heartache, but something held her back. "He told me the truth. Finally. Read it for yourself." She turned away instead and began walking out into the fields to be alone.

She had no family. She didn't belong anywhere.

Elam came out of the house and leaned a hip against the porch railing later that evening. Katie sat on a rocker on the front porch with Rachel in her arms. He had found the letter from her brother and read it. His heart ached for what she must be going through. He studied Katie's faraway look. "You barely touched your supper."

"I'm not hungry."

"*Mamm* has a custard pie cooling on the counter. If you'd like a slice, I can fetch one for you."

Katie smiled. "I imagine when you were a boy you brought home all manner of birds with broken wings and stray kittens."

"A few," he admitted.

"I'm fine, Elam. I don't need to eat."

"You must keep up your strength for your daughter's sake."

Kissing the baby's forehead, Katie then leaned her cheek against her child's head. "Yes, she's all I have now."

He sat down in the rocker next to her. "I'm sorry for the way Malachi delivered this news, but isn't it best to know the truth?"

"I guess you're right. I just feel so lost. All my life I wanted my family back. I hated that God took them all from me, and now I find out they weren't my family at all. My mother gave me away. I have no idea who my father is. I'm truly without any ties to this world."

"A family is more than blood, Katie. You know this. Those who live in our hearts are our family." He reached across and laid a hand on her arm.

He longed to ask her to become part of his family, to marry him, but fear held back his words. He had asked Salome to marry him and she had taken her vows to the church without meaning them. The result was that she was shunned by her family and friends for the rest of her life. He couldn't bear to have that happen to Katie.

She seemed so remote, as though she needed to separate herself from all that had gone on. Rocking back and forth, she held her baby, looking as lost and alone as she had that day at the bus station.

"It's going to be all right, Katie."

She didn't seem to hear him. He moved his hand to her cheek. "What can I do to help you?"

Pulling away, she said, "Nothing. I just want to be alone for a little while."

He stood but couldn't bring himself to leave her. "I wish you would not take this so hard."

Rising to her feet, she gave him a brave smile. "I'm not. I'm going to stop dreaming of things that can't be and make my own way in the world. It will be Rachel and me and that will be enough."

She left him and went into the house, closing the door softly behind her.

Elam sat back down in the rocker. It might be enough for her, but it would not be enough for him. He wanted to be included in their lives. He loved them both.

Katie was on the right path. When she had made her

baptism and her hurts had healed, he would offer her his heart, his home and his family as her own.

His mother had told him about Katie's job and her plan to move into town. He was prepared to bide his time. Katie Lantz was a woman worth waiting for.

Kate's first day of working for Emma Wadler proved to be easier than she expected. The Wadler Inn sat at the west end of town, overlooking a valley dotted with white Amish farmsteads. The view was unspoiled by power lines, as none of the families beyond the edge of the city in that direction used electricity.

Emma's rooms were small and quaint. The beds were covered with bright Amish quilts, and the furniture had all been made by local craftsmen. Her large gathering room boasted a wide, brick fireplace and soft sofas that the tourists seemed to love.

Katie's duties were to answer the phone, to take reservations and to keep Grandma Wadler company. The latter proved to be the easiest task of all. Grandma Wadler had made it her mission in life to spoil Rachel the moment she met her.

Knowing she was lucky to find a job where she could keep Rachel with her, Katie allowed the wheelchair-bound woman to hold and rock the baby whenever Rachel was awake.

Emma's current group of guests were a family from Arizona. They were genuinely interested in learning about Amish culture. Katie was happy to answer their questions. They were disappointed to learn that they should avoid photographing the Amish, but heartily promised to drive slowly and watch out for buggies on the area's winding, narrow roads.

When five o'clock rolled around, Katie was ready

to go home and put her feet up. When she walked outside with Rachel in her bassinet, Elam was waiting to take her home.

"How was it?" he asked, as she climbed in the buggy.

"It wasn't bad. Emma is very nice and her mother is easy to please."

After guiding the horse into the traffic, he settled back and took a peek at Rachel. "How did *moppel* like being a working woman?"

"She isn't a fat baby. I wish you and your mother wouldn't call her that."

"Ach, she's just plump enough to suit me."

"That's right. You don't like skinny women."

He eyed Katie up and down. "I make an occasional exception."

She felt the blood rush to her cheeks. Was he implying he found her attractive? Perhaps there was hope for her after all.

Before she could think of a comeback, he changed the subject.

"Mr. Imhoff is bringing over one of his ponies and a cart for you to use until you move into town."

"That's very kind of him."

"*Jah,* it's kind but we both know why he's doing it." Elam rolled his eyes and grinned.

Katie giggled. "To impress your mother."

"She was baking a lemon sponge cake when I left the house."

"Let me guess. It's Mr. Imhoff's favorite."

They looked at each other and both ducked their heads as they began laughing. Still smiling, Katie studied the man beside her. It felt good to laugh with him. She'd shared so many things with him that she hadn't shared with anyone else.

She loved his quiet strength, his bright eyes and ready smile. He was a good man. She was blessed to be able to call him a friend.

Content to ride beside Elam, Katie enjoyed the rest of the trip home. As Judy turned into a lane, Katie tucked the memory of her time with Elam into a special place in her heart. When she had her own place, these rides with him would stop. But until then, she would cherish their time alone.

The following day was "off" Sunday, a day of rest, but without a preaching service. It was a day normally devoted to reading the Bible and visiting among friends. Katie was reading from the German Bible and struggling a bit with the language. Elam was helping her. She was determined to finish the chapter while Rachel was napping.

"Is that a car I hear?" Nettie looked over the top of her spectacles toward the door.

Katie glanced up. "Maybe Amber has come for a visit."

Rising, Katie walked to the screen door to look out. Her heart jumped into her throat and lodged there. It wasn't Amber.

Matt stepped out of a dark blue sedan in front of the house.

Chapter Seventeen

Shocked beyond words, Katie could only stare. What was Matt doing here?

Elam, sipping a cup of coffee, didn't bother looking up. "Amber is always welcome."

"It's not Amber." Katie didn't explain. She simply opened the door and walked outside.

Matt had changed a bit in the four months since she'd last seen him. Had it only been four months? It seemed like a lifetime.

He was still good-looking in a reckless sort of way. His long, dark hair had been cut and was neatly styled now. The diamond earring he normally wore was missing from his earlobe. His clothes were casual and expensive.

She hadn't realized until this moment how much better looking Elam was than her former boyfriend. Elam's goodness came from within. His clothes might be homemade and simple, but his heart was genuine.

Matt's face brightened when he caught sight of Katie. He held out his arms. "I found you at last."

When she didn't move, he slowly lowered his arms and slipped his hands in the pockets of his pants.

Katie found her voice at last. "What do you want, Matt?"

"What do I want? I've come to bring you home. I see your brother's got you wearing one of those sacks again."

She smoothed the front of her apron. "I chose to dress Plain, Matt. My brother had nothing to do with it."

"You're still mad at me, aren't you?" He sent an apologetic look her way, then approached.

When he was standing in front of her, he said, "I've come to say I'm sorry for the way I left you. I can explain everything, and I've come to see our baby."

Katie heard the screen door open behind her. Elam said, "Who is it, Katie?"

A big smile creased Matt's face. He held out his hand to Elam. "Hello. I'm Katie's partner, Matt Carson."

When no one said a word or took his hand, Matt let it fall. "I know my showing up like this must be something of a shock to you. Is it a boy or a girl?"

"It's a girl," Katie answered. "I named her Rachel."

Matt smiled. "I like it. Can I see her?"

Katie glanced toward Elam. Should she refuse? How could she?

Before she could form a reply, Elam stepped forward and squared off with Matt. "You are not welcome here."

Matt took a step backward. "I think that's up to Katie."

"She has nothing to say to you."

Katie laid a hand on Elam's tense arm. "I will talk to him, Elam, and then I will send him away."

His jaw tensed, she could see the muscles twitch as he held back his anger. Finally, he nodded once. "I will be in the workshop if you need me."

Elam crossed the yard with angry strides. Matt took

a step forward and blew out a breath. "Wow, I thought the Amish were nonviolent."

"We are."

Matt nodded toward the house. "I'm not sure about *him*."

"Elam would rather die than harm another human being. That doesn't mean he doesn't feel anger or annoyance. It just means he will not act on them."

"Good to know. Look, Katie, I know I have a lot to apologize for, but there is a lot you don't know. Let me explain before you kick me off the place."

She glanced toward the house where Nettie stood watching them. Katie said, "Why don't we take a walk?"

As they strolled side by side down the lane, Katie worked to keep her anger in check. Matt seemed to sense her feelings and said, "Katie, I was stupid. I shouldn't have left you when I did. I got scared. I didn't want to be a father. I'd never even told my parents about you."

"Because you were ashamed of me," she bit out.

"Like I said, I was stupid. Anyway, my folks were taking this trip to Italy. I got my dad to spring for my ticket and I joined them. They were thrilled because I hadn't seen them in almost a year. I honestly intended to tell them about you and the baby and then come back in a week."

Was he telling the truth? She found herself believing him. "So what happened?"

"My dad had a stroke the night we arrived in Rome. He lingered for another two months in the hospital, but then he died. He never even knew he was going to be a grandfather." The quiver in his voice wasn't faked. Katie could see the sorrow in his eyes.

"I'm sorry, Matt."

"I really messed up. Mom was a basket case. She'd

never done anything without dad. By the time we flew the body home and arranged a funeral, you had already left the apartment."

"I was kicked out because I couldn't pay the rent… three weeks before our baby was due. You could have called."

"I know, I know. None of this was your fault. I messed up. I messed up big time, and I've come to ask your forgiveness."

Katie sucked in a deep breath. She had to forgive him. It was a fundamental part of being Amish. She searched her heart for God's grace and found the words she needed. "I forgive you, Matt."

Hope filled his eyes. "Do you? Do you really?"

"Yes."

Stepping forward, he took hold of her hand. "I want my mother to meet you and to meet the baby. You and I and our child are all the family she has left. She was lost without my dad, but as soon as she learned about the baby, the light came back into her eyes."

"Matt, don't do this to me." Katie pushed him away gently. "I have learned to get along without you. You didn't care enough to see that we had a place to live, or food, or medical care."

"I can keep saying I'm sorry for the rest of my life if that will help. Give me another chance, Katie. I'm begging you. We can make it work. Will you marry me?"

Shaking her head, she turned away. "It's getting late. We should get back."

"Think about it, Katie. Think about Rachel and what it will mean to her if you come with me. We can be a family."

"Please, Matt. I need some time to think."

She left him and hurried toward the barn, but she

didn't go to Elam's workshop. Instead, she climbed the ladder that led to the hayloft, looking for solitude. Matt's arrival had been completely unexpected. He was asking for a second chance. He was Rachel's father. He was offering her everything Katie once thought she wanted.

Reaching the loft floor, she moved toward the dim interior at the back of the barn where bales of hay were stacked to the rafters. Dust motes drifted in lazy arcs across the bands of sunlight that streamed from the double doors at the end of the loft. Overhead, pigeons fluttered about in the rafters, disturbed by her presence.

Matt had come back for her. He had asked for her forgiveness and she had forgiven him. Now what? He was offering her something she'd never truly had—a family. But a family away from the Amish life she had finally grown to love.

She had a choice. Go with Matt or stay near Elam. Elam, a devout man of the Plain faith. Would he be able to return her love? Would Elam trust that she had truly found her way back to God?

She heard a rustling behind her and turned to see Elam, pitchfork in hand, standing at the wide doors.

He said, "I'm sorry if I frightened you."

She smiled at him. "You could never frighten me."

He came toward her. Laying the pitchfork aside, he took a seat beside her in the hay. His hand lay close to hers but not touching. She wanted him to hold her hand. She wanted him to kiss her and wipe away this feeling of being alone.

"I saw you out walking with Matt. Will he be staying long?"

She sighed. "That depends."

"On what?"

"On me." Suddenly, she couldn't stand it any longer. She grasped his hand. "Elam, I don't know what to do."

He didn't draw her close, didn't kiss her, didn't promise to make everything all right. Some of the hope she'd held in her heart began to fade.

"What are you doing, Katie?"

A chorus of chirping began overhead. Katie looked up to see a mother swallow returning to her mud nest in the rafters. Katie held on to Elam's hand. "I am like that swallow. I had a home here once but I couldn't stay. My life was like a long winter. I wanted someone to show me the sun."

"So you flew away."

"I never planned to come back."

"Yet like the swallow, you did return and you began to raise your young one. The swallow will nest here, but she won't stay. When the days grow short and winter comes and her little ones no longer need her—she'll fly away again. Is that what you will do, Katie?"

She turned so she could face him. "I don't know."

"Do you love Matt?" he asked quietly.

"I did. I think I did, but maybe he was just a means to an end. I felt used when he left me, but maybe I was using him, too. To escape Malachi's strictness. I'm so confused. Why couldn't it be simple?"

"It is simple, Katie."

"How can you say that?"

He looked away. "Because it is simple."

"I don't want to go, Elam. I want to stay here with you and your family."

"Do you?"

"Give me a reason to stay, Elam."

Sadness filled Elam's eyes. "Ah, Katie. Have you learned nothing?"

"I don't know what you mean."

"I wish with all my heart that I could give you a reason to stay, but I can't. The reason must come from your own heart or it won't be strong enough to withstand the trials that will come your way in life."

"I could withstand them if you were beside me."

"Only faith in God can give you that strength, Katie. I love you, but I will not use that love to bind you to a faith you have not accepted with your whole heart."

"My faith can grow." He was breaking her heart.

Leaning forward, he kissed her forehead and whispered, "I pray that it will."

Rising to his feet, he left her alone in the loft. When she was sure he was gone, she broke down and cried.

Elam walked sightlessly between the rows of ankle-high new corn. He wasn't ready to face anyone yet. He couldn't believe how close he had come to gathering Katie in his arms and telling her nothing mattered but their love.

If only it could be that simple.

Perhaps for the English it was. He wanted Katie. He wanted her in his life, wanted her to be his wife and he wanted to raise Rachel as his own child.

The temptation to race back to Katie was almost unbearable. Why had God laid this burden upon him again?

If she chose to return to the outside world with Matt, Elam didn't think he could bear it.

The Lord never gave a man more than he could bear; yet if that were true why did his heart ache like it was being torn in two? He could barely draw a breath past the pain. Tears filled his eyes and he stumbled on the rough ground. Pressing the heels of his hands to stem the flow of tears, he dropped to his knees in the rich earth.

"Why, God? Why didn't You send me a woman of my own faith to love? Why must You test me? What have I done to deserve this sorrow?"

If he had given in to the pleading in Katie's eyes and asked her to stay, how much worse would it be to lose her later?

Elam sank back onto his heels. How could it be worse than this?

I could go with her into the English world.

Even as the tiny voice in his mind whispered the words, Elam knew he could not act upon them. He had made a vow to God and before the members of his church. If he broke that promise, what value would any promise he made in the future hold?

He tipped back his head and blinked away the tears to stare at the blue sky. "Your will be done, Lord. Give me Your strength, I beseech You."

When Katie came out of the barn, she saw Matt smoking a cigarette while leaning on the railing of the front porch. He held up the butt. "I'm trying to quit. Don't tell my mom. She thinks I already have."

Katie stared at him a long moment.

Poor Matt. He's trying to become a better man, but he's still willing to backslide and deceive others.

A passage from *Luke* 16 flashed into her mind.

He that is faithful in that which is least is faithful also in much: and he that is unjust in the least is unjust also in much.

Matt bent forward to look at her more closely. "Have you been crying?"

How can I judge him harshly when I am guilty of the same thing? Forgive me, Father, for failing You in so many ways. She drew a deep breath. "I was, but I'm fine now. You should be truthful with your mother."

"You're right."

"Matt, we need to talk."

He ground the cigarette butt beneath the toe of his shoe. "That's why I'm here."

"I can't go back with you."

"Katie, I know I treated you badly, but it won't happen again. My father's death made me see things in a different light. I'm all the family my mother has. I want you and Rachel to become part of that. She's beautiful, by the way. She has your eyes and your hair. Mrs. Sutter let me hold her."

"I'm Amish, Matt." As she said the words, she knew in her heart that they were true. She was Amish. Not by blood or because of her family, but by choice.

He looked at her funny. "I know."

"That means so many different things that I don't expect you to understand it all, but one thing it means is that marriage to someone outside of my faith is forbidden."

"I thought you had to go through some kind of baptism for that to happen."

"I will be baptized in a few months."

"How can this be the life you want? It's crazy. Are you sure?"

"I'm sure. This is the Plain life. Each day I will try to make my life pleasing to God. That is what I want."

"And what about Rachel? What about my daughter? What if she doesn't want to live in the Stone Age?"

"Matt, she will be loved, cherished and accepted among the Amish."

He paused, at a loss for words, but then he said, "She'll only get an eighth-grade education."

"She'll read and speak two languages. She'll know everything there is to know about running a household, raising a happy family and running a farm or a business."

"And what if that's not enough for her? What if she wants to be a doctor or a lawyer?"

"Then she will not stay among the Plain people." She reached out to lay a hand on his face. "And she will have a father to go to who can show her a bigger, if not a better world."

"Why do you have to sound so rational?"

"Because that's the way it is. You didn't really want to marry me, did you? Let's be honest with each other."

He looked taken aback. "I came here to do just that."

"You came to appease your conscience and because you wanted to offer your mother the comfort of having a grandchild. It was a good thing, but it isn't reason enough to marry me."

"So you're going to stay and marry the Amish farmer, is that it?"

"No."

He drew back, a look of confusion on his face. "I don't get it. You just said that's what you want."

"I love Elam and his family. I always wanted a loving family, but it wasn't until I met Elam that I came to understand I've always had one. I belong to the family of God. Elam helped me to see that I am Amish."

"Okay, I'm missing something. Why don't you want to marry him?"

"I do, but Elam doesn't believe that I'm staying out of my love for God. I didn't know it myself until a little while ago."

"What are you going to do?"

"I'll go to Malachi in Kansas. I can stay with him until I find a job and a place of my own."

"You'll be getting child support from me. That should make things a little easier."

"Thank you, Matt."

"It's the right thing to do. I just wish I hadn't blown my chances with you."

"You and I weren't meant to marry. We should both thank God we didn't get the chance to make each other miserable for fifty years."

"You're probably right."

"I know I'm right. Matt, I promise I will bring Rachel to visit both of you as often as I can."

He smiled for the first time since he had arrived. "That'll give us both something to look forward to. How soon will you be heading to Kansas?"

"The bus doesn't leave until tomorrow evening. I have a friend in town I can stay with until then." The memory of Elam finding her at the bus station threatened to bring on her tears again, but she fought them back. She was sure Amber would put her up for the night.

"Can I give you a lift to your friend's place?"

"That would be great." Katie glanced over her shoulder, but there was no sign of Elam. Perhaps that was for the best. In her heart, she knew they had already said their goodbyes.

Katie led Matt inside the house where she told Nettie her plans and had a tearful farewell.

Chapter Eighteen

"They have only been gone a day and yet I can't believe how quiet the house is without them." Nettie sighed heavily at the kitchen sink.

"You said that already." Elam sipped his coffee without tasting it. Katie was gone and so was the sunshine that warmed his soul.

"I just can't get over what a difference it made having them here."

He wouldn't mourn something that was never meant to be. "We got on well enough before they came. Mary will have her babe in another month. You'll be so busy helping her you won't notice that Katie and Rachel aren't around."

If only he had some way to block out his thoughts of them. Had he been right to rebuff Katie or had he pushed her into Matt's arms?

She said she wanted a reason to stay. He could have given it to her. Setting his cup down, Elam rested his elbows on the table and raked his fingers through his hair. Why didn't he give her that reason?

She might have been content, even happy with him. With his help she might have had a chance to grow in her faith and understanding of God's will. He glanced at his mother slowly drying the supper dishes and putting them away. Her boundless energy seemed as lacking as his. Katie and Rachel had taken the life from this home.

"*Mamm,* can I ask you a question?"

"Of course." She set the last glass in the cupboard and closed the door.

"When did you first know that *Dat* had lost his faith?"

She turned around, a look of shock on her face. "Why are you asking about that now?"

"I have wondered for a long time if there were signs."

She came and sat beside him at the table. "You know that our first child died when she was only two months old. She was such a beautiful babe. It broke our hearts to lay her in the cold ground. Your father struggled mightily with his faith after her illness and death."

"It must have been terrible."

"It was *Gotte wille.* He needed her in Heaven more than we needed her here on earth, although we cannot understand why. You father never got over her loss."

"But he was a good and faithful servant all the years I was growing up."

"He went through the motions for me. There were times I almost believed he had found his way back to God, but then I would see something in his eyes and I would know he had not. I was not surprised the day he announced that he wouldn't go to the preaching anymore. He could not forgive God for taking his baby girl from him."

"Do you wish he'd gone on pretending?"

"No. I wish he could have opened his heart to God's healing power the way Katie was able to. I'm sorry it did not work out for the two of you. I thought you cared for each other."

Elam set his cup on the table. "She was only pretending or she would not have gone back to the English."

"What do you mean? She has not gone back to the English."

He looked up sharply. "She left with Matt. I saw them."

Cocking her head to the side, Nettie said, "Yes, he gave her a ride to Amber Bradley's place. She's taking the bus to her brother's. She plans to stay with him only until she can get a job. I thought you knew this."

Elam jumped to his feet. "She's taking the bus?"

"Did I not just say that?"

She hadn't left with Matt. He still had a chance. "I must get to the bus station."

"Why?"

"Because I love her. I drove her away with my false pride instead of believing she was the one God chose for me."

He snatched his hat from the peg and jammed it on his head on the way out the door.

Katie sat in the front seat of Amber's car as she drove them to the bus station. Rachel slept quietly in the infant seat in the back. "Thanks for giving me a lift."

"No problem. Are you sure you won't change your mind and stay in Hope Springs?"

It would be too painful to live in the same community with Elam. To see him at worship and at gatherings and to know he didn't trust that her faith was genuine.

"I think it's better that I go to Malachi. He will take care of us until I can manage on my own."

"I'm going to miss you and Rachel."

"We will miss you, too."

When they reached the station, Amber carried Katie's suitcase to the pile waiting to be loaded on the bus. The two women faced each other then hugged one another fiercely. "Take care of yourself and that beautiful baby," Amber whispered.

"I will. God bless you for all you've done for us." Drawing away, Katie straightened her bonnet and picked up Rachel, now sleeping in her bassinet. She entered the bus station with tears threatening to blind her.

The same thin, bald man stood behind the counter. Katie wondered if he would remember her. She said, "I'd like to purchase a ticket to Yoder, Kansas."

He didn't glance up. "We don't have service to Yoder. The nearest town is Hutchinson, Kansas. You'll have to make connections in St. Louis and Kansas City."

"That will be fine. Is it still one hundred and sixty-nine dollars?"

He looked up at that. "Yes, it is. Do you have enough this time?"

"I do." She laid the bills on the counter.

"No, you don't," a man said behind her.

She recognized the voice instantly. It was Elam.

"I have enough." She didn't turn around. She didn't trust herself not to start crying.

"You haven't paid me for Rachel's baby bed." He was right behind her. She could feel the warmth of him through the fabric of her Amish dress.

Reaching around her, he took the money from the counter. "Now you cannot leave."

"I don't have a reason to stay." Her heart was beating so hard she thought it might burst.

Quietly, he said, "God willing, I shall spend my life giving you a thousand reasons to be glad you stayed."

She turned at last to face him, the love she'd tried to hide shining in her eyes. "Malachi says it's very hot and dusty in Kansas."

Elam covered her hands with his own. She could feel him trembling. He said, "It doesn't sound like a good place for Rachel."

Behind her, the man at the counter said, "Do you want a ticket or not?"

She smiled at Elam. "It seems I can't afford one."

Elam drew a deep breath. "Come. I'll give you a ride home."

Outside, Katie climbed sedately into the buggy, although she was so happy she wanted to shout. Elam helped her in, then handed her the baby and climbed up after them. With a cluck of his tongue he sent Judy out into the street.

They rode in silence until they were past the outskirts of town. As the horse trotted briskly down the blacktop, he turned in the seat to face Katie. "I ask you to forgive me. I judged you unfairly, Katie. I pushed you away when you needed my counsel."

"I forgive you as I have been forgiven."

"Will you marry me, Katie Lantz?"

Her heart expanded with happiness and all the love she'd kept hidden came bubbling forth. "*Jah,* Elam Sutter. I will marry you—on one condition."

His smile widened. "I knew it could not be so easy. What is your condition?"

"I want Rachel to be able to visit her English family."

His grin faded. His gaze rested on the sleeping baby. "And what if she is tempted to leave us and go into the English world when she is older?"

"Then we will face that together, and we will pray that she finds God in her own way."

"This is a hard thing to ask, Katie. I love her like my own child."

"And she will love you and honor you as her father. Just as I love you and will honor you as my husband."

He was silent for a time and Katie waited, not daring to hope. The clop-clop of Judy's hooves and the jingle of her harness were the only sounds on the empty highway. At last Elam said, "And you will obey me in all things and without question."

She heard the hint of teasing in his tone and all her fear vanished. With a light heart and prayer of thanks she leaned close to him. "You will be in charge of the house. It shall be as you say."

Elam chuckled. "A man who claims he's in charge of his own home will lie about other things, too. When do you want the wedding to take place?"

"Tomorrow."

He slanted a grin her way. "Be sensible, Katie."

"If tomorrow isn't possible, then I think a fall wedding will be good. How about the first Tuesday in November?"

"Tomorrow sounds better, but November will do. It can't come soon enough to suit me."

Happier than she had ever imagined she could be, Katie linked her arm through his and looked out at the passing landscape. The once-empty fields were springing to life with new green crops. Wildflowers bloomed in the ditches and along the fencerows. Larks sang from the fenceposts and branches of the trees. Her life, once bleak and empty, was now full to overflowing.

She laid her head against Elam's strong shoulder. "It's a beautiful evening, isn't it?"

"Beautiful," he replied, happiness welling up in his

voice. He wasn't looking at the countryside. He was smiling down at her.

She smiled at him. "Do you think your mother and Mr. Imhoff will see more of each other when you marry?"

"I think that's a good possibility. Mother deserves to be happy. She would like having stepgrandchildren to raise."

"Who knows, maybe there will be more than one wedding this fall in your family."

"It will be hard to keep our betrothal a secret. Do you know how much celery I'll have to plant for two weddings? The whole township will know something is going on."

"I can live with that if you can."

He nodded. "*Jah,* I can."

When they finally reached the lane, Judy turned off the highway and picked up her pace. As the farmhouse came into view, Katie thought back to the night she'd arrived.

How she had dreaded returning here. Now the farm had become something different, something it had never been before. It was a place of joy. A place where she could raise her child to know God. A place where she and her family would work together and pray together as God intended.

She said, "'Even the sparrow has found a home, and the swallow a nest for herself, where she may have her young—a place near your altar, O Lord Almighty, my King and my God.'"

"*Psalms* 84:3, I think," Elam said quietly. At the top of the rise, he pulled the horse to a halt. Katie looked up at him, at the love shining in his eyes, and she knew she was truly blessed.

"Why are we stopping?" she asked, hoping she already knew the answer.

He drew his fingers along her jaw and cupped her cheek with his hand. "Because I've been wanting to kiss you since the first time I picked you up at the bus station."

"Then you've waited long enough. Don't waste another minute." She raised her face to him and closed her eyes.

As Elam's lips touched hers with gentleness and love Katie knew in her heart that God had truly brought her home.

* * * * *

PLAIN SECRETS

Kit Wilkinson

To my sister, Elizabeth Ann, whose faith never falters. Thanks for all the support, love and direction over the years. And to my editor, Elizabeth, for her patience and guidance. Danke. Merci. Gracias. Arigato… I really cannot thank you enough :-)

Live a life worthy of the Lord and please Him in every way: bearing fruit in every good work, growing in the knowledge of God, being strengthened with all power according to His glorious might so that you may have great endurance and patience… For He has rescued us from the dominion of darkness and brought us into the kingdom of the Son He loves, in whom we have redemption, the forgiveness of sins.
—*Colossians* 1:10–14

Chapter One

Where is that girl? Hannah Nolt could hardly believe her seventeen-year-old stepdaughter had spent the entire night away from home. But here it was morning as sure as the rooster crowed in the new day, and not a single sign that Jessica had come home.

Hannah stepped from the warmth of the cottage, bracing for the chill of morning air. She tried to ward off all negative conclusions about the girl she'd raised as her own. It wasn't like her to stay out all night even on *Rumspringa*—that time when Amish youth have their "run around." And shirking morning duties was never a part of that.

Hannah should have been angry with Jessica, but instead it was only worry that filled her bones as she shivered in the darkness on her way to morning milking.

Jessica had been acting strangely for weeks now—demanding privacy, running off for hours with no explanation, even leaving the farm on weeknights. Things she had never done before. Hannah did not question the change in her behavior. She and Jessica had been closer than ever since Hannah's husband's death, just two years ago, and she had faith in Jessica's good sense and kind spirit. Surely these estranged few weeks were just a simple bump in the road—a growing pain, nothing to be alarmed over. Now Hannah wondered if perhaps she had been wrong to put so much trust in the girl.

Hannah rushed on to the barn. Maybe Jessica had gone straight there from wherever she'd been all night.

Maybe.

But as she scurried up the steep hill, her hope that Jessica was inside milking the Jersey heifers diminished. Fear as thick as the morning fog clouded her thoughts. Something was wrong. Something terribly, horribly wrong. She could feel it in her bones. None of this made sense. Jessica was not the kind of girl to stay out late, much less all night. She just wouldn't do such a thing. Not by choice. No. Something had happened. Something *Farrichterlick—frightful*. She closed her eyes and lifted her head to the skies. *Please let her be safe, Lord. Let her be safe.*

Hannah turned back to the path. A bright flash grazed the hillside, then disappeared. She paused. *What is that? A coming storm?* She heard no thunder. Saw no clouds.

Her dread doubled as she climbed the last slope to the barn. She pushed open the back door and stepped inside. Another flash of light blinded her eyes. It speared through the inside of the stable. That was no storm. *Those were car lights.*

The *vroom, vroom* of a powerful engine broke through the silent morning air. Hannah's heart raced. Her mouth went dry. Who could be at the barn at this hour of the day? She shuddered. Whatever the reason, it could not be good.

She lifted her lantern. Cold air whooshed around her. Had someone just passed her? Brushed against her?

"Hallo? Jessica? Is that you?" The dead space swallowed her voice. Not even the animals responded. Another flush of air brushed around her. The door behind her slammed shut. She turned, only to have the lantern knocked from her hands. Its flame was extinguished as it hit the dirt floor. As she scrambled after it, something bumped against her once more, this time knocking her to all fours.

Please, God. Be my light. Help me to safety.

Scrambling to her feet again, Hannah lunged toward the closed door, but the large wooden slider wouldn't budge. She was trapped. The only other door out was at the other side, where she'd seen the car lights. Where she still heard its engine. She took one step forward and stopped. She had not the courage. Sliding into an empty stall, she crouched low, pressing her back against the wall. Footsteps padded down the aisle behind her. Hard, heavy steps—those of a man, a large man. The man who had locked her in and knocked her to the floor.

Beams of light once again filled the eaves of the barn. Hannah sucked in her breath and pressed deeply into the wooden boards behind her, wishing somehow she could disappear into the wall.

Please be leaving. Whoever, whatever you are… please be leaving.

A car door slammed. Gravel crunched. The hum of the car motor grew dim. Her prayer had been answered. She slinked upward and peered over the edge of the stall. Through the open front doors, Hannah spotted a long, shiny black sedan heading away.

Hoping but not truly believing she was alone, she crouched again, feeling over the earthen floor for her dropped lantern. She refilled her lungs, taking in the soothing, familiar smells of animal and hay. She tried

to calm her panicked mind. She listened to the cows'
lows and sheeps' vibrating *baas*.

With trembling hands, she found her lantern and relit
the flame. A warm orange glow filled the space around
her, and her eyes adjusted to the soft light.

Slowly, she stood and stumbled her way to the front
of the stable. Her mind reeled. What had just happened?
Who had pushed her to the ground and locked her inside, and why? What mischief had brought an *Englischer*'s car to their barn? Hannah's legs trembled under her
as she moved across the dirt floor. She jumped when
one of the cows swung her head into the aisle, then
again when the gray barn cat sauntered over her path.

"The Lord is my shepherd. I shall not fear." Hannah whispered the Psalm to herself and the animals. *I
should not be so frightened.* She wondered if the dis-
turbance had something to do with Jessica's absence.
In fact, for a moment the car had given her hopes that
Jessica had come home. But that idea had died when
she was locked in and knocked to the floor.

The cat cried. Hannah stooped to scratch its head. A
lamb skirted beside her, down the aisle and out the front.

"What are you doing loose, little girl?" Hannah
placed her lantern on the ledge of the sheep pen. Someone had left the gate wide. She peered in only to see
that the space was mostly empty. Twenty-plus sheep
were out scampering the hillside no doubt. Once it was
light, she'd fetch one of the dogs to help round them up.

Hannah turned back to the aisle but stopped as something in the far corner caught her eye. One sheep still
sleeping. How odd that he hadn't stirred when the others roused. Perhaps he was hurt. She reached back for
her lantern and moved nearer with care not to startle
the creature. But as she closed in on the figure, she re-

alized it was no animal. It was a human. A girl. An Amish girl. Her Amish girl.

Hannah knelt beside her stepdaughter, who in all this time had not moved, nor made a sound.

"Jessica? Jessica?"

Putting the lantern aside once again, she touched the girl's shoulders and rolled her slightly, drawing her face toward herself.

Jessica's body was cold. And there was blood. On her face. On her apron. On her neck and hands.

Jessica! Jessica! Oh, Father in Heaven, what has happened?

Hannah whispered prayers as she felt the lifelessness of the body beside her. Shock flowed over her and flashes of Peter erupted into her thoughts. Images of the night he'd been killed. The ice. The untrained horse. The car coming toward him, traveling too fast. Her dear husband, Jessica's father, thrown from the buggy and trampled. There had been much blood that night, as well.

Hannah reached for the girl's arm to feel for a pulse. There was none. No life. No spirit. Jessica was no longer in this body. No longer with her.

She touched the girl's cheeks and turned her face toward the light. There on her soft neck hung open flesh. The throat had been cut—deliberately. The marks were deep. A wound as deadly as the one her father had taken just two years ago.

"The Lord giveth and the Lord taketh away. Blessed be the name of the Lord." Hannah whispered the familiar words from Job then fell over the girl's body and wept.

"Yo! Miller."

Elijah Miller, Philadelphia Internal Affairs detective, swung his head in the direction of Captain O'Dell's deep voice.

"Need to speak with you. Pronto." The captain gestured toward his office.

Elijah pushed away from his desk. His partner, Mitchell Tucci, stood, too, and started to follow.

"Not you, Tucci. Just Miller."

Eli jerked his head around to glance back at his partner, who shrugged. It was rarely a good thing when the captain called you to his office. *Never* a good thing if he called you in by yourself. Elijah crisscrossed his way through the maze of desks and entered O'Dell's corner space.

"Shut the door. Take a seat," his captain said.

Eli did as he was told. O'Dell flung a pile of five-by-seven evidence photos across the desk. "The Lancaster police sent these over. Their chief wants your help with a homicide."

"Why would they want me on a homicide? I'm Internal Affairs."

When the captain didn't answer, he looked down at the first picture. A dead teenaged girl. She wore a frock and an apron and a prayer *Kapp*. A wave of nausea coursed through his veins. This was no normal homicide. This was an *Amish* homicide.

"Where in Lancaster is she from?" he asked.

"Willow Trace."

His hometown. Elijah's teeth clenched. His mind raced with the images of old faces, friends and family. He shuffled to the next picture. *A stable.* And the next. *Her slit throat.* The next. *Bruises and cuts.*

When he'd gone through the entire stack, he placed the pictures back on the edge of the desk and tried to keep down his breakfast of toast and black coffee. Silence filled the room. Eli stared at the floor, trying to squeeze the horrid images from his mind. But he couldn't stop his racing thoughts. Who was this girl? A neighbor? A friend's daughter? He pitied the family. Mourned for them. Then wondered at the idea that they encouraged an investigation. Could that be possible? Had things changed that much since he'd left home? The Amish didn't usually encourage any sort of police aid—or interference, as they thought of it. They liked to take care of their own problems. Eli didn't imagine this community trait had altered since he'd lived there.

"You okay?" the captain asked.

Eli shook his head. "I don't want to work an Amish homicide… She could be a relative."

"She's not. I checked. Her name is Jessica Nolt." O'Dell grabbed a page from the tiny file folder and began to read. "Daughter of Peter Nolt. Also deceased. Lived with stepmother Han—"

"Hannah Kurtz Nolt." Eli's voice was cold as he pronounced that name for the first time in a decade.

"Oh, you know these people?"

"Yes. My family shares a property line with them. I knew Peter well. He was a bit older than me. I was friends with his younger brother. And Hannah…" His throat closed tighter. "Hannah was my girlfriend." *Once upon a time…in a faraway land.*

"Girlfriend?" The captain looked skeptical.

Eli swallowed hard. "Yep. I dated Hannah while she worked as a nanny to Peter's daughter. Peter's first wife died soon after giving birth to Jessica—a bad case of hepatitis. Peter was devastated. Hannah's parents sent her to help the Nolt family."

"Then daddy fell for the nanny?"

Eli shrugged; he did not like having that heartache

rubbed in his face even after eleven years. "Something like that. Hannah started working for the family when she was twelve. The Nolts became her family—marriage just made it official. And Jessica was a very sweet girl. I remember her well." He shook away the memories—both good and bad. "So, how old was she? Fifteen? Sixteen?"

"Seventeen."

Seventeen. He frowned, thinking how an unexplained death like this would affect all of the community. And especially Hannah. "I see a deep laceration on her throat in this picture, but there's no blood. Not even on her clothes. This isn't the crime scene? Or has it been cleaned up?"

"I thought you didn't want to work the case."

"I don't. But I can't help being a little curious."

"The notes here explain that the uncle, Thomas Nolt, called Chief McClendon, but by the time he arrived, the family had already changed the girl's clothes and burned them. They claim there was no blood around her, only on her clothes. If they are telling the truth I think we can assume she wasn't killed in the stable."

"They are telling the truth… What's the story on the girl?"

"A perfectly good girl, as far as the family tells it. No evidence of drugs or alcohol."

"But the family wouldn't necessarily know what she's involved in. She was probably on *Rumspringa.* Kids don't have to tell their parents anything much during that time." Eli sighed and glanced again at the horrid photos. "There's bruising on her arms and neck in those pictures. A struggle before death? Abuse? I can't imagine it of the Nolt family, but there are cases of abuse in the Amish community."

"I don't know. This is all we have." The captain held up the thin file. "The only other information in here is that her stepmother, Hannah, is the one who found her in the milking stable. Maybe you could start by questioning her."

Question Hannah? The woman who dumped me. No way. No Hannah. No Willow Trace. No investigation. "I don't think that's a good idea."

"Oh, come on. You don't have to be official about it. Just go and pay respects or whatever."

"Why me? If you just want someone to figure out what's going on, why not one of the local guys?"

"Chief McClendon says his own men aren't always Amish-friendly. He'd heard of you, the Amish cop in the city, and thought the people would respond better with one of their own asking the questions."

Eli shook his head—that made no sense. Very few people knew he was raised Amish. "They'd be even less likely to answer me—because they'd think I should know better than to ask. The Amish don't seek revenge or restitution or even answers for unexplained events. They accept it as God's will and move on. So they would have no reason to seek answers and therefore would have no interest in answering them. I can't imagine the family even wants an investigation."

"Well, they don't. That's why there was no autopsy. All we have are these pictures. And Chief McClendon took them himself. He thinks there's something major going on here and that you're our best shot at finding out what it is."

Eli shook his head. "I haven't seen these people in eleven years. I'm not one of them anymore. They won't talk to me about any of this. They probably don't even talk to each other about it."

The captain frowned. "McClendon thinks you'll have a chance."

Eli groaned. He did not want to go back to Willow Trace. Not now. Not ever. "I'm sorry, Captain. But I can't do this."

"You have to."

"But Tucci and I are right in the middle of a case against that officer in District Seven."

"I'll put someone else on it."

Eli shook his head. "You don't get it. I really cannot go back there."

"You have to." O'Dell folded up the record file. "I'll be honest with you, Miller, I don't quite get it, but this is *way* over my head."

Eli narrowed his eyes on the captain. "What? How can it be over your head from the Lancaster County police?"

His boss crossed his arms over his chest. "The request came from Chief McClendon via the governor."

"The governor?" Elijah stood and began to pace in front of his boss's desk. "How does the governor even know I exist?"

"No idea, Miller. But when the governor asks for you, you go."

An hour later, Eli was navigating the rolling hills of eastern Pennsylvania reluctantly on his way to Willow Trace. With every passing mile, the tension in him racked tighter and tighter. After eleven years, how would he be received? Would he be received? The only person who'd stayed in touch with him was his sister, Abigail. But even she did so in secret—their father, the local bishop, had told Elijah never to return if he chose to take up weapons as a part of his life and work.

Eli knew it was difficult for his family to understand the choice he'd made, not just to leave the community but to become a police officer. Yet the reasons for it went far back into his childhood. He'd only been about five years old when, during a trip to the city with his father, a crazy man on the train had kidnapped him and his sister, Abigail. If it had not been for the help of the Philadelphia police, Elijah and his sister would never have been reunited with their family. That incident had always made him admire and respect the police. When Hannah had chosen to marry Peter instead of him, Eli had felt certain that leaving the Amish community behind and becoming a policeman was what God had called him to do. Ironic that the very reason he'd never returned to Willow Trace since then was exactly the thing forcing him home today.

About as ironic as heading out to see Hannah—the woman he'd tried so hard to forget. They'd been so in love. Or at least he'd thought so. Then she'd married Peter. He'd felt like such a fool.

His thoughts rambled as he maneuvered his convertible through the hills and around the horse and buggies. He kept his head down and lifted a quick word. *Guard me from their judgment, Lord. If there is a job for me here, then make me strong so I can do it. If not, let me return to what—*

Eli looked up just in time to slam on the brakes as another horse and carriage crossed right into his lane while attempting to avoid a sleek black sedan speeding around the buggy on the right shoulder.

Crazy driver. Couldn't slow down one second for a buggy. *Good grief.* Someone could have been seriously injured. He shook his head, remembering all too well the days of being in the buggy himself and having those sorts of incidents. They happened more frequently than they should. He patted the dash of his Mustang. He felt much safer in his convertible.

Checking his rearview mirror, he searched for the car, but the black sedan had already fled the area. Thankfully, the horse and buggy were recovered and back on their side of the road. Eli drove on.

Minutes later, he turned onto the dirt path leading to the Nolts' farmhouse. A chill of unease rippled down his spine with the strangest feeling that he was being watched. He parked in the gravel turnaround in front of the quaint two-story stone cottage and stepped out of his car. The old house hadn't changed. The sight of it flooded his head with hundreds of memories—gatherings, Sunday church, buggy rides.

A woman stepping onto the long white porch restored his mind to the present. She wore a blue frock with a black apron. Her raven hair had been tucked tightly away under a white prayer *Kapp.* She dried her hands on the skirt of her apron, then pressed away the creases, all the while studying him from the safety of the porch. At length, a soft, pleasant smile fell over her lips.

Hannah.

Eli froze to his spot on the front walkway. She was stunning as ever—her sweet face, her deep emerald eyes. As soft and beautiful as the last time he'd seen her so many years ago. She smiled wide, although from the redness around her eyes he guessed she'd been crying recently, no doubt over the loss of her daughter. Still, as she moved toward him, she was easy and natural. Seeing her felt like a cool breeze against his skin on the hottest of summer days. A lump the size of a stone grew into his throat, and his heart pumped four times its normal speed.

I can't do this. I can't do this.

"Can it be? Elijah Miller?" Her alto voice sounded smooth and rich. "After all these years?"

"It is." He struggled to speak. Seeing her again seemed to have sucked the air from his lungs and brought back so many memories his head was full. "How are you, Hannah?"

She tilted her head to the side, grinning wider. "How long have you been home? I have not heard a word about your visit. How is that so?"

"I just arrived, actually." He forced out each word carefully. Painfully. He shifted his weight and pressed his lips together. Her friendliness surprised him a little but not as much as his own reaction. Where was all the pain and anger he should be feeling?

"And you have not been first to see your *Mamm?* How is that?"

A buzzing sound zipped through the air between them. Eli turned his head to the woods. *Was that gunfire?*

Suddenly all of his wavering uncertainty vanished. Years of training and experience had hardwired his response to that sound—even when it came at the most unlikely of moments. Without a second thought, he dove forward, covering Hannah with his body and forcing her to the ground. Eleven years working the city streets had taught him to react first and think later. A skill that had saved his life on more than one occasion.

A second buzzing flew over them. A nanosecond later, the front window of the house shattered.

Oh yeah. That was gunfire.

Chapter Two

"What's going on?" Hannah tried to sit up and take stock of the situation. Elijah pushed her back to the ground.

"Stay down. Someone's shooting at us." He rolled onto his back and pulled his Glock from its shoulder holster, aiming it toward the woods.

Hannah stared wide-eyed at his gun. She scooted back a few feet, then started to stand.

"What are you doing?" He jumped up after her, shielding her body again but continuing to face the woods with his firearm cocked and ready. "You're making yourself a target. Those are real bullets, Hannah."

"*Jah,* all the more reason to move inside, no?" She hurried toward the porch.

Okay. Maybe she had a point.

Eli covered her as they made their way to the front door. He kept his eyes on the edge of the nearby forest. "Is anyone else home?"

She shook her head.

"I'll go first." He slipped in front of her and into the house, gun raised. Glass from the broken window had sprayed out across the hardwood floor. Otherwise, the large open space looked untouched. He pulled her in behind him and placed her in a corner away from the open door and window.

"Stay here while I check upstairs and in the *Dawdi Haus.*"

Hannah nodded. Eli ran up the stairs. He checked the bedrooms and single bath of the main cottage. He opened the connecting door leading to the *Dawdi* or grandparent addition and hurried through the small, attached living space. The entire place was empty.

"Clear." He descended to the living room. Hannah was still crouched in the corner. He put away his gun and knelt in front of her. "I'm going to search the woods. Don't move until I get back."

"You're going back out there?" Her eyes widened.

He placed his hands on her shoulders, trying to catch one of her nervous glances, but her eyes would not rest. She shook all over. And he didn't blame her. Someone had just blown out her front window. He hated to leave her, but he had to check the woods. "I'll be right back. And I'll keep an eye on the house the whole time."

She nodded, her body still trembling and her eyes avoiding his. But he could see the tears in them. As her head sank lower, Elijah's heart dropped. He hated the fear she was feeling on top of the pain she'd already been through. This wasn't the time for condolences, but the words burst out anyway.

"I'm sorry about your daughter. I'm sorry about Jessica."

He quietly slid through the front door and took off across the front lawn, finding cover behind an unfinished wooden shed, his car, then an old stone well. His mind spun hard and fast with muddled questions and strange emotions…and Hannah. And he didn't like any of it one bit.

At the forest edge, Eli did his best to estimate the position of the shooter and he scanned for any evidence—a footprint, a thread of material, bullet casings. Anything besides a plethora of flora and fauna. But there was nothing, not even a squirrel skittering about. So when a twig snapped behind him, he immediately turned and raised his gun.

He lowered it just as quickly. A small child stood there—an Amish child, dressed in a blue shirt, black trousers with suspenders and a straw hat.

"Sorry." Eli clicked on the safety of his gun and slid the piece back into its holster. "Don't be afraid. I thought you were someone else."

The boy frowned and pointed through the woods. "He went that way."

"Who went that way?"

"You look for man with, uh, *der Pistole?*" The boy looked at the Glock.

"You saw the man with the gun?"

The boy nodded and pulled his hand from behind his back to reveal a large black hat, the kind the Amish men wore.

"The man was Amish?" Eli's voice cracked with surprise.

The boy shook his head. "*Nein.* English he was."

"But he wore this hat?"

"*Jah.* He wear hat but also he have a…*Oberlippen-bart.*" The boy pointed to his upper lip.

"A mustache?" Eli was thankful the kid was observant. No Amish man grew a mustache—only the beard. So, the kid was right. The shooter could not have been Amish. Not that it was likely a shooter was Amish any-

way, as the People did not support the use of weapons—
and hence the main reason his own father could not
accept his choice of professions. "Did you see where
he went?"

"In black car. Big black car." The boy's eyes were
wide with admiration.

A black car? Like the one that nearly caused the
wreck earlier? "And the car?"

"It goes."

Of course, the car was long gone, but at least he'd
been searching in the right place. Whoever he was, he
had taken his shell casings with him, meaning he was
probably not an amateur. Although if he was a pro, and
had been aiming at Eli or Hannah, then why had he
missed? They'd been standing out in the open, without
a thought of danger, until the first shot had been fired.
Could his poor aim have been deliberate? Like warning shots? Eli looked back at the boy. "Okay, son. Let's
get you home. Where do live?"

"Miller's Grove."

Elijah nodded. Miller's Grove was the home of his
uncle. "What's your name, son?"

"Nicholas." He grinned. "Nicholas Miller."

"Well, you get on home, Nicholas Miller." Eli smiled
at the child. "Can I have that hat?"

The boy lifted the hat to him. "Are you a policeman?"

"I am," Eli said, then watched the child, his very
own cousin, scramble down the same path he'd taken
so many times, so many years ago. At the other edge of
the woods, an older girl with golden braids walked the
path in her bare feet. No doubt it was Nicholas's sister
come to fetch her brother home.

Elijah sighed and headed back to Nolt Cottage.

Great. That cute cousin would head home now and tell all his siblings about the cop in the woods…and then everyone would know he was back in Willow Trace.

But would he be staying long enough to make a difference to his family? He wasn't sure yet. From those surprising first few minutes, it looked as though he was needed in Willow Trace—at least judging by the flying bullets. But even that didn't make him want to stay. Seeing Hannah had been strange enough. He couldn't imagine a confrontation with his own father. No. The sooner he was out of there, the better.

Hannah wrapped her arms around her legs, hugging her knees to her chest, as if she could squeeze away her own fears. But when her eyes fixed on the shards of broken glass spread across the floor, she continued to tremble.

Today had been the first time she'd dared be alone since that morning in the barn, since Jessica's "accident"—as Thomas, her brother-in-law, referred to the girl's death. But Hannah didn't believe Jessica's death was an accident. Dead bodies don't get placed in barns by accident. People probably don't shoot at you and your house accidentally, either. Losing Jessica had been devastating enough on its own—she had never once imagined that whatever had gotten Jessica killed could put herself or any others in danger, too.

Perhaps Thomas and she should not have kept silent about the events surrounding Jessica's death. About the blood and how she'd been away all night. About her many secrets. About the black car at the barn and the intruder who pushed Hannah down and locked her inside. If only she could relive that last week. As her mother, she could have prevented this. She should have prevented this.

In her mind she replayed the moments when she could have stopped Jessica and asked her what she was about. Each time she'd failed. What she would give to have just one more day with her precious daughter. Hannah dropped her head in a fit of sobs. What she would give not to have found her in the stable that morning. It seemed the more she tried to push away the memory of that morning, the more she relived it in her mind...

"Oh, Jessica, I'm so sorry. I'm so very sorry. If only I had been a better mother to you." Hannah had turned the girl's hands over in her own as she knelt beside her in the stall. The girl was so disheveled, bloodied, dirty. "This is all my fault. I should have known what you were about. Rumspringa or not, I should have taken better care of you. I can never forgive myself."

Hannah had brushed the dirt and loose hairs from the girl's face.

"What's the trouble?" A deep voice had sounded at the front of the barn.

It was Thomas. He must have wondered why she wasn't in the house making breakfast. She moved to the side so that he could see his niece in the sheep's bed of straw.

He froze, the color draining from his face. He rushed forward. "Is that—is that Jessica?"

Hannah met his dark eyes. "I—I found her here. She's dead, Thomas. Jessica is dead. I have failed her and Peter and God...and you."

"This is not your doing," he said. "You must not blame yourself. You were a gut *mother to her, Hannah. As* gut *as her own mother could have been. As good as if you had given birth to her yourself."*

His words were meant to comfort, but Hannah fell limp at the reminder of her infertility and the end of what was to be her only chance at motherhood. She just sat crying silently as Thomas placed Jessica's hands together on her belly and patted them.

"Our God is sovereign, Hannah. He alone is ruler and judge. We must accept what has happened. Be strong." He touched his hand to hers. "I will call the elders."

"No. Please. I don't want anyone to see her this way."

He had seen she could not be calmed. "Stay with Jessica until I return. I will bring her clothes. I don't want Nana to see her this way, either. I will also have to call the police, Chief McClendon. He is sensitive to our ways."

"Yes. Call the police. They will find who did this to my precious Jessica. I will tell them about the car I saw, and—"

Thomas put a finger to her mouth to stop her speech. "You will tell them nothing, Hannah. You know it is not our way to search for answers. It is in God's hands. Promise me you will say nothing."

She promised. He was right, of course—investigating was not what the Amish did. But she couldn't help wishing, as impossible as it seemed, that someone would come and help her find the truth.

Footsteps sounded on the front porch and she stiffened, turning her face toward the door. Elijah's solid frame blocked the sun from the room, and his dark shadow covered her. Both startled and relieved, Hannah placed a hand over her mouth and released a tight breath.

"I'm sorry. That took longer than I expected. I didn't

mean to startle you. Are you okay?" He entered the house slowly.

"I am okay." She nodded. "Did you see anyone?"

"Yes. But not the shooter. I saw a child. And according to him, the man with the *Pistole* drove away in a big black car."

A black car? Like the one at the barn when she'd found Jessica? She swallowed hard. "A child?"

He nodded. "Nicholas Miller. My own cousin, I believe."

"He is. Son of your cousin John. He comes to see the young horses from time to time. Loves them, he does. He wasn't hurt, was he?"

"No. He's fine. Went home down the path. I watched him through the forest." He walked closer. His eyes narrowed on her. "Do you know something about a black car?"

"How would I know about a black car?" She tried to keep her voice steady, but Eli's penetrating eyes kept her on edge. "I pay no attention to such things."

Closing in the space remaining between them, he offered a hand to help her up. "You sure you're okay, Hannah?"

"*Ach.* It's not every day people run around Willow Trace with guns and bullets." She stood without his help, took a step back and tried to face him. But the intensity in his eyes made her more nervous than she already felt.

He walked back to the front door and checked that it was secure. She hoped that he had put away his gun. He must remember that guns were *verboten*. Although there was something—a dark object—in his hands. As he moved back to the kitchen, she saw that it was a black broad-rimmed hat like the one Amish men wore when they weren't working in the sun. She wanted to ask him where he'd gotten it, but there was a more pressing question at hand. "Do you intend to stay awhile?"

Eli frowned taking a look down at the hat, which he then tossed onto the tabletop. "No, I don't—just long enough to figure out what's going on. According to my little cousin, this hat belongs to our shooter."

"Sure." She lifted a brow and glared at him. "An Amish man with a gun. Shooting at my house. Maybe you've forgotten but we don't have or use guns."

He gave her a dissatisfied look. "Any joker off the street can buy one of these hats in a tourist shop or online."

Right. Hannah dropped her head.

"So, let's get started, shall we? Who is shooting at you and why?"

Eli didn't sound angry, but in his eyes, she could see how uncomfortable he was to be there, talking to her again. She told herself that that was why he was being so abrupt, so different from the boy she remembered. She also told herself—and tried to believe—that his detached tone didn't hurt.

"I have no idea." And that was the truth. "In fact, maybe that someone was shooting at you? Your life involves guns much more often than mine, does it not? Or maybe it was a hunter with a bad aim?"

He tilted his head to the other side. "Except that it's not hunting season. You said yourself no one around here owns a gun. And for the other possibility, well… if someone wanted to shoot at me they would have better opportunities than driving out to Lancaster County and aiming through the woods."

She let out a nervous laugh. "Then it must be a mistake. Who would shoot at me?"

"A mistake?" His face was grim as he pulled his pistol from under his jacket, did something with it that made some clicking sounds, then returned it to his side. He looked up at her again and clenched his jaw. "Two shots within inches of each other, that's no mistake."

Hannah turned away and continued to stall the conversation. "Your weapon should be outside."

"Someone just shot at you. The gun stays here with me where I can use it."

"Then maybe *you* should go." She lifted her head high as if to challenge him.

"Gladly, just as soon as you tell me what's going on around here."

"I do not know what you mean."

"I'm talking about your stepdaughter's death and someone shooting at you." He folded his hands over his chest. "I'm here to investigate what happened to Jessica."

His words sent a quiver over her lips, but she fought through it. She would not cry in front of Elijah Miller. "Again, you—you must be mistaken. There was not to be an investigation. There was…nothing to investigate."

Elijah tossed a photo on the table next to the black hat. "Her neck was cut. She's bruised all over. Four days later someone is shooting at you and you say there is nothing to investigate?"

"How did you get that?" She glanced at the photo, immediately recognizing the wound to her dear girl's neck. Grabbing at her stomach, she turned away. She must be strong. There was no need to involve Elijah in this.

"Chief McClendon of the Lancaster police." Eli removed the photo from the table and put it away in his jacket pocket. "He asked me to come here and see what I could find out."

"And what do you find so far?"

"I think there is something to investigate. I think you should talk to me. This is no game, Hannah. You need to protect yourself. Someone is threatening you and your family. You cannot sit and be silent."

"I know you want to help. And it's very kind of you." She forced a smile. "But it's not our way. We will accept what has happened."

"It's *not* very kind of me. I don't want to be here one bit. But it's my job and I take that pretty seriously. Now please stop avoiding my questions and tell me how and when all this started."

She glanced at him and saw the frustration but also sorrow in his eyes. Like so many years ago when she told him she'd decided to marry Peter. Then, too, she had not told him the entire truth. Here she was again, keeping secrets. But she had promised and she must keep her word.

She fetched a broom and dustpan from the cupboard, and with short, quick strokes, she began to sweep the broken glass that covered the floor. "Even if there was more to the story, it does not change the fact that Jessica is gone. So what is there to investigate?"

"Perhaps something about this black car that you know about but don't know about?"

She continued to sweep, not looking his way. He watched her for a few moments, then moved next to her and gently took the broom and dustpan from her hand.

She still refused to look up as she said, "We are all fine. Really."

"Really? Someone just shot at your house. That doesn't seem so 'fine' to me. I haven't forgotten the way things work around here. I understand that you want to let go and accept what has happened. I'm not trying to stop that—in fact, you may be able to let go more easily if you know what happened. Don't you even care about who killed your stepdaughter?"

"Of course I care. I miss her every minute. She was everything to me." Hannah began to tremble again, but she would not give in to her emotions. She would not show such weakness of faith. "But knowledge does not bring peace and understanding. That comes only from God."

The back of his hand caressed her cheek. The warmth was comforting, and for a strange, fleeting second, she longed to fall into his arms and weep. Instead she turned away.

He stepped back. "I wish this wasn't why I was here. I'm so sorry. I know you raised Jessica as your own child. I can't imagine what you are feeling and after what happened to Peter..."

She looked up and he must have been able to read the surprise in her face.

"Abigail told me. As a midwife, she has a cell phone in order for her patients to contact her when they go into labor. We talk occasionally. She told me about Peter." He pressed his lips together. "He was a good man, Hannah. If he hadn't been, I... Well, that was a long time ago. I didn't come here to rake up the past. You must want to know what happened Jessica. So please, come sit with me. Talk to me. Tell me about her. She must have been a wonderful good girl with you as her *Mamm*."

With all of the charisma and ease he'd possessed as a young man, Eli put the broom and dustpan aside and led her back to the kitchen table. But she did not take a seat.

"Perhaps we should go to the porch?" she suggested.

"I don't think the porch is a good place for you today." He pulled out a chair for her. After she sat, he removed his coat and hung it over the back of one of the other kitchen chairs and sat opposite her. His gun was still in the holster at his side.

"Have you forgotten everything, Elijah Miller? We don't have guns in our houses."

"Actually, it's you who has forgotten that someone shot at you only fifteen minutes ago." He smiled and patted the gun under his arm. "It's staying right where it is."

"Nana Ruth will be horror-struck."

"Nana Ruth will never know." Eli's ridiculous expression nearly caused her to giggle. She lifted a hand to her mouth to cover her slight smile.

"Please, don't cover up such a beautiful face," he said. "It is the one perk of the assignment."

Perk? She could feel the warmth grow in her cheeks. "You speak with strange words, Elijah Miller."

"I've been gone a long time."

His lips curved with the hint of a smile. How handsome his face was to behold. She remembered how the sight of him had always stolen a little of her breath. She feared she would reveal too much if she said a single word. It was best to do as she had promised—to keep silent. This would all pass, even if there was a part of her that wanted to know the truth.

"You won't talk to me, then?" He rose from the table.

"I cannot."

"No. You choose not to talk. It isn't the same, Hannah." He lifted a small black mobile phone from his pocket. "I'm going to call the Lancaster police and report the shooting. They'll have to come out and file a report."

"No. Please. You're the police. Isn't that enough?"

"You can't have it both ways. Either you talk to me and tell me the truth or I call Chief McClendon." He held his little phone in the air, waiting for her decision.

Hannah dropped her head between her hands. She did not want to see Chief McClendon again. But to speak the truth to Elijah…that might be worse.

Chapter Three

Eli walked onto the porch, frustrated and defeated—not so different than he had all those years ago when Hannah had refused him without so much as an explanation. Being back in Willow Trace was harder than he'd anticipated. He hadn't counted on all those old emotions resurfacing the second he laid eyes on her. Yet he knew he needed to be there no matter what he'd said to Hannah or how badly he'd like to go back to the city.

Hannah needed protection. Maybe the Amish had survived centuries with very little police or other government interference, but the governor had called him there. Clearly this situation was even more dangerous than Eli had suspected. Anyway, Elijah didn't believe in coincidence. He'd prayed for confirmation that his presence was needed there, and God had answered that in a big way. Jessica's death was no accident—even if Hannah wouldn't talk, he could tell that she didn't believe that. Nor was the shooting at her house a mere coincidence.

The sad truth, though, was that if he couldn't convince Hannah to talk to him, then there was no chance anyone else would. She had the most to gain by learning the truth, and there she was ordering him away—Hannah whom at one time he'd been so close to and shared all his dreams with. She saw him as an outsider now. It shouldn't upset him. He shouldn't take it so personally. He was just there to do a job. Right?

He watched through the window as back inside the house, Hannah went back to her broom and dustpan, cleaning the broken window up from the floors. What was she hiding? He had a wild impulse to hold her gently until she cried and told him all her secrets, to make her see that he was still the same person he'd always been.

Focus on the case, Miller. Do your job and get out of Willow Trace. Hannah had never been for him. How could he even think such a thing after the way she'd broken his heart and never looked back? His grip on the phone tightened. He turned his back to Hannah and dialed the private number given to him by Captain O'Dell.

"McClendon."

"Hello, sir. This is Detective Miller in Willow Trace, as per your request. Within five minutes of my arrival, there was a shooting incident—someone firing from the woods toward the Nolts' home. No one is injured, but I thought—"

"I'll be right out." The line disconnected.

Not much of a conversation. Eli put the phone away in his pocket. Then again the whole situation was strange—so much secrecy? No media coverage? The governor involved? He hoped to have a nice chat with McClendon when he got there.

Maybe there was a political connection. But to the Amish? That was a stretch. Who could find a group of people more unconnected to the political world? They didn't even vote. A young widow and her teenaged daughter were not likely to be involved in anything that would snag the governor's attention.

Soft footfalls behind him made him turn. Hannah had joined him on the porch with a tall glass of lemonade. "Drink."

"Denki." He took the glass. They both smiled at his use of Pennsylvania Dutch language. He laughed. "I haven't said that in years and already twice today."

Her cheeks became a lovely color of pink. Her green eyes shone brighter. For a second, Eli felt like a sixteen-year-old boy again—that very same boy who would have leapt ten feet into the air after feeling the tingle of Hannah's fingers brush against his own as she passed him a glass of lemonade.

Tender emotions rushed through him. How he'd loved her all those years ago. Every woman since, he'd compared to her beauty and her kindness and her soul. None had been able to match up.

Get a grip, Miller.

He stepped back, trying to smile nonchalantly. Good grief. He was there to investigate, not to rekindle an old flame, especially an old flame with the woman who had dumped him. Once in a lifetime was enough for that.

Eli drank down the crisp, sweet mixture and returned the empty glass to her. *Keep your mind on the investigation.* "McClendon is on his way."

She frowned, clearly displeased with him, and his heart sank all over again. "You have changed, Elijah Miller. I thought you would understand and remember our ways. I thought you would respect them."

"I do respect *our* ways." He paused, a bit surprised at his choice of words. "But when the outside world comes to you, you have to respect it, too. You don't have to be in it, but you have to let someone help you protect yourself from this danger. Hannah, remember when I was six and my *Dat* took me into the city for the first time? I was abducted the second I stepped off the train."

"*Jah.* I remember that story. God brought you home safe to us again."

"Yes, but with the help of a police officer. Let's face it. If that cop hadn't fired his gun and shot the man holding me, then I would have been the one who'd died that day. Not the criminal. Someone wants to hurt you, Hannah, you and your family. They've already succeeded once. Please, let me help keep you safe," he pleaded. "Tell me what you know instead of cleverly avoiding every one of my questions."

She shot him a furtive glance as if she considered his words. Then she moved away from him. "It is not our way. As you must already know, it was decided that Jessica had a terrible accident."

"A terrible accident?" He shook his head in disbelief. "If one of those bullets had hit us earlier today, would that have been an accident, too?"

Hannah kept her eyes low, avoiding his face. "I don't know why anyone would be shooting at the house. But, in any case, the Nolts do not want the police involved. Thomas said so himself. You know how it is."

"I remember, Hannah." He remembered more than he liked. "And sometimes that is best—to move on. But if you are now in danger, then it's time to be proactive. You don't want to give the shooter a second chance."

She backed away.

"Don't you even want to know what happened to your daughter?" He reached for the crook of her arm. "Forget the *Ordnung* talk for one second and be straight with me."

She yanked her arm away.

Good. He was getting to her, even if he was pushing her in an uncomfortable way. She had to see that she needed to both accept God's will here and protect herself. And for that, he would push as hard as needed.

"You do, don't you?" he continued. "You do want to know what happened. The report said that you found her. Hannah, is that true? You found her in the barn at milking time? I saw the pictures. Tell me what happened that morning."

Hannah kept her eyes to the floor. Her jaw clenched.

"I can see you want to tell me something. Why don't you just say it?"

"I can't. I'm sorry, Eli. You should go home and leave us be."

A different question—what if he tried a different question? "Not until you talk to me. Where was Jessica before she died? Had she gone into the city? You know something, Hannah. I can see it in your face."

"You're wasting your time, Elijah. Jessica is gone and there's nothing to be done about it. Go back and tell your people that we do things differently here."

"I can't. McClendon is on his way. The governor asked me to be here. Please, Hannah." He stepped closer and spoke at a whisper. "Tell me what happened."

She looked up at him, tears glistening in her eyes. "I don't need to know what happened to Jessica. Without her, I don't even know if I care that I live. I have nothing left."

He swallowed hard. His heart ached for Hannah. More than ever he wanted to pull her the rest of the way into his arms and hold her tight. He wanted to let her release all of her pain and confusion. He wanted to remove her sweet prayer *Kapp,* run his hands through her locks of raven curls and remind her of how beautiful and precious she was. He wanted to press his lips to hers and kiss away her sorrow. But he knew she didn't want him to. Maybe she never did.

Elijah's firm grip on her arms gave Hannah a feeling of support she hadn't experienced in many years. His breath brushed warm and soft against her face. She should not let him hold her so close, but there was no strength in her to push him away. Her brain was befuddled as his questions swirled in her head while his touch both comforted and frightened her. She wanted to tell him everything—about Jessica, about Peter, about how she could never have children. But fear kept her mouth tight.

"*Hannah, gehts-du innen*—get into the *Haus*." Thomas's deep voice boomed across the porch.

Hannah and Elijah broke from their near embrace. She turned to face her brother-in-law where he stood at the edge of the porch carrying a large satchel of horse feed that made his muscles bulge. He looked as angry as she had ever seen him. "Thomas, brother, you remember your friend, Elijah Miller."

"I do." He gave a curt nod.

"He has come to pay his respects," Hannah explained.

"Actually, I'm here to investigate your niece's death," Elijah said. "I was trying to get Hannah to talk about the day you found Jessica. From the pictures of your niece postmortem, it looks very possible that she was murdered. Some of the police feel the matter should be looked into. Perhaps you can fill me in on things? Hannah doesn't feel she should talk to me."

"Looked to me like you were investigating something else." Thomas eyed Hannah. "I am certain Hannah explained our wishes in both matters."

"*Both* matters?" Elijah's confusion was apparent.

Hannah shrank back toward the door of the cottage. She wanted to run into the house, but she knew that that would only make matters worse. How could Thomas bring up such a topic only a few days after Jessica's death? It was not unusual for a widow to marry the unwed brother of her deceased. But nothing had been decided, and they had not talked about such a union in months.

"Oh…oh…you—you are betrothed? No. Hannah didn't mention that." Elijah glanced back and forth between the two of them, then moved toward Thomas. "But no need to upset yourself, old friend. I'm here on business. Just after I arrived, shots were fired at the house. I think for your safety you should tell me what you know that could be relevant."

Thomas's look of anger softened quickly into concern as he turned to Hannah. "Is this true? Someone shot at you?"

She glared at Elijah, her mind full of his touch. How unaffected he seemed by the moment and the news that she was betrothed—even if it was false. She looked back to Thomas and tried to ignore the disappointment that weighed on her. "It is true, brother. You can see for yourself the broken window."

Thomas dropped his large pack and hopped up the steps. "But you are fine, no?"

"*Jah,* I am fine." She gathered her wits as best she could. "Mr. Miller has been kind enough to call your friend Chief McClendon. I believe he is expected soon, ain't so? I will finish cleaning the glass and make coffee."

Hannah scrambled inside the house, leaving the two men to puff their feathers for each other. She was mad at them both. She had never promised to marry Thomas, although he had asked her once and she had requested time to think on it. And Elijah should not have taken hold of her in such a bold way, grabbing on to all her senses the way he did.

That impulse she felt in that moment when she'd wanted to tell him everything…that was clearly just Elijah's bad influence at work. Thomas had made the decision that they would not seek answers as to what had happened to Jessica, and it was her duty to follow his wishes. Elijah had no business asking her to open her heart and share her thoughts and fears with him. He had shown their community that he could not be relied upon when he left them all behind, abandoning his family and breaking his father's heart.

At least now Thomas was home and he could tell Elijah to leave. He did not belong there. He was no longer one of them.

Chapter Four

Evening came fresh and cool. After a large helping of Hannah's hearty shepherd's pie, Eli followed Chief McClendon and Thomas Nolt onto the front porch.

He stopped at the edge of the stoop and looked into the clear night sky. He had forgotten how many stars one could see on a clear night in the country sky. He'd forgotten the rushing sounds of the wind, and of the leaves, and of the livestock milling about. Even the smells, he'd forgotten—that earthy blend of grasses and compost and animal and home cooking and unfinished wood.

It's true, Lord. Here, it is easier to see You, to hear You, to be with You. He breathed in deeply all the familiar odors and smiled up at the night sky. If only he could record all the sensations for when he returned home to the city.

The other men's voices pulled him back to the moment. Chief McClendon turned to Thomas. "I thank your family for such kindness to me this evening."

"*Gut* to see you, Chief. Not so *gut,* your reason for coming." Thomas gave Eli a frosty glare. Then the two men shook hands like old pals, while Eli stood there, feeling about as welcomed as the Plague.

He had not expected a warm welcome from his old school friend and neighbor, but he hadn't expected one quite this glacial, either. He supposed it was his fault seeing as the man had caught Hannah practically in his arms. Even though Thomas and Hannah were not engaged, as Thomas had insinuated, Thomas's intentions seemed clear. At the very least it was readily apparent that he felt completely responsible for Hannah and very protective toward her. Hannah's feelings on the matter were less obvious. She attended to Thomas as head of the household, but she didn't show him any particular regard—not that Elijah was taking notes or anything. He couldn't have cared less. He had no interest in Hannah. He'd just been trying to get her to talk to him, and if Thomas hadn't shown up when he did, she would have. He was sure of it.

Eli glanced through the broken window at her, washing up dishes in the kitchen. She turned as if aware of him, offered a smile, then quickly averted her eyes back to her work.

Right. He felt nothing for her. The spike in his pulse must have been agitated nerves from his unexpected return to Willow Trace. Eli sighed and tried to focus once again on the case. "So, Hannah found the girl as I saw her in the pictures that you, Chief McClendon, took and filed away without further inquiry?"

McClendon shook his head, some regret in his expression. "I've been working with the Plain folk long enough to know what is acceptable. I do try not to interfere, but this case is different. I don't feel comfortable simply walking away. Thomas, consider making allowances this time."

"We appreciate Chief McClendon's respect. That is why Mr. Miller need not stay in Willow Trace," Thomas said.

McClendon frowned at Thomas. "As I said, I don't usually interfere, but I think this case is different. Call it instinct. I should have some of it after working the job for twenty-five years. Thomas, I hope you'll accept my advice to have Detective Miller stay on at the farm for a day or two. Losing *one* of you has been hard enough. And with the incident that occurred today, I cannot turn a blind eye."

Thomas and Eli looked uncomfortably at each other.

Eli had about as much desire to stay at the Nolts' as Thomas had for him to be his guest. But from the way McClendon was behaving, it seemed as if the alternative was to have a patrol car on the farm, and neither McClendon nor Thomas would have any part of that. Eli tried to hide his skepticism. The Lancaster County Police Department was a large organization. It was hard to believe there wasn't one trustworthy individual among its ranks to work with the Amish. As far as Eli was concerned, McClendon, Hannah and Thomas were all hiding something, and he intended to find out what that was. How the governor fit into all of this he couldn't even imagine.

At dinner, he had not gleaned much new information. But one thing was certain—they all knew Jessica's death was no accident. There was an undercurrent of fear riding through the house.

Thomas frowned. "I made a mistake to leave Hannah alone at the house today. It will not happen again, I assure you both."

The chief nodded. "I know you'll make every effort to take care of your own. And normally, I wouldn't press my ways on you. But I'm asking you this one time to keep Mr. Miller close. He's got a phone and a radio and—"

"And a gun," Thomas finished his sentence.

"And a gun." The chief nodded and turned toward his car. "I'll check with you tomorrow, Detective." He stepped into his squad car and drove away.

Don't call us, we'll call you, Eli thought. *Thanks, Chief.* What was that? No explanation of the pictures. No mention of what had happened to the girl's clothing. No hint of a theory as to who had been behind the shooting earlier.

As the Lancaster chief drove away, the tension between Thomas and Elijah returned in full. They stood in silence on opposite ends of the porch.

"I didn't ask for this case," Eli said at length. "But now that it has been assigned to me, I intend to see it through."

"Meaning what exactly?" Thomas glared back at him.

"Meaning I'll be around for a few days asking questions about Jessica, about her friends and about her death."

"Questions to Hannah? Questions *about* Hannah?" Thomas folded his arms over his chest, making him seem even larger than he already was.

"I'll be asking questions of all of you." Eli shifted his weight. "It is what I do. Solve crimes. Find the bad guys. I don't want to be here any more than you want me here. So if you want to make my stay shorter, then tell me what happened to Jessica so I can do my job and get out of here."

"And what if there are not any bad guys, as you say?" Thomas said. "What if Jessica's death was an accident?"

"I find that a little hard to swallow after what happened this afternoon. I'm pretty sure you do, too. Look, I had planned to stay at the bed-and-breakfast. You're clearly uncomfortable with—"

"No." Thomas put his hand up stiffly. "It will not be said that I did not protect my family. Come. I will show you where you will stay tonight…in the horses' stable."

Hannah could not sleep. The sound of bullets zipped through her brain. The crash of glass breaking. The cold feel of Jessica's hands. The black car whizzing away from the barn.

And Elijah Miller. The warm touch of his hands on her elbow, that soft way he gazed at her—even after all these years. A softness she did not deserve. She'd broken his heart when she'd chosen Peter. Or so his sister, Abigail, had told her. And for what? To have a family with Peter and his daughter—a family she would lose before she turned thirty. Even though she was unable to birth children, she'd wanted so badly to be a mother. She couldn't have known how it would end. But not once had she regretted her choice in Peter. He had been a wonderful husband and *Dat* and friend.

She noticed, too, that Elijah seemed happy in his choice not to take vows. Still he had sat so comfortably at the dinner table among them—despite the awkwardness with Thomas. He'd put his weapon away and eaten a king's portion of her cooking. That was most pleasing to her. He had talked freely about his work. And what work he did! She couldn't imagine the frightening things he faced in the outside world. She could never…

Under streams of white moonlight, Hannah stared through her small window down the path to where Eli slept in the horses' stable. Thomas was a bear for making him sleep out in the cold. Although the way Mama Ruth snored, Eli might find it a kindness not to be in the house with them.

What truly wasn't right was that Elijah still had not been told anything about Jessica's death and the black car. He was not stupid. He knew they weren't telling him everything. And while she did believe that God wanted them to accept what had happened to Jessica, she also believed that there could be good in discovering the truth—if it kept her safe, if it saved another from Jessica's fate. As Elijah had pointed out to her earlier, there was good in the work of the police. It was not merely to pass judgment and serve vengeance. They were there to protect, as well.

That's why tomorrow she would talk to Thomas and convince him to tell Elijah the whole story of the black car, the change of clothes, the bloodstains and the intruder in the barn.

Elijah, who after all these years still made her heart race. He'd grown even more handsome since she'd seen him last—stronger, taller. When he'd arrived at the front of the house, her heart had nearly flipped inside her chest. He'd looked so fine and fancy in the tight-collared shirt and jeans. And those huge blue eyes of his had always muddled her thoughts. What fun they had had together so long ago. How quick he had always been to make her smile.

The groan of wood bending sounded from the stairwell. Hannah sat up quickly and held in her breath. Someone was on the stairs. Who could it be? They'd all gone to bed hours ago.

She listened, but Ruth's snores filled the air again and there was nothing else to be heard. Maybe it was Thomas? He usually slept in *Dawdi Haus,* but he wasn't much of a sleeper. He could be up checking on things. And, really, who could sleep with all that snoring?

Hannah sighed and pulled the covers over her shoulders. Thomas was a good man and very protective of those he loved. She knew that he cared for her, as she did for him. He was sweet to offer her marriage. But something had kept her from giving him an answer to his proposal. Today, after seeing Eli Miller, she couldn't help wondering if her hesitation had something to do with racing pulses and easy smiles.

Should that matter, Lord? Should the shivers and chills a man gives us with a glance make a difference to our hearts?

She didn't know. Truth be told she'd forgotten all about those kinds of feelings. Until today.

I must be the silliest woman on the earth to wonder such things, she scolded herself. *I know what matters, Lord. That I serve You in all I say and do.*

She doubted that included thoughts of Elijah Miller and his blue jeans. *Goodness.* What had gotten into her head? It wasn't as if she and Elijah could ever be together. He was an outsider. She'd be shunned by the People—never allowed to return, or have a meal with them, or pray, or even speak with them. She would never even consider such a thing...

Anyway, Elijah Miller wasn't interested in her. *Ach!* He'd shown nothing but disdain at being back in Willow Trace. Her thoughts must be the result of a tired mind.

It was late. She needed sleep. Without Jessica, she had twice as much work to do around the house. Hannah closed her eyes tight. But still sleep did not come. In between the rhythmic crescendos of Nana Ruth's loud expirations, Hannah heard the downstairs floorboards creak again. She sat up again and fumbled on the nightstand until she found her small candle and lit it. Should she go downstairs?

If Thomas wasn't sleeping, either, she would go down now and talk to him. She slipped from bed, pulled one of her dark frocks over her head and hooked it quickly up her back. After tucking her long braid into a bun, she grabbed a bonnet that lay on the chest at the end of her bed. It was Jessica's, but it fit well enough. Then she blew out her candle and slipped down the stairs in bare feet.

"Thomas?" she whispered into the dark room. At the foot of the stairs, she searched the corners of the large room. A few beams of moonlight lit the space, as well as the dying embers in the fireplace. It must have been later than she thought. A shiver trickled down her spine. The hole in the window had left the room quite chilly. Thomas would have to get a new piece of glass for that right away.

Speaking of Thomas, where was he? The downstairs seemed to be empty. "Thomas? Are you there?"

Hannah shuffled to a chair in front of the fire where a nice warm quilt lay. She unfolded the heavy blanket and draped it over her shoulders.

Click.

Her head turned fast to the front door. It popped open and swung wide, letting in another blast of cool air.

"Thomas?" she called loudly this time. Still no answer. Had the door opened on its own? No. Thomas had locked it.

Hannah's pulse spiked as she had that feeling again—that feeling she'd had in the barn the other morning. The feeling she was not alone. Coming downstairs had been a bad idea.

She peered out onto the dark porch. "Thomas? Are you there?"

Another floorboard creaked; her heart plummeted. Thomas was not outside. But someone was there, in the kitchen. She had to get back upstairs and wake Nana Ruth. Forgetting the opened door, Hannah raced back over the hardwood floors to the bottom of the steps.

She looked up, ready to ascend, when she realized her mistake. The intruder was not in the kitchen. He was on the stairs.

A man dressed in all black came at her from the stairwell, face hidden in the shadows. He pushed her down to the floor, almost as if he had tripped. Her hands became pinned beneath her chest. Her head landed with a *thunk* onto the hardwood.

"Don't make a sound," he said. "I won't hurt you. I just… I need the journal. You have it. I know you do."

He came down on her, pressing a knee in her back so that she could not get free. "So, where is it?"

Where was what? What was he talking about? She knew nothing about a journal. "I have no journal," she pleaded. "I know not of what you speak."

He pushed her harder into the floor. "But you *have* to. You *have* to have Jessica's journal. She said you knew about it, about where it was. I need it. You need it. Where is it?"

Jessica's journal? What was he talking about? How could Jessica have a journal? Hannah and Nana Ruth had already been through the girl's things. There was nothing like a journal. She knew not what to say to this man. But she wondered if this journal he spoke of was the reason for Jessica's death.

Help me, Lord. What do I do?

Chapter Five

The trainer's quarters in the horse stable proved more accommodating than Eli had expected. But its location was lousy for keeping an eye on the main house. At midnight, instead of sleeping with the Nolts' prize-winning horses, Eli sat in his car with the motor running, watching the house and having a conversation with his partner, Mitchell Tucci.

"What do you mean you're working with another partner?" he asked his partner of five years.

"O'Dell assigned me to work with Sid Kaufman. Said you would be too busy to get back in time to wrap up the Mason-Hendricks case."

"But I shouldn't be here long at all. A couple of days tops. And we've been working on that case for months." Eli tried to control the sudden mixture of anger and fear that overwhelmed him—the feeling that he would never escape Willow Trace or have a job to return to when he did.

"So, what's the assignment?" Tucci asked. "O'Dell made it sound top secret, like FBI stuff."

"Top secret? In my hometown? Tucci, this is Willow

Trace. The only thing top secret around here is Emily Matheson's recipe for apple pie."

"I thought you said bullets were flying as soon as you got there," Tucci reminded him. "Maybe it's more complicated than you think."

Eli slumped in the driver's seat. His partner was right even if he didn't want to admit it out loud.

"You think they were shooting at you and not at the old love of your life?" Tucci asked.

"Yeah, I thought about that angle. But it doesn't really add up. Only O'Dell knew I was here at that point. And consider that the shooter missed purposely and cleaned up his casings. If a professional were after me, he wouldn't have missed. Any of my enemies would just want me dead."

"Maybe a warning for you to get off the case?"

"But from whom? O'Dell? He just sent me here."

"Hey, man, I'm just looking at possibilities. Trying to help out. I thought you said the local chief suspects some strong anti-Amish sentiment in his ranks."

"Chief McClendon, yeah. He's hard to read. On the one hand, he seemed to really care about the safety of this family."

"And on the other hand?"

"And on the other hand, he's leaving everything up to me…and he doesn't even know me. I don't get it. In some ways, I feel like I'm being set up to fail and this is the one place on Earth where I absolutely cannot fail. That would just show my people that I was wrong to leave. I can't let that happen."

"What does it matter to you what they think if you know you did the right thing for you? You never worried about that before, did you?"

"Yeah. I guess. I don't know." Eli pushed the troubling thoughts away.

"Well, let me know if there's anything I can do to help out. Don't be a stranger."

Help. That was exactly what he needed. "Really? You wanna help me out?" Eli asked.

"Of course, I've always wanted to come out there and see where you're from."

"Oh." Eli paused. His loudmouthed Italian city slicker partner in Willow Trace was not exactly what he'd had in mind. "Actually, I wanted you to run some names and take some photos to the coroner."

Tucci laughed. "I can do that, too. Shoot me the names and pics."

"Names…well, anything on Jessica Nolt, Hannah Nolt, Thomas Nolt, Chief McClendon and Governor Derry. I'll email the photos."

The line went silent.

"Tucci? You copy?"

"I copy. The governor? You want me to run a check on Governor Derry? Where did that come from? And how? You know I don't have clearance for that."

"O'Dell said Derry asked for me on this case. But Governor Derry doesn't know me, so I want to know how he came about this idea. I think he must have some ties to the Willow Trace community, know what I mean? Anyway, maybe it would help if I knew what that connection was. I was thinking you could call that friend of yours at the bureau. He owes us a favor, right?"

"That he does." Tucci chuckled.

"And don't check everything. Just connections to Willow Trace or the Lancaster police. Maybe you won't get anything, but it's worth a try. Got to start somewhere."

"I hear you. Wow. The governor asked for you? This is making the Mason-Hendricks case look pretty lame. You sure you don't need me to come out there? Shake things up a little?"

"Maybe later," Eli said. "I'll send the pics through my phone as soon as we hang up."

"I'm off to run the names," Tucci said, and ended the call.

Eli clicked off. He missed his friend and he found it disturbing that O'Dell had replaced him on the Mason-Hendricks case. But he could hardly worry about that now.

From his lap, he lifted the small file folder created by the Lancaster police concerning Jessica Nolt's death. He hadn't had a chance to review it since leaving his office.

Eli flipped through the folder reading the pages with a penlight. There wasn't much there. Only pictures and the information on the family. With his cell phone, he took photos of each image and then emailed them to his partner with a message. Run these by Michelle at the coroner's office. Tell me what she sees.

If Tucci could get anything from Michelle, it would be helpful, as he did not even know the probable cause or time of death. Never before had he worked a case with so little to go on.

Tomorrow, he needed to talk to Jessica's friends. He'd get a list of them from Hannah. Perhaps she could also show him how and where she found the body. Although with Thomas hanging around, he feared it would be difficult to get her to open up.

Eli tossed the file folder into the passenger seat and leaned back, struggling to get comfortable in his small car. His phone battery was still low. Might as well keep the engine running and let it charge for a few. Wasn't as if there were a lot of electrical outlets where he could plug in for the night. He needed to shut his eyes for a few minutes. It had been a long day and tomorrow would probably be longer. The more time he spent in Willow Trace, the bigger chance of his having to confront his own family. It was certain by now, with the help of Nicholas, they knew of his return.

He squirmed, still trying to get comfortable, his eyes focusing on the upstairs window of the cottage, where a dim light appeared behind the green curtain. It was the window he guessed to belong to Hannah's bedroom, as per his estimation from running through the house earlier that afternoon. The Amish had no fancy closets but hung their clothing on pegs. He was pretty certain he'd distinguished between Hannah's frocks and those of the slightly larger Nana Ruth. But why a light in Hannah's room at this hour? It was late. What could she be doing awake? She must be exhausted. But perhaps she was troubled after the scare she'd had that afternoon. That could not have been easy. Poor Hannah. She had lost so much. Although part of him was angry with her, as it was clear she knew more than she was telling him, he couldn't help empathizing with her pain. He glanced again at the photos of her daughter. How horrible it must have been to find her.

Faint shadows fluttered behind the dark green shade of Hannah's room. Maybe she and Thomas were talking. His body tensed at that thought. Or was that his gut telling him that something was wrong up at the house? As if he would know. Seemed his instincts had gone on holiday the minute he saw Hannah. His head was a mess. He should probably be doing more than sitting in his car.

Eli killed the engine and rolled down the window.

It was a stretch to think he could hear anything at that distance, but certainly he could hear more with the window down than up. Having one person in the house killed and another shot at, there was no such thing as being too careful.

His cell phone vibrated in the seat beside him. He checked the screen. Tucci.

"That was fast," Eli answered the call. "Did you get my pictures?"

"I did. I'll send those to Michelle in the morning," Tucci said. "Got something else, too."

"What's that?" Eli tried to focus on the conversation with Tucci, but the flickering light inside Hannah's room was extinguished. He sat up straight, his senses on full alert.

"My friend Jim at the FBI was up late and ran your names."

"And he found something that fast?"

"Yep, it may be nothing but I thought I'd pass it on."

"Please."

"So, apparently there was one prize-winning cross-draft pony stallion sold about six months ago by a T. Nolt to our very own Governor Derry for the sum of eighty-six thousand dollars." Tucci emphasized the price of the sale.

"Whoa. A pony for that kind of money? And to Governor Derry?"

"Paid in cash, too. I thought you might—"

"Shh." Eli shushed his friend. The faint sounds of a distant shriek reached his ears. "Did you hear that?"

"Hear what?"

Eli's heart began to pound. Had that been Hannah? "You didn't hear anything?" he whispered into the phone.

"Nothing," Tucci said.

Eli listened but the night had fallen quiet again. "Uh...I don't know. Probably a cat, but I'm going to run a perimeter check on the house and barns. Keep digging, Mitchie. I'll call you in the morning."

Eli was already sliding out of the car, grabbing his flashlight and pocketing his phone, before his partner could respond. Eli didn't really believe he'd heard a cat. That was a woman's scream. And he believed it was Hannah's. Thomas might not want him to, but he was going back inside the house.

Without a sound, he closed the door to his car. Then slinking his way under the tree-covered path, he dashed toward the house. Another muffled cry broke through the night. This one louder than the first and confirming his hunch. It *was* Hannah. She was in trouble.

Glock drawn, Eli sneaked to the porch, sucking in a gasp when he saw that the front door to the cottage hung wide open. From the bottom of the steps, he could hear a muffled voice inside speaking fast and low.

Eli clenched his teeth, resisting the temptation to bust into the house and attack whoever was making Hannah scream. Of course, he knew that would be dumb. It was too dark and the downstairs was too large and open. If he raced inside, he'd be nothing more than an easy target standing in the doorway with a flashlight to help the bad guy aim better.

Instead, Eli tucked the flashlight into his belt and lowered himself into a squatting position. He could creep up the front stairs and slink into the house slowly, unnoticed. That way he could get a better handle on the situation. But as he pressed his weight over the first step, it groaned loudly under him.

Stupid old house. Heavy footsteps scrambled across the floor inside. The intruder was getting away. Again.

Eli leaped like a cat through the front door, aiming both his gun and flashlight in the direction of the footsteps. Target or not, he wanted a chance at this guy. At the other end of the kitchen, he caught the backside of him. A man in all black. Thin. Tall. Quick.

"Hold it. Freeze. Philadelphia police." Eli cocked his gun and aimed for the man's heart.

Chapter Six

The dark figure in the kitchen door did not stop as Eli commanded but continued straight through the opened screen and out into the darkness. Eli knew he should chase after him, but a more pressing concern came first.

"Hannah!" Eli moved across the room, the beam from his flashlight finding her lying facedown near the bottom of the stairs. "It's me, Eli. Are you okay?"

He knelt beside her. Putting a hand to her shoulder, he could feel her shaking.

"So glad that you are come." Her voice quivered as he unraveled her from the quilt that seemed to have her trapped to the floor. Her prayer *Kapp* had slipped from her hair, her apron unpinned; her face was red, splotchy and swollen.

"Can you move?"

"I think so."

Eli helped her to a seated position. "Are you going to be okay?"

She gestured to the back door. "Yes. Go. Go after him."

Elijah took off through the back and searched for the fleeing intruder. All was dark. The backyard and garden

were empty. But as he turned to go back inside, his eye
caught a flicker of movement in the distance. There, in
the distance, he could barely make out the silhouette of
a man. He seemed to move his arms rapidly through
the air over and across something large and dark. For
a second, Eli feared the man had a weapon, but when a
second later his figure lifted high from the ground. Eli
realized he'd mounted a horse and was already gallop-
ing away into the night.

Eli turned and went back into the house.

Who was that? Who pushed me down? Had she
known his voice or had she just imagined that? Hannah pushed herself up from the hardwood floor and
turned on the oil-powered overhead light. An agoniz-
ing pain stabbed through her head, followed by a steady
rhythmic throbbing, making her want to tear her hair
out by the roots and vomit. She stumbled her way to the
small couch by the woodstove and carefully sat back
into the cushions. The movement filled her with nausea and she doubled over her lap, hoping to swallow
away a dry heave.

Eli stepped back through the back door. Slowly, she
turned her aching head toward him.

"Whoever it was rode off on a horse." He shrugged.
"Only in Willow Trace, right?"

No black car, she thought. But someone on horse-
back, that brought things a little too close to home.
"What kind of horse?" she asked.

"Uh…black? But don't they all look black in the
dark?"

"No." She looked away from his attempt to make her
smile. How had that almost worked? Two minutes ago

she'd been scared out of her mind. His presence had such an effect on her. It should not be so.

"Where are Thomas and Nana?" he asked.

"I can hear Nana still sleeping," she said. "I don't… I don't know about Thomas. He's not usually a heavy sleeper."

Eli nodded thoughtfully, then moved toward her, slowly taking the seat next to her. He reached for her hands and covered them over with his own. *Thomas.* She hadn't even thought of him since the attacker confronted her. When she'd been afraid, it had been Elijah she'd wanted and welcomed. Her hands felt warm and safe inside his. She should have been ashamed, the feelings he stirred in her. She should have pulled away. He was not her beau. He was not one of their community anymore. And yet his eyes held her in a tender gaze from which she could not look away.

"You need a doctor," he said.

She felt her eyes widen. "No. No doctor. I'm fine."

Eli looked doubtful.

"That is, I'll be fine," she amended.

"Then tell me what happened tonight," he whispered.

No. She closed her eyes tight. She didn't want to remember. But her mind rushed back to the hard push to the floor. Tears flooded her eyes and crashed down her cheeks. She looked away, pulled her hands back and turned from him. "What if you had not come when you did? I—I am so thankful to God—"

"Me, too." His voice was soft, reassuring. "Glad I wasn't in the stable or I would never have seen your light on and heard you scream."

She nodded and slowly opened her eyes to him again. How the strength and softness in him blended and touched her through his deep gaze. He reached up and wiped away the moisture from her cheek. "I know you don't feel well, but…can you tell me what happened? It's best with victims if they talk about things right away."

Victim? Was that what she was? It was hard to put such a title to herself, to think she was different from anyone else. Special. The idea conflicted her. She took in a deep, shaky breath and wiped away the rest of her tears.

"Tell me what happened, Hannah. I need to know about everything."

"Everything?" Her gaze went down to the wooden floor. "I—I wouldn't know where to begin with everything. I feel so confused inside since—"

"Then start with tonight. You turned on a light, didn't you?"

She nodded.

"Start there."

"I could not sleep. My mind was racing with thoughts of…" Hannah pressed her lips together. Her thoughts had been on Eli and all that he made her feel inside. But she would not speak of that. He must never know she still loved him. Had always loved him. If it had not been for Jessica…

"Your mind was racing. Mine, too." He smiled and patted her shoulder sweetly.

"*Jah.* So, I am awake and I think I hear someone moving downstairs. I think it must be Thomas. I dress and come down to talk because I have things to say about…" How did she keep getting back to Elijah?

"But it wasn't Thomas." Elijah tried to help her refocus.

"No. It was not Thomas. I realized that right away, but I see the front door is opened, so I go to close it. Then I hear someone moving. Oh, Elijah, I was so scared. I run to the steps, but...he got to me first. I was so frightened."

"I know. I know. But you are safe now." He put a gentle arm around her shoulders and pulled her close to his side. "You're safe. Relax."

Hannah could not tell if she stiffened from his touch or melted into his arms. There was such a mixture of emotions inside her. For certain, her heart beat faster and her breath shortened. But it was no longer from fear that her body reacted, but from Elijah's scent and touch and kindness to her.

"What happened next? You were near the stairs when I got here."

"*Jah,* so I run for the stairs but he pushes me down and asks me for... he asks for...for something. I don't remember."

"Did you see his face?"

"No. It was too dark. Pushed me to the floor. Very strong."

"Yes, you have a nasty bump on your forehead. How about we get some ice on that? You should put your feet up, too."

Eli propped her feet on the table in front of the couch then left her to fetch a few ice cubes from the oil-powered freezer. He wrapped some ice in a dish towel and returned to her side, placing the homemade cold pack on her head.

"Aye." She backed away from his hand. "It must be more than a bump." She reached for the ice bundle and took it from his fingers.

"It's quite a knot." He smiled and sat down again. "I should call my sister and have her take a look at you."

"No. Thank you. I'm sure I'll be fine." Hannah located the giant bump on her head with one hand, then gently placed the ice around but not directly on the sore.

"Okay, but I'm going to stay here and keep an eye on you for a while. It's a nasty bump."

Hannah smiled at his concern, knowing she wanted him to stay for more than just to see about her health—his presence gave her a comfort she longed for.

"Can you remember anything else?" he asked. "I heard his voice when I got up to the house. Seemed he was saying quite a bit."

Hannah thought hard. "He did. He spoke like he was nervous. He mentioned Jessica. It was…it was almost like he knew me. And I knew him."

"What do you mean? Like he was Amish? Or someone from town?"

"I—I don't know." She closed her eyes, but her mind was blank. "I only remember thinking that there was something familiar about his voice. That is all. I am so sorry, Elijah. I wish I could keep it all straight in my head." She looked up again into his soft blue eyes. Why was it she could not remember five minutes ago while old forgotten feelings seemed so completely alive to her? Maybe Eli was right and she should have his sister look at her head. "We should inform Thomas of what has happened. He will not be pleased."

Eli didn't look so pleased, either. "Yeah. Okay. I'll go and wake him."

Hannah closed her eyes as he moved away. Her head pounded. "I'm sorry I cannot remember."

"It's okay, Hannah. It's been a long day. And you're doing as well as can be expected. Just relax and let the details come back na…"

Hannah opened her eyes when Elijah stopped mid-sentence. When she looked up, he was standing at the bottom of the stairs staring downward with a strange expression. "What is it?" she asked.

"The bottom step. It's been opened. You know, the storage area under the stairs. Did you keep anything in it?"

"Opened?" Hannah swallowed hard. Panic flashed through her as she remembered her attacker reaching over her toward the step. "Yes…or at least Thomas used to keep some things there. Why?"

Eli turned back, shaking his head. "Because it's empty. What was in it?"

"I am not sure. Maybe nothing. Perhaps Thomas or Nana Ruth keeps something there, but I do not think so." The intruder had asked her for a journal, for Jessica's journal. What had the poor girl done? Gotten herself into? Hannah could not imagine. The room seemed to spin like the confusion in her head. Her chest tightened. The lump on her head ached.

"What is it, Hannah? Tell me."

Hannah could hardly hear Elijah's words over the noise in her own mind. She began to shake, her thoughts jumbled. In her head, voices, noises. The intruder. Jessica. Thomas. Elijah. Chief McClendon.

If only she had been a better mother to Jessica. None of this would be happening. "I should never have tried to be Jessica's mother. God did not want me to have children. I should have understood that. I should have—"

Eli stood before her. His warm hand touched her cheek. Hannah opened her eyes. He lifted her chin tenderly. "You were a wonderful mother, Hannah. I don't know what is happening here, but I am certain that it is not the result of your parenting skills."

Tears spilled from her eyes. How many people she had hurt in her own selfishness. How Elijah could be so kind to her after she had refused him she did not know. She grabbed his hand and the wrist and pressed her face against his warm palm. "You are gracious."

"No. Hannah, I'm not. But I can put the past in the past. And I can assure you that you are in no way responsible for the things happening here."

Tears flushed from her eyes. He did not understand. Perhaps it was better that way. Perhaps he should never know the truth about why she had refused him, about how she had never stopped loving him, about how feeling his warm touch against her cheek brought her more comfort and pleasure than he would ever know.

He drew back. "I know there is more that you have to tell me. I can see it in your eyes, but you're tired. I'm tired." He smiled. "Let's continue this in the morning. I'll go and tell Thomas what's happened. Stay here. I'll be back to help you up the stairs."

Hannah nodded in agreement. She *was* ready to tell him everything about Jessica, whether Thomas agreed to it or not.

Screech! The back door swung open.

Hannah squealed. Someone was there. Someone tall and dark and hidden in the darkness of the kitchen.

Elijah stepped forward, pulling his Glock from his waist. She turned her head away, not wanting to hear the gunfire. Nor see death. She had seen enough of that for a lifetime.

Chapter Seven

"I take it you did not expect me back so soon."

Eli relaxed his defensive stance. The man at the door was Thomas, dirty, disheveled and wet with sweat. Eli couldn't help picturing him as the man he'd seen mounting the horse and riding off in the night. Anger tightened Eli's fist around the butt of his gun as he put it away.

"Expect you back? We didn't know you had gone anywhere," he said. "At least now I understand why you didn't hear Hannah scream for help. You weren't here. Are you crazy leaving her after what happened this afternoon?"

Thomas's angry expression dropped. He came farther into the kitchen, his eyes wide. "But was it not you who sent me to go to Hostetlers' farm?"

"Me?" Eli laughed. "Why would I do such a thing?"

"I—I…"

"I'm not the enemy here, Thomas, and the sooner you figure that out, the safer we're all going to be." Eli clenched his teeth. His hands rolled into fists. "Hannah was attacked. Good thing I wasn't asleep in the stable or I would never have heard her scream."

"This is true?" Thomas looked worried now.

"Yes, Thomas. There was an intruder. I—" Hannah tried to stand, but not having the strength wobbled off balance.

Eli reached an arm to steady her. Thomas, having the same idea, moved forward as well, but stopped, as he was not needed.

"You are not well, Hannah. Allow me to fetch Abigail Miller or Dr. Peters for you," he said.

"No, brother. Truly, I am fine. Just a bump on the head." She pulled away from Elijah and made her way to the stairs.

"Would you not tell me what has happened?" Thomas asked.

"There will be time to talk tomorrow. I am tired."

"Good night, Hannah." Elijah smiled at her brave front. He knew inside she was hurt and very scared. He wanted to help her to her room, tuck her into her bed and kiss her soft cheek. He wanted to let her know he would keep her safe…if he could.

Thomas turned to Elijah. "Forgive me. I'd found a note at the front door saying that there was an ill foal at the Hostetlers' farm and that they requested my help. It is not unusual for a neighbor to ask such a thing, but when I got there and saw there was no trouble I rushed back and found you two together. I…I—"

"Do you have this note?" Eli asked. "Could I see it?"

Thomas produced a small white sheet of paper from his sleeve. The message was just as he'd said, written in carefully scripted block letters. Elijah studied it then handed it back to Thomas. "Hold on to this. I doubt it will be of use, though, as the script looks stilted. Probably anyone could have penned it. Although if it were the intruder… Hannah did say she thought she knew his voice. Did any neighbors know what you kept in the bottom stair?"

Thomas blanched and turned toward the staircase. A deep frown forced creases around his eyes. "This is… this is most disappointing."

"What *did* you keep there?" Eli hated to pry. It was not the Amish way, but he needed to know. He needed Thomas and Hannah to tell him the truth. He regretted that Thomas had cut his time with Hannah short. He sensed that finally she had been ready to tell him more about Jessica and the events leading up to her death. Hopefully, tomorrow he would get another chance.

"Cash." Thomas lifted up the step and examined the empty hole. He turned back, looking even more ill than before. "A lot of cash. I made some good trades recently. I was saving for…" He removed his hat and shook his head. "Oh, what does it matter? *The Lord giveth and the Lord taketh away.*"

"God didn't take your money, Thomas. A man did. A man that wore dark clothing and rode off on a horse. Was there anything else in there?"

Thomas nodded. "Some documents concerning the horses and a journal I keep on all their breeding and trades."

"Your trades?" Eli repeated, thinking of Thomas's high-dollar horse recently sold to the governor. "How involved was Jessica in your trading and training?"

"Not at all, really. Jessica was here in the house with Hannah, learning to cook and sew and garden. She fed and groomed the horses from time to time but nothing more and not much of that since she started courting."

"Jessica had a beau?"

"Daniel Hostetler, of course. They've been insepa-

rable since they were children. It was no surprise to us
that they began courting last year."

"And he is a large boy? Full grown?"

Thomas looked away. "I will not accuse my own
brethren, nor help you to do so."

Elijah ground his teeth in frustration. What were
they all hiding? And how was he ever to figure any of
this out if they didn't help him instead of keeping secrets? "I'll need to talk to Daniel and any other friends
of Jessica's first thing in the morning."

"If you must."

"I must…" Eli sighed heavily. "I'd like to see where
you found Jessica's body, as well."

"Why? She is no longer there."

"Of course not, but I can imagine the scene as it was
and try to piece together in my mind the events of that
night she died."

"It is not our way to wonder about what has happened."

"No. But it's mine and I've been asked to look into
it. Anything you can tell me about Jessica or anything
unusual around here would be helpful."

"I can't imagine I know anything that would make
a difference."

"How about your horse trade with Governor Derry?"

Thomas's face twitched. "Yes. A pony for his daughter and a good sale it was. But it has nothing to do with
us now." He walked over and put a hand on Elijah's
shoulder. "I am thankful you have helped Hannah this
day. She is in a fragile state. But you will not take advantage of that to pry into things that are none of your
concern—or to get any closer to Hannah than is proper.
In any case, now that I think on it, I can keep a better
eye on you if you stay here in the house." He gave a

quick laugh. "Come now. We must get to bed. All this talk leads us to nothing."

"Did you want me to call McClendon about your break-in and the money that was stolen?"

"You see what good calling the police has brought us so far. No. And no more talk of it. Come. I'll show you to the spare room."

Eli locked the doors both front and back, something the Amish rarely did, and followed Thomas into the *Dawdi Haus* and up to the extra bedroom, too tired to think over all that needed sorting out. In particular, Mr. Daniel Hostetler.

Morning came all too quickly and Hannah rose, reminded of the lump on her forehead as standing brought a wave of pain to her head. At least the swelling had reduced during the night, she decided as she ran a cold, damp cloth over her face. A little headache never hurt anyone. She would be brave and face the day no matter how much she'd like to crawl back into her warm bed. There were still things to be happy about. She missed Jessica terribly, but she was in heaven now and at peace. Life on Earth moved on. She would move with it and her God would be enough. He would get her through this just as she had gotten through losing Peter. Oh, how thankful she was that He had already saved her from saying too much to Elijah last night. She must take care to guard herself better. He was not for her and she was not for him. Baring her soul to him would only make things harder when he left. And he would leave. That she was sure of. Just as he had left before.

Hannah dressed, taking great care when she pinned on her prayer *Kapp,* then went down and began breakfast. Nana Ruth came behind her and then Thomas, who looked as if he had not slept at all.

"You should fetch Elijah from the stable," Nana Ruth suggested to Thomas. "I am sure he will not be used to waking at this hour."

"I don't think Elijah Miller will be joining us for breakfast," Thomas said. Hannah nearly dropped the pan from her hands. What did he mean by that? Had Elijah left? Had Thomas sent him away?

She cracked an egg and dropped it into the hot skillet. It sizzled and popped and the room filled with its rich aroma of butter and breakfast. "Nana Ruth, would you watch over this egg while I fetch more from the hen-house? I'm afraid we're down to the last three."

Nana Ruth smiled. "I will go and fetch them my-self," she said, taking the basket. "My old bones need a shake this morning."

She left through the back door.

Hannah fixed Thomas his plate and brought it to the table.

"How's your head?" he asked.

"Better." She stood back as Thomas prayed over his food. "Did he leave?"

Thomas took a bite of his breakfast and mumbled something inaudible. "It would be best that he would go back to the city. He's brought nothing but trouble here." He studied her. "Be careful, Hannah. He is not the boy you once knew."

"I do not know what you mean."

"I see how you look at him."

"I give him no better treatment than I would any guest in your home."

"Is it not your home, too?" He gazed into her eyes.

Hannah looked down. "I—I do not know. Now that

Jessica is gone you do not need me here. I have no one to teach the sewing and cooking to. Nana is in good health. You can care for yourself. You did not even tell me that you were leaving the house last night. I thought…"

"We could marry this November, Hannah. Everyone expects it. That would give you the security you want."

"You cannot ask me to think on marriage so close to Jessica's death. I cannot." She hurried to the stove, embarrassed she had revealed her fears to him. Her question sounded like a push for him to renew his offer of marriage. And it was not. How could she think of marriage to him when her head was full of nothing but Elijah?

"Elijah showed you the bottom step? I told him I didn't think you kept anything in it," she said.

"There was the money there, Hannah."

"I'm sorry. I did not know."

"I have always kept a bit of cash on hand for emergencies. I am not troubled by its loss. It is nothing. The money was not mine. It belonged to God. I'm sure He knows where it is. I am only thankful you are safe."

Hannah looked back at him. "What if all of these events are related?"

"How do you mean? The money and Jessica? Were you listening to our conversation last night?"

"I was not."

"Did Elijah suggest this idea to you?"

Hannah began to feel angry with Thomas. He was being obtuse because of his jealousy. "He did not. I am perfectly capable of having the thought all by myself, I assure you. It makes sense. The man last night asked for a journal—he said it belonged to Jessica. He must have thought that he might find it there in the step."

"A journal? Did Jessica keep a journal?"

"I do not believe so. But I obviously knew very little about Jessica."

"Perhaps you are right. The events are related somehow. There *was* a journal in the step—my journal, listing my trades. That must have been what was meant by the man's demands. And now that this person has our money and journal, there can be nothing left for anyone to come for. We are safe."

"You have already sent Eli home, haven't you?" Hannah turned back to the stove, her heart sinking. "I think your decision is unwise."

"You may think what you like. But I believe the intruder got what he wanted. There was a lot of money there, Hannah. That is what he wanted. Nothing more. And this is what we will report to the bishop and to Mother. There is enough talk amongst the people already because of Jessica's accident. This will end it… Fix yourself some breakfast and trouble yourself no more over this."

Hannah began to fix a plate of fried eggs even though she wasn't hungry in the least. In fact, Thomas's talk of marriage had made her nearly ill. "But this man said he wanted *Jessica's* journal. Not yours. And not money. He was quite serious. He may have taken your money, but he will come back when he sees your journal is not the one that he wanted."

"He was after the money, Hannah. That is always what they want. He will not come back. You are safe now."

Hannah wanted to scream out her frustration, but the arrival of a horse and buggy in front of the house put an end to the conversation.

Hannah glanced through the kitchen window. A

woman dressed in a maroon frock and white apron descended the vehicle.

"Is Nana expecting a visitor?" she said.

Thomas shrugged. A light rap sounded at the front door. Hannah moved quickly to open the latch.

"*Guten Morgan,* Hannah Nolt. *Wie gehts?*" Abigail Miller looked as bright and cheerful as the morning sun itself. Her peppy voice washed through the room and Hannah allowed herself to smile for the first time that day.

"Come in, Miss Miller. Please. How nice to see you." Hannah opened the door wider so that Elijah's younger sister could enter.

"I have come to see my brother. He is here, ain't so?" She was nearly giddy with excitement.

"He is," Hannah said. "Or at least he was last night. I have not seen him this morning."

Thomas grumbled from the kitchen. Hannah felt her cheeks heat up. Abigail continued to smile, seemingly oblivious of the tension in the room until she moved closer to take a look at the lump on Hannah's forehead. "Oh dear, Hannah, your head. What has happened?"

"I'm afraid it looks much worse than it is." Hannah backed away. All she needed was one more person asking questions. "Thomas, could you tell Elijah that he has a visitor?"

"So he is still sleeping, is he?" Abigail smiled.

"Nope, I'm right here." Elijah stepped into the kitchen. His eyes fell softly on her. Hannah tried hard to be indifferent at the sight of him. Not that he cared or would have noticed the thrill he gave her. All too quickly, he looked away to his sister, grinning like a child with a new puppy.

Thomas stood from the table, took his hat from its

peg on the wall and backed up to the kitchen door. "If you'll excuse me, I have work to do. Enjoy your morning. I'll return in time to head to the Millers' for the harvest this afternoon. Good day."

What? A harvest gathering at his family's place? That was exactly what Eli had hoped to avoid. Although seeing his sister there so happy to see him gave him great joy.

"Abby." He came forward and gave her a hug.

"You are just as I imagined," she teased.

"I hope not." He brushed a hand through his bed-head hair and made a wide-eyed face. For certain, he needed a few more hours' sleep and a shave. The Amish might not talk about outward appearances, but one as bad as his could hardly escape their notice. "You look well yourself, Abigail. So glad you're here. How is everyone? *Mamm?* Elizabeth?" He looked down before adding, *"Dat?"*

"Come see for yourself? I came just so. To invite you to cousin John's. Today we pick his strawberries. He has so many this year he decided to have a gathering to bring them in. I'll give you a ride myself if you like."

Eli shook his head. "No way. That is a terrible idea and you know it."

"And why is it a terrible idea?" Hannah asked. "I'm sure all of your family would like to see you."

"You're wrong about that. *Dat* said he never wanted to see me again, and unless I hear otherwise I'm not going to face him. It will be a disaster."

"Oh, come, now, Elijah. You are overreacting." Abigail gave him a disapproving glare.

"Am I?" Elijah frowned and tried not to resent the way his sister reminded him that he alone was the outcast child. How was it that Abigail had not yet joined the church and still lived among the People when he so much as mentioned the police academy and was instantly disowned? "I don't think so."

Hannah came back to the table with a cup of coffee for each of them. She served them and stood back from the table. "You should go, Elijah. Many will be there and among them most of Jessica's friends. You could ask them about the night before she died…if they had seen her, where they had been."

"So that is why you have come home?" Abigail was wide-eyed. "To ask questions about poor Jessica?"

"Yes," he answered, thinking over Hannah's words. It was true. He needed to talk to the community, especially Jessica's friends. But seeing his family was a bad idea. Not to mention that it would be hard to protect Hannah there. "No, I'm not going and neither are you, Hannah. It could be dangerous for you to be out in the open all day like that."

"Why would Hannah be in danger?" Abigail asked, looking confused. "What harm could come to her from a simple gathering?"

"It is of no consequence," Hannah replied.

Elijah frowned. This pattern of secrecy was going too far, making her actively ignore the danger she was in. But he wouldn't embarrass Hannah by arguing with her in front of a guest.

"What if I could promise you that *Dat* will not be there?" Abigail said teasingly.

"Yeah, right. Bishop Miller miss an opportunity to eat? I don't think so."

"No. I'm serious. It's the main reason I thought I'd come by and ask you to join us. *Dat* was called away to meet with the bishop from Grenlicht today. That's a long buggy ride even on a good day. He'll be gone for hours," his sister said.

"I don't know. It could still be dangerous…but I do need to talk to her friends."

"Exactly. Then it's settled. I'll be back at noon to pick you up." Abigail gave his cheek a kiss and headed back out.

Elijah watched her off, then turned, crossed his arms over his chest and glared at Hannah. "So, I guess now would be a good time for you to tell me about this journal of Jessica's? And about everything else you've been keeping from me."

Chapter Eight

"Father, we are thankful for what we are about to receive…"

Elijah's cousin John Miller stood at the head of the long table leading the blessing and giving thanks for his fine harvest of strawberries, which the entire community had come together to gather, sort and place in baskets to sell at market.

John was a Plain man—the ideal Amish man, so to speak. His dirty-blond hair was cut in a simple bowl shape around his head. It fell slightly below the brim of his straw hat. His shirt was a loose-fitted button-up, the color of the sky. His trousers, black—no pockets, no zippers, no cuffs. His reddish-blond beard framed the outside of his chin and was trimmed away from his mouth and upper lip. It was a style belonging uniquely to the Amish.

If Elijah had stayed in Willow Trace instead of leaving when he turned eighteen, he guessed he'd look much the same as his cousin. He certainly wouldn't be wearing a fitted pair of Levi's jeans and a golf shirt. His hair would be longer like John's and his face smooth, unless of course, he'd married…

A dry lump formed in his throat. He looked to Hannah. Marriage. He had wanted that with her so many years ago. He had wanted a family with her. He remembered how they'd talked about having three or four children. They had even decided on names. How was it that she changed her mind so suddenly?

Oh, what did he care anyway? He didn't. He could never come back to Willow Trace. Nor did he want to. If only Nana Ruth hadn't walked into the house the very second he'd asked Hannah about the journal, maybe he'd already be on his way back to the city.

Elijah knew he was trying to push away the pleasant experiences of home that had filled his senses all afternoon—the buggy ride, which he'd given in to despite his better judgment that they go in the car; working alongside his kinsmen and friends in the fields, the fine meal they took together, the sight of all the children dressed like miniature grown-ups running barefoot through the fields, playing tag and hide-and-seek and swinging from the same tire swing he had played in as a child. The sights had quite overwhelmed him.

And as his cousin prayed, full of grateful thanks to both God and his family and friends, Elijah was moved to tears. He had forgotten the sense of community and traditions of his People. He'd forgotten his sense of belonging. He looked to his sister's wagon and remembered his gun and badge hidden under the blanket. What was wrong with him? Sure, it was great to be home for a few days, but he did not regret his choice to become a police officer. Nor was he ashamed of it. In fact, it was time to get back on the job and start asking around about Jessica.

After the meal, Eli zoned in on a group of young teens that sat on John's front porch, enjoying the evening breeze. He did not recognize their faces, as they would have been babies when he left town, but they would know him. Of that, he was certain. He hoped that would work to his advantage.

"Were any of you friends with Jessica Nolt?"

The group fell silent.

"You can talk to me. I'm Elijah Miller," he said. "I'm sure you knew me when you were little. I've just been gone awhile."

"You're the cop," one boy said.

Elijah neared them. He made the courteous gesture like tipping a hat, even though he wore none. "That's right. I'm the bishop's son that became a cop."

"Are you moving back here?" another child asked, turning a nice shade of red.

"No, just visiting." He looked around at the beautiful land. In the distance, Hannah was cleaning one of the dinner tables. Near to them, his mother, Nana Ruth and a few other women sat chatting in a small circle. His chest tightened at the sight. "Just visiting," he repeated as if to drive home his answer.

"Do you kill bad people?" a boy in the group asked.

"No. I've never had to kill anyone," he answered.

"Would you?" the boy continued. "My dad says guns are bad."

"Almost anything can become an instrument of evil in the wrong hands." Elijah gave them a compassionate look. "So, did you kids know Jessica Nolt?"

They all nodded.

"Well, can you tell me about her? Like what did she like to do for fun? Who were her closest friends? Stuff like that."

"She hung out with Daniel and Kasey and Geoffrey," one answered.

"They're over there by the horses," another said.

"They go to town sometimes," one of the girls added. "And to parties."

"Yes, they do," another boy confirmed. "They are on *Rumspringa*."

"Any idea what they do in town?" Elijah followed the kids' gaze to a group of three older teens sitting on a fence rail. Geoffrey, Daniel and Kasey, he presumed.

"We don't know. They don't really talk to us."

"Are they good kids? Do they go to singings and do their chores?"

The kids exchanged quick glances, probably afraid to answer and get their older friends in a pickle.

"Come on," he encouraged them. "I'm not here to get anyone in trouble. I'm just trying to see if I can figure out where Jessica was the day before she died."

"*Jah,* they are good. But you should ask them your questions." A boy pointed to the kids on the fence rail.

"Okay." He smiled and backed away. But the young kids scattered as if the porch had caught fire.

What was that all about? I'm not that scary.

But when he turned to go talk to the other group of kids, he understood why they had run off. Just down the hill, the bishop was coming toward him. So the meeting hadn't kept him away after all. And now his *Dat* had come to send him home. Some things would never change. Once the bishop decided on something, he never changed his mind. Accepting his own son's decisions wouldn't be any different.

Elijah's heart sank. If he left the gathering, how could he protect Hannah? Didn't anyone understand that she was in danger and that they needed help and protection from something beyond their borders? But even his fear of leaving Hannah unprotected couldn't compete with his fear of the conversation about to take place.

His heart pounded in his chest like a drum and his throat grew so tight he could barely take in the air he needed. After eleven years, his *Dat* was coming to speak to him. He'd dreamed of this moment. Imagined it over and over in his mind in many different ways... none of the scenarios had ever ended well. He doubted this would, either.

He stood frozen to his spot on John's porch and waited. There was no smile on his *Dat*'s face, no welcome in his manners. Not that Eli had expected otherwise, but he had hoped somehow for a miracle. He still believed in them. As his father grew nearer, his appearance shocked Elijah. How old he'd grown. The lines on his face deeper, his hair whiter, his shoulders rounder. He stopped a few steps away, squared his feet under himself and crossed his arms over his chest.

"I know why you have come and about the recommendation of Chief McClendon, who is a good friend to our People. I spoke to the elders. We give you three days. After that, you will leave." His words were sharp and spoken in the Pennsylvania Dutch. And as soon as they were said, he dropped his arms, turned and started to march away.

Elijah shook his head at the unfeeling encounter. *Three days.* He wished they were already past.

Hi, Dat. *Good to see you,* Dat. *Miss you, too,* Dat. *Yeah, right.*

Almost as if he'd heard the words, the bishop stopped and turned. Eli's heart jumped for a second as his father opened his mouth to speak again. *"Und kleine Pistole,"* the bishop added, marching away. "It isn't our way."

Eli swallowed away the hurt of his father's cold

words and manner. Then he glanced over at his sister's buggy where he'd stowed away his Glock.

Of course, Dat, *no guns. If someone shoots at us again, I'll just hit him with a farm tool.* He broke no law by having a gun. He had not taken vows. And if that cop so many years ago had not shot his abductor, he and his sister, Abigail, would both be dead. Did that not mean anything to his father? Did the bishop not see that protecting the innocent was a good thing?

Elijah dropped his head and walked toward the other small group of teens.

"Elijah Miller, after all these years?" Margaret Brenneman whispered to Hannah as they cleared away the evening meal dishes. "I heard he showed up completely unannounced. That must have given you quite a shock."

"Yes, a little," Hannah answered.

"Wonder why he's back after all this time," Margaret continued, not really listening to Hannah's answer.

"And wasn't he always a favorite of yours?" Mary Payne jumped into the conversation. "In fact, if I remember correctly we were all astonished when you announced your engagement to Peter Nolt instead of to him."

"I'm sure I can't remember anything that happened so long ago," Hannah said, a little angry at their choice of topics. "It is surely of no consequence now. Peter is gone. Jessica is gone."

Hannah walked quickly to the kitchen with her stack of plates, hoping Margaret and Mary would give up their gossiping mission by the time she returned, but it seemed that was not to be.

"Levi says Elijah is staying with you during his visit?" Mary Payne added.

Hannah cringed. She hated any sort of gossip, but she especially hated it when the gossip involved her. And she could see exactly where this topic was leading. She wanted to silence their tongues. "He is estranged from his father. You know that. And he's here on business. Perhaps you should ask him about it yourself. 'Tis no secret."

"About that troubled Jessica, no doubt," Margaret said. "I've heard all sorts of tales of her goings-on at parties and such. It must make it all so difficult for you."

"Not a bit of truth in any of that talk. Idle prattle, I assure you." Hannah sighed in frustration at the turn in the conversation. "Jessica was a good girl."

"Of course she was, dear." Margaret shot Mary a worried look. "It must be such a terrible time for you."

"It's been difficult," Hannah said, lifting her chin high. "It was so unexpected."

Mary came and patted her hand. "And it can't help with all of this terrible talk going around. Well, at least you can count on the two of us not to join in."

Mary and Margaret saw the sadness in her eyes and finally turned to their work. Hannah wanted to flee, but forced herself to stay and help them with the dishes.

"Do you think you'll stay on at the Nolts' now that she's gone?" Mary started again.

"Where else would I go?" Hannah felt her tears begin to form. Normally, she wouldn't listen to such silly talk, but today, after all she'd been through, she didn't need to hear this from these women, who had nothing better to do than speculate about her business.

"You have kinfolk in the town of Esperance, do you not?" Mary said.

"A cousin." What was this? Hannah shuddered at their words. They wanted her sent away. Out of their sight.

She could take no more. She rushed from the kitchen before the tears came. Abigail was just coming into the house. She nearly knocked her over.

"I'm sorry. I'm so sorry."

"Hannah, what is it?" It only took Abigail a second to look past her into the kitchen and see Mary and Margaret there. "What did they say to you, those gossiping twits?"

Hannah tried to stop her tears. How foolish she felt to be rattled by the silliest women in all of Willow Trace. "There was talk about Jessica. Bad talk. They were suggesting I go to Esperance to live with my cousin."

"I ought to give them a piece of my mind," Abigail said. "You're not going anywhere. Come, Hannah. Let us walk and take in some fresh air. It's gotten much too crowded in here." She said the last part loudly so that the other ladies could hear.

Hannah took Abigail's arm and they walked out behind the farmhouse.

At least, they were giving him three days, Elijah thought. That was more time than he'd expected. He almost laughed thinking how upset Thomas Nolt would be having to put up with him for a few more days. Eli gazed over the others at the gathering. He wondered if anyone had seen the awkward encounter with his father.

No. The men were chatting and putting the tables away, the women cleaning.

He continued to look around, checking for Hannah regularly. He did not see her. Nor Abigail. Nor Thomas, for that matter. In fact, Elijah hadn't seen Thomas since the meal had begun, and that surprised him since the entire day his old friend had been quite intent to make certain that he and Hannah did not get within a stone's throw of each other. Thomas was hiding something, of that Eli was certain. He feared it might have to do with the horrible things happening to Hannah. He could indeed picture Thomas as the man atop the fleeing steed he'd spotted racing off from the cottage. But what he couldn't imagine was Thomas knocking Hannah to the floor and hurting her. In fact, he couldn't imagine Thomas causing Hannah any harm whatsoever. Thomas cared for Hannah greatly. That was not debatable. Still, where was Thomas? Why wasn't he keeping a better eye on Hannah? Or perhaps they were together now? Eli had to admit he didn't like that idea one bit, and it made him all the more anxious to find them.

But first he needed to talk to the other friends of Jessica's. With only three days, he had no time to spare. So far, the only thing he had to go on was a big pony sale and a journal that, from the stairwell, he had overheard Hannah telling Thomas she knew nothing about. Two things, which added up to nothing.

Elijah moved toward the other group of teens—Daniel, Kasey and Geoffrey. Daniel Hostetler was easy to pick of the three. The Hostetler family had been around forever, every one of them tall, lanky and dark-headed. And interesting that no one other than Thomas had bothered to mention that Jessica had had a boyfriend. He wondered what else they hadn't told him.

Eli approached them quickly.

"Hello, Daniel. I'm Elijah Miller. I went to school with your sister Miriam. I heard she married and moved away to Indiana." Eli reached out his hand and gave the kid a firm shake.

"That's the truth." The teen avoided looking him in the eye but returned the handshake with gusto.

"I'm Geoffrey Payne." The other boy stood from the fence and offered a hand to Elijah. "My family moved here from Ohio a few years back. We live on the other side of your cousin John. John told us that you're a cop—Internal Affairs, ain't so?"

Eli nodded.

Geoffrey smiled. "And this is Kasey Phelps. She's staying with the Lapp family for the year."

"Hi." Elijah shook her hand. "I understand you all were close friends to Jessica Nolt?"

Kasey and Geoffrey nodded with long, sad faces.

"I'm hear to look into—"

"*Jah,* we heard why you are here from John Miller," Geoffrey interrupted. "But we don't know anything."

"That's for sure. We don't know anything," Daniel said. "I used to see Jessica a lot. We courted, you know. But she broke it off with me. Didn't see her much after that."

So, were they courting or weren't they? Elijah listened to the strained inflections in Daniel's voice.

"Did you see her last week?" he asked the group.

"No." They all shook their heads, but looked away. Elijah had a suspicion that one or more of them were not telling the truth now. Maybe all of them.

"Did you know if she kept a journal?" He continued with his short list of questions.

"A journal?" Daniel repeated, forcing out a nervous laugh. "Like something you jot down thoughts in?"

"Yeah, a journal."

"I don't know anything about a journal. Do you?" Daniel looked at his friends.

They shook their heads. "No."

"So, when did you last see—?"

"Oh. Gash. Sorry. I hear my *Dat* calling," Daniel interrupted. "Have to go help. I'll find you guys later." The tall boy ran off, down the green, grassy hill and toward the long line of buggies getting ready to depart before dark.

"He still gets really upset talking about Jessica," Kasey said.

"I understand." Eli nodded. "But maybe you can tell me more about her?"

Kasey nodded. "She was so nice, a really good girl. Always trying to help people. I still can't believe she's gone. I keep thinking she'll be sitting there with us, coming to the next singing, you know?"

"Did the four of you hang out often?"

"Sure. Almost every Saturday," Geoffrey said.

"What did you guys do?"

"You know, the usual courtin' stuff. Dinner in Strasbourg. Sometimes we'd see a movie. A couple of parties. But none of us really like that sort of thing so much."

"Did you go with Jessica into the city the night before she died?"

"No. That was a Monday night. I work at the SuperMart on Mondays until eight," Geoffrey said. "Every Monday."

"Me, too," Kasey added. "Anyway, Jessica had her accident in the barn, didn't you know? She didn't go out."

Elijah chose to change the subject. "What's in the city?" he asked them. "Why might Jessica have wanted to go there?"

"Well, a few weeks ago, Jess started spending time with an *Englischer* friend she met at a *Rumspringa* party." Geoffrey shrugged. "Supposedly the girl was from Philadelphia."

"Does this *Englischer* friend have a name?"

"Brittney," Kasey said.

"Brittney Baker," Geoffrey said.

"You remember her last name?" Kasey looked at Geoffrey with a wounded expression. "You never remember anything."

Geoffrey shrugged. "Sometimes I remember stuff."

Kasey jumped off the fence rail and pouted. "Yeah, he remembers because she's drop-dead gorgeous. Very exotic looking—long dark hair, long legs, big eyes."

Eli tried not to smile at the lovers' spat. "And she's from Philly?"

"That's what Jess said. We never really talked to her. Only saw her *once* at that *one* party." Geoffrey emphasized the important words to Kasey.

"But you think Jessica saw her again?" he asked.

"She told us that she did." Kasey narrowed her eyes. "Hey, why so many questions about Jessica's friend? She died in the stable, right?"

"Her clothing and other evidence suggest that may not have been the complete truth," Elijah said carefully.

The two kids looked at each other, but didn't say anything else.

Eli frowned. "Sorry for all the questions. The police are just trying to do a little more research since it's not clear exactly what happened. Um…but you must have talked this through with the local police and your deacons, right?"

"No," Kasey said with a thoughtful air. "You're the first person to ask us anything."

Geoffrey nodded in accordance.

Eli thought back to the illegible notes in Jessica's

investigative file. Maybe they were illegible because the conversations never actually took place. "Was Jessica close with any other Amish in this area? Any other teens?"

"She was friends with everyone. But she and Daniel were steady, you know," Kasey said. "She spent all her free time with him—well, until she broke it off."

"So she did break it off?"

"*Jah.* He was crushed. Thought she'd found another beau."

Like mother, like daughter. "And when did that happen?"

"Just a few weeks ago."

It sounded to Elijah as if Jessica had met her friend Brittney about the same time as when she broke things off with Daniel. He pressed his lips together, wondering how hard it would be to find this Brittney Baker of Philadelphia. It would be important to speak with her. "One last question. Did Jessica keep a journal that you know of?"

The kids shook their head with vehemence. "In this *Ordnung,* you aren't allowed to keep journals. Too much inward reflection."

"Right. But it doesn't mean that no one has one."

"It means that Jessica didn't have one," Kasey said back.

"Okay. Thank you." Elijah pulled out his phone and sent a quick text to Tucci, asking him to dig up any information he could find on a Brittney Baker living in Philadelphia. When he finished, he saw other men in the distance clearing away the tables and benches. It was time to go. And he should lend a hand with the work and thank his cousin John. "Well, if you think of anything else, I'll be at the Nolts' for another night or two."

He turned away and headed toward the buggies. He still had not spotted Hannah or Thomas, and this was starting to make him nervous. Everyone should be gathered below ready to head home. Where were they? He spotted Abigail by her horse and buggy. She was talking to a young man, but it was not Thomas. Eli scanned the farm. It was growing dark. The sun had begun to set and cast an orange-red glow over the land around him.

There. At the top of the hill behind the farmhouse, he spotted a man large enough to be Thomas. He needed to tell him about his father's decree and the three days. Moving quickly, he rounded the house and started upward. But as he climbed higher he saw that the man was not Amish. Or at least not dressed Plain but only wearing a black Amish dress hat like the one Nicolas had found in the woods the day before. He was tall, and gripped a small rod or a stick of some sort in his left hand.

A spurt of adrenaline shot through Elijah. Was this their shooter come to seek Hannah out again? Or did he already have Hannah? Elijah tore up the big hill. No way would this guy get away from him this time.

Chapter Nine

Elijah knew the land, and on the other side of that hill was nothing but open fields in every direction. There was nowhere for this man to go. No road to hide a car on. He would have him.

Elijah was close enough now to see that the man was tall, but fair and much too thin to have been Thomas. He spotted Elijah coming at him. He turned immediately and headed over the back of the hill. It didn't matter. There was nowhere for him to go. Elijah was nearly there.

He topped the hill and looked down over the vast pastures on the other side. He saw cows and sheep and goats and acres and acres of grassy fields. There was no man.

Impossible. Impossible. It was as if he'd chased a ghost. Only he didn't believe in ghosts. He'd seen someone and just like yesterday that person had vanished.

Defeated, Elijah dropped his gaze to the ground. Beside him in the grass he saw the stick. It was the right size to have been the one the man had carried. He must have tossed it aside in his flight.

Elijah picked it up. It was nothing special, just an or-

dinary stick one would find on the forest floor. Fresh
dirt clung to the small end. Elijah's focus switched back
to the earth. Perhaps the tall man had been digging.
To his right, he found not a hole but several deliberate
markings drawn into the rich soil. Elijah stepped back
and studied the image. It was a symbol he knew well—
a Dutch hex sign. Hex signs came in many forms but
his one was in the shape of an eight-pointed star. It was
encompassed in a large circle except for the north point,
which extended beyond the circle's arch.

He studied the symbol for a moment, wondering what
kind of message could be meant from it. The meaning
of Dutch hex symbols had long been a source of confusion, even in Lancaster where these painted designs
often hung on houses and barns. Many believed them
to be nothing more than a decorative pattern. In fact,
some of the patterns were sewn into quilts or painted on
wood and sold to tourists. But other folks thought there
was some religious attachment to the symbol. But what
that religious significance was no one seemed to agree
over. Still, this uninvited man who'd been watching
over them had taken the time to draw it into the ground
and in a manner of speaking had lured him up there to
look at it. Perhaps it was some sort of clue? A warning?

Elijah pulled out his cell phone and snapped a picture
of the design. He messaged it to Tucci with a message.

In addition to Brittney Baker. Check this out. Another
uninvited visitor. Male. Thin. Over six feet. Fair skin.
Ran off, but left this symbol where he was standing.
Please reference. Will call later.

A few seconds later, Tucci wrote back that he would.
Leaving the hilltop, Elijah turned back to the crowd

on the other side of the farmhouse. And at long last he saw Hannah and Thomas standing with Abigail. Well, at least Hannah was safe. But this case was getting more complicated by the minute, and Eli was beginning to think that three days would never be enough to figure out the mysteries of Willow Trace.

Hannah stood away from the others, pretending to busy herself folding and refolding a quilt that she and some of the other women had spent the afternoon working on, all the while staying close enough to listen while Elijah and Thomas talked.

"I have a meet with the elders this evening," Thomas said to Elijah. "Mother wants to tag along and chat with the other women. If you and your sister would be good enough to take Hannah back to Nolt Cottage, we'd welcome both of you as our guests tonight."

"We'd be delighted to take Hannah home," Abigail answered quickly.

"Denki," Hannah said to Abigail. She did not look at Elijah for fear Thomas would see those feelings in her, which she did not want exposed.

"I will join you soon." Thomas turned and left them.

Abigail smiled and sang a sweet tune as she checked the hitch and reins, readying the buggy for the drive home. Hannah hoped they would allow her to sit in the back. She couldn't imagine a twenty-minute ride giving Elijah Miller the view of her bare neck. She was uncomfortable merely thinking of it. Even now as he took the quilt from her hands to place it in the carriage, she felt herself trembling with nerves.

"Here you go, brother." Abigail handed him the reins. "I hope you remember how to drive."

"Huh? Where are *you* going?" His face showed genuine confusion.

"Mr. Phelps's cousin from Indiana is visiting for the spring. He's a widower," she explained. "He's asked me to Strasbourg this evening for an ice cream."

"You're going on a date?" Elijah's eyes widened.

"We call it courtin'." She smiled at Hannah. "Make sure he doesn't traumatize my mare, would ya? I'll see you all first thing in the morning. Thank Thomas for his kind offer, but my house is much closer to Strasbourg than yours. I like Mr. Phelps, but I don't know if I like him enough to drive me all the way back to Nolt Cottage. Anyway, once he sees that Hannah is five times sweeter and prettier than I am, he'll be inviting her for an ice cream. So I might as well enjoy the attention while I can."

"Not so." Hannah blushed. How could Abigail say such a thing?

Abigail gave her brother a hug and headed down the long line of buggies toward the Phelps family.

Elijah turned to her and offered her a hand up into the buggy. His light touch over her fingers sent a tingle across her arm.

"You enjoyed the gathering?" she said.

"I did." He moved in beside her and tapped the reins to Abigail's mare, urging the horse forward.

They rode in silence, one by one separating from the other family buggies. Evening was upon them. The sun had sunk low and filled the sky with a purple glow. Every so often he glanced at her, his eyes bright and his smile dazzling in the evening shadows.

"So, it was *gut* to see your family?" she repeated, feeling that such a long silence had become awkward.

"Yes. It was fine." His head dropped a little. "Although my *Dat* came to the gathering, ya know?"

"I did not know," she said with a smile. "I did not see him there. But he came to greet you. How nice—"

"He didn't come to greet me, Hannah," Elijah interrupted. "He came to say that I have three days to find out whatever I need to know and then I have to leave whether I'm finished or not. So now might be a good time for you to tell me all about that journal and everything else."

"Yes. I would have done so this morning but Nana came in. Then you and Mr. McClendon went to the stable to…" A dry lump filled her throat. "So, how did you know about the journal?"

"I could hear you," he explained. "I could hear you and Thomas talking this morning over breakfast."

"Everything?" Heat crept up her neck as she remembered Thomas's jealousy and innuendos of her feelings toward Elijah.

"I heard what I needed to hear," he said.

What was that supposed to mean? She turned away, her face flushing with warmth. She was thankful Mary and Margaret the gossips weren't there to see her blushing.

"And a good thing, too," he continued, oblivious of her embarrassment. "With only three days to figure out what's going on around here, I can't afford to waste a second. Neither can you. Don't play games, Hannah. I need to know everything, so start talking. Don't leave out a thing."

"I do not play games, as you say."

He cut his eyes at her. He was not happy.

"I have wanted to tell you, Elijah. It's just that…" She pressed her lips together. "I didn't realize the danger."

"Obviously."

"You have to understand we thought we were doing the right thing in protecting our traditions and keeping all of this out of the press. Seems ignorant now. I apologize." She looked off into the evening, thinking sadly about her stepdaughter. "In any case, I don't know about a journal. When the man last night asked for one, it was the first time I had ever heard of such a thing. But that doesn't mean she did not have one. Maybe her friends would know about it. I saw you talking with them."

"They said they didn't know about a journal. I asked. But I don't know that they were telling the absolute truth."

Hannah looked down, shaking her head. She should have known her own daughter better. "She was on *Rumspringa*. I gave her every freedom. I did not ask questions or give her cautions. I should have."

"Hannah, I know you want to blame yourself, but until you know what you're dealing with, I think that's premature and, frankly, it's a waste of the little time we have to get this straight." His eyes stayed focused on the road. "I think we should make a search for this journal. If she had one, it must be around somewhere. But hidden in a place where you and Thomas and Nana Ruth would never look."

"How about in the barn since I found her there? Maybe the person who hit me the morning I found Jessica was already looking for this journal when I arrived for milking."

"There was someone in the barn when you found the body? I don't remember reading that in the police report. Well, if you could call that a report. Did you know that Jessica's friends haven't even been questioned about Jessica before?"

"No. They wouldn't have been. McClendon knew we didn't want an investigation."

"Then what? He changed his mind and had the governor send me here?"

"I do not know about that." Hannah stopped a moment, realizing why maybe the horse sale to the governor might have seemed relevant. But what could Thomas possibly have to do with this? "And McClendon didn't even know about the person in the barn. So it would not have been in the police report. I didn't tell anyone but Thomas. And he—"

"Told you not to tell anyone?"

"Jah." Hannah dropped her head. "Like I said. We did not know the danger."

"Someone attacked you in the barn and you didn't think there was a danger?"

"I'm sorry, Elijah. I don't understand any of this, either. That much I can promise you."

"I know."

"What about the journal?"

"I don't know if the journal would actually be in the barn. Whoever is after it most likely already looked there, and we know they haven't found it."

Hannah looked down. "Can I ask you something which I do not understand?"

"Sure."

"Why do you think they brought her to us and left her in the barn? Thomas said that she could not have died in the barn because there was not enough blood. God forbid, if someone did kill her and they did it somewhere else, why bring her home?"

"A good question. And unfortunately there could be a million answers to that. For example, to look for this so-called journal. To scare you. Because the Amish don't pursue killers and that would give the event a low profile. Can you imagine the press if she'd been found outside the community?"

"I cannot." She knew very little of the world outside Willow Trace. How different she was from Elijah. How naive and simple he must find her.

"Whatever the reason, it is a threat that says, 'We can get to you.' As they keep proving over and over."

A threat. Hannah swallowed hard. "I—I hadn't thought about that," she said.

"And a black car? Like the one Nicholas saw? You saw one, didn't you?"

She nodded. "I'm sorry. I should have told you as soon as you arrived. It's just that I'd promised Thomas."

She went on to tell Elijah about Jessica's strange behavior before her death. He listened in a detached, businesslike manner, which felt cold to her after his tenderness to her the evening before. That should not make her sad, she told herself. But then again, since he'd arrived her thoughts were not always where they should be.

"Tell me more about Daniel Hostetler. Why did Jessica break it off with him?"

Hannah shook her head. "I do not have an answer to that. She told me that she didn't want to spend her whole *Rumspringa* in the same courtship—that she needed to branch out. That always seemed less than the complete truth to me. But like I said, I didn't push her."

"Was it like Jessica to want to take a break? To want to have a lot of freedom?"

"No. It wasn't. She was very much like me in that way. Very loyal. No matter what people are saying about her now."

"You consider yourself loyal?" Elijah huffed.

"I don't want to quarrel about the past." *And I don't want to cry in front of you again.* But she felt the tears coming. His comment, though, almost made her angry. He could think what he wanted. He didn't know she thought not only for herself but for him, too. He didn't know she couldn't have children. That she could never give him the family he'd said he wanted. And he had wanted a family. He had told her that many times when they talked of their future together.

"I don't, either, Hannah. It's okay. You did hurt me, but that was a long time ago. I was torn between the two worlds and you made the decision easy. If you and I had married, well…it doesn't matter."

"It was not an easy decision." She blinked back the tears. "But you know how I made it?"

"I don't. I don't think we've talked much since," he teased.

"*Jah,* that is true."

"So, tell me…why Peter?"

"He needed me more than you did."

"Because of Jessica?"

She nodded. "I couldn't imagine leaving her. I didn't want to leave her. And Peter, God rest his soul, was a good man and a good father and a good husband."

Elijah turned to her. He reached for her hand and gave it a squeeze. "You made a good choice, Hannah. I never questioned that. I just missed you."

"I am sorry—" Hannah shook her head.

"It was the right choice, Hannah. We don't need to talk of it again," he said. "I'll be gone soon and all will be as it was. You'll marry Thomas soon. He loves you. And I'll go back to doing the work that God called me to do."

You are wrong. You have come back into my life

now. Nothing will be as it was. She kept her thoughts inside and turned her head so that he might not read them from her expression. "And you? Any hope for a family? I was most surprised yesterday when you said that you did not have any children."

Eli laughed. "I did used to talk of that, didn't I? No. Never happened. I probably work too hard and what woman could put up with me for a lifetime? And children are such a handful—I'd probably make a mess of being a parent."

She smiled. "Jessica was wonderful. But I suppose there was much I did not know about her. I saw you talking to her friends. I wanted so badly to ask them questions myself. But I know that would only create more talk."

"Did you know Jessica had a friend named Brittney in the city?"

Hannah turned to him wide-eyed. "No. In the city? I didn't even know she had been to the city."

She tried not to feel hurt by discovering that Jessica had kept secrets from her. It was normal for a girl at that age to break away from her parents. But it all seemed so shocking and unexpected. At least, it took her mind from thoughts of Elijah. Well, sort of.

"Would it make you feel better to travel with me into Philadelphia tomorrow? My partner, Mitchell Tucci, is finding out where this young lady lives—this friend of Jessica's. I'm going to find her and see what she knows. I think you should come with me."

"Me? In the city?" Hannah almost laughed.

"Yes. You in the city."

"I don't know. I doubt Thomas will agree."

"Well, then I'll just have to insist— Whoooooah, girl!" Elijah grasped at the reins as Abigail's mare spooked and pulled the vehicle so hard to the left that Hannah slammed up against his side. Her stomach leapt into her throat.

"We need to turn here." She pointed to the gravel path to the Nolts' cottage. "If you can manage it."

"The mare does seem mighty reluctant, doesn't she?" Elijah held fast to the reins and steadied the horse. She slowed her steps and proceeded but with much hesitation. Elijah tapped her rear with his crop and urged her on again with a strong voice. "You know my car never fights me like this."

"Maybe you're just out of practice." Hannah reached over. "Hand me the reins I'll take it from here."

"Are you kidding me? I used to race these buggies." He kept the reins from her. "I haven't forgotten a thing."

"I remember." She eyed him. "I remember you used to lose races."

They both laughed. He looked down on her with a kind smile. The first one he'd shown her since the ride home started. A spark of heat flushed through her core.

Three days, she reminded herself. In three days Elijah Miller would be back in the city where he belonged. He wasn't one of them. She knew that fact as well as he did. They had made their choices years ago and could never be together now. No matter what her heart seemed to be thinking.

Hannah's laughter sounded sweet to his ears. He would gladly have listened to it all evening. Every evening. Any evening, for that matter.

Time with family, good hard work, fine people with no agenda other than to help one another, Hannah's smile and laughter—those were things that would have been a part of his life every day if she'd agreed to marry him, if he hadn't left the *Ordnung.* Boy! Today had been a big fat dose of all the things he missed. Part of him wanted to share all that was in his heart with Hannah and tell her how the experience had moved him—how she moved him. How he loved the chance just to sit next to her in the buggy. Alone. Listening to her laugh and catching flashes of her beautiful smile.

But the other part of him was wary and bitter. And angry at his own heart for being so tender toward her. He couldn't take any more tears and confessions. She had crushed his feelings, refused him, yet made it impossible for him to love another woman. And now with one explanation, with one breath he was forgiving her everything? Inviting her to the city with him? Sitting beside her and thinking of nothing but how sweet her laughter was? Maybe three days was too long for his weakening heart. Maybe he was in more danger than Hannah—in danger of falling in love and getting hurt again.

Just get her back to the cottage, Miller, he told himself. If only this silly mare of Abigail's could keep a steady pace, he would. But as it was, he could barely keep her moving straight ahead. Hannah seemed amused by the animal's behavior, but more and more Elijah was beginning to suspect there was something to the horse's skittishness.

"I should have insisted we take my car," he muttered under his breath, grabbing the blanket from the back of the buggy—the blanket that concealed his Glock 19. He thought of the man on the hill who'd disappeared. A lookout to see when they were coming? To be sure they hadn't been at home? There was something to it. "I have a bad feeling about this."

"Maybe the mare is not used to being driven at night?" Hannah suggested.

"No. Something's not right." His body tensed. "She sees or smells something we don't."

"Like an animal?"

"Yes." *A two-legged one,* he wanted to say, but didn't want to scare her in case he was merely being paranoid. If they could just get past this front part of the farm where the woods were thick and enclosed them, he'd feel much better. But there was another five hundred yards or so to go and—

Eli caught a flash of movement in his peripheral, something shiny in the forest reflecting the buggy's headlights. He stiffened. He wasn't being paranoid. Someone was there. Animals didn't run around in the woods with shiny metal.

"Sit back, Hannah." He cracked his whip over the mare again, asking her to move forward. The faster they got through that canopy of trees, the better. The mare bolted forward as if she sensed danger, too.

Even Hannah seemed on alert. She grabbed on to his arm. "You're right! There's a car coming at us!"

Eli spotted the car but it was too late. Its lights flashed bright as it tore out of the woods and turned directly toward their buggy. Elijah could see nothing but white. His ears heard nothing but Hannah's scream.

The mare whinnied, jerked forward, then kicked back. The front of the buggy lifted from the ground, then titled to the right as the horse balked again and pulled them toward the grassy ditch. The car continued straight for them. Elijah reached for Hannah. It looked like they would have to jump. He pulled her against him, but hesitated as the car swerved hard to the left at the last second, just missing the horse.

The car did not, however, miss hitting the buggy. Its back fender caught the front left wheel and the wooden spokes crunched and split like twigs.

"Take the reins," he shouted to Hannah.

Elijah aimed his Glock at the back of the vehicle. Time to find out who that was and put an end to all of these unwanted visits to Lancaster. How dare anyone come into this safe haven and cause such havoc and fear to the people he loved? Anger pulsed hot through his veins as he shot at the car's back tire. The driver shot back, hitting the taillight on the buggy. It shattered to bits, exploding like the anger inside him. He fired again. This time he succeeded in blowing out the back left wheel, which caused the car to spin. The driver could no longer shoot but was forced to focus on steering. Elijah knew if could also hit the front tire he could possibly stall the car and driver long enough to approach them. Elijah raised his gun to the front end of the car, but the swaying buggy wouldn't give him a clean shot.

Hannah had not been able to take control of the reins. Unguided, the mare recoiled at the gunfire and tugged the collapsing buggy farther into the ditch. Elijah swept his hand down to grab the loose reins, but there was nothing to be done—the buggy was toppling over.

"Jump!" He took hold of Hannah's arm and pulled her from the moving vehicle.

Chapter Ten

Elijah took hold of Hannah's arm with a strong grip and lifted her from the floor of the buggy. As the vehicle began to roll on its side, he pushed her through the driver's-side door, then followed with a great leap of his own. They hit the gravel path as the buggy tumbled and slid into the deep ditch.

"You okay?"

Hannah didn't answer. Ignoring the gravel that seemed to have embedded itself in her palms and face as it had his own, she hopped up and raced toward the front of the buggy.

"What are you doing?" he called after her. "You're going to get hurt." She was much too close to the anxious mare, which seemed to be pinned under the hitch. "Let her calm down."

"She can't calm down. She has to be set free. Otherwise she'll hurt or kill herself, if she hasn't already." Hannah moved on, ignoring him as she reached for something behind the crazed beast. Elijah cringed but moved in behind her, ready to yank her from harm's way if need be.

"Hannah, come on away from there. Let her be."

But determined to help the stressed horse, she continued to bend over the joint, working her arm at the hitch and harness.

Stubborn woman.

Finally a *click* sounded and Abigail's mare took off down the road at a full gallop, still in her harness with the reins flapping behind her. Within seconds she was out of sight.

"She could still hurt herself." Hannah turned as he sidled up next to her. "But chances are she'll find her way home or to another barn and we'll get her back."

Elijah didn't care about the mare. He didn't care about the trashed buggy or Thomas or Abigail or his *Dat*. He didn't care about anything that had been on his mind of late. He put his hands on her arms and pulled her closer. "We could have been crushed. That was no grazing bullet. That was meant to end us. What do these people want, Hannah? Tell me now so that I can help you." *I don't want to lose you again.*

"I don't know. I don't know." She trembled against him. "I told you everything."

He pressed her closer—close enough to feel her breath on his shoulder. Close enough to take in her scent and feel her warmth. Together they stood in each other's arms, trembling.

Hannah tried to wiggle from his tight embrace, but he knew she needed to feel him as much as he needed her. She was as frightened as that mare. As he stroked her shoulder, she relaxed and leaned against him, her wet, warm tears soaking the collar of his shirt.

"I've lost everything," she whispered. "Everything."

Her words and the feel of her against him slowed his racing adrenaline. "I felt like that a bit today, Hannah. Looking around at all I gave up when I left here. You have lost a lot. But you haven't lost everything. You still have your love and compassion and your drive to help others. You have a lot, Hannah Kurtz."

She laughed as he used her maiden name. "No one has called me that in a long, long time."

"Yeah, well, you'll always be Hannah Kurtz to me. No matter who you marry."

He tightened his arms around her. He kissed the top of her head. How he had loved this woman—and how he loved her still. It made him ache to see her suffering so deeply. Anger and fear coursed through him, too. This was his home, his people and his heritage. This was Hannah, *his* Hannah. He would keep her safe—even though he'd never see her again after these three days.

"Lord, give Hannah the strength to endure this hard time in her life. Keep her safe and protect her from these people who wish her harm. Lead us to this journal so we can move forward and restore the joy in living for You."

Hannah nodded her head against his chest, as he prayed, her tears still streaming. "Thank you, Elijah Miller. Thank you for being here with me at this time. I know that the Lord has brought you to me."

"I wouldn't be anywhere else," he whispered. "Now let's get you home." He took a flashlight from the broken buggy and turned them down the path, the flashlight in one hand, Hannah's hand in his other.

With each step toward Nolt Cottage, Hannah's fear and panic slipped away. Elijah's hand seemed to feed her his strength and courage as they walked together. The other more tender sentiments released from his touch she tried to dismiss.

"I'm glad Thomas and Nana Ruth will be coming to

the cottage from the other direction. I wouldn't want them to see the wreckage."

Eli nodded, looking back at the destroyed buggy. "I know. And I dread telling Abby."

"Abigail will understand. And if I know Thomas, he will take care of everything for her. That's how he is." She stopped and pressed her lips together. "Your prayer was most kind. I didn't know you were still in the faith."

"Living in the world doesn't mean I have to be of the world," he said. "It's harder. There's more distractions to be sure, but I think in the end not joining the church has made my faith strong, not weakened it."

Hannah almost smiled. "But that doesn't fit too well with Amish thinking, does it?"

"No. I don't suppose it does. I guess you could say I have a tolerance for other life choices. I think there are good English people who love God as much as we do. For me, being Amish isn't a choice to have faith or not to have faith," he said. "It's a choice of how and maybe even where we are called to live."

"But how do you give reason for the gun and the taking of human life? This is a part of your job, no?"

"No. Well, the gun, yes. But the gun is for protection. I've never killed anyone. Don't want to, either."

"Would you? Would you kill someone? You fired the gun tonight, did you not?"

"I shot at the tires of the car. I was trying to stop them. Not kill them. But I'm not so sure they weren't trying to kill us this time."

"They weren't before?"

"I don't think so. Tonight was different. The attack, it was much more aggressive. More risky. More dangerous. They have upped the ante and I don't know why.

Maybe we are on to them and we don't even know it."
He laughed.

"On to them? Upped the ante? Sometimes it's hard
to remember you were here among us once."

"Sometimes I feel that way. But not today, Hannah.
Not today. The gathering was nice. Thank you for in-
sisting that I go. I'm glad I did."

"I knew you would be…and seeing your *Dat?* Not
as bad as you anticipated, no?"

"The verdict is still out on that."

"There you go again, with your strange expressions."

Elijah stopped on the gravel path and turned his head
toward the horse stable. "Is that…?"

She followed his dark gaze to the holding pen. Abigail's chestnut mare paced back and forth in front of
the gate. "I told you she wouldn't go far. Let's go and
bring her in."

They made their way behind the horse, guided her to
the holding pen, then removed her harness. She snorted
and paced between them still very agitated, but at least
they had found her.

"I'll go fetch a lantern from the kitchen. Then we can
take her to a stall and give her some hay. She will feel
better to be with the other horses inside, *jah?*" Hannah
gave him a slight smile, glad to have a task to fix her
mind on. She turned away toward the house.

Elijah grabbed her by the elbow. "You're braver than
you should be. I'll go with you."

She did not like the wariness in his eyes. They'd already been attacked and shot at. What else could happen in one evening? It must have been tiresome to go
through life worried about one's safety at every turn.
Hannah had always been thankful for the safe haven
that was her Amish community, but now even more so.

If this was what life was like on the outside, she wanted no part of it. Elijah's presence might produce sparks in her heart, but she would forgo that for a quiet place to serve the Lord. Right? Yes. She was sure of it. Perhaps she'd always been sure of it and that's why she'd chosen Jessica and Peter. Oh, why did she keep going back to that moment so long ago? Clearly, Elijah had let it go. Why couldn't she?

Eli walked quickly to the dark cottage. She could barely keep pace with his long strides. And despite her momentary flash of confidence, angst crept into her skin and filled her senses. Eli seemed tense, as well.

"What is it?" she asked.

"I thought I heard something." He reached back and took her hand.

"Fear thou not; for I am with thee," she began her favorite verse. *"Be not—"*

"Be not dismayed; for I am thy God," Eli interrupted. *"I will strengthen thee; yea, I will help thee; yea, I will uphold thee with the right hand of my righteousness."*

Hannah swallowed hard, looking up into his beautiful blue eyes. Remorse for the pain she'd caused him all those years ago sank her heart low and she closed her eyes against her regret.

"Don't fall apart on me now." He moved closer, offering his embrace but not forcing it upon her.

Hannah stepped back. "I'm—I'm sorry. I am just glad you are come. So glad you are here."

"Me, too." Eli tilted his head and lifted his arms again.

This time, Hannah sank into his embrace. She placed her hands on his chest and felt the steady beat of his heart. His arms surrounded her. And she felt...she felt safe.

After a long moment, he lifted her hand to his lips

and kissed her fingers gently. "You need to rest, Hannah. You must be—"

Crash! They turned toward the back door. Something inside the house had fallen. Something big and heavy.

"Can't seem to get a break, can we?" Elijah slipped his gun from its holster and slid open the back kitchen door.

"I didn't know you had brought the gun," she whispered.

"Would you feel better if I had left it in the buggy?" He stared back at her.

She shook her head no. She had to admit that although the gun made her uneasy, she would have felt worse without it. Once inside the kitchen, she clicked on the overhead oil-powered lights.

As soft light spilled over the room, they each sucked in a quick breath. Elijah was right to have followed her to the house. Someone had most definitely been inside and probably still was.

Chapter Eleven

"I think they're gone," Elijah whispered, putting an arm around Hannah as the tears spilled over her cheeks.

The house was a horrible chaos. Not one thing seemed to be in place. Tables and chairs had been overturned. The cupboard emptied. Flour and oats and other grains tossed and spread across the hardwood floors. The upholstered sofa had been shredded with a knife and unstuffed. Broken plates and kitchen utensils were strewn about. But the crash had come from the corner where Daniel Hostetler sat bound, gagged and duct-taped to one of the kitchen chairs. It looked as if in trying to free himself he'd turned his chair over and landed on his side.

Eli rushed to the young man and carefully lifted the tape from his mouth. "You okay?"

He nodded.

"Who did this? Are they still here?"

"I don't know. I don't think so."

Elijah frowned as he began to cut the boy loose. "So, what happened? How did you get here like this?"

Elijah righted the chair and helped Daniel up and into it, as there was nowhere else to sit. When Daniel

did not answer, Elijah righted a few of the other chairs
and pulled one next to the kid.

"Listen, Daniel, I let you run off earlier today, but I
shouldn't have. Whatever you know about all this, you
need to come clean. Now."

The kid swallowed hard. He lifted his eyes to Hannah, then back to Elijah. "But I—I don't really know
anything."

Elijah folded his arms over his chest. "Then how did
you end up here and in this chair?"

He looked at Hannah. There was shame in his eyes.
Slowly, he reached into his shirt and pulled out a cloth
bag with a drawstring top. "I—I was returning this."

Elijah took the bag and opened it. Inside was a large
amount of cash in hundreds.

"Thomas's money!" Hannah ran over to the boy, covering her mouth with one hand. "Oh, Daniel, it was *you*
in the house last night. I knew I had heard the voice
before." She paused and looked confused. "But why?
Why did you come in the night? Why not just come and
ask for what you need? Why sneak in and scare me to
death and hurt me? Thomas is always generous with
his earnings. You must know that."

Daniel's head dropped below his shoulders, but still
he said nothing.

"That's it." Elijah stood, grabbed his phone from his
pocket and showed it to the kid. "Time to call Chief
McClendon."

"No. Please. No." Daniel's voice sounded panicked.
"They'll kill Mrs. Nolt. They'll kill me. I promised them
I wouldn't talk to the police. They're watching me. I
saw them at the gathering."

"The man on the hill?"

Daniel nodded. "Please don't call the police."

"So, who are these people? Why would they want to kill you or Hannah or Jessica? What is this journal that you keep talking about?"

"I don't know." He shrugged. "But Jessica took it and she shouldn't have. We have to find it. *I* have to find it."

"Did they say what's in this journal?" What could a young Amish girl take from *Englischers* that would have them willing to kill?

Daniel shook his head. "I don't know. I don't know," he said, nearly crying now. "They just keep telling me to get it."

Eli sighed heavily. He sat back in the chair across from Daniel, then motioned for Hannah to sit also. "Why don't you start at the beginning, Daniel? Don't leave out a thing. When and how did these people come into your lives?"

Daniel nodded. "Well, you know that Jessica told me to not come a-callin' on her anymore. At first, I thought this was just her way. You know, to take some time and think us over a bit before we could…well, before we get real serious. But then I find out that she's going into town every chance she gets. I could not think why she would do this but that she had found herself another beau. So I—I followed her to town on the train one night."

"When was this, Daniel? What night?" Elijah asked.

"Two weeks ago."

Hannah covered her mouth again, this time to muffle a sob.

"Okay. Keep going," Elijah prompted him.

"So, she took the train. I followed her. She carried a large bag and walked fast. Many blocks. I could hardly keep up with her. She seemed very…enthusiastic. I think she must be off to elope or run away. I was so angry and so broken."

Broken. Elijah glanced at Hannah. He remembered feeling broken himself at that age. The moment Hannah had told him she'd accepted Peter's proposal.

"Finally I catch up to her," he continued, "and ask her what she is doing. I tell her she is stupid, acting like a child and should come home with me now."

The more Daniel talked, the more Hannah tensed. Elijah reached a hand over and touched her shoulder. "Are you sure you want to hear all of this?"

She nodded. "Yes. What did my daughter say?" She looked to Daniel.

"She told me to go home. That I was going to ruin everything. I asked, what can I ruin? She was ruining everything all by herself. But she says I don't know anything. That she is making a difference. Whatever that meant. Then she just keeps going. I followed her to a big apartment building. Outside, there are some boys, men really, mean-looking, bully-types. I am scared for her. But she goes through them like nothing. They say hi to her and let her pass. But it's not so easy for me.

"They stop me. They take my hat. They push me. Make me go on my knees. They are going to beat me. But Jessica returns and tells them not to waste time. She and another girl. This other girl tells them to walk me to the train and make sure I get on."

"Another girl?" Elijah asked.

"Yes, I think they called her Brit."

"Brittney Baker?"

"Yes. Maybe. I don't know. But she came out, like I said, with Jessica. Then I was walked to the train and forced on by these boys."

"Did Jessica come home with you?"

He shook his head. "No. She didn't even go to the station. She stayed with her fancy friend."

"Did you ever see Jessica again?"

Daniel paused, looking from Hannah to him and back again to Hannah.

"We need to know the truth, Daniel. The more I know, the better I can help you…and Hannah." Eli tried to give an encouraging look to help the boy to trust him. "This isn't about you getting into trouble. This is about stopping a killer. You have to understand that."

Daniel still hesitated.

Hannah leaned forward and touched the boy's knee. "It's okay, Daniel. I know that you loved her. And she loved you, too. I don't blame you for following her."

A tear rolled down the boy's smooth cheek.

"When did you last see her?" Eli asked again.

"I did not see her again." Daniel stared at the floor, avoiding Eli's gaze.

Elijah sighed. The boy was lying or leaving something out. "But you went back to the city?"

Daniel lifted his eyes, then froze when they reached Elijah's gaze. "I did. I went back to the city after…after Jessica was found. I wanted to know who this friend was. Why Jessica had left me. Why I'd lost her." He dropped his head in his hands. "Jessica was gone—I couldn't ask her. And I had to know."

"What happened when you went back? Did you talk to Jessica's friend?"

He nodded, looking away. "Yes. She looked bad, this time. Not like before. There was a cut on her face. And she wouldn't tell me anything about Jessica or what had happened that night. And then those boys come again and they made me leave."

"They beat you up?"

"*Jah.* They said that if I didn't find this journal, I'd end up like Jessica. When I told them I didn't know where or what it was, they said to ask her mama. One of them held a gun to my head and pulled the trigger just to scare me."

"Is that who came here today?"

"I don't know. But I don't think so. Those boys they talk like kids, you know…"

"Street. They talk street."

"*Jah,* they talk street. Very hard to understand. But the men tonight. They sound older. Educated. Good English. Not street."

Elijah shook his head. Was this kid telling the truth? If so, this story painted a rather grim picture of Jessica—stealing, lying, involved with a gang.

He didn't know exactly what he'd expected to find out about Jessica—perhaps that she'd been dragged into the city, forced somehow—certainly not that she'd taken a train there alone. Intentionally.

"Do you know the address of the apartments you went to when you followed her?"

"Kensington. From the train stop, it was three blocks west and two north. There was a restaurant across the street called the Imperial."

One of the worst parts of town. Elijah pulled his phone from his pocket.

"Pease don't tell the police about me," Daniel said. "Please."

Elijah could see the fear in the boy's eyes.

He walked to the corner of the room and called his partner. "More bad news here," he said to Tucci, catching him up on the case. "How about on your end?"

"It's pretty interesting, Miller," Tucci said. "I got the info on your symbol and on your girl. First of all, there are about twenty Brittney Bakers in Philadelphia, but only one with a record and between the ages of thirteen and twenty. So I figured that must be her."

"Got an address?"

"Yes," Tucci said, "4203 Yanger Street, number 502, across from the Imperial."

Then that part of Daniel's story was true. Yanger Street was exactly three blocks from the train at Broad. It was also the worst area of the city—the roughest and dirtiest. It was no place for a young girl and certainly no place for an Amish one. Elijah glanced back at Daniel and Hannah still sitting in the corner. Maybe the kid *was* telling the truth. But that prospect made his stomach churn for Hannah's sake. It was so important to her that she'd been a good mother, that she'd done all the right things, that Jessica had been a good girl. He knew this story of Daniel's must have been the hardest for her to hear.

"Why is she on record?"

"She's run away from home four times," Tucci said. "One time she was gone for a month. Got all the way to New York. She was working the streets."

Elijah rubbed his face. That was not anything he wanted to share with Hannah. "What's up with her home life? Why run?"

"There's not much there, only that she lives with the dad, who is really the second stepdad. No record of the actual father," Tucci said. "But this guy is acting guardian and get this—he is former D.C. Metro. His name is Jackson. Had some serious charges brought up against him three years ago, so he resigned from the force. He's been off the grid ever since. Supposedly, he's working as a security guard for Philadelphia Party Rentals Incorporated. I found a huge file on him, pictures included. I'm going to forward it to you."

"I don't have internet out here."

"Your BlackBerry, man."

He laughed. "I'll have to sit back out in my car and recharge. So, what about the symbol?"

"I'm getting to that. The symbol, turns out, is the marketing logo for a Fortune 500 company called Dutch Confidential. They own and operate a lot of business up and down the east coast, but mostly they work in electronic security systems. But guess what else they own? Philadelphia Party Rentals."

"The company that Brittney's stepdad works for as a security guard, right?"

"Right."

"Hmm. Why does a party rental operation need an ex-cop or security guard working there?"

"Exactly. I was wondering the same thing. So I called a friend of mine at Metro and he said this guy, Jackson, is slick—a dirty cop with big-time connections. Watch your back, Miller."

"Will do." Elijah folded the phone and put it back into his pocket. Slowly, he walked back to Hannah and Daniel, wondering what to do next. He could clean up the house. Get Abigail's buggy from the ditch before Thomas would be left to deal with it. Or he could tell Hannah that exactly what she feared most was true— that Jessica had befriended some pretty bad people.

Hannah wasn't sure what she thought of Daniel's story. It surprised her that Elijah had not called Chief McClendon to make a report, neither about the ransacked house nor about Daniel's participation in the whole affair. When Thomas and Nana returned, he solicited Daniel's help in pulling the broken buggy back to the barn and later in cleaning up the house.

Nana and Thomas remained quiet as they all worked to restore order to their home. It was late when Elijah drove Daniel home. Even later when he returned and they all went to bed.

Another short night and Hannah did not sleep well even knowing Elijah had camped out on their living room floor in order to watch all points of entry into the downstairs.

He was still sleeping when she descended to help with morning milking. She stopped and studied the angular cut of his jaw. A warm pang flashed through her belly. She leaned forward and replaced the quilt, which had fallen from his shoulders. Her fingers brushed over his tight chest.

"You do not need to help with milking, Hannah." Thomas stood at the bottom stair, rolling up the cuff of his sleeves. Disapproval in his eyes. "Our nephew Samuel is coming. You could sleep another hour."

Hannah shrank away from Elijah. Once again she had hurt Thomas's feelings and looked ungrateful for all he had done for her. How he must loathe her and think her a reckless woman. Was she? She had always been so prudent in her actions, as a youth and as a woman. Had that changed? Had seeing Elijah again made her forget her place? She prayed it was not so but that she acted only in sisterly love for her old friend even though she knew that in this matter, her head and heart were not in agreement.

"You must be glad your money has been returned," she said, wondering what Thomas thought of last night's events. "Will you go to the elders with what the boy has done? And with the break-in?"

"I will not. This is Elijah's puzzle to solve. I want only that you are safe. If he sees no need for it, then I do not, either." He turned away, placing his straw hat over his long brown locks. "Anyway, the youth seemed punished enough in his fear. His involvement with my own niece forced his behavior. I cannot punish him for that. He will work the next two Saturdays with me in the fields. And I will welcome his help."

She bowed her head to him, then scurried to the kitchen and began to brew the tea and coffee. "I am glad your money has been restored. You are a good steward."

"The money belongs to God." He corrected her praise, as such things were not to be said aloud. "Even when it is taken, it belongs to God. But since it is again in my care, I have an idea. We will purchase a new buggy for Abigail. And when you return from the city, she will take my dun-colored gelding. He is an easy fellow—a much better match for her than that young, green mare. We will keep the mare for training and return her smooth and steady in a year's time."

Hannah was not surprised by Thomas's generosity. He was a good man. She *was* surprised that he had approved the plan that she go into the city with Elijah and Abigail. Elijah must have spoken with him last night. She had not really agreed to go, and after the break-in and the story from Daniel, it did not seem the rational thing to do. "Thomas, I have no desire to go into the city. You must know that. I admit I wonder what Jessica had gotten involved in, but I am perfectly satisfied to let Elijah find those answers on his own. I have plenty to tend to here."

"I do not care for you to go to the city, either, Hannah, but I think perhaps you are safer with Elijah. I am not trained in the ways of the world as our friend is. I must trust you to him for the day. And I do trust him. It seems his intentions toward you and his motivations for being here are truly noble. I understand as well as any man wanting to prove that past choices were justified. Be careful." He tipped his hat to her. "I will take no breakfast this morning. Good day."

As he left through the kitchen door, Hannah struggled to comprehend Thomas's meaning. After she and Nana had retired, the two men had spoken of the day's events and apparently of other things as well, such as her. She must conclude from Thomas's attitude and Elijah's words the previous night that Elijah had no lingering feelings for her. He was only there to prove to all of Willow Trace that his profession was respectable. She should be relieved that her heart was therefore not in danger, but she was not. She was disappointed, but that would pass. Elijah would go home when this journal or whatever was found, and she would stay there. The realization left Hannah feeling more alone than ever before.

Elijah watched as Hannah, seated beside him in the Mustang, clung with one hand to her starched prayer Kapp. A serene smile fixed on her lips. He wasn't sure if she enjoyed the open-top ride into town, but she had asked for it and he had obliged her. An occasional laugh slipping from her lips as Abigail leaned forward between the two of them, recounting the details of her "date" with Mr. Phelps. Although Elijah paid more attention to the way the sun sparkled over Hannah's porcelain skin. He studied the happy curve of her mouth. And when the wind would blow just the right way, her scent would tease him into wanting a taste of her lips and a touch of her hand.

Good thing he'd left Willow Trace when she married Peter. It would have been torturous being around her all the time with her married to someone else. It was hard enough being back there and even thinking about the fact that she would soon marry Thomas. Not that he didn't wish them well. He wanted Hannah to be happy and he obviously wasn't the man for that job. Didn't mean he loved her any less.

He'd been careful the night before to convince both Hannah and Thomas that he had no interest in a relationship beyond friendship with Hannah. But the truth was, he did. He missed home. He missed the Amish ways. He missed feeling that close to God all of the time. He missed Hannah.

But then there was his *Dat* who would never change his opinion. His father would never understand his calling to police work. He would never accept Eli back in Willow Trace. So there was no reason to even entertain the idea of making amends, much less bring it up with Hannah or his sister. Abigail would push him to come home, no doubt. But Hannah? She had tender feelings for him. That was clear. But she had always had those feelings and it didn't lead to anything before. Who was to say it would now? And if it didn't, could he take another rejection from the same woman? He wasn't willing to find out.

Once he knew Hannah would be safe again—that they *all* would be safe again—he would get as far away from Willow Trace as possible.

"So, no second outing with Mr. Phelps?" he teased his sister, trying to push his mind away from his own emotions.

"No. An old *Maidel* I am and always will be." Abigail laughed.

"And what about you, my brother? Have you never thought to take a wife?" she asked.

"No. I haven't really," he said. "I've been married to my job."

"That is a strange expression." Hannah turned to him. "Surely you do not mean that. In our spirit we should be married to Christ, no? Not our work."

Elijah swallowed hard. Hannah had misunderstood and his words had disappointed her. "Yes. It's a strange expression. I just meant that I spend more time working than I do courting."

"Oh, I see." That seemed to relieve her somewhat, but she still seemed a bit displeased. "But you used to want a family so badly. Is this not a desire of yours any longer?"

He wanted a family with *her* so badly. But he would not say that aloud, as she had chosen to have a family with someone else. "We want many things when we are young. But our paths don't always take us where we think they will," he said instead.

Hannah's face washed over with sadness. Of course, her path had brought her many losses. He should have been more careful of his words. He hadn't meant to upset her.

Abigail leaned up between them. "That's what makes life so exciting. You never know which way your path will go next. Who knows? God could have new spouses for us all."

Hannah didn't comment. She seemed to suddenly realize she was in the heart of downtown Philly.

"I'm sorry your first trip into the city is to this part of town," Elijah said to her.

"I only want to find out about Jessica," she answered.

"Are you sure this is the right address?" Abigail asked.

"Yes, this is the place." Elijah indicated a large high-rise apartment on the corner. He circled the block until he found a spot to parallel-park his car against the curb. "This neighborhood is worse than I remembered. Maybe you ladies would like to stay in the car? Abs, you remember how to drive, right?"

"No way. I wouldn't drive in all this traffic for anything. I'll take my chances on the street."

"Me, too." Hannah nodded, though he could see she was filled with fear. "I've come this far. I might as well meet this friend of Jessica's."

Eli nodded. He closed up the car and led the ladies to the front of the building. A group of young men appeared as they turned the corner. There were six of them, all wearing caps, chains and jeans so large they fell halfway down their thighs. Elijah could only assume it was the same welcoming gang that had escorted Daniel to the train.

When they saw that the three of them wanted to enter the building, they formed a barricade in front of the door.

"Can we help you?" one of them asked.

Elijah put the ladies behind him, standing like a wall in front of the gang of young men. "We're not here to make trouble. We're on a social call."

"A social call, huh?" the kid continued. "Perfect. 'Cause we are the social committee. Welcome to the hood."

Another young man in the group stepped forward. "Hey, guys, they dress like that other girl—remember? That girl with Brit?"

Elijah tried to remain calm. "You know an Amish girl?"

"We know everybody. Amish. Polish. Italian. It's our job."

"Yeah, it's our job to know everyone…especially the ladies."

"And these ladies are fine." One of the gang circled around and came close to both Hannah and Abigail. He reached out and touched Hannah's bare neck. She flinched, and lowered her eyes to the ground.

"Even under all that dress. Can't hide what looks fine," said another boy, joining his friend.

"Mmm-hmm," they hummed together. The two largest boys stepped between Elijah and the two women. Elijah was wishing he'd brought Tucci with them. At least then he would not feel so outnumbered and unable to protect both his sister and Hannah.

In any case, he did not want to fight with these hooligans in case they had any information about Jessica and the night she was killed. Possibly even they were the killers as Daniel had suggested. However, seeing them in person, he doubted that. He knew the type—at this age, they liked to throw their weight around, but they were mostly talk. They certainly didn't have the discipline yet to rise to any kind of high level within a gang. And that made him wonder if any information they had was worth subjecting Hannah and his sister to their rough language and crudeness.

He looked back to Hannah. "Let's just get inside. We can talk to them later if we need to," he whispered.

But the group had circled around them. They laughed and continued to make offensive suggestions.

"That's enough, guys," Elijah said. "Let the ladies pass. We have someone to talk to."

"You married to these girls?" one of them snarled. He reached out and touched the strings of Hannah's prayer *Kapp*.

"Who cares if I am or I ain't?" Elijah let his cop street training fall into practice. "I said to let the ladies pass or I'll—"

The most aggressive of the group pushed Elijah at the shoulder, knocking him back into the boys behind, who stiff-armed him, shoving him back forward. "Or you'll what, Blondie? We ain't afraid of you."

"You're assaulting a police officer," Abigail announced. "I'm a witness. How about you, Mrs. Nolt? Are you a witness?"

Hannah nodded, while Elijah reached into his coat.

"That true? You a cop?" one kid said. The others backed away.

Elijah pulled his ID card from his pocket and showed the boys.

"You Philadelphia P.D.?" the leader asked.

"That's what the card says, doesn't it?"

"I ain't never seen you on this street."

"I'm I.A."

"You don't look like no cop," he said.

"Look like one of those guys in a BVD ad," another said. The others laughed and snorted.

"Why are you here?" the leader said. "Nothing funny goes down on this block. You would know that if you were really Philly P.D."

"Like nothing funny happened here when an Amish girl came to visit, then returned home murdered?" Elijah asked.

The boys moved away faster. "Hey, we was just kidding. We don't know any Amish. We don't know what you talking 'bout, man."

"Tell me about Brittney Baker," Elijah said.

"What's there to tell?" one boy answered. "She lives here. We don't talk to her much. She's quiet, you know."

"That's not what we heard. We heard you are good friends and that you do anything she asks."

"Look, man, no one touches Brit. Her dad's..." He looked around to his friends, who had backed up even farther.

"Her dad is what?" Elijah pushed.

The kid eyed Hannah and Abigail, took a step backward and shrugged. Then he turned and hightailed it away from them as fast as possible, catching up to his buddies already a block away.

Chapter Twelve

Hannah looked over at Eli. "Are you okay?"

"More like are *you* okay?" Eli gave her a cockeyed smile. "I'm fine. But I am anxious to get going. We need to get to Brittney before she and her father hear that we're coming. Are you two able to handle that? Or was this too much already?"

"We are fine. Maybe not used to being eyed like animals for the purchase. But fine," Abigail answered.

"I will be fine." Hannah nodded. "This is why you did not tell them you were a police officer? Because they will bring more trouble? Do you not think that they—that they..."

"Killed Jessica?"

"No. I don't think they are killers. Not yet. They are just the lookout. Brittney's father must have some power over them. I'd guess they are on their way right now to warn him that we are here."

They entered the building and took an elevator to the fifth floor. The apartments had a strange odor, although the interior proved to be much nicer than what the outside had first promised. The paint was clean. The woodwork and carpets were fancy and colorful.

Elijah knocked at door 502. He held his little card to a
small glass hole in the center of the door and announced
himself as Detective Miller of the Philadelphia Police
Department. The door creaked open though it was still
connected to the wall by a link chain, as if someone
expected a person to knock and then come bursting
into the house. These English were most strange. She
didn't know how Elijah had made his way among them
for so many years.

"My stepfather isn't…" The dark-headed girl at the
door stopped speaking as her eyes fell on Hannah and
Abigail and their clothing.

Through the tiny slit of a doorway, Hannah could
tell the girl was thin and tall. And very pretty. Much
like the dark looks of her girl Jessica. Most certainly
they were close in age. Was this girl the reason for Jessica's death? Hannah bit her lip, trying to shut out the
wild surge of desperate emotions that filled her heart.

"Not here to see anyone's father. We're here to see
Brittney Baker," Elijah said. "Are you Brittney Baker?"

The girl was wide-eyed. "Why do you need to talk
to Brittney Baker?"

"We understand that she's friends with a girl named
Jessica Nolt. We have some questions for her."

The girl seemed to consider his words for a few seconds, and then the door closed fast. Hannah heard the
metal of the chain slinking behind the door, and then the
girl opened it again, completely, and bade them enter,
but only into the foyer.

"I haven't seen Jessica in a week." She stared at Hannah. "Are you her mom? She said her mom was young
and had green eyes."

"Are you Brittney Baker?" Elijah asked before Hannah could reply.

"Yeah, I'm Brittney." She shuffled her weight from side to side and pulled the small, short jacket tight around her shoulders. "So what?"

"Can we ask you a few questions about Jessica? It won't take long."

She nodded, albeit reluctantly.

"Tell us about the last time you saw her," Elijah said.

Again, she looked at Hannah. "This isn't going to get her in trouble, is it?"

"No," Elijah assured her. "You aren't going to get Jessica in trouble."

"Then…why do you need to know about her?" She folded her arms across her chest. "Cops only come around asking questions when someone's gonna get in trouble. I don't have to answer any questions."

"No, you don't have to answer any questions. But we are hoping you will. This is Jessica's stepmother. She came a long way to meet you and find out what happened to her daughter."

Hannah gave the girl a pleading look and nodded. "Please. I want to know what happened to my daughter."

Brittney's defiant expression changed to one of concern. "What do you mean what happened to her? She came by and we hung out a couple of times. No big deal, right? She told me she was on *rum-spring* or something which meant that it was okay for her to hang out."

"Did you see Jessica last Monday?" Elijah said.

Brittney looked down as if recalling a bad memory and nodded gently.

"Please. Please tell us what you know. It's important." Hannah came forward, placing her hands on the girl's forearm. Brittney retracted as if Hannah's touch were fire.

"What's wrong with your arms?" Abigail interrupted. "You stand like you have pain. You are hurt, aren't you? That's why you're holding that jacket around your shoulders. Brother, I have seen this before with some of my patients."

"No, I'm fine." Brittney backed away. "I just don't like anyone touching me."

Elijah shot his sister a look, which Hannah supposed meant Abby should leave that alone. And Hannah, despite her overwhelming desire to put this behind her and go back home to normalcy, could not help her worry and disappointment.

Elijah turned back to Brittney. "So, you girls hung out a lot?"

"Yes, I guess. She was cool." Brittney stopped and looked at each of them. "So, is she missing or something?"

Hannah wondered that Elijah did not tell her that Jessica was gone.

"Do you know anything about a journal that Jessica had?"

"Oh, man." Brittney shivered and backed away from them. Her eyes darted between the faces of the adults. "My dad sent you here, didn't he? He's so mad about that stupid journal. Look, I don't know where she took it. Okay? Just go. Get out of here."

"Your dad didn't send us here," Elijah said. "We got your name from some of Jessica's friends in Willow Trace and we're here to find out what you and she did last Monday night. Where did you go? Who did you see and talk to? Can you help us out or not?"

She turned her back to them, holding herself as if she were cold. "I want to talk to Jessica first."

"I'm sorry, you can't do that," Elijah said. Hannah could tell now that the poor girl was starting to cry.

"Yeah, why not?" she asked.

"Because she's dead," Elijah said quietly.

Brittney turned back. Her face went pale and her eyes widened. She held a hand to her mouth as if she might get sick. Curses slipped from her lips, then regrets, and a single tear spilled over her cheek. She hurried to the window and looked out. "You should go."

"Because of your friends downstairs?" Elijah asked. "Did they hurt Jessica? Did they hurt *you?*"

"You'd better go," Brittney said. "For all our sakes, just go." She started shooing them toward the front door.

"You won't tell us what happened?" Abigail said.

"I don't know what happened. Really. And I'm really sorry about Jessica. I am. But go. Before it's too late. Go. And don't come back." She herded them out into the hallway.

Hannah felt she did not need any encouragement. She was quite ready to leave this place. But Abigail hovered at the doorway and pulled a slip of paper from her apron. She handed the card to Brittney.

"What's this?"

"My address," Abigail said. "I'm a nurse. Someone should look at your injuries."

Brittney took the card, then slammed the door behind her. The sound of the metal chain sliding closed rang through the long hallway.

"I don't think she had anything to do with Jessica's death," Elijah said.

"How can you tell?" Abigail asked.

"Her body language. Her expressions."

"Then why did she seem so scared? Is she afraid of those boys? Daniel made it sound like they listened to everything she said."

"She wasn't so scared until we brought up the journal," Elijah said.

"And that made her think of her *Dat*," Hannah added.

"You would make a good detective, Hannah." Elijah gave her a nod. "Exactly. She's afraid of her dad and that journal. Looks more and more like Daniel's story was the truth. If only she could tell us what's in that journal, or what happened the last time she saw Jessica, but I don't think she'll talk unless we get her out of this place, and that's not going to happen with the friendly neighborhood watch downstairs."

Hannah knew Elijah was talking about the repulsive young men that had surrounded them. She slumped and broke into tears. "I can't believe my girl came to this horrible place. What was she thinking? Why did she tell Daniel that she was doing something good? What good is there to do here?"

Abigail put her arm around Hannah. "There, now. We may never know what she was about. But God does and He is a loving, kind, forgiving God. Do not fret, my sister. Jessica is safe now and in the hands of her Maker. She was a good girl. We will never think of her any other way."

Hannah wished she could feel so sure. She wished she could push the ugly words of her neighbors out of her head. But she feared when news of Jessica's visits to the city spread through Willow Trace—and word would spread—the talk about Jessica and her poor parenting skills and weak faith would only increase. Not that she cared so much what others thought. She did not. What bothered her was the doubt in her own heart that she had been a good mother. What bothered her was the inner fear that others spoke the truth. Otherwise, how could she have let this happen?

* * *

Elijah was thankful that Abigail was there to soften this experience for Hannah. It was rough even for him to imagine a sheltered Amish teen in such a setting. And Jessica had definitely been there. Brittney even seemed protective of her. Eli wasn't sure if that was a good thing or a bad thing. And only God knew what Jessica had been up to in such a place. Elijah had a hard time believing that Jessica's visit had been of an innocent nature—not in this part of town.

Drugs and prostitution certainly came to mind. Poor Hannah. If she weren't clearly in imminent danger, he'd have to agree with Thomas that all this searching for answers over Jessica's death was a bad idea.

He stopped in front of the elevator and pushed the call button.

"I'd prefer the stairs," Hannah said weakly.

Elijah nodded. Of course, Hannah didn't want to ride in an elevator. He should have thought of that himself. With a sigh, he made a move toward the stairwell, but at the same time the elevator door opened.

Abigail grabbed Hannah's hand and pulled her into the lift. "Oh, come on. It's probably the only day you ever will travel on an elevator. Once more. Trust me, it's better than walking down so many flights of stairs."

Elijah entered after them. A sinking feeling in his stomach made him wish they had listened to Hannah and taken the stairs.

"What's the matter, Eli?" Abigail studied his face.

"Nothing." He turned and tried to smile. No need to worry the ladies. They were nervous enough after the encounter with the gang and the not-so-wonderful conversation with Jessica's friend, Miss Brittney Baker. What he wished he had time to do was comb the neighborhood further in order to gather more information about the type of friendship that had existed between the Amish girl and the city one. But he couldn't do that today. For one, it was already out that he was a cop. More than likely that meant that no one in the neighborhood would talk to him. And more important, he could not imagine exposing poor Hannah to any more of downtown Philadelphia. She looked ready to faint as it was.

He tried to give her a reassuring smile as the doors opened behind him to exit the elevator. But instead of Abigail and Hannah smiling back at him, their eyes widened and they backed away from him.

"Watch out!" Abigail squealed.

Dread flowed through Elijah and he anticipated an attack from behind.

Elijah didn't even get a chance to turn his head. A strong force struck him in the back of the head. His knees gave way and he fell like a bag of rocks to the floor. Everything went black.

Chapter Thirteen

"Wake up! He's got Hannah!" Abigail's words came to him in pieces like a bad phone connection. His head and neck ached. Two hands pulled at his shoulders. Elijah rolled onto his back and forced his eyes open. Abigail stood over him with a frantic expression.

"Get up!" she said.

"What—what happened?" He put a hand to his head and with the other pushed up to a sitting position. It was then he remembered vaguely the scene in the elevator. Someone had been behind him. Someone large and strong. He'd been struck in the back of the head.

"It was terrible, it was. He came so fast. Hit you in the head. Took Hannah. I tried to stop him, brother, but he swatted me away like a fly, he did." Abigail grabbed hold of his hand and tried her best to help him to his feet.

"What do you mean, he's got Hannah?" Elijah balanced his weight over his two feet. His head felt like an anvil and throbbed with nearly debilitating pain. He lifted a hand to his aching cranium. Warm blood stuck to his fingers. He'd been struck with something blunt like the back end of a gun. "Who has Hannah?"

"I don't know," she said. "The man was tall and thin with reddish-blond hair. I've never seen him before. He was so fast, I tell you. Put you down and took Hannah in one motion. He had a gun."

Reddish-blond hair. *Tall. Strong.* Eli had seen photos in the file his partner, Tucci, had forwarded him the night before. The description sounded just like Flynn Jackson, Brittney's stepdad. Jackson must have heard from the front door gang of their arrival. But if they worked for Jackson and also did whatever Jessica and Brittney requested, that painted a strange picture—and not one too favorable for Jessica.

As these thoughts raced through one side of his aching head, the other could think of nothing but Hannah. "Which way did he take her?"

"I do not know. Maybe this way." Abigail pointed away from the building entrance and toward the back of the first-floor hallway.

The stairwell, maybe? Or he could have taken her out the back. Eli's heart sank. He had no idea.

"How long was I out?"

"Not long, brother. The elevator doors, they close and then they open again. Two times."

That was not too long. But, still, they had a head start and he wasn't even sure which way to begin looking. His chances of finding them by himself were too few.

He limped out of the elevator, pulling his keys and cell phone from his pocket. He dialed Tucci.

"I need backup. Hannah's been abducted. Possibly by Jackson. He's armed."

"Location?"

"The address you gave me yesterday."

"Roger, that," Tucci answered. "Be there in ten."

"Bring a team."

"Already on it, Miller. And wait for us. No Rambo moves, Amish boy."

Elijah clicked off and handed his keys to Abigail. "Run to my car. Lock yourself in and stay hidden. If you have to, drive away. I know you remember from your *Rumspringa*."

She reached for the keys but hesitated. "You can hardly stand, Elijah. Shouldn't I stay and—"

"Go," he ordered her. His voice sounded weak and stressed. No wonder she didn't want to leave him. "I don't want to be distracted by worrying about you, too, Abby. Just go. That is the most helpful thing you can do."

Abigail took the keys and ran from the building. Elijah prayed she would make it to his car safely. What had he done by bringing them there? It had escalated things—that was for sure. Now he only hoped that he could get Hannah back safely and then make this terrible incident work in their favor.

Elijah looked in every direction. Which way would he go with a hostage? Maybe to a place he knew well. Like home. Sure. That was a good place to start. Back at Jackson's apartment.

Elijah ran toward the door to the stairs, ignoring the shooting pain in his head. Pulling his gun from his jacket, he slipped into the spiraling stairwell. *Please, Lord, lead me to them. Keep Hannah calm and safe.*

With a quick move, he aimed his Glock upward and stepped into the center of the stairwell, looking both up and then down. Twelve stories of stairs. No basement access. That meant there was another set of stairs. What if he'd picked the wrong ones? How could he know? And not a puff of air stirred. One or two minutes were like an eternity to be behind in a chase. Too much time had passed since Jackson had attacked him and made off with Hannah.

Pushing his discouraging thoughts away again, Elijah hurtled up the stairs, his adrenaline helping to numb the pain in his head. At the top of the fifth flight, he plowed through the stairwell door and raced down the hallway. He knocked hard at the door to 502.

"Flynn Jackson, open up! Philadelphia P.D."

From inside, Elijah heard a loud *click* that sounded all too familiar—the lock and load of a shotgun. *Please let Hannah be safe,* he prayed as he dove out of the way of the door.

He hit the floor to the left side of the door and rolled onto his shoulder. A terrific blast blew through the front door of the apartment. Definitely a shotgun. No wonder his head hurt if he'd been hit in the head with the back end of one of those.

Eli protected his face from the flying debris. Then he sat up and aimed his Glock at the hole in the door, ready for Jackson to peek through the destruction.

But no one moved. From inside sounded Jackson's low grumbles, a woman's cries and furniture scooting across or toppling to the floor.

"Hannah?" Elijah hurried to get up and pressed his back to the wall next to the blown-out front door.

"Elijah!" Hannah cried from within. Terror sounded in her voice.

He had to save her. But alone? Jackson could blow him away with one step inside the apartment. But to wait five to ten more minutes for his backup? Was he willing to risk that? To wait?

"Send the woman out, or I'm coming in," he said. He cocked his gun so Jackson would know he was armed.

"It's over, Jackson. I called backup. You got nowhere to go. A SWAT team will be here in no time."

"How's your head, Miller?" he yelled back with a laugh. "Seems like I'm always looking at the back of it, don't it?"

"And seems like you're always hiding, Jackson…in the trees, outside the elevator, in a stable, on the side of a road…from the Metro police." Elijah leaned to the side and looked through the front door. He saw nothing. Jackson and Hannah were nowhere near the entry.

"You don't know anything about me, Amish boy. But I know everything about you—you and your pretty girlfriend here. I think she likes me. And what do I care if you come in? You are out there all by yourself. Now, if you Plain folk would just give me what I need, I will let her go. But not until I have it in my hands."

"No one has anything of yours." Elijah slid into the entrance hall. From there he spotted Jackson in a mirror. He dropped low to stay out of sight. Jackson reloaded the shotgun with one hand. With the other, he forced Hannah against his chest, holding her by a fistful of her luxurious hair. "Let her go."

"No can do. The little Amish girl said her *Mamm* knew where to find the journal. And this is her *Mamm*. You should be thankful I found you before any of the other interested parties. They'd just cut both your throats like they did that troublemaking Jessica."

Elijah slid farther into the apartment. "Hold it, Jackson. Put the weapon down. I have a clear shot."

Jackson tossed the gun at him. When it hit the ground, it fired at the wall, blasting shrapnel into the long hallway. Elijah covered his face and had to back away.

Jackson let out a low, husky chuckle. "How's your shot now, Amish boy?"

"Let her go, Jackson. She doesn't know where the journal is," Elijah repeated. "I'll turn my head and let you run. A favor from one cop to another. Do it now before my team gets here."

"Thanks, but I really need that journal. Bring it to me and then you can have her back."

Elijah scooted back into the hallway and across from the mirror. Not only had Jackson moved close to a back door and window leading onto a fire escape, but he had another gun in his hand. This one a small pistol aimed right at Hannah's head. Even from that distance, he could see the huge gold ring on his third finger, sporting the symbol of Dutch Confidential. No mistaking, this was the tall, fair-skinned man from his cousin's farm, also Brittney's stepfather.

Hannah had her eyes closed tight with tears on her cheeks.

Where was his team? Where was his backup? Elijah had to rush forward and save Hannah. He had to because if he lost Hannah, he'd lose everything.

Protect Elijah, Lord. Protect me. Deliver us from this place. Hannah kept her eyes closed and tried to be absent from the body and present with the Lord.

"Let her go." Elijah's voice sounded in the foyer.

Thank You, Lord. Thank You for sparing him. God had sent Elijah to help her. Just hearing his voice made her feel better. She hadn't been able to see him yet, but she could hear him, first through the door, and then from inside the apartment. The man holding her had shot his horrible weapon twice. Each time Hannah feared he'd harmed or killed Elijah. But then she'd hear his voice again, as strong as ever.

The horrible man dragged her by the hair. Her neck felt as if it might snap from her head. Even with her eyes closed, she could feel the barrel of his gun pointed into her temple.

"Let her go," Elijah said again. He sounded calm but authoritative. It reminded Hannah of the way the elders spoke when making a ruling no one in the *Ordnung* was to question.

But the redheaded man did not let her go. Instead, he tightened his grip, digging his fingertips into her scalp. Agony pealed through her body. Each time he turned, each time he moved, the pain increased. How could a human treat another human so?

Give me strength, Lord.

"She doesn't have what you want." This time he spoke, Elijah came boldly into the room. At the sound of his voice, her eyes flew open. His gun pointed straight ahead. "Now let her go and I'll let you go."

The man yanked Hannah placing her directly in front of him like a shield. He laughed. So close to her she could feel his breath.

"Elijah! Please!" She could not stop her tears as he pressed the cold end of the gun harder into her head. The trigger clicked in her ear and she trembled. Her weight, ironically, was held up by the hair on her head.

"He can't help you, lady. He wouldn't pull that trigger and risk hitting you. Actually, I don't know if he could even pull that trigger. He is Amish, after all. You're just going to have to tell me where my journal is," he said.

"I do not know," she cried. "I do not know."

"Let her go." Brittney appeared in the corner of the large living space.

"What are you doing here? You should be at school." He sounded truly surprised.

"Drop your weapon." Elijah had moved closer. Behind him several other officers filed into the apartment.

Jackson cursed. "No. And if you want to keep this lady alive, you'll back out of here. Brittney, you, too, get out of here."

"Just let her go." Brittney moved closer. "If she knew where it was, she'd tell you."

The police ordered Brittney to step back. Instead she moved closer and once she was in reaching distance, Jackson grabbed hold of the girl, after shoving Hannah as hard as he could to the other side of the room.

She stumbled out of control toward Elijah and the others, blocking any access to Jackson or Brittney.

Elijah lowered his gun and scrambled toward her to help her up and out of harm's way.

"It's okay now. You're safe," he told her.

Shock distorted her reality. Hannah could barely register the words he spoke. She could barely feel his tender touch leading her from the apartment. She could still feel that hand in her hair yanking at her scalp.

"Did he hurt you badly?" Elijah's voice was a whisper compared to the commotion behind them.

"The building is surrounded," she heard one of the other officers say. "Let the girl go and come with us."

"Not today, boys," the man replied.

Although he sounded less sure of himself, when Hannah looked over her shoulder she shuddered. Jackson had grabbed his stepdaughter around the waist and positioned her in front of him, just as he had held her seconds ago. But instead of controlling the girl with a handful of hair, he held a knife to her throat.

Hannah froze in the doorway watching as the knife

pressed against Brittney's soft skin. The policemen didn't press toward Jackson, but stopped short, lowering their weapons. No one doubted he would hurt the child.

Oh, Lord, please, not another child.

"Elijah, please, can we not do something more?"

Chapter Fourteen

I can pray, Elijah thought to himself as he tried to move Hannah from the apartment. She wouldn't budge. She was as still and heavy as a sack of stones staring back at that girl. And how could she not be? The sight before her was one that would never fade from her mind. As it would never fade from his.

Jackson's ring and the blade of his knife flashed under the poor girl's chin.

"You got nowhere to go, Jackson," Tucci yelled from beside Eli. His partner and three SWAT team members had positioned themselves around the room—each with a rifle pointed at Jackson.

"Put the guns down." Jackson's voice made Eli's skin crawl.

Slowly, they lowered their guns to the floor.

"You're cornered," Tucci said.

Jackson smirked before pulling Brittney along with him as he slowly slinked to the back of the room where a single window was cracked open. Jackson bent his knees and reached down, lifting the window wide. Then he backed through the open space like a panther onto the fire escape. The whole while he kept his stepdaughter as a shield with the knife to her neck. He dragged Brittney with him, then slammed the window closed and jammed it with the knife.

"No, Elijah. Why do they not stop him?" Hannah sounded hysterical, clutching on to him with a death-like grip.

"We can't risk Brittney's life to get him, Hannah," he said to her. "But don't worry. We will catch up with him yet."

At last, she relaxed her frozen stance and he was able to pull her away.

She cried and shook against him. He held her close, supporting her and helping her out of the building. An emergency team rushed to them as they exited the building. A couple of EMTs whisked Hannah away from him to check her over for injuries. Other police hurried over to him.

"Tucci just radioed down. Jackson has vanished," they said. "The girl, too."

Elijah felt a surge of frustration and disappointment, but his thoughts remained mostly focused on Hannah.

Seated at the edge of the emergency truck, a worker handed her a blanket. She tried to smooth and tuck her loose hair. Her apron was smudged. Her frock was ripped at the shoulder. She looked pale. Shaken. Exhausted.

He'd almost lost her. Again.

Thank You, Lord. Thank You for getting her out of there. He lifted the prayer and tried to release the fear that gripped him.

And the guilt. If something had happened to Hannah…

An EMT appeared before him. "The lady says you have a head injury?"

"I'm fine." Elijah stood suddenly, and homed in on Hannah. He had to hold her. He had to feel her in his arms and know that she was safe. That she was still alive.

In a second, he stood before her. He touched his hand gently to her smudged cheek. "I can't lose you, Hannah," he whispered. "I can't lose you again."

Then he lifted her into his arms and held her tighter than he'd ever held anyone.

"I can't lose you again."

Jackson and his stepdaughter were not caught. Mr. Tucci and Elijah's colleagues from the Philadelphia Police Department had come up empty-handed after a complete search of the building. It was as if Jackson and Brittney had vanished into thin air.

For a long time, Elijah, Abigail and Hannah had to answer questions for the team of police. The EMTs strongly recommended a trip to the hospital, but Elijah seemed to know that Hannah couldn't take any more of the city.

She tried to focus on the fact that she and Elijah and Abigail were blessed to be alive. And she was so thankful for that. So very thankful. But she had seen and heard such atrocities that day and her mind could not leave the idea that her Jessica had seen and heard it all, as well. Maybe worse. She was starting to think that the gossips back in Willow Trace had been right to speculate about her daughter. Maybe Jessica's heart had not been so pure. The girl had certainly been spending time with terrible people. Today's trip into the city and the discovery of Jessica's secret life had made Hannah feel cheated and deceived. She was ashamed that she'd not been a better mother and prevented this. If she had, Jessica would still be alive. And Elijah wouldn't be there, making her confused and feeling so many things. Right now all she wanted to do was to collapse in a fit of tears until she washed away all the filth of the outside world.

Surely, some quiet prayer and hard work would set her right—no more thoughts about how she should have done things. No more thoughts about Elijah and the past...or the future. No more thoughts of how he'd held her in his arms.

"Do you think your partner and his team will find Jackson and Brittney?" Abigail asked from the seat behind her.

Hannah looked away and stared out the window at the rolling green hills. She didn't want to hear any more talk of Flynn Jackson or Brittney Baker or even of Jessica.

"I hope so," Elijah said. "I think if we can get Jackson into the station, we will be able to get the information we need. What exactly this journal is that he wants. And why he thinks Hannah has it. Tucci will also talk to people in the neighborhood and see what he can find out. Jackson said he wasn't the only one looking for the missing journal. I think that worries me most."

"You mean like those young men, who were so awful when we first arrived?" Abigail asked.

Hannah shuddered at the reminder.

"No. I think the gang is linked somehow, but remember Daniel said that they were friendly to Jessica and Brittney. That they even took him to the train station when Jessica asked them. I think Jackson is into things with much higher stakes than those kids on the street."

"Higher stakes?" Abigail asked.

"Yes. I think this journal must have some pretty serious information in it. Something that could hurt a lot of people. Maybe even get them killed or incarcerated."

"But why? Why would Jessica…" Hannah could not make sense of it all. How could her girl have gotten involved in such schemes?

Elijah reached over and held her hand. He was so strong. She could feel the power and strength flowing in him.

"My strength comes from the Lord," he said.

Hannah turned to him. "I understand better now what it is that you do."

He nodded. "Yes, thank you. I wish my *Dat* could see it, too."

Abigail smiled. "Give him time. He will see that you try to bring some order to the world."

"I didn't bring much order today." He frowned. "I nearly got us all killed…"

Abigail nodded. "Well, we are here to help. Even though I know it is hard." She patted Hannah's shoulder. "I think we must find this journal."

"Or at least figure out what information is in it," Elijah said.

"Ah. I can see in your eye you have an idea." Abigail grinned. "What is it? If we all think hard, maybe we can figure this out."

"I don't really know anything," Elijah said. "Just that Jackson was a dirty cop. He did and could still have access to all kinds of things."

"Dirty cop?" Hannah asked. "What does this mean?"

"It means he did police work and carried a badge, but at the same time he took money from criminals by overlooking their crimes and helping them get away. Maybe making evidence disappear. Or selling secret information. Jackson is no longer a cop, but the rest of what he does could be the same. He could use old contacts inside the police department to get information, to get inside the system, to help bad people make money so that he can make money."

"But why would anyone in the police department work with such a man?" Abigail asked.

Elijah tilted his head. "Because, sadly, there are some cops on the force who want money more than they want to do what is right. And if they're greedy just once and agree to do one thing, then Jackson has a way to end their career and can blackmail them into doing more work for him. They don't want to lose their jobs. Trust me. I work Internal Affairs. This happens more than you really want to know."

"What a terrible man is this Flynn Jackson," Abigail said.

Hannah had tried not to listen, but no matter how much she wanted to block everything out, she could not. More than ever, right or wrong, she wanted to learn the truth. Without the whole truth, she might never accept that Jessica had turned out to be a bad girl. And she had to accept what had happened. She had to accept God's will. Elijah had been right about that. He had been right about a lot of things. She turned to him. "Do you think he killed Jessica?"

Elijah turned to her. Regret shone out of his blue eyes. "I don't know. He said that someone else wanted the journal. He made it sound as if that person harmed your daughter and not him. But the way he grabbed Brittney with that knife...he certainly seemed capable of it."

Hannah put a hand to her stomach. She felt ill. She wondered how a mother could leave her child with such a man. But who was she to judge? She'd done no better with Jessica.

"Brittney could be lying, Hannah," Elijah said as if reading her thoughts. "Jessica might not have taken this journal. Maybe Brittney told Jackson this just to save her own skin."

His words were meant to comfort her, but they did not. She could only think of her own failing.

"So, what we really need," Abigail said, "is to find out what the journal actually is and what information it holds?"

"Yes," he answered. "And as hard as it is, we should start looking for it in Willow Trace."

"So you *do* think she took it?" Hannah asked.

"It doesn't matter what I think. *They* think she took it and they think *you* have it… I just wish I knew better what I was looking for."

Hannah did not follow. "What do you mean? It's a journal, right?"

"I'm not sure that they mean an actual journal. Not like what you are thinking, a book with someone's personal thoughts in it."

"Then what?" Abigail asked.

"Okay. I just thought of this, but it makes sense. So, there's this retired guy I know from the Philly P.D., Mike. Mike works in security now on the weekends to earn a few bucks. He's at the downtown courthouse. Really tight security. Very high-tech systems. And Jackson supposedly works in security, too."

"And what?" she and Abigail asked at the same time.

"Well, all of this security is controlled by bar codes and card swiping. Mike said they are constantly changing the cards and the codes. And in case there's some sort of blackout or computer malfunction, the security people keep all these codes on a special storage device. It's changed out each week and synched with the mainframe system. For lack of a better word, they call this device the journal."

"Would having it be worth killing over?" Abigail asked.

"Sure. If a place has that kind of security, there must be something inside worth guarding."

"But Jessica? Taking something like this? Hiding it? Why?" Hannah closed her eyes and sighed, her stomach still churning. She didn't want to talk about any of these horrible things her daughter had gotten involved in.

"*If* she even took it, Hannah," he corrected her. "And I think when we know the answer to that question, we'll know the whole of this."

But would they? Hannah wondered.

No one spoke as they pulled back in front of Nolt Cottage. Thomas stood waiting. He'd replaced the broken window, making his stone cottage look as homey as ever. A brand-new carriage, and the gelding Thomas had spoken of earlier was tied to the hitching post. What a good man Thomas was. She should love him and want to marry him, but in her heart she knew she could not.

Strange emotions swept through her as she exited the car. She could not lift her head to Thomas. She could not look back to Elijah. The heaviness of the day weighed down on her. The loss of Jessica and Peter gripped her so tightly she felt as if she would snap. No hope for her future.

She rushed up the front porch steps and into the house. She would not love again. She could not risk the pain of losing anything else.

Elijah didn't think he could feel any worse than he already did. But when Hannah ran into the house, his heart ached ten times more than his head. He should never have taken her to Philadelphia. He'd thought it would help make Jessica's so-called friend feel comfortable and talk. And perhaps that connection did help somewhat, but it hadn't been worth the dangers that they'd all been exposed to. He'd always believed that seeking the truth was worth any risk, but that was only because he had never risked something he loved as much as Hannah.

He'd always thought that going home would turn his people further against him and make him feel even more alienated from the world he had grown up in. That was what he had feared—well, that and his *Dat*'s disapproval. He'd been right about his *Dat*. But he had been very wrong about his own experience. Instead of feeling alienated from the Amish, Elijah was finding that their beliefs and rules and laws made more sense to him than they ever had before. For the first time in a long while, he started to wonder what it would be like to come home for good. Lead a Plain life. The thought was very tempting—but also very distracting. He was getting too attached, too emotionally involved, and it was keeping him from solving the case. He wasn't doing a good job as a detective—and if he couldn't do that, then there was no reason for him to stay. No reason other than his love for Hannah, which seemed to grow stronger—and more hopeless—every day.

She'd made her choice long ago, and it was long past time for him to accept it. But accepting it meant he needed to go. It had been easy to leave before when Hannah hadn't wanted him, when his father had challenged him. Leaving this time would not be easy at all, but it was exactly what he needed to do and he needed to do it now.

Elijah kicked a stone in the path, watching Thomas go in after Hannah. That was another reason to leave. He needed to get over that feeling of jealousy and be able to wish Thomas and Hannah well. They would be good together. And he had no doubt that Thomas cared for her. He turned to his sister.

"I need to have my captain send someone else here to protect Hannah. I should never have come back home. I've only made things worse."

Abigail frowned. "You are wrong, brother. What you feel now is fear. But you must not let it take you. Be strong. Listen to your own advice."

"Today was a disaster. Abby, I have no idea what we are looking for or why. I was just spouting off a bunch of thoughts, but the truth is I just don't know."

"But you said we should look here. Let's at least do that. You said we could check the stables and maybe some other places," she said. "You can't give up. Hannah…no, *all* of us, even Thomas, we are counting on you."

"I don't know, Abby. Being back here hasn't been what I thought it would be. I feel—I feel confused like I don't know what I'm doing."

"Looks to me like you have these bad guys pretty nervous. So you must be doing something right. Anyway, who would you call? Who else could help, but you? You're the one to help Hannah. God sent *you*." Abigail walked to the hitching post and gave her new gelding a pat. "You will do your job. Of that I have no doubt. But that is not what you are most afraid of, is it? You know, brother, you should speak your heart before it's too late."

"What are you talking about?" Elijah swallowed hard. "Facing up to *Dat,* you mean?"

"No. That's not what I mean, you daft man." Abigail

frowned and lifted an eyebrow at him. Then she gave a nod back toward the house. "You wish it were you in there with Hannah in place of Thomas."

"Oh, please, Abby, she's got a killer after her and I'm doing a lousy job of keeping her alive. That's all that is between us right now. Hannah rejected me years ago. I have no interest in going through that again."

"What makes you so sure she'd reject you this time?" Abigail said. "Hannah and Peter were happy. She was a good wife to him. But it was you she loved enough to set free."

"Enough of this. You're making my head hurt worse than it already does." He turned away. "Let's go check the stables for this journal. Then I'll call McClendon and he can stay with the two of you tonight. I've got to go back before I…"

"Before you what, Elijah?" Abigail crossed her arms over her chest.

He looked up at the house, then back to his sister. "Before I do or say something that will hurt everyone."

Chapter Fifteen

Hannah's spirits lifted when Abigail invited her to spend the night at her home near Strasbourg. She couldn't remember the last time she'd slept away from Nolt Cottage—a night away from the constant reminders of Jessica and Peter, from her life before, would be a welcome reprieve.

After dinner, she packed one dress and climbed into Abigail's new carriage, while Abigail thanked Thomas for the gift of the horse and buggy. But when Elijah climbed in and sat beside her, a whole other feeling infused her blood.

"I thought you were going into the city to help with the search for Jackson, brother?" Abigail asked, sparing Hannah the need to frame the question as to why he was joining them.

Elijah flinched. "My partner, Tucci, has that under control. And…"

Hannah's heart froze at his pause.

"And what?" Abigail prodded.

"Well, tomorrow is my last day. *Dat,* he gave me three days. I'm going to use them. Hannah has decided to spend the night with you. So, if my first priority is to protect her, then you'd better make space for two guests."

"I knew you weren't a quitter." Abigail gave her new gelding a tap with the reins and they were off.

"Elijah, how would you feel about 'tending service with us in the morning?" Abigail asked.

Hannah had nearly forgotten that tomorrow was the Sabbath. A good word from Preacher Miller would do her well.

"I was welcomed at the gathering…but Sunday church? I don't think so."

"It is Providence that has brought you here, brother." Abigail smiled. "And it would please me very much. Mother, as well."

"And what do you think of my coming to Sunday church, Hannah?"

"Me? Well, I—I cannot say." Suddenly the image of Elijah in Plain dark trousers, a blue button-up shirt and black felt hat fell into her head. She hoped she did not blush. Why would she think such a silly thing? "I have no objections. But I cannot speak for others."

"Then you would welcome my coming?"

"Aye, I would."

Hannah was glad to see Abigail's home just in front of them and to have the end of this conversation.

It had been years since she'd been to see Abigail; Elijah's sister was a bit of an oddity in the *Ordnung,* not marrying, and living alone. Her place was large and fine. For years, she had been consulted for her knowledge as a *Doula* and as a doctors' aide at the hospital. Often, women would seek her help with womanly pains or other ailments when they did not need the consultation of a medical doctor.

Because of her clinic space, the house was more

modern than most Amish. She even had more than one bathroom.

"One for clients. One for me," she explained.

And a fancy climate controller, which maintained seventy-two degrees even in summer.

"I can't have it too hot," she explained. "Breeds germs. I only use it in summer and it's still run by my oil tank."

It was late by the time they arrived, and after nearly no rest the night before, they were all ready to get to sleep.

Elijah insisted on sleeping downstairs on the couch, so Abigail showed Hannah to the spare bedroom, then brought her a clean towel and an extra blanket. Then she took a seat on the bed and smiled.

"You still love him, don't you?"

Heat rushed to Hannah's face. "Who do you speak of? Peter?"

"No. Of course you loved Peter, but he's gone with God now. I mean Elijah. You still love him. I can see it when you are together. You love him. Just as much as you did when you were young."

Hannah pressed her lips together and did not speak. To deny her statement would be a lie. To admit to it could be troublesome and unwise.

Abigail waited a moment. Then she stood and walked near to her. "You don't have to answer, Hannah. I see it in your face. What I really want to know is what you plan to do about it."

"To do?" Hannah tried to hide her face. She pretended to wipe it with the towel. "There is nothing to do. Your brother is part of a world that I care not to join. And today I saw what good he does." She dropped the towel and looked at her friend. "It is what he always wanted… I will admit that he is a good man, bound to the church or not. But he will be gone in another day. And I will go home. Where I belong."

"You admit nothing, Hannah." She turned toward the door. "God is giving you a second chance to be happy. But you and my brother are too proud to see it."

"Too proud?" Hannah stepped after her. "How am I proud by choosing the Plain life? It's Elijah who…"

"It's Elijah who what?" Abigail asked.

"He will never forgive me for choosing Peter."

Abigail came back to stand next to her. She took one of her hands in her own. "Why did you choose Peter?"

"I loved him."

"You loved my brother. There was a reason. Was it for Jessica? To be her mother? I often wondered that you and Peter were never with child."

Hannah closed her eyes. She felt the tears coming. *Your brother wanted a family. He wanted to be a police officer. I could not give him those things.* Hannah wanted to say it, but she could not. She could not open her heart again. "It does not matter the reason. I hurt your brother and damaged what there was between us. What you see now is the pain I put there. Not love."

"Love can heal any hurt. Talk to him," Abigail said. "He has never loved another girl, Hannah. Only you."

Abigail left the room, but her words stayed and pressed on Hannah's heart. Exhausted and drained in every way, she lay on the bed and wept.

Elijah tossed and turned on Abigail's couch, unable to fall asleep despite his exhaustion. His aching skull was partly to blame, but it was more his racing mind that kept him awake—his thoughts jumping between the strange complications of Jessica's death, his mixed-up feelings about coming home and his even more complicated relationship with Hannah.

It wasn't just how he felt about her. He knew he loved her. He'd always loved her. She'd chosen someone else and he still loved her. None of that had changed. He had gone his own way and he knew he had been an instrument of God working as a police officer. So why did he feel called to come home now?

Was it for Hannah? Was it because he sought his father's approval so desperately?

It was both of those things and yet it somehow seemed like more than that. He half laughed to himself. His *Mamm* would have said it was further proof of his contrary nature, that he had dreaded coming home again, but now that he was there he wasn't sure he wanted to leave.

He missed the simple life. He missed his family. He missed that easy connection to his Father above. It was as if in coming home he'd come to a deeper understanding and need for all that he had once walked away from.

But how? How could he come back? His father did not accept him. Hannah would marry Thomas come November. That he could not bear to see. And God had called him to do police work.

He tossed again over the hard couch. Why did he feel so conflicted? God did not make mistakes. Elijah shook away the thoughts. He needed sleep and a clear head if he were going to figure this case out. There was still so much to work out and tomorrow, per his *Dat*'s decree, was his final day. He feared it would not be enough time and that he'd say goodbye to Hannah without giving her the peace of mind she so desperately needed.

A shadow fell over the room. Elijah welcomed the

cloud. It would be much easier to sleep without so much moonlight, glaring in through the large windows.

He rolled onto his side and started to close his eyes. The shadow flickered. It grew larger. It went to the right. Then to the left.

That is no cloud. Someone is on the porch.

Without making a sound, Elijah slipped from the couch and moved away from the couch and window. The shadow formed once again on the wall across from him. Yep. He'd been right. That was not a cloud. It was a person, peering into the window—another uninvited guest, he thought, remembering the last two evenings.

Well, this time, Elijah was going to do the surprising and not the other way around. He slid away from the living room and moved quietly toward the back door of his sister's house.

Chapter Sixteen

Hannah awoke with a start. Heart racing, she sat upright in the bed, soaked in a sticky sweat. She'd fallen asleep over the bedsheets, fully dressed. Her cheeks were moist from half-dried tears. Her arms asleep from resting at strange angles. She scooted to the edge of the bed, trying to orient herself to the strange surroundings.

Abigail Miller's house. The shelves over the desk were heavy with books on homeopathic medicine and midwife practices. For the last five years, Abigail had helped to deliver the babies of almost every young Amish wife in Willow Trace and the surrounding towns. All of the young married women except for her. And that was the very reason she had been crying. Jessica was the only child she'd ever had—and now not only was Jessica gone, but the memory of her had been tainted by all the dreadful things Hannah had seen.

Hannah walked to the bathroom and washed her face. How had she gotten to be in this nightmare? It was all so confusing, so frightening, so…she didn't know what. She didn't know what to feel or how to feel it. She didn't know what to believe anymore. She thought of Abigail's encouraging her to talk to Elijah about her feelings. But hadn't she tried that last night in the buggy on the way back from the gathering? He had not responded. In fact, he had changed the subject and even seemed angry with her.

Not that any of it mattered. He was leaving. Tomorrow.

Hannah sighed away the sad thought, only to have it replaced with the other confusion in her head—that of this business with Jessica. Despite all the horrors she had seen that day, she could not bring herself to believe that Jessica would steal and lie and bring such shame to herself and all that she had professed to believe. It could not be possible. There had to be another reason Jessica was connected to all of this. Something that they were missing.

In her mind, she passed over her conversations with Brittney and Daniel. She suspected that both kids had lied at some point in their story. They were afraid, and rightfully so. But surely some of what they had told was truth. How did it all piece together?

Hannah couldn't help worrying about them both. Watching Brittney be dragged away had been terrifying. Neither she nor her father had been found.

At least, Elijah had "put a car on" Daniel, as he had phrased it, meaning he had police friends keeping an eye on the boy. Elijah had explained that not only would they keep him safe, but following Daniel might also lead them to the people tied to Jessica's murder.

How she both hoped for and feared the truth about her daughter. So many horrible things had been said about her. She had been to such a terrible place. Been so secretive and almost cruel to Daniel.

Only one thing gave Hannah a glimmer of hope, and that was Brittney. Brittney, who had been so worried that she would get Jessica in trouble. She'd sounded cognizant of the Amish ways. And she had stopped her stepfather when the man had had a gun to Hannah's head. Traded places with her. Maybe Brittney was not so bad as Daniel had made her sound.

Hannah also remembered a few other things that Daniel had said. First, that Jessica had carried a large bag with her. What large things would she be carrying? None of her clothing was missing. He'd also recounted that when he stopped her at the apartments, Jessica had claimed she was doing something good. For him to go home and that she would explain it later.

If Jessica were going to explain it later to Daniel, then she wasn't planning to run away. But doing something good? It was hard to believe there was any good to be done in that horrible place…unless…

Hannah straightened herself and headed out to wake Elijah. Finally she had an idea about Jessica that made sense to her. She hadn't figured all of the pieces out, but this part, this part about Jessica, this she felt certain of. She had to tell Elijah as soon as possible.

Passing through the small hallway into the living room, she found that the couch was empty. Hannah walked through the kitchen and then passed by the clinic.

"Elijah?"

There was no answer. Hannah shuddered. There was no chance Elijah had left them alone. Not after getting so cross with Thomas for having done that very thing.

Hannah turned back toward the bedrooms. She would wake Abigail. But something in the window caught her eye before she reached the hallway.

Hannah froze as fear prickled through her limbs. Had Jackson found them? She could still feel his massive fingers yanking at her head. Had he already gotten to Elijah? Hannah didn't know whether to run or scream or both.

She watched as the dark figure melted back into the night without a sound. Then she sprinted back to Abigail's room. She wasn't going to sit there like an easy target. Not tonight. Not again.

"Abigail, wake up. Elijah is gone and I saw someone looking in the windows."

"What?" Abigail sat up. "Hannah? Are you okay?"

"Wake up. Something is happening." Hannah repeated the situation. "I think they found us."

Abigail looked pensive for a second. Then she got up and headed to her own window to peer out. "Yes. Could be so," she said. "Or it could be a patient?"

"But where is your brother? He wouldn't have left us without saying so."

"Probably so. We should call the police."

"You have a phone?"

"Only for work. I have to know when a patient is going into labor, you know." Abigail headed for the hallway. "Come. It's in the kitchen."

A light knock sounded at the door.

Abigail and Hannah looked at each other. Hannah could feel her heart pounding in her chest. But Abigail relaxed some and headed to the door.

"What are you doing?"

"Intruders don't knock." Abigail turned to the door and called out. "Who is it?"

"Please, let me in. Hurry. Please." The voice was weak and soft like that of a child.

Abigail looked back one more time at Hannah and then headed on to the door. Heaven help them if this were a trick. But they could hardly ignore the desperation in the voice behind the door. Still, where was Elijah? She wished Elijah were there.

"Do I know you?" Abigail asked with a shrug.

"It's Brittney. Brittney Baker. I know it's late. I'm sorry. I didn't know where else to go. You said I could come. Please let me in."

Abigail unlocked the front door. Hannah hit the light switch. Brittney hobbled into the house. She was cut, bruised, bleeding.

Elijah came up behind the porch behind her. He was putting his gun away. "I nearly took you out, young lady. You shouldn't go around peeking into the windows like you did. Next time try the front door first."

"I am sorry. I—I—"

Elijah caught her before she hit the floor. "Good gracious. She's been beaten nearly to death."

"Quick. Take her to the clinic," Abigail told him.

Elijah picked the girl up and carried her to Abigail's examination room.

Her eyes fluttered as Elijah placed her on the table.

"Dear child, what has happened to you?" Hannah asked.

"I just don't know where it is." She tried to lift herself up.

"Shh. Don't try to talk. Just rest." Hannah turned to Abigail. "What can I do to help?"

"Keep her quiet. And still." Abigail busied herself preparing bandages and solutions. "We'll have to cut off those clothes and dress all those wounds. She may need blood."

"Can you tend to her, Abby? Without paramedics?" Elijah asked.

"I can try. I think Jackson did this to her," Abigail

said. They checked her limbs, face and neck for more bruising and other injuries.

"I know Jackson did it." Elijah pointed to a cut on the girl's face. "See? Here is a mark from the ring he wears on his right hand." He put a hand to the girl's forehead and she opened her eyes. "Do you know where he is?"

She was too weak to answer.

"You can interrogate later." Abigail shooed him from the clinic space.

Hannah was filled with anger thinking of the horrible man who'd put this girl in such a state. It made her sick and enraged all at once. And there was so much blood. She couldn't help thinking of Jessica.

But for the next few hours, she and Abigail tended to the poor beaten girl. She was in and out of consciousness. Mercifully, nothing was broken, but she was still suffering from a severe concussion and bruising such as Hannah had never seen. And it all confirmed the idea she'd had earlier about her stepdaughter.

When they'd finished, they dressed her in some of Abigail's clothing, moved her to the couch and Abigail began pouring tea down her throat.

"Drink up. It will help with the swelling and the pain."

"It's a wonder you made it all the way out to Lancaster without passing out," Elijah said. "Where is Jackson? Where did he take you?"

"What is this?" She choked at the taste of the tea.

"Lotus." Abigail smiled with pride, then looked at her brother. "You have to report this."

"No. No." Brittney coughed out the words. "No report. I thought that was the Amish way. No outside help. That's why I came here."

"Well, yes, but you aren't Amish," Abigail said. "And this isn't something we can ignore. He could kill you."

"He won't kill me," she said. "He always knows when to stop. You are wasting your time if you report this. Actually, it will just make things worse. I'll have to go back to him. They'll call him. They always call him. What I really want is to stay here. Please promise me you won't call."

"We can't promise that, Brittney," Elijah said. "I am a police officer. You are underage and have to be either in the care of your legal guardian or Social Services. I can hold off for a bit, but eventually I have to report a case of child abuse. At least that will get you out of his custody."

"But don't you see? He is the police, too." She shook her head. "You make a report. He makes it disappear. You say Flynn Jackson. He makes the report says Christopher Jones, or George Smith. He has the system in his pocket."

"He doesn't have *me* in his pocket," Elijah said.

"Jessica was trying to get you out of there, wasn't she?" Hannah asked.

"Yes. She was. I saw Jessica at a party. She looked so perfect. So peaceful. So happy. I knew she had something that I didn't. And I wanted it. So I asked her. I asked her about your God. And when I heard of His love and acceptance, I knew I belonged to Him. I just didn't know how to get away from Flynn."

"But Jessica had a plan?" Elijah asked.

The girl nodded. "She said I could come here. Because of the Amish way. No help from the authorities. She said that Flynn wouldn't be able to find me here."

"She was trying to help this poor girl," Abigail repeated proudly. She patted Hannah's hand. "See? You were a great mother. Jessica was a sweet girl. She was trying to help."

Hannah fought tears.

"Now I'm off to fix everyone some tea." Abigail hurried off to the kitchen.

Hannah took a step toward the girl. "So all this is due to Jessica trying to help you?" Brittney nodded, and the tears slid down Hannah's soft cheeks.

He walked over and touched Hannah's shoulder. "Your daughter made a difference. I know it doesn't bring her back. But knowing must give you some peace. She made a difference. *You* made a difference. This girl will never be the same."

She looked up and smiled at him. "It does not take my sadness. But, yes, it gives me peace."

Abigail bustled back into the room with a tray of steaming teas.

"I don't think you can get her to drink anymore." Elijah pointed out that Brittney had dozed off.

"This is for you." Abigail handed a cup of tea to both Hannah and him.

"For us?" they said together.

"Yes, it's passion flower."

Passion flower? Hannah could already feel the blush on her cheeks. Why was Abigail pushing this so hard? Didn't she see that it wasn't meant to be?

"It's for sleeping," Abigail said with a teasing tone. "You both need to rest."

Although still stiff and bruised, Brittney was much recovered by morning. The ladies tended to her with a full breakfast and much fussing.

Elijah sat at the other end of the table with his cup of black coffee and slice of buttered toast, alternating thoughts between the case and how today was his last day in Willow Trace.

"You look much better, Brittney."

"Thanks. Thanks to all of you," she said. "And especially for not calling the cops. You don't understand—"

"We do," Elijah said. "We do understand. And we want to help, but you have to talk to us so that we can stop Jackson once and for all. Did he kill Jessica?"

Her eyes went wide. "I don't think so."

"But he was with her that night?"

She nodded hesitantly. "Yes."

Elijah leaned forward with his cup of coffee. "Who else was there? Why didn't you tell us any of this when we were there?"

"I couldn't talk in the apartment, you know." Brittney pushed a loose lock of hair out of her eyes. "You never know who's listening. That's what happened with Jessica."

"*What* happened with Jessica?" Elijah pressed her.

"Well, I don't know all of it." Brittney pressed her lips together and took a long sip of her tea. "She came over and we were going to leave. Leave Flynn. She said I could come here and he'd never find me. But..."

"It's okay," Hannah encouraged her. "Keep going. We want to know."

"Well, it was all going great, until Jackson showed up."

"*What* happened with Jackson?" Elijah was impatient for answers. It wasn't that he didn't trust that Brittney wanted a different life and now knew God's love. He just didn't trust that she was telling the hundred percent truth. She was scared. And used to a world where steering people the wrong way to protect yourself was a way of life. But lies were often mixed with some truth, and if she told the right things, if he asked the right questions, he could put it all together and maybe figure out where Jackson was. Today. His last day.

"Well, like I said, she came to the apartment. But we didn't get out in time."

"Who found you?"

"Flynn and Mr. Krups," she said as if they should have already known.

"Mr. Krups?"

"Yeah. That's who wants the journal. Mr. Krups. Why else do you think Flynn is so crazy? If he doesn't get that journal back, Mr. Krups will…well, *he* won't do it…but let's just say it won't be too good for Flynn."

"Wait a minute. Wait a minute." Elijah shook his head. "Your dad works for Norton Krups? I thought he worked for Philadelphia Party Rentals?"

"Stepdad," she corrected him quickly. "The party rental place is a front. I thought everyone in Philly knew that."

"So, it's Norton Krups's journal that everyone is looking for? How or why did Jessica get a hold of something like that? Or *did* she actually get a hold of it?"

Brittney looked around the room at each of them. Her eyes almost popped out of her head. "Man, you guys really don't know anything, do you?"

"Apparently not." Elijah ran his hands through his hair. How could he take down someone as connected and powerful as Norton Krups?

"And it's not really a journal, either," she added. "It's an electronic device that holds security codes. And not just for Krups. I heard Flynn bragging to someone that the journal had all the codes connected with Dutch Confidential security systems and that he could steal information without being detected. Can you imagine? Even government systems use that company."

"I do not understand. Who is this Krups?" Hannah asked.

Elijah paused. How did you describe a guy like Krups to a lady like Hannah? "He's a respected businessman who has been suspected of illegal activities, gunrunning, drugs, murder. But no one has ever been able to prove it." Elijah turned back to Brittney. "So, why did Jessica take this journal? What was she planning to do with these codes?"

"Actually, I took the journal." She dropped her head. "One day, I was so mad at Flynn. He kept bragging about how great it was and how Krups was going to make him top dog. Then as usual, he got drunk and hit me for leaving a dish out or something. Anyway, I took it and I asked Jessica to hide it."

"And she agreed to this?" Hannah asked.

"Yes. I told her what it was and what Flynn and Krups could do with it and so she thought it was good that they not have it anymore. *A good thing to do,* she said." Brittney smiled.

Elijah couldn't help grinning. He turned to Hannah and explained. "If what Brittney says is true, you can be sure that Krups and Jackson were going to use these codes to do something illegal. Jessica thought that it was a good thing to stop them."

"Right," Brittney said. "And she also figured that Flynn would be so freaked out about losing the journal that he wouldn't notice me leaving. She said once I turned eighteen I could hand it over to the authorities and get Flynn in lots of trouble."

"So, where did Jessica put the device?"

"That I don't know. Jessica thought it would be better if she didn't tell me. And then if Flynn asked me about it, I wouldn't have to lie."

"What happened the day Jessica came to see you?" Hannah asked.

"We were going to come here. It's only a few weeks until my birthday. Then I would be eighteen." A sad expression covered her face. Her eyes teared and she stared at the floor, speaking slowly. "Jessica thought her mom would let me stay for a bit. She said as long as I did my work and went to church, I'd be *Welkommen*."

"So, what happened?"

"We didn't make it. Flynn showed up. Krups showed up. Somehow Flynn realized that I took the journal. I don't know how he figured it out, but he did. I was so scared. But Jessica was brave. She talked right back to Flynn and Mr. Krups. Told them they could have the codes back as soon as Flynn signed over my guardianship."

Elijah shook his head. "Jessica was brave. Too brave."

"What do you mean?" Hannah asked.

"Well, a man like Krups isn't going to…" Elijah paused. "He isn't going to negotiate with a couple of teenagers."

"So he killed her." Hannah sighed.

Brittney looked down. "I don't know. They separated us. Flynn took me inside the apartment. Krups grabbed Jessica…that was the last time I saw her."

Elijah rubbed his face with his hands. Krups. Jackson worked for Krups. Everyone worked for Krups. And Jessica had died at their hands keeping this secret in hopes of saving a poor girl from a home where no one wanted her. Hannah had been right all along. She'd raised a noble and brave daughter. Her actions reminded him of how he'd felt when he first had joined the force—he'd thought stopping a criminal would be as easy as finding them.

Hannah stood, wringing her hands in her apron. "Okay. Now I understand why they searched our house and our stable, but why me? Why do they think I know where this journal is? I know nothing."

Brittney shrugged and started to cry again.

Eli frowned. The girl knew why Hannah was a target. But still there was something she wasn't saying. He wondered how detrimental her silence would be.

"Well, I'd say that's enough questions for now." Abigail walked over to where Brittney sat. She knelt down beside her and spoke. "I am very glad you have come, Brittney. And we thank you for the truth. You know it is okay to be sad." She glanced at Hannah as she spoke. "But wasn't it good to have someone in the world to love you? Even if it is just for a short time. Treasure your friendship with Jessica. It was from God, who loves you. That is the Amish way. We don't understand why she had to leave us so soon, but we are ever thankful that we had her here with us for the time that we did. Same as her *Dat*. He would have been proud of her."

Abigail rose again and helped the girl up from the couch. "Come now. Time for another lotus tea."

She led Brittney away to the kitchen.

Elijah agreed that she needed a break even though he had more questions. He wasn't even sure the girl could answer his questions.

What they really needed was to find Jackson. And maybe, with the help of God, find the journal of codes. If they could do that, they could possibly take Krups down, too. There was still so much uncertainty, so many things they didn't know. Well, at least, Hannah had one account of Jessica that was favorable. No one could be pleased with the outcome, but it seemed the girl's heart had been in the right place.

He turned to Hannah. He caught the curves of her profile as she looked away from him. He admired the fullness of her lips and long dark lashes that blinked away the abundance of moisture in her eyes. How beautiful she was. How he longed to comfort her in her moment of suffering. He watched a moment as she continued to play nervously with the white cloth of her apron.

"Jessica died trying to help this girl." Elijah turned away as he spoke, for fear she'd see the love in his eyes. "She was brave and bold. I'm sorry I didn't know her better."

"Aye, but she was a *gut* girl." Hannah was trying to control her voice and yet it faltered with emotion.

Elijah glanced to the kitchen, where Brittney had gone. "I think we should finish what she started. We should help this girl."

Hannah rose from her chair and moved toward him. She grasped his hands and looked deep into his eyes. "Always, I knew Jessica was a *gut* girl. She had a heart only to help others. Like you, Elijah. God has brought you here to make this right."

Elijah released her hands, placed his gently against her cheeks and wiped her tears with his thumbs. Closing her eyes, she leaned into his palms, welcoming his touch. Her hands lifted up and rested on his shoulders. His pulse raced as he lowered his head toward her soft lips.

The beep of his cell phone sounded. He wanted to ignore it. He wanted to kiss her. Instead, he stepped back and pulled his phone from his pocket.

"Miller here," he answered.

"We got Jackson," Tucci said. "But you've got to get here fast. I won't be able to hold him long."

"What is it?" Hannah asked when he pocketed his phone and turned away.

"They got him. They got Jackson. I have to go."

Without a kiss.

Chapter Seventeen

Hannah had thought this would feel different. She had thought that finding out about Jessica would give her some closure. But instead it seemed as though there were only more questions. Where was this journal? And why did anyone think she had it?

Not that it mattered anymore. Elijah had Jackson. Jackson would give them this Krups person and the whole thing would be over.

Which meant not getting to see Elijah anymore. She definitely felt confused about that. And there she had just nearly let him kiss her. What was she thinking? Good thing his phone had rung. And now he was gone.

"Where is Brittney?" Hannah asked as she and Abigail dried the morning dishes.

"She's gone to rest." Abigail eyed her with suspicion. "What's on your mind? I know when a woman wants to talk."

Hannah shrugged. "What's not on my mind—the journal, this poor child's father, what I'm going to do when this—"

"Your feelings for my brother…" Abigail added.

Hannah took another plate and began to dry. Yes, that was on her mind but it shouldn't be.

"I know I shouldn't pry, but you both are so worried the other doesn't want to hear what you have to say that…" Abigail took the drying towel from Hannah's hands and steered her toward a chair at the kitchen table. "I saw you holding his hand. Did you talk about your feelings? About the future?"

"I told you, Abigail, it's not meant to be."

"How do you know what God's plan is? You don't."

"No. I don't. But I know I'll be shunned if I take on seriously with your brother. And I'll hurt Thomas, which I would never want to do. He's been very kind."

"Thomas is your brother. And he loves you. He isn't going to be surprised by this. If he is protective, it's because he doesn't want you to get hurt. And that's only because he doesn't know my brother. But I do and I know Elijah loves you."

Hannah shook her head. "Sometimes love isn't enough. Sometimes people need different things. You know I don't regret the decision I made. I was a good wife to Peter and I cared for him. I missed Elijah's friendship, but I knew he was happy being a cop and I was so happy to be a mother to Jessica." She sat down and sighed.

"But what about now?" Abigail smiled and took the seat opposite her.

Hannah smiled and nodded. "I don't think your brother wants to come back here."

"You are wrong about that. I saw him yesterday. Coming back is exactly what Elijah wants. He wants family. He told me so himself."

Exactly. And I cannot give him one. "I don't know.

I tried to talk with him last night. He did not seem interested in hearing my feelings."

"*Ack*. He is only afraid. That is why I push you. You are brave, Hannah. Just like Jessica."

"Not anymore. Not after losing Peter and Jessica."

"You must be brave." Abigail patted her hand. "Be brave with your heart again."

"It's not my heart that I fear. It's that I cannot…" Hannah paused. *I cannot tell him that I cannot give him a family…*

"You cannot what? Will you not speak to him?"

Hannah shook her head. "There are things you do not know, Abigail. It is not as simple as you believe."

"I never said it would be simple." Abigail smiled. "I only said you should be honest. At least, think on it. I'm going to check on our patient. Then perhaps we could head to Sunday service."

Hannah stopped her. "What do you think will happen to the girl? Will she have to go back to her stepfather?"

"No. Elijah will not let that happen. She's almost eighteen, which means she'll soon be legally independent—but she will still need some guidance and a way to support herself." Abigail clasped her hands together at her chest. "Elijah is arranging for her to stay here until I make some arrangements for her. It's complicated, but I think she'll be okay."

"I'd like to help," Hannah said.

"Good. I'd like for you to help."

The exchange of words was like a pact between sisters and it warmed Hannah through. Maybe Abigail was right. Maybe everything would work out somehow. She started away to fetch her best dress for Sunday church. Service was at the Stottlemeyers', just a five-minute walk from Abigail's.

"Hannah?" Abigail walked back in from the hallway. "I was thinking if you can't talk to my brother and you don't want to stay on with the Nolts—"

"I never said I didn't want to—"

Abigail waved her hands in the air. "Hear me out. I was just thinking that it must be hard for you to stay on without Jessica there."

"*Jah.* It is."

"Well, you are welcome to stay here. As long as you need. I would welcome the company."

"That is most kind. But I couldn't pay you."

"You could work for me," she said. "I need someone to tend to the garden and the cleaning while I am seeing patients."

Hannah took in her words.

"Think that over, too," Abigail said, and turned away.

"I will," Hannah said. "Now let's off to church and some time to pray. You have my head spinning, Abigail. I need some time to listen to God and settle it again."

After the call from Tucci, Elijah knew two things. First, that his partner was sticking his neck out in a big way by bringing Jackson in under a false name for him.

Secondly, Elijah knew this was his best chance to help Hannah and Willow Trace. He had to ask the right questions. There was no time to make mistakes. If only he could focus, he could be sure to do that. But that wasn't so easy to do, when he couldn't stop thinking about that near kiss.

Get a grip, Miller. Strange vibes flowed through him as he entered the station. Something was different. He ignored the uncomfortable feelings and found his partner waiting for him in the hallway.

"I got him in interrogation five," Tucci said. "I

haven't asked him a thing. He's just been sitting there for an hour. He's starting to sweat."

"Where did you find him?"

"At a coffee shop in Kennett Square," Tucci said. "A patrolman walked in and recognized his face from the bulletin yesterday."

"Great. Then all his friends will know he's here."

"Not much we can do about that," Tucci replied. "But he was stupid and sloppy yesterday. Too many people saw him. He assaulted you. Held a woman at gunpoint—"

"Beat his teenaged stepdaughter to near death," Elijah added. "She showed up at my sister's in the middle of the night. Abigail took pictures."

"Rape?"

He shook his head. "My sister is a midwife and nursed her last night. She says no signs of rape. But the girl told us a lot this morning."

Elijah filled Tucci in while pouring himself a tall cup of coffee, and headed into the room with Jackson.

"Good morning, Flynn. So good of you to come visit me and see how I'm doing. I really appreciate that because I have some questions for you."

Jackson barely lifted his eyes. "I don't know you. So I don't know what you're talking about."

Elijah spotted the large ring that had marred Brittney's face. "Tucci, I need someone to bag and analyze this ring, please."

"Don't you need a warrant for those?" Jackson said. "I want my lawyer."

"We're trying to get your lawyer, Flynn. But he's not answering his phone. And no, I don't need a warrant. I don't even need the ring or the boot." He pulled out his cell phone and showed Jackson a picture of Brittney's bruised face and then a picture of the cut on his head. "Between these pictures and many eyewitnesses, I think you'd better hand it over. The best thing you can do is confess. Even your lawyer would tell you that. Plead guilty and maybe the courts will have some mercy. What do you say, Jackson?"

"Confess to what?" Jackson laughed. "You got nothing. In about thirty minutes I'll be walking out of here."

"Well, then why don't we chat for those thirty minutes?"

"I don't have anything to say to you."

"What if I told you I found that journal of codes that you've been looking for? Have anything to say then? If I hand that over to someone—like, let's say, Norton Krups—then maybe you won't be walking in thirty minutes."

"You don't have that journal." He sneered. "You're bluffing."

"How does Mr. Krups feel about you getting duped by a couple of teenaged girls, huh?" Elijah taunted him. He had a feeling that Jackson was the type to lose it if he got mad. And if he lost it, he might say something useful. "So that was probably a career buster for you. Even though you're the one who stole the codes from Dutch Confidential, you also lost them before getting them to Krups. Sort of knocked you down the crime ladder a good ways."

Jackson shifted uncomfortably in his chair. Elijah continued with the humiliation tactic.

"I'll bet Mr. Krups had some big plans for all those codes. But you blew it. Let a couple of little girls steal it right out from under your nose."

"What do you want, Detective Miller?" Jackson

crossed his hands over his chest. "You want me to help you get Krups? I'm dead if I do that."

"You're dead if you don't do it."

"What are you talking about?"

"I'm talking about you murdering an Amish teen-aged girl. I'm talking maximum security for an ex-cop. The guards will hate you. The inmates will hate you. It will be a long, long life sentence."

Jackson stood, throwing his hands in the air in protest. His anger now was turning to fear. "Murder? I didn't murder anyone. I trade information and do favors for people. I don't kill."

"Jessica Nolt. She was last seen with you before she was found with a slit neck. We have pictures of what you did to your own stepdaughter. We saw you with a knife under her chin. I doubt a jury will think it much of a stretch to believe you used that knife on another child." Elijah stood and walked to the door. "You should have stuck to being a dirty cop. Murder is a deadly business."

"Wait," Jackson said before Elijah had stepped out of the room. "Just…just wait. Let's talk."

Chapter Eighteen

Hannah and Abigail dressed and helped Brittney into an old dress of Abigail's since her own clothes had been so badly stained and cut.

"It's a little long." Hannah giggled. Abigail was a good three inches taller than the teen. "But it will do."

"It's a little stiff and itchy," Brittney said.

"*Jah*. Just be thankful you don't have to pin it together like some of the Amish," Hannah said.

"Pin it?" Brittney scrunched up her nose.

"*Jah,* many Amish think hooks and eyes are too fancy," Abigail said. "They use straight pins to fasten the skirt and apron together."

Brittney seemed to consider that for a moment. "Don't they stick into you when you move?"

"*Nein.* Not if you pin it correctly."

Brittney giggled. "Jessica told me how different it is here. She said that you try not to be noticed here. And there *we* are, back in the city, squeezing into the tightest jeans possible, hoping someone will look."

"We look upward," Abigail said. "To the Lord."

"I want to learn how to do that, too." A worried expression covered Brittney's face.

"You know they won't be able to keep Flynn," she said. "He gets questioned all the time, but never charged with anything. And if he did, then where would I go?"

Hannah looked to Abigail and back to Brittney. "I do not understand the English system, Brittney. But I have faith in God and in Elijah that you will not be harmed again. If I have to stand between you and that horrible man to prevent it, I will. Just like Jessica. I give you my promise.

"And now we are off to church?" Hannah asked Abigail, wondering if the girl was too frail to walk the short distance to the Stottlemeyers' for church.

"How would you like that, Brittney?" Abigail said. "It's not far today. Just around the corner. If you get tired, we can find you a comfortable spot there to rest. Or we can return."

The girl's expression perked up a bit. "I suppose I'm already dressed for it. Let's go."

"Gut." Hannah was pleased. "Daniel and Jessica's other friends will be there. You can socialize with them after the service, if you feel up to it."

"Daniel?" Brittney looked worried again. "I'm sure he won't be glad to see me."

Hannah patted her shoulder. "That is not true. You have much to learn about the Amish. We are very forgiving."

"Have you talked to him about Jessica and the journal?" Brittney asked.

"Jah, he was looking for it in our house the other night." Hannah said. "Why?"

Brittney paused before speaking, as if she weren't sure how she wanted to answer. "Just wondering if he had talked to you about stuff. That's all."

Hannah could see behind Brittney's brown eyes that

that wasn't all. There was something else the girl knew and it had something to do with Daniel.

The day was warm and after the service Hannah helped the other women set tables on the front lawn for the midday meal.

Abigail had taken Brittney to the back porch to rest for a bit. Hannah could only imagine that listening to a two-hour sermon in a language one didn't understand would be fatiguing for even someone in the best of health. After all that Brittney had been through, she had to have been exhausted. Hannah figured that as soon as she'd helped set up the meal, she and Abigail could help Brittney back to Abigail's so that the girl could get some proper rest.

Before leaving, Hannah had also thought to speak to Daniel. She had seen him earlier sitting with his family. He had looked more than surprised when he saw Brittney sitting with herself and Abigail. Earlier at the house, Brittney's comment about Daniel had her thinking that maybe he knew more than he had told them. As Elijah had said to her, *sometimes we know things that we don't think are important to a case, but they are.* He had explained that part of his job was to get all of that information from witnesses and victims and other parties and put it together, until it made sense.

She wished Elijah were there now so that she would know what questions to ask Daniel. She wasn't sure at all how to start a conversation with him about the journal and what he knew about it.

Truth was, she wished Elijah were there anyway. During the service, she had thought and prayed heavily about the things Abigail had mentioned. She wanted to talk to Elijah about her feelings, but she didn't know if she could be that brave. And in the end, what would it matter? Elijah would go back to the city and his work and she would stay in Willow Trace.

Hannah carried out the drinks and saw that most of the work had been done. She would look for Daniel. Glancing across the lawn, she saw him crossing the grassy paddock in front of the stable. He glanced her way. Hannah put down the two pitchers of tea she carried and tried to motion him over, but he turned away and slipped quickly behind the Stottlemeyers' barn. There wasn't anything she knew of behind that barn. Curious, she decided to follow after him.

She was halfway across the lawn when she realized she should tell Abigail her plan. It would take but a second to walk by the back porch. Abigail sat upright in a white wooden rocker and was sleeping like a baby. Hannah would have laughed aloud except that as she got closer she noticed the long swing next to Abigail—the swing on which Brittney had been resting—was empty.

Brittney was missing.

"I didn't murder anybody. You got the wrong guy for that." Jackson shook his head back and forth.

Elijah turned and glared hard at him. The brutish man ran his thick hands through short red hair.

"Then who did? You were with her. You dumped her at the barn. Your black sedan was seen leaving the site. I'm thinking we'll find trace evidence once the car is examined."

Jackson grumbled, "She's my daughter's friend. I gave her a ride."

"You don't think we'll find her blood? What about the other Amish kid, Daniel? He can identify you, too."

"But he can't say I killed her, because I didn't. I

didn't touch that little girl. I swear. And if Brittney or that other punk kid says I did, then they're lying." The color of Jackson's cheeks now matched his hair. "Krups did it. He's crazy all of a sudden. He'll kill anybody to get those codes back. He thinks that afterward he can get into the right system and change the history on the computer."

"And that's why he doesn't kill you? Because he needs you to get the codes?" Elijah slammed the file folder down on the table and looked into the two-way mirror with a shrug. This discovery was not going to work in their favor. Jackson was mad enough to point the finger at Krups for the murder charge, but he wasn't scared because as long as those codes were still out there, Krups wouldn't hurt him.

"Okay, let's say I believe you for one second. Tell me why Krups killed the one person who knew where the codes were?"

"He didn't mean to kill her," Jackson said. "Don't get me wrong. He probably would have anyway, once he got the journal. But he didn't mean to when it happened."

"When what happened?"

"Krups was knocking her around, trying to get her to talk. He broke a bottle against the wall to scare her. But when he pushed her a little too hard, she fell. Krups reached out with the sharp glass in his hand. It went clean across her throat as she tripped down the stairs. Then he was just angry because he still didn't have the codes."

"If your story is true, that's still murder and you're an accessory." Elijah walked back and leaned his weight over table toward Jackson.

"I can't give you Krups," he said.

"Then tell me why you and Krups are after Daniel

and Hannah. What makes you think they can lead you to the journal?"

"The girl said so." Jackson was very matter-of-fact. "Krups was scaring her and pushing her around and her last words were 'don't hurt my *Mamm* or Daniel.' They must know something. Otherwise, why would we hurt them?"

"A dying child calls out for her mother and friend and that's what you guys are going on? Are you kidding me?"

"I'm not. And Brittney confirmed her claim. She'd told my daughter nearly the same thing—that no one knew exactly where the codes were but that Daniel and her *Mamm* could find them if they had to. That's all we had. Brittney would have told us if she'd known anything else. Krups can be very persuasive."

"But, let me guess, you made her talk." Elijah felt his head begin to ache. "Just tell me where Krups is and we'll drop the accessory to murder charge."

"You're not a D.A. You can't negotiate that." Jackson shook his head. "Look, even if you have the journal, which I don't believe you do, you can't tie it to Krups. You can't get to him. It's impossible. He dots every *i* and crosses every *t*. You are wasting your time."

"Like getting you was impossible?" Elijah smiled. "Everyone has an Achilles' heel."

"Yeah, well, if he's got one it's that journal, which you don't have, or this conversation would be going in a completely different direction."

Elijah sighed in frustration. He'd hoped for more from Jackson, but he should have known he wouldn't get it.

A knock sounded at the interrogation room door.

Tucci cracked the door slightly and popped his head in. "Phone call for you, Miller."

Elijah nodded. He stepped out of the small interrogation room, closed the door behind him and reached for the phone from his partner.

"Miller here," he answered.

Tucci hung close as if waiting to see his response.

"Elijah, we need your help." The voice on the line was not any he'd expected—it was deep and tight and speaking the language of his youth. "We need your help, son."

"*Dat?* What it?" Elijah's pulse spiked.

"They're all missing—Hannah, Abigail, the *Englischer* girl, even Daniel. They were here at the Stottlemeyers' for Sunday church. And now they aren't. Thomas drove over to Abigail's place and they aren't there, either. We're quite afraid something has happened. The People are all together praying. Come, my son. Come and help us find them."

"Keep everyone praying. I'll be right there, *Dat.*"

Chapter Nineteen

"Hurry, Abigail," Hannah said. "There she goes, behind the stable, just like Daniel. We don't want to lose sight of her."

Hannah hurried toward the Stottlemeyers' stable, tugging Abigail behind her.

"Where in the world could she be going?" Abigail said. "She doesn't know her way around here."

"No, but Daniel does. She's following him. I saw him go around the stable first. Then I came to check on you, and Brittney had just left. I looked up across the lawn and spotted her exactly where I had seen Daniel."

"But what can they be about, running off from Sunday gathering into these woods?" Abigail asked.

"Actually, I think I know where they are going." Hannah shook her head. "And I cannot believe I did not think of this place before. It makes perfect sense now."

"What makes perfect sense?"

"The hiding place. Jessica's hiding place."

"You mean Brittney and Daniel are going after the journal? You think they know where Jessica hid it?"

"*Jah,* that is exactly what I think."

* * *

"Don't you think we'd get more information if we stayed and continued to question Jackson? He knew Krups was headed out there. He as much as said so. He probably set the whole thing up."

"I don't think so. We have to get started while the trail is still at least warm."

"But we couldn't find Jackson yesterday and he'd been right under our noses in the city with nowhere to go." Tucci glanced over at Elijah as they sped over the Pennsylvania countryside. "If Krups has Hannah and your sister, then how in the world do you think we're going to locate them in the boondocks of Lancaster County? He's had an hour start on us."

"You forget that I know those boondocks." Not to mention his *Dat* had asked him to come. His *Dat* actually called him and asked for his help as a cop and as his son. Elijah closed his eyes and tried to visualize what might have happened at the farm to Hannah, Abigail and Brittney. They'd gone to Sunday church. Listened to the preaching. Everyone would have seen them. Brittney would have been introduced to the other teens—Daniel included. Hannah would have helped with the Sunday meal. He'd seen at his cousin John's that Hannah sort of took charge in this activity. She would have been missed if she had not been there helping. By the time his *Dat* had called him at the station, the Sunday meal would have normally started. Now everyone was gathered to pray that they found Hannah, Abigail, Daniel and the *Englischer* girl.

He too prayed.

"Are you sure you know the way?" Abigail asked Hannah for the third time since they'd started into the woods behind the Stottlemeyers' barn. "We haven't seen either Brittney or Daniel since we first came into the trees."

"Well, this isn't the usual way to get to Cyprus Cabin, but I know we're heading in the right direction." Hannah climbed over a patch of briars. "In fact, we should be getting very close." She lowered her voice. "Did you know the hunting lodge is over one hundred fifty years old? This land used to belong to some wealthy *Englischer* from the city before the Stottlemeyer family bought it up. At one time, I think the cabin must have been quite nice. Not much to it anymore. But when Jessica was very young, I took her there and let her play 'house' while I worked on some knitting or whatnot."

"So you and Elijah had a secret love shack?" Abigail teased.

"*Ack*. No." Hannah blushed. "Your brother was a perfect gentleman…although he might have stolen a kiss or two. Shh. There it is."

Hannah directed Abigail to look through a small clearing so that she could see the dilapidated cabin ahead. As she had remembered, not much was left of it, no windows and doors. Just the clapboard siding and roof remained. Vines and trees had grown thick around it—its grays and greens still soft and inviting.

"It's charming." Abigail smiled.

"I hear voices," Hannah warned her.

The two women stalked closer to the small structure, trying to keep themselves hidden in the brush. Through the window holes, Hannah spotted Daniel and Brittney. They seemed to be in the midst of an argument.

"Come on," Hannah said to Abigail. "Let's see if

they found the journal. I want to see this thing that has wreaked havoc on all our lives."

Elijah and Mitchell arrived in Lancaster from the city in record time and drove straight to Stottlemeyer's where much of the Sunday gathering had disbursed. A few families had gone home in order to be on the lookout for their missing friends. Only a few remained huddled in prayer and communion. Among the women, Elijah spotted his mother.

He gave her a strong, steady embrace.

"Your father's gone home in case of any news there." Her face was drawn with worry.

"What can you tell me? Where did you see them last?" Elijah asked her.

She shook her head and shrugged. "After service, Abigail and the *Englischer* girl were resting on the back porch. Hannah was directing Sunday meal as always. Then all of a sudden they were all gone. It was time to sit down and eat and we couldn't find any of them. Kasey and Geoffrey said that Daniel was gone, too. Your father sent Thomas to Abigail's to see if they had walked home, even though I can't imagine them doing that without speaking to a soul."

Elijah nodded. "Has anyone seen any strangers about today? Tourists? Passing cars? Vans? Anything unusual?"

The women shook their heads.

Elijah's hope was fading as he looked around at the vast countryside around them. "Did the women arrive in a buggy?"

"No, by foot."

"And Daniel?"

"Rode in with his family," his *mamm* answered. "They are still here and so is the buggy."

"Any of Stottlemeyer's horses missing?"

"Nary a one. Mr. Stottlemeyer went and counted them all."

"Are Kasey and Geoffrey still here?"

"*Jah,* just there." His mother pointed across the lawn.

He nodded for Tucci to follow him over to the group of teens. "Maybe Daniel said something to his friends?"

"I sure hope so. 'Cause otherwise, we got nothing. No vehicle to follow. No trail. Nothing to put out an APB on. They haven't been missing long enough to conduct a search."

"Well, under the circumstances, we can call in some local cars to troll the surrounding areas." Elijah shook his head. "I should have insisted that car stay on Daniel. Or that he stay with me."

"He had a detail?"

"Yes, but only for twenty-four hours. You know, budget cuts. Lack of officers on duty. Not enough manpower to keep anyone on him for longer."

"So, we have nothing," Tucci said. "We certainly can't chase around every one of Krups's company cars."

"No. But a GPS. We could chase a GPS." Elijah stopped fast and grabbed his partner hard around the upper arm.

"Who out here has a GPS?"

"Abby does. Abby has a cell phone. Maybe, just maybe, she has it with her." *Oh, Lord, please let Abby have that phone with her.*

"Hey. It's worth a try. I'll get a locator on it right now." Tucci turned back to the police car. "You go ahead and talk to the kids."

The young couple sat on the ground in a patch of clover near the stable. Geoffrey stood as Elijah approached. "Are you here to find Daniel?"

Elijah nodded. "Did he say anything to either of you about leaving this afternoon? You have any idea where he might be?"

"I have no idea where he is," Kasey said as she stood from the ground and dusted her skirt. "But he was not happy to see Miss Brittney Baker at church today. And as soon as the service was over, he made a beeline for her and they exchanged a few words."

"Did you hear any of what they said?"

The kids shook their heads.

"Okay. Thanks. If you think of anything else—" Elijah started to turn away.

"Sir, I don't know if this is helpful or not. And I only just thought of it because we are at Stottlemeyers' today, but…" Geoffrey hesitated.

"What's that?"

"Well, Jessica and Daniel, they had a special place," the teen explained.

"A special place?" Elijah repeated his words just as they stirred a flowing of memories of his own special place.

"*Jah,* it was near here. In the woods somewhere, I believe."

Elijah was filled with hope again. "Yes, I know exactly the spot."

"Is it here?" Hannah walked into the shack and confronted the two arguing teens. Abigail followed in after her.

Daniel stopped feeling around the boards on the floor and looked up. Hannah still could not see his eyes below the brim of his black hat. "Mrs. Nolt, Miss Miller. You shouldn't be here. I was just telling Miss Baker that she, too, should leave. It's not safe here."

"Brittney, you should be resting," Abigail said. "I don't know how you had the strength to walk all this way."

"I knew when I saw Daniel at church that he was scared. When I saw him running into the woods, I had to come. This is all my fault. I have to fix it."

Abigail put her arm around the girl. "Here, come and sit. Rest because you will have to walk back in a bit."

"You should walk back now," Daniel said. "It's not safe here."

"Not safe?" Hannah repeated, looking around at the old wood. "Daniel, why do you think Jessica hid the journal here?"

"Well, she told me that the hiding place had something to do with you. She told Brittney the hiding place had something to do with me. I know she wouldn't lie to either of us, so I think both are true."

"This hunting cabin would make sense, then, if she brought you here." Hannah smiled.

"*Jah,* everyone was thinking this journal was at Nolt Cottage or in the stable," Daniel explained, "but this morning when we were sitting at Stottlemeyers', I thought of this place. Jessica showed it to me years ago. She said it was your special play place when she was a child. That you brought her here, Mrs. Nolt. And she brought me here, too, so…"

"Then where is it?" Brittney asked. "Daniel's right. We all need to get out of here. Krups has people watching all of you. It won't be long before they are here."

"Did you look behind that loose brick in the old fireplace?" Hannah said.

Daniel paused for a moment, then rushed over to the fireplace. He ran his hands over the rows of brick.

"Lower." Hannah also made her way to the old chimney. "Here."

She pulled away a dark brown brick. "It's this one."

Daniel reached his hand into the dark space. "There's something here." He pulled out a small quilted bag like the ones that she and Jessica used to make to sell in the local tourist shops. He opened the bag and inside was a tiny electronic device that looked like a big cell phone or a small tablet.

"That's it," Brittney said. "That's it. Recorded on it are security codes to half the buildings and accounts that belong to Krups and others."

"So much trouble just for this little piece of nothing I can hold in my hand. I would like to take a hammer to it so that it cannot hurt anyone else." Hannah took the piece from Daniel and lifted the electronic tablet. She truly wanted to smash it to pieces for all the pain it had caused her. "How does it work?"

"My stepdad said that it has a USB port and will hook up to any computer," Brittney said. "If you know the password, you can read anything on it. But only he knows the password."

"That's right, little lady," a deep voice sounded from the front of the cabin. "That's why we'll go spring your dad right after we get what we need from here. Take her to the car. And bring me the journal. Now."

Hannah, Abigail and Daniel huddled together against the fireplace. At the door was a short, gray-headed man dressed in a fine suit. He held a gun and directed two other muscular and mean-looking men with him, who also had guns.

"You can't, Krups. I won't go back to him," Brittney

said. "Isn't that right, Abigail? Your brother said he wouldn't let that happen, right?"

"Get her out of here," Krups yelled. "Tie the others up."

One large man with dark, oily skin grabbed Brittney without care and slung her over his shoulder. Hannah and Abigail both cringed thinking of her bruises and how tender she must still be.

The third man was bald, angry and as strong a man as Hannah had ever seen. He snatched the journal from Hannah's hands and tossed it to Mr. Krups. He pulled a rope and knife from his pocket.

"Stand over there." He pointed them away from the fireplace.

"You look strong," he said to her. "Here. Tie up the others. Ankles and wrists."

He handed her the rope. She reached for the knife as well.

"Nice try." He laughed. "I'll cut the rope when you're ready. Thanks."

Hannah trembled as she worked the ropes around Daniel's ankles and wrists.

"Be brave," she whispered to them in their Pennsylvania Dutch. "The Lord is with us."

Tears were in the boy's eyes as she tied his ankles. "I'm sorry," he repeated. "I'm so sorry."

"Quit your yacking in German." The man waved his gun. "This is America. Speak English."

He came close, checked to see the ropes were tight, then cut the ends. "Now her."

Hannah moved around to Abigail.

Abigail stared hard at her. Her face like a stone. "Hold it," she whispered in their own tongue. "When he checks the ropes."

Hold what? Hannah's trembling fingers fumbled and she dropped the ropes to the floor.

"Hurry up." The man gave her a scolding look. "Haven't you finished tying her yet?"

Hannah picked up the rope and started to wrap it around Abigail's wrists.

"I don't know why you're going to all this trouble. It will take us thirty minutes to get back to the farm. You'll have plenty of time to get away," Hannah said.

"You're not going back to the farm, darling," he said. "You're going to have a little campfire."

Krups stomped back into the cabin. "You're taking too long."

In the one second they looked away, Abigail slipped something into Hannah's hands.

Her cell phone. Abigail had her cell phone and didn't want that brute of a man to find it.

"Leave it on," she whispered.

Hannah froze, the ropes and cell phone in her small hands. Already she could smell the cabin beginning to burn.

"Come on," Krups said again. "Just shoot them and let them burn. We got to get out of here."

Was it possible that the old hunting cabin was still there and that was where they had all gone? Elijah ran from talking to the teens toward the car to get his partner.

Tucci was already waving him to the space behind the barn.

"GPS?" he asked.

"Yep," Tucci said. "Your sister's cell phone says she's two miles into these woods. I've got a headset and device on me. Leslie back in I.T. is going to guide us through to the location."

"May not be necessary." Elijah started to run. Tucci followed. "There's a cabin back here. I thought it had been torn down long ago. But according to those kids, it's still here and Daniel and Jessica used to frequent it."

Elijah and Tucci sprinted through the woods, half going on his memory of the cabin's location, half listening to Tucci's tech speaking to him from the city.

It was difficult terrain as the path had grown over. There were many briars. And the space was thick with trees.

"Leslie says we're close," Tucci said. They slowed as they were both breathing heavily from the exertion.

"Do you smell what I smell?" he asked.

Tucci nodded. "Smoke!"

Elijah and Tucci both pulled their weapons and proceeded toward the burning cabin, which they could just now see through the thick foliage.

"They're there." Elijah made a halt motion with his hand. "There's only one door. I see one man at the car. Let's go in at the same time from opposite sides."

"Roger." Tucci took off to the right. Elijah continued to the left side of the cabin.

On the count of thirty, they both rushed the front of the cabin. Tucci aimed at the car. Elijah at the door of the cabin.

"Company!" The driver, a large dark-skinned man, got out from inside the car and aimed at Elijah. Elijah dodged the bullet while Tucci took the guy out from the back. A scream sounded from inside the car. *Brittney.*

Another man appeared at the door to the cabin. Elijah hoped there weren't many more of them. The man from the cabin ran forward to the driver of the car, who had just been shot. As he looked down, Tucci stepped out of the woods and put his gun to his head.

"Drop the weapon." Tucci slapped a pair of cuffs on the guy and pushed him to the ground.

Elijah peered into the car. Brittney was tied up in the backseat.

"Stay down," he said. "Where are the others?"

"Inside. Krups is in there."

"Any others?"

"Just those two," she said.

Tucci cuffed the man to the steering wheel, and then the two of them flanked the cabin.

On three, Elijah mouthed to his partner.

As they rushed in, Elijah prayed that Hannah and his sister were alive and well.

Chapter Twenty

"Don't take another step." Krups held Hannah at arm's length with his fingers around her throat and a gun at her back. Less than a foot in front of her were large flames licking away at the rotted cabin.

Abigail and Daniel sat on the floor tied to each other. It was a stalemate situation. If he made a move, Hannah would get hurt or killed. Krups, on the other hand, was too arrogant to realize that he couldn't win.

"Give it up, Krups," Elijah said. "We've already got Jackson. He's going to testify against you."

"Not if he's dead, he won't."

"He's in protective custody," Tucci said. "Your claws only go so deep. You can't get to him anymore."

"We'll see about that." Angry, he pushed Hannah closer to the flames.

"No." Elijah froze, his stomach knotted with fear.

Hannah whimpered as he stretched her out over the fire.

"Back up or I'll drop her," Krups warned.

Elijah backed up. Krups relaxed his grip around Hannah's throat.

"Come on, Krups," Tucci said. "Let me get these people out of here. There's no need to harm them."

Krups seemed to consider his words. "Yes, you take those two out. Leave me with her."

Leave Hannah with him? No way.

Tucci moved quickly to release Abigail and Daniel and get them out of the smoky cabin.

"I told you to leave," Krups said, cocking his gun at Hannah's back.

"I can't leave without her." Elijah took a step closer.

"Stop. St-stop right there." Krups shook his gun. "It doesn't matter. I've got all the codes. I can change anything. Break into any system. You can't stop me. And you'll not be able to trace me, either."

"You can't get out, Krups," Elijah said, inching just a bit closer to them. "You're never going to get to use the codes."

"I will. They're mine. I've got the journal right here." Krups trembled, sweat pouring from his face. As Jackson had said, he'd gone mad.

"Let her go," Elijah said.

Krups was shaking his head; his eyes looked wild. He moved Hannah away from the flames and now had her directly between himself and Elijah.

"That's right," Elijah coaxed him. "Pass her over to me."

Elijah saw Tucci in his peripheral. His partner signaled him to go ahead with the exchange. Tucci would come up from behind and disarm him.

Finally this would all be over.

Elijah inched just a bit closer and reached out for Hannah. Krups released her and she hurried toward Elijah.

As planned, Tucci ran at Krups from behind. But

Krups had anticipated him. The crazy man turned and aimed at Tucci.

As Hannah ran into his left arm, Elijah lifted his right hand and fired just a moment before Krups. Krups fell to the floor. It was all over.

Hannah was still shaking when the fire truck and emergency unit arrived. Behind them was another string of cars. Out of the first one, Thomas came running. McClendon was with him and also another man Hannah did not know.

Thomas hugged her tight. "I have prayed to God every minute that you would be safe and that He would spare you. I'm so sorry that I have not told you the whole truth."

Hannah lifted an eyebrow. "The truth? What can you mean?"

Thomas released her and waved Elijah and the strange man over. He took Elijah's hand and patted his shoulder in a manly fashion; tears had filled his eyes. "Elijah Miller, this is Governor Derry. Mr. Derry, Detective Miller and my sister-in-law, Hannah Nolt."

Elijah shook hands with the governor. "You did this, Thomas? You arranged with the governor for me to be here?"

Thomas gave him a quick nod. "I did. And I had to keep it from *Ordnung.* I had to make it sound as if you had to be here."

The governor pumped Elijah's hand, then kissed Hannah's. "Mr. Miller, you and your partner have stopped what was about to be the biggest breach of security in American history. I cannot thank you enough. I'll be in touch with you both very soon."

With that, Derry returned to his large blue car and

left. Chief McClendon and his men worked the scene, taping the area, taking pictures, removing the two bodies. Brittney was taken to the hospital. It was enough activity to make Hannah's already-spinning head explode. She turned to Thomas and Elijah. "You two seem to be okay with all of this, but would one of you please explain?"

Thomas hugged her again. "Jessica asked to borrow my cell phone the day before she died. She was nervous. Not like herself. When I saw her body the next day, I knew that she had gotten mixed up in something bad. I knew we needed help. Governor Derry had said to let him know if I ever needed a favor and so I told him about Jessica and the phone call. And that our people would not allow an investigation. But I thought of Elijah and I knew that if anyone could get in here and ask questions and protect us, it would be him. I asked Mr. Derry if he could somehow get you here."

"You could have called me yourself, Thomas," Elijah said.

"I see that now," Thomas said. "But I was worried at first about your response, and about what the elders might say."

"Why didn't you tell me about the phone call?" Hannah asked.

"It was untraceable. And you were feeling bad enough about things."

"But why not tell Elijah? Why act like you didn't want him here?"

"I did want him here. But I didn't want him courting and confusing you and leaving again." Thomas shrugged. "And as I said, I did not want any trouble with the elders. I did not think they would look upon my calling the governor too kindly. And McClendon said the phone call wouldn't help you out."

"It wouldn't have," Elijah said. "Real photos and the clothing—"

Hannah reached up and touched both their shoulders. "It's over. Let us not second-guess ourselves."

"You are right, sister," Thomas hugged her once more. Then the police working the scene asked him to step back.

Hannah could hardly remember the rest of what happened. The fire was put out. Another ambulance took Tucci to the hospital. The bullet Krups had fired in his direction had grazed his leg. Thomas and Abigail had left to speak to the People. They would meet and pray and part of her longed to be among them. It was late when Elijah drove her back to Nolt Cottage.

She sat in his car not wanting to get out and say goodbye. Elijah would not be back and they both knew it. They would both go back to their own worlds now. Now that the terror was over.

"How long will your partner be out?" she asked him.

"Not long," he said. "The bullet didn't hit anything important."

There was silence between them and she sensed his inner struggle over having taken a life. "It's not for me to judge, Elijah. But if you ask me, I think you did the right thing. The man you killed would have shot again, then turned and shot the both of us. David killed Goliath with a stone, did he not? It is not our way to choose violence but today it was forced on us. You stood your ground. That is also Amish thinking."

Elijah's lips turned up slightly at the corners. "I appreciate your words more than you know."

"What will happen to Brittney?" she asked, looking

away, afraid that if she saw his tender blue eyes, she would not be able to finish, not be able to say goodbye.

"She's with Child Services," Elijah said. "In any case, she turns eighteen in a few weeks. I think Abigail offered for her to come and stay with her. What she really wants is to find her mother that Jackson beat and ran off. We have some people with the FBI working on that for her. And the codes are safely back at Dutch Confidential."

"Thank you, Elijah," she said. "Thank you for coming. For helping me find out about Jessica. It was so good to see you and see what you do. After having a gun at my back, I understand your desire to protect others. I understand why you were driven to leave Willow Trace and become a detective."

He looked deep into her eyes and took her hand. "That wasn't the only reason I left."

So, now he finally opens up about the past? Now that he was leaving. Hannah sighed hard. "I would not have been happy outside of the faith. You know that."

"I would have stayed for you."

She glanced away but left her hand in his, enjoying the warmth of his touch. "But I couldn't give you what you wanted, Elijah. I chose Peter because that was the only way we could both be happy and have what we wanted."

"I wanted you, Hannah," he said. "I still do, God help me. But you have Thomas. He's a good man. You will be loved and happy here. You did the right thing. I am not Plain. Especially after today. I showed that to everyone." He started to open the door and get out of the car.

"You mean because of using your weapon against Krups?"

He nodded. "Yes, I didn't make good on my promise to my *Dat,* that I wouldn't use my gun."

"But didn't you also promise to serve and protect?"

"I did. But *Dat* will never understand that. In any case, Hannah, I couldn't stand to be here and see you wed to yet another man. I won't be back again." He got out of the car. She could tell he was choked with emotion as he walked around to open her door. "Come on. I'll walk you in and say goodbye to Thomas."

"I won't be marrying Thomas." She took his hand as she stepped out of his fancy car. "We don't love each other that way. He's my brother. Nothing more."

"You say that now, Hannah. But…"

"It's true. I talked to your sister about it. Ask her."

He shook his head. "It won't matter. I can't come back. My actions today only sealed that fate. I don't belong here. You know it."

"I don't know it, Elijah. I think that was true of you when you were younger. You wanted to go out and help the world, but now I think you want something else."

"Hannah, you're only making this harder. I know you've wanted to talk about the past and about us. But can't you see? There is no us."

"Then, at least, let me finish telling you what happened back then." His harsh words brought tears to her eyes. But she was determined to tell him the whole truth.

"I cannot have children, Elijah. When I was eighteen, I had a tumor. It was removed and with it went all my possibilities to be a mother. Peter happened on my mother and me as we were leaving the hospital. He saw me in the wheelchair and of course he came and asked. So I told him I could never have children. He could see that I was devastated. That's when he asked me to marry him. So that I could be a mother. So, yes, I chose Peter because I chose Jessica. I chose him because he could make me a mother. I chose him because I could not make you a father."

Elijah stepped back around the car door. She couldn't read his expression. Shock, pity, anger, sadness. Whatever was there, he kept it all hidden behind his steely blue eyes.

Then he looked away and she saw the pain on his face—the one thing she had never wanted to give him.

"You chose well, Hannah," he whispered, close to her ear. "Peter and Jessica were blessed to have you in their lives." He leaned over and kissed the top of her head. "You chose well, Hannah Nolt."

He walked her to the front door, gave her hand a squeeze and then turned. "Take care of yourself."

She watched him from the front porch as he drove away and out of her life again.

Chapter Twenty-One

Two months later

Elijah filed away the last of the Mason-Hendricks case paperwork and shut down his computer. He wanted a drink of water, but instead of walking to the cooler he stayed at his desk running his finger around and around the rim of a coffee cup in a continuous circular motion. His thoughts fixed on things far, far away from the Philadelphia Police Internal Affairs Department.

A hand waved in front of his face, breaking his trance. It was Tucci standing before him, hands on hips with that I-know-what-you're-thinking-about-again look on his face.

"Sorry," Elijah said, sitting up tall, trying to feign interest in whatever it was his partner had come to tell him. "Did you say something?"

"Would it matter?" Tucci lifted an eyebrow.

"Yes, Mitchie. It matters. I don't know why I can't focus these days," he said.

"Really? You don't know?" There was an edge of playful sarcasm in his words. "Let me help you. Her name starts and ends with the same letter."

"Yeah, well…Hannah and I have said goodbye for the last time. She's happy the way things are. And I'm happy here. This is where I belong."

"Yeah, you're Mr. Sunshine these days." Tucci pulled up a chair and sat in front of his friend. "Why don't you just go back and talk to her? See how she feels about you? Wouldn't that be better than sitting around here wondering all the time?"

"Come on. I explained it to you before. There's no place for Hannah and me. She belongs there and I— well, I don't know where I belong but it's not in Willow Trace. Anyway, my father doesn't want me back. He made that very clear."

"So, I guess you don't want to talk to him, then?"

"My father? Like he wants to talk to me. Ha, ha. Right."

"Well, he's here. And he's not asking to see anyone else."

"*Dat* is here? In the Philadelphia Police Department?" Elijah stood and looked toward the reception. Just beyond the door he could see him, his father, pacing back and forth.

Tucci stood and motioned toward the door. Preacher Miller stepped through dressed in his Sunday best, black trousers, white shirt, black hat, suspenders. He made his way toward the center of the room where Elijah stood, mouth half-opened in disbelief.

"Father. I—I—"

"No, son, it is I who have come to do the talking today." His father spread his feet, leaned back on his heels and placed a hand firmly on Elijah's shoulder. "Let me speak."

Elijah nodded, his eyes fixed toward the floor. Even though he was not sure he could bear to hear any more harsh words, especially in front of his colleagues. Most likely, his father had come to deliver a formal statement, something kin to a shunning. He'd been waiting for it. Possibly that was why he hadn't gone back to face Hannah and his inescapable feelings for her. Now he was glad he had stayed away from Willow Trace.

"What I have to say is simple," he continued. "The elders have decided that it is unfair to punish you for using your weapon when you, in fact, have never taken your vows to the church. You are in no way required to follow our beliefs. I was wrong to speak so harshly to you. You are welcome to come home anytime. To visit. Or to stay, should you find yourself called to join the church. That would be a most pleasing event to your mother and me. In either case, Elijah, I am proud of you. You chose a different path than I wanted for you, but on it you have made a good life and you have become a good man. I am as proud as any father could be."

"Is this true, Father? I am welcome to join the church?"

"If you feel this is where the Lord has called you, yes."

"It is." Elijah nodded. "I want to come home."

Hannah wiped down the exam table and instruments in Abigail's clinic with a mixture of alcohol and water. It was five o'clock and Abigail had no more midwife appointments for the day. In fact, Abigail and Brittney had taken the horse and buggy to the butcher's to fetch some lamb for a stew, and Hannah, instead of joining them, was able to enjoy a delectable moment of solitude. Life with Abigail Miller didn't allow for many of them. There were always so many people coming and going. And much more conversation than Hannah had ever been a part of at the Nolts'.

Which was why she did not jump when a knock sounded at the door after hours, a "walk-in" patient, Abigail called those without an appointment.

"Coming." Hannah put away the cleaning rag and checked to see that her hair was still tightly tucked away in her *Kapp.* She pressed the white apron with her hands and opened the front door. "Miss Miller is not in at the moment. You are welcome to…"

She stopped, seeing as the man at the door was most likely not a patient. In fact, it was Elijah and he was dressed in Plain clothes and was clean-shaven. He looked so different that it had taken Hannah all of that time to realize who he was.

"I take it from the expression on your face that Abby didn't tell you I was coming to call on you," he said in a sort of apologetic tone.

"I—I um, no. She did not." *To call on me?* Hannah was sure she had misunderstood. After all, her heart was beating so loudly she could barely manage to speak over the pounding. She must gain control of herself before she embarrassed herself yet again with him. "Abigail went to Mr. Hochenlooper's. She's not been gone long. I'm sure if you hurry you can catch her."

Elijah removed his black hat and twirled it in his fingers. "Well, this is a lousy beginning if I have to explain more than once that I've come to call on *you,* Hannah Nolt. I have not come for a visit with my sister. I've come to see you and ask if you will take a ride with me on this fine night. I'll have you home early. I already promised my sister I would. Not a minute past ten."

Hannah frowned. Was he kidding? She had heard that he had come to stay with his father a few weeks ago. But for how long? Did he think he could simply change his clothes and shave and that would put them in the same world? "No, Elijah. I cannot. My place is here with the People."

"And so is mine." Elijah stepped forward and took her hand. "I've come home. I have my father's blessing. I've been working in his mill. I bought the old abandoned Manders' place and I'm fixing it up. It will take a while, but I've got time. I'm not to join the church until the spring. Until then, I can call on you and once I've taken my vows, well…if you'll have me, Hannah Kurtz Nolt, I'd like to be your husband soon after."

"But will you be happy giving up your police work? Will you be satisfied knowing you can never have children?"

"Once I saw you again, I knew there was only one place I could ever be happy," he said, pulling her hand to his lips. "Beside you."

Hannah smiled, every happy emotion swirling inside her so much so that she felt she might burst from it. "In that case, I'll just fetch my wrap and leave your sister a note."

Elijah smiled wide at her consent and grabbed her round the waist, lifting her and spinning her in a circle. "And might I start our outing with a sweet kiss?"

Hannah laughed with joy and threw her arms around his strong neck. He stopped spinning her and pulled her in to his lips for what she hoped to be the first of many, many kisses.

* * * * *

WE HOPE YOU ENJOYED THESE **LOVE INSPIRED®** AND **LOVE INSPIRED® SUSPENSE** BOOKS.

Whether you prefer heartwarming contemporary romance or heart-pounding suspense, Love Inspired® books has it all!

Look for 6 new titles available every month from both Love Inspired® and Love Inspired® Suspense.

Love Inspired®

Save $1.00

off the purchase of any
Love Inspired®,
Love Inspired® Suspense or
Love Inspired® Historical book.

Available wherever books are sold, including
most bookstores, supermarkets, drugstores
and discount stores.

Save $1.00

on the purchase of any Love Inspired®, Love Inspired® Suspense
or Love Inspired® Historical book.

Coupon valid until July 31, 2016. Redeemable at participating retail outlets in the
U.S. and Canada only. Limit one coupon per customer.

52613630

5 65373 00076 2 (8100)0 12155

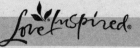
When Kayla had discovered she had a bodyguard, she
hadn't expected this. He should be in the background,
quietly observing. Her father was a lawyer and a
politician; she'd seen bodyguards and knew how they
did their jobs. And yet here she sat with this family, her
bodyguard talking of cattle and fixing fence as his sisters
tried to cajole him into taking them to look at a pair of
horses owned by Kayla's brother.

A hand settled on her back. She glanced at the man
next to her, his dark eyes crinkled at the corners and his
mouth quirked, revealing a dimple in his left cheek.

Boone opened his mouth as if to say something but
a heavy knock on the front door interrupted. He pushed
away from the table and gave them all an apologetic look.

"I think I'll get that." His gaze landed on Kayla. "You
stay right where you are until I say otherwise."

"They wouldn't come here," she said. And she'd meant
to sound strong; instead it came out like a question.

"We don't know what they would or wouldn't do,
because we don't know who they are. Stay." Boone

walked away, his brother Jase getting up and going after him.

Kayla avoided looking at his family, who still remained at the table. Conversation had of course ended. She knew they were looking at her. She knew that she had invaded their life.

And she knew that her bodyguard might seem like a relaxed cowboy, but he wasn't. He was the man standing between her and the unknown.

Don't miss
HER RANCHER BODYGUARD
by Brenda Minton, available June 2016 wherever
Love Inspired® books and ebooks are sold.

www.LoveInspired.com

James Harrison's radio crackled, something about a break-in
at the bridal salon. He was about to respond when a black
sedan shot past him at a speed approaching fifty miles an
hour. Had the car come from the salon parking lot?

James turned on the siren and gunned the engine, taking
off in pursuit and praying no pedestrians were in the path
of the crazed driver. Hawk sat up, rigid, and bayed so loud
James's ears rang.

"Quiet," he called. They took the bend out of town, the
sedan shimmying and bucking as if the driver was not fully
in control. James tried to catch the license plate number, but
it was covered in mud. As he turned a corner, he rolled past
a tiny grocery store. Out in front was a truck half in the road,
the deliveryman loading a dolly full of vegetable crates.

With a last-minute correction, the sedan jerked past,
barely missing the deliveryman, who fell over, heads of let-
tuce tumbling everywhere. The sedan plowed into the side
of the truck, sending bits of metal and glass flying. James
leaped out and drew his revolver.

"Put your hands where I can see them," he shouted.

There was a momentary pause before the driver
slammed into Reverse and backed straight toward James.
There was no choice except to leap up onto the front of

his police car. The sedan smacked the bumper, sending James to his knees and upsetting his aim before the driver put the vehicle into Drive and shot away down the road. James scrambled off his cruiser, Hawk barking madly in the backseat.

James got back behind the wheel, hastily checked on Hawk and drove a few hundred yards but realized he'd lost the guy. His radio chattered.

Not just a break-in at the salon. Someone had been attacked. The shop owner? He fought the sick feeling in his gut as he wrenched the car around and hurtled to the salon, the first officer to arrive on scene. He hastily secured Hawk to a pole outside, shaded by a crooked awning. Hand on his gun, he raced to the back door, which stood ajar.

Listening, he picked up on soft crying. That made him move even faster, pushing through the back hallway and emerging against a rack of hanging dresses. Frances, the shop owner, knelt on the floor, tears streaming down her face.

Frances gasped, "I think she's dead."

A woman lay on the floor, facedown, spectacular red hair fanned out around her, in a puddle of blood. His heart thunked as he recognized Madison Coles.

Nerves pounding, he radioed for an ambulance. As gently as he could manage, he lifted the hair away from her face and slid his fingers along her neck to check for a pulse. The gentle flicker of a heartbeat sent a wave of relief through him. Not daring to move her, he stayed there, monitoring her pulse, waiting for help to arrive.

Don't miss SEEK AND FIND
by Dana Mentink, available June 2016 wherever
Love Inspired® Suspense books and ebooks are sold.

www.LoveInspired.com

REQUEST YOUR FREE BOOKS!

2 FREE INSPIRATIONAL NOVELS

PLUS 2 FREE MYSTERY GIFTS

Love Inspired®

YES! Please send me 2 FREE Love Inspired® novels and my 2 FREE mystery gifts (gifts are worth about $10). After receiving them, if I don't wish to receive any more books, I can return the shipping statement marked "cancel." If I don't cancel, I will receive 6 brand-new novels every month and be billed just $4.99 per book in the U.S. or $5.49 per book in Canada. That's a saving of at least 17% off the cover price. It's quite a bargain! Shipping and handling is just 50¢ per book in the U.S. and 75¢ per book in Canada.* I understand that accepting the 2 free books and gifts places me under no obligation to buy anything. I can always return a shipment and cancel at any time. Even if I never buy another book, the two free books and gifts are mine to keep forever.

105/305 IDN GH5P

Name	(PLEASE PRINT)

Address	Apt. #

City	State/Prov.	Zip/Postal Code

Signature (if under 18, a parent or guardian must sign)

Mail to the **Reader Service**:
IN U.S.A.: P.O. Box 1867, Buffalo, NY 14240-1867
IN CANADA: P.O. Box 609, Fort Erie, Ontario L2A 5X3

**Are you a subscriber to Love Inspired® books
and want to receive the larger-print edition?
Call 1-800-873-8635 or visit www.ReaderService.com.**

* Terms and prices subject to change without notice. Prices do not include applicable taxes. Sales tax applicable in N.Y. Canadian residents will be charged applicable taxes. Offer not valid in Quebec. This offer is limited to one order per household. Not valid for current subscribers to Love Inspired books. All orders subject to credit approval. Credit or debit balances in a customer's account(s) may be offset by any other outstanding balance owed by or to the customer. Please allow 4 to 6 weeks for delivery. Offer available while quantities last.

Your Privacy—The Reader Service is committed to protecting your privacy. Our Privacy Policy is available online at www.ReaderService.com or upon request from the Reader Service.

We make a portion of our mailing list available to reputable third parties that offer products we believe may interest you. If you prefer that we not exchange your name with third parties, or if you wish to clarify or modify your communication preferences, please visit us at www.ReaderService.com/consumerschoice or write to us at Reader Service Preference Service, P.O. Box 9062, Buffalo, NY 14240-9062. Include your complete name and address.

LII15